SECOND SIGHT

Books by Gary Blackwood

WILD TIMOTHY

THE SHAKESPEARE STEALER

SHAKESPEARE'S SCRIBE

SHAKESPEARE'S SPY

THE YEAR OF THE HANGMAN

SECOND SIGHT

Gary Blackwood

DUTTON
CHILDREN'S
BOOKS

DUTTON CHILDREN'S BOOKS

A division of Penguin Young Readers Group

Published by the Penguin Group

Penguin Group (USA) Inc., 375 Hudson Street, New York, New York 10014, U.S.A. / Penguin Group (Canada), 90 Eglinton Avenue East, Suite 700, Toronto, Ontario, Canada M4P 2Y3 (a division of Pearson Penguin Canada Inc.) / Penguin Books Ltd, 80 Strand, London WC2R 0RL, England / Penguin Ireland, 25 St Stephen's Green, Dublin 2, Ireland (a division of Penguin Books Ltd) / Penguin Group (Australia), 250 Camberwell Road, Camberwell, Victoria 3124, Australia (a division of Pearson Australia Group Pty Ltd) / Penguin Books India Pvt Ltd, 11 Community Centre, Panchsheel Park, New Delhi - 110 017, India / Penguin Group (NZ), Cnr Airborne and Rosedale Roads, Albany, Auckland 1310, New Zealand (a division of Pearson New Zealand Ltd) / Penguin Books (South Africa) (Pty) Ltd, 24 Sturdee Avenue, Rosebank, Johannesburg 2196, South Africa / Penguin Books Ltd, Registered Offices: 80 Strand, London WC2R 0RL, England

Library of Congress Cataloging-in-Publication Data
Blackwood, Gary L.
Second sight / by Gary Blackwood.— 1st ed.
p. cm.
Summary: In Washington, D.C., during the last days of the Civil War,
a teenage boy who performs in a mind-reading act befriends a clairvoyant girl whose frightening visions
foreshadow an assassination plot. ISBN 0-525-47481-1
1. Washington (D.C.)—History—Civil War, 1861–1865—Juvenile fiction. [1. Washington (D.C.)—
History—Civil War, 1861–1865—Fiction. 2. Magic tricks—Fiction. 3. Entertainers—Fiction.
4. Clairvoyance—Fiction. 5. Lincoln, Abraham, 1809–1865—Assassination—Fiction.
6. United States—History—Civil War, 1861–1865—Fiction.] I. Title.
PZ7.B5338Se 2005 [Fic]—dc22 2005041350

Published in the United States by Dutton Children's Books,
a division of Penguin Young Readers Group, 345 Hudson Street, New York, New York 10014
www.penguin.com/youngreaders

Designed by Heather Wood

Printed in USA / First Edition
1 3 5 7 9 10 8 6 4 2

For those unforgettable
characters, Claire and Erin

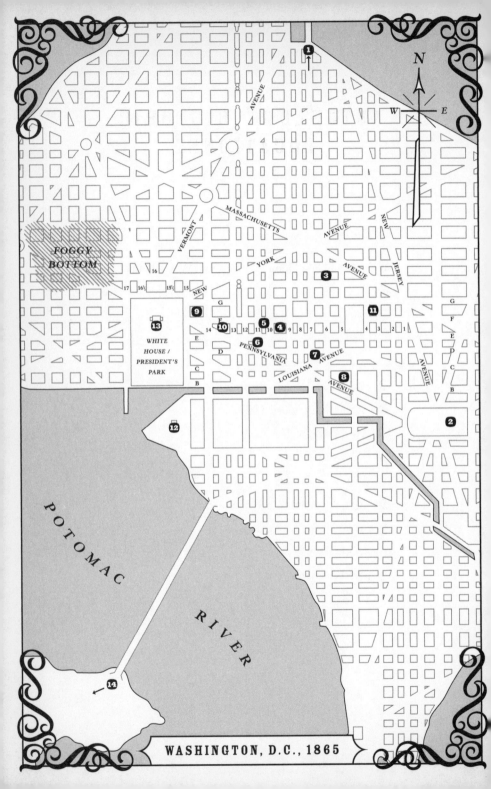

WASHINGTON, D.C., 1865

NOTABLE *and* HISTORIC
LOCATIONS
in WASHINGTON, D.C., 1865

1. To Soldiers' Home, the Summer White House
2. Capitol
3. Mrs. Surratt's Boardinghouse
4. Ford's Theatre
5. Foley's China and Lamp Store
6. People's Circulating Library
7. Canterbury Music Hall
8. National Hotel
9. Willard's Hotel
10. National Theatre
11. Mrs. McKenna's Boardinghouse
12. Washington Monument
13. White House
14. To Alexandria

SECOND SIGHT

CHAPTER ONE

Come with me.

Why do you hesitate? Perhaps you're wondering whether you can trust me. I understand. We will be heading into unfamiliar territory, full of unaccustomed and sometimes unpleasant sights and sounds. You may find it all a bit daunting and disorienting, a bit dirty, even dangerous.

But that's why I'm here. Think of me as a guide, an interpreter. Though I may take a wrong turn now and again or introduce you to some characters of a questionable nature, you can rely on me, I assure you. I've done this before.

There are a few rare individuals in the world who are blessed (or cursed) with the ability to look into the future, an ability known as precognition, or second sight. I am not one of them. The best I can offer you is a sort of *retro*cognition— the ability to look into the past. None of what you'll see is real, of course. It is only an illusion, a novelist's trick.

The time I want to take you to is the fall of 1864. That horrible and fascinating conflict variously called the War of Secession, the War of Northern Aggression, the Southern Rebellion, and Mr. Lincoln's War has been dragging on for three years, and it seems possible that it may go on forever. It has begun to resemble some enormous, ravenous beast with a life and a will of its own, beyond the control of governments or generals.

You hesitate again. Don't be alarmed. We won't be visiting any bloody battlefields, strewn with dead soldiers and wounded ones in such agony that they pray for death. Our destination is the nation's capital. Though there is no shortage of maimed and dying men here, they are confined in hospitals, safely out of our sight.

The Washington of 1864 is very different from the way it will look in your time. The White House is surrounded by acres of tents and ramshackle wooden shanties occupied by refugees from the ravaged countryside and by freed Negro slaves. A new wing is being added to the Capitol building, so its grounds are littered with piles of lumber, blocks of marble, and workmen's sheds. The war has halted work on the Washington Monument; the stump stands like a finger severed at the first joint. At its base is an army slaughterhouse; the guts and body parts of butchered pigs and cattle lie a foot deep, rotting in the sun. I wouldn't breathe deeply if I were you.

Perhaps you'd like to move on. I think you'll find that the streets aren't what you expected, either. Very few are paved. You're fortunate to be here now. In the summer, the streets are blanketed in dust that swirls like a choking fog each time a carriage or horsecar passes. In the spring, they turn to mud.

Though the city's main thoroughfare, Pennsylvania Avenue, is covered in cobblestones, the military's heavy wagons and cannon have cracked and churned them up so that it is hardly better than the side streets.

The Avenue divides the city into two distinct sections. To

the north of it lie the respectable residences, the hotels, restaurants, stores, and theatres. The area to the south, commonly called The Island, is home to unsavory saloons, gambling halls, tenements, brothels, and lawless gangs. One section is even known as Murder Row.

I think it's best if we stay clear of that neighborhood; you wouldn't like the sort of people you'd find there. But we won't be mingling with Washington's high society, either. They're a rather tiresome lot—mainly congressmen, cabinet members, ambassadors, and merchants who have grown rich by providing the beast of war with the supplies that sustain it.

We'll find someone you can feel more comfortable with, someone more like yourself, someone who seems—at the risk of offending you—more ordinary. There. The boy who just emerged from John R. Foley's China and Lamp Store. He looks ordinary enough. A little taller than average, perhaps, with an unruly head of light brown hair, a square, trustworthy sort of face, and close-set brown eyes that have a certain intelligence about them, but no more than the ordinary amount.

He turns to his employer, who is locking up the shop, and, with obvious relief in his voice, bids him a good evening. "Good evening to you, Joseph," replies Mr. Foley.

Joseph's sense of relief is understandable. He's just spent another long and tedious day attempting to sell coal oil lamps and other furnishings for the home to customers who can't afford them. He longs to find some more rewarding and interesting career but doesn't really hold out much hope of that happening, for he has no outstanding aptitude or skill of any sort, at least none that he's discovered yet.

When he comes nearer you will see that, despite his size, he can be no more than fourteen or fifteen—too young, you may think, to be working ten hours a day. He should be in school. But any education past the elementary level requires money, and there is none to spare. The war has driven up the cost of everything. Even the modest boardinghouse where he and his mother and father live charges the shocking sum of sixty dollars a month—which is now overdue—for a small room and two meals a day.

The last time he was in a classroom was three years ago, when they were living in Baltimore. Joseph doesn't miss school much. He had no real friends there, or at any of the half-dozen other schools he attended. His family never stayed in one place long enough for him to get to know anyone very well.

And, though he was a capable enough student, he had a hard time keeping his mind on his studies. His thoughts were continually wandering off to the Wild West, or the Caribbean, or the Far East, or some other exotic setting encountered in one of the rousing adventure novels that he devoured in his free time, and still does.

In fact, he's about to stop at the People's Circulating Library to check out another one. Without telling his parents, he's put by a few cents each week from his meager wages and purchased a subscription that lets him borrow as many books as he likes.

One of the valuable devices available to authors is the ability to jump forward in time at will, neatly avoiding anything that might bog the story down. We'll do that now, and catch our protagonist as he leaves the library. The book in his hands is open, and he's already three pages into it.

Since we may also observe our characters as closely as we like without disturbing them in the least, let's have a look at the title. *The Scalp Hunters* by Captain Mayne Reid. Not exactly serious literature. It is, in fact, just the sort of low-class entertainment that, according to reformers, is largely responsible for the country's moral decay. But it does make for exciting reading. And for a brief time it makes his life, which is quite ordinary, seem less so.

If you're worried that Joseph may be too ordinary even to bother with, be patient. Within a few chapters some extraordinary things will begin to happen to him. (The fact that I know this does not mean that I have powers of precognition. It's only another trick of the novelist's trade, known as foreshadowing.)

Outside the Canterbury Music Hall and Theatre, Joseph comes up against a wall of people, all of them with their faces turned to the sky. On the roof of the Canterbury, workers are anchoring one end of a wire cable that stretches across the street to the roof of another building. One of the workers gingerly tests the cable with his foot to make certain it's secure. Then he moves back, and his place is taken by a much smaller figure—a boy who appears to be no more than eight or nine, dressed in a skintight white costume decorated with spangles.

"What is he *doing*?" asks the fashionably dressed young woman next to Joseph.

"He's going to walk from one building to the other," Joseph replies.

The girl turns to him, her eyes wide. "On that *wire*?"

"Don't worry," says Joseph. "He's as sure-footed as a cat."

The boy atop the building picks up a long, thin balancing pole and places one foot on the cable. For a moment he sways back and forth, finding his balance. Then he brings up the other foot and takes a careful step forward, then another. The crowd below has gone utterly silent, holding its collective breath.

At first the boy does, indeed, seem as sure-footed as a cat. But just when it appears that he may make it safely across, his forward foot slips a little. He begins to teeter danger-ously, sickeningly, from side to side. A chorus of gasps and groans goes up from the crowd. The young woman next to Joseph unconsciously grasps his arm, as though she is the one who has lost her balance. "Oh, my goodness!" she whis-pers. "He's going to fall!"

CHAPTER TWO

Let me reassure you that the boy on the wire will not go plummeting to the ground. We can't afford to lose him; he'll be needed in the story later on. He goes down on one knee, juggling the balancing pole, until he has steadied himself again. Then slowly, shakily, he gets to his feet and moves on. There is a unanimous sigh of relief from the spectators, who break into applause and cheers as the boy springs lightly to the roof of the second building and makes a sweeping bow.

The fashionably dressed young woman releases her hold on Joseph's arm. "I beg your pardon," she says.

"It's all right," replies Joseph. Actually, he was enjoying it.

"I was so afraid that he was going to fall."

"You didn't need to be." Joseph leans closer to her and says confidentially, "If you want to know the truth, he didn't lose his balance at all. He was only pretending, so the audience would applaud more."

The young woman places her hands peevishly on her hips. "Well, that's a thoughtless thing to do. You've seen him perform before, then?"

Joseph nods. "In fact, we live in the same boardinghouse."

"Oh? Are you a performer, too?"

"No, no." He laughs uncomfortably. "At least . . . at least not yet." He blushes slightly and, perhaps in hopes of impressing the young lady, admits, "My father and I . . . we have a sort of . . . a sort of mind-reading act. But we're still perfecting it." He has never told this to anyone before, since he's unsure that they ever will manage to perfect it. But there's little danger in telling it to someone he doesn't know, someone he will likely never see again.

The young lady does seem impressed. "Really? What's your name? I'll watch for you."

"Joseph Ehrlich."

I won't bother telling you the young woman's name. Joseph is right; we won't be seeing her again. Now, you may think that you'd rather follow her as she makes her way through the crowd. I don't blame you. She is an attractive and amiable girl, with a charming smile. But she's not going anywhere you'd care to go. She's on her way to a meeting of the Sanitary Commisssion, which raises money to aid the wounded—an admirable undertaking, but not really very interesting.

If, on the other hand, you stay with Joseph, you will meet some characters who are far less ordinary than he is—including the young high-wire artist, who is known as El Niño Eddie. That's only his stage name, of course. His real name is Eduardo Montoya, and, though the playbills and newspaper advertisements claim that he is eight, he is in fact a twelve-year-old who is unusually small for his age.

As Joseph heads up Louisiana Avenue, he hears his name being called and turns to see a boy in a brown coat and cap hurrying toward him. "Eddie?" says Joseph.

"Ssh!" says the boy. "I don't want them to know it's me!"

"Who?"

El Niño Eddie jerks a thumb over his shoulder. "The bloodthirsty ghouls."

"The spectators, you mean?"

The boy nods. "If they recognize me, they'll want my autograph."

"What's wrong with that? I wish somebody wanted *my* autograph."

El Niño Eddie shrugs. "I liked it at first. But after three or four years, it gets tiresome. Besides, I don't want to miss supper."

Eddie and Joseph aren't paying much attention to what's going on around them; their main concern is getting back to Mrs. McKenna's boardinghouse before all the food is gone. So we'll ignore them for a moment and have a look at the city for ourselves.

Three years ago, Washington had the air of a sleepy Southern town, one that reluctantly came to life only during those months when Congress was in session. The war has changed all that.

In addition to freed slaves and landowners forced off their land, the city teems with soldiers—and not just Union men. The number of Rebels who have given up the cause and fled to the North grows daily. It's startling to see Confederate officers strolling the streets, too, in full uniform. They are not actual deserters; they were captured and then paroled, after giving their word that they would not return to their commands.

Along with the refugees, soldiers, and former soldiers, the city has attracted a large number of opportunists. They know how carelessly, even foolishly, enlisted men will part with the wages for which they have risked their lives, and they are determined to profit from it. Some are legitimate businessmen and women, selling necessary goods and services. But there are also the gamblers, the confidence men, the ladies of the night, the pickpockets . . . and, of course, the entertainers.

The city boasts three bona fide playhouses, which have imported such renowned performers as Charlotte Cushman, the Booth brothers, Edwin Forrest, Jenny Lind, and the scandalous dancer Lola Montez. But there are also half a dozen music halls, which feature more common fare—minstrel shows, farces, comedians, vocalists, performing animals, and the like.

The entertainers who play the music halls can't afford rooms in the city's best hotels. They lodge mostly in boardinghouses, such as the one run by Mrs. McKenna, a humorless and childless widow whose husband fell at the first battle of Manassas—or so she says. There is a rumor among the boarders that in fact her husband skedaddled (another name for desertion) and was later seen prospecting for gold in Colorado.

The boarders have heard some interesting things about Joseph's parents, too. It's rumored in theatrical circles that Carolina (pronounced Cahr-oh-leena) Ehrlich is descended from Gypsies and that she once made a living reading people's palms. Nicholas Ehrlich, they say, once had a promising career upon the stage. He still works in the theatre from time to time, but always behind the scenes, prompting or handling properties or running a spotlight. When nothing is available—and this is one of those times—he makes a little money coaching aspiring singers and actors who can't afford anyone better.

By the time Joseph and El Niño Eddie arrive at Mrs. McKenna's, most of the boarders have already finished their supper and are getting ready to depart for their respective theatres or music halls. Aside from the landlady herself, who is cleaning up, the only ones left in the dining room are Nicholas Ehrlich and the Thomsons, a father and daughter who have a trained dog act.

Joseph sits down next to Nicholas and says softly, "Did Mother come down to supper?"

Nicholas nods. "For a few minutes. I don't believe she ate more than half a dozen bites." He glances wryly across the table at El Niño Eddie, who is, by contrast, loading his plate with everything in sight.

"Is your mother unwell?" asks Fanny Thomson. Boarders who have been here longer than the Thomsons don't ask such questions. They're well aware by now how little appetite Carolina Ehrlich has for either food or company.

Joseph stares at his plate, unable to meet Fanny Thomson's gaze. He's rather smitten with the girl, who is only a year older than himself, and he would prefer not to discuss his family's idiosyncrasies with her. He simply mumbles, "It's her nerves."

"Oh, I see," says Fanny, as though no more explanation is necessary. And in fact the term *nerves* is in such common use these days that everyone—at least everyone above a certain social level—knows what it means. It is applied almost exclusively to women, specifically those whose natures are so refined and sensitive that the pressures and demands of modern life make them physically ill. Though there's more to Carolina Ehrlich's problem than the pressures and demands of modern life, it's easiest just to chalk it up to nerves and let it go at that.

The Thomsons, who are due onstage in an hour, excuse themselves from the table. Joseph wishes them a good show and silently wishes he could go along and watch their act. He's rather envious of them and the other boarders, for each of them has some special ability or gift. The Montoyas are athletic and daring. Mr. Hayes, the clog dancer, is elegant and graceful. Mick O'Boyle can keep an audience in stitches with his portrayals of comical Irish characters. Monsieur Paul, the Modern Hercules, can outpull four horses with the reins held in his teeth.

All Joseph can do is sell lamps and dishes, and he's not even very good at that. If he were, perhaps Mr. Foley would pay him more, and he could at least afford to go and watch the other boarders perform occasionally. But even the cheapest bench seats, among the rudest and rowdiest segment of the audience, would set him back twenty-five cents. In any case, he's needed here.

Ever since the Ehrlichs moved into Mrs. McKenna's well over a year ago, Nicholas and Joseph have spent at least two hours each night working on the mind-reading act he mentioned. Joseph has come to dread these hours. It's not that his father is harsh or unpleasant to work with; on the contrary, he is kind and patient. It's just that he expects so much from Joseph—and from himself.

Tonight Joseph gets a temporary reprieve, for Nicholas Ehrlich has another victim to deal with first—a Mr. Murray, a sad-looking, stoop-shouldered young fellow who hopes to become an opera singer and hasn't the remotest chance of realizing those hopes. Since none of his pupils (there are only three) has yet found work in the theatre (and perhaps never will), Nicholas has had to schedule their lessons in the evenings so they don't conflict with the students' day jobs.

You have heard it said, I'm sure, that those who cannot do, teach. Certainly this is true of Nicholas Ehrlich. He hasn't acted or sung on the stage since the day, ten or fifteen years ago, when he damaged his vocal cords irreparably.

He is often asked how it happened, and he seldom tells the same story twice. Sometimes it involves a doctored drink given him by a jealous fellow actor. Other times it's a badly aimed sword thrust during a fight scene that is to blame, and yet other times the damage is brought on by his doing back-to-back performances of *King Lear* despite a raging cold. Joseph suspects that all these versions are, like many of the stories Nicholas Ehrlich tells about his career, highly questionable.

Whatever the cause, the rasping stage whisper he's been left with gives him a rather tragic air that seems to appeal to his pupils. They're also impressed by his distinguished appearance. Though he's no more than forty-five, his hair is silver, and he wears it longer than is the current fashion. This, along with his prominent cheekbones, gives him a certain resemblance to the famous Hungarian composer Franz Liszt, whose portrait hangs above the piano in the parlor. The likeness is not lost on Nicholas's students. They assume that anyone so distinguished and artistic-looking must have a touch of genius.

Nicholas does his best to sound distinguished and artistic, too, working quotes from great writers into his speech as often as possible, along with impressive words whose exact meaning no one is quite sure of.

Though Joseph is fond of his father, he doesn't consider him distinguished or artistic so much as . . . well, frankly, a bit pretentious. He has some doubts about Nicholas's qualifications as a teacher, too. The exercises he gives his pupils seem designed more to embarrass them than to improve their range and projection. At the moment he has poor Mr. Murray standing sadly next to the piano in the parlor, repeating the phrase *Hiiii-yaaa!* at the top of his lungs, as though he is training not to sing but to drive a team of horses. As Joseph heads upstairs, shaking his head, Mr. Murray finishes urging on his horses and begins instead to yodel "Coo-coo!" like a demented bird.

Outside the Ehrlichs' rooms on the second floor is another parlor, a tiny private one, furnished only with two armchairs, a round marble-topped table, and a single gas lamp on the wall. Joseph sinks wearily into one of the armchairs and takes his book (*The Scalp Hunters*, you will recall) from the inside pocket of his coat. Before he has read a single sentence, the door to their room opens and his mother appears in the doorway.

CHAPTER THREE

If Carolina Ehrlich could be summed up in a single word, that word would be *dark*. It's easy to conclude that she has Gypsy blood: her hair is sleek and black; her eyes are black, too, and slightly slanted, giving her an exotic look; her skin is dark as a quadroon's; she wears only dark clothing, even in the spring and summer. Her mood, too, is dark more often than not.

Joseph can't help wishing sometimes that she were more like the mothers in the books he reads. He doesn't expect her to lovingly embrace him and call him her darling boy, as so many fictional mothers do, or to offer him a glass of milk and a plate of fresh-baked cookies. It would be a pleasant surprise, though, if, just for once, she greeted him with something resembling a smile and asked how his day went or whether he got enough to eat at supper.

But if Carolina Ehrlich models herself after any sort of character found in books, it must be the melancholy, self-absorbed heroines who populate the romantic novels of which she is so fond. She gives him a rather puzzled look, as though she were expecting to find someone else sitting there, and says, "Where is your father?"

"With a pupil. Do you need something?"

"I thought a cup of tea might settle my stomach."

"I'll get it for you." Reluctantly, he sets aside *The Scalp*

Hunters and goes downstairs. When he returns with the tea, his mother has retreated to her sanctuary, as she calls it—a small room adjacent to the bedroom. Sighing, he sets the tray outside her door and settles down in the parlor with his book again. Within seconds, he is transported by Captain Mayne Reid to the western frontier, just as you were transported here by me.

Imagine if someone within Captain Reid's story were to also pick up a book, perhaps one in which the protagonist is reading yet another book in which another person is reading a book about someone reading a book. We might have an endless chain of stories within stories, like those images in a house of mirrors that stretch on forever, except that each one would be set in a different time and place.

But that, I'm afraid, would be beyond my ability to write— and perhaps yours to read. For better or worse, we must stay here in the tiny parlor with Joseph, who, despite the rather lurid and compelling nature of Captain Reid's story, is falling asleep. He has had a long day, and the parlor is warm and close and, thanks to the flaming gas lamp (which was purchased not at John R. Foley's China and Lamp Store but someplace more affordable), a bit short on oxygen.

After an hour or so (how convenient it is to be able to jump forward in time!), he is startled awake by his father pulling the book from his hands. Nicholas Ehrlich reads the title aloud in his curious voice, which sounds as though there is something bound tightly around his neck—though of course there is not: *"The Scalp Hunters: A Thrilling Tale of Adven-*

ture and Romance in Northern Mexico." He hands the book back to his son. "It doesn't seem to be."

Joseph squints sleepily at him. "Be what?"

"Thrilling. In fact, I'd have called it soporific."

"Soporific?"

"Sleep-inducing."

"Oh. No, it's exciting enough; I'm tired, that's all."

His father places a sympathetic hand on his shoulder. "I'm sorry. I wish it were not necessary for you to be employed, at least not such long hours, and for such a pittance. But things will change for the better very soon, you'll see. As Tennyson says, 'Forward, forward let us range! Let the great world spin for ever down the ringing grooves of change!' Once we have the act working flawlessly—"

"I know, I know. We'll be—" Joseph yawns broadly. "We'll be the toast of the town. We'll abide at the choicest hotels, and feast upon capons and capers—whatever those are—and I can bid a fond adieu to Mr. Foley forever."

His father smiles sheepishly. "You've memorized my spiel. I didn't realize I'd said it so many times."

"Oh, not really all that many. You know what a quick learner I am. I can pick something up after hearing it only four or five hundred times."

"Don't be hard on yourself, Joseph. It's a complicated system we're using. If it were not, the audience would deduce too easily how it's done."

Joseph nods—he's heard this a good many times as well—and yawns again. "I don't suppose we could skip a night."

"The sooner we perfect it, the sooner you can say that final fond adieu to Mr. Foley." He gestures toward their room. "Shall we commence?"

Joseph rises reluctantly from the armchair. "If we rehearsed out here, it wouldn't disturb Mother."

"True," says his father, in more of a whisper than usual, "but we might be overheard. I don't want anyone to suspect what we're up to until we unveil the act before the astonished eyes of the public."

"And when do you think that might be?"

Nicholas Ehrlich claps a hand on his son's shoulder again, more firmly this time. "When we're ready."

Though Joseph is beginning to suspect that they have as much hope of performing the act successfully as Mr. Murray has of singing *Pagliacci*, he does his best. Nicholas Ehrlich is right; the system with which they intend to create the illusion of clairvoyance, or mind reading, is quite complex.

He first conceived of it well over a decade ago, when he shared a bill with the great magician Robert-Houdin. Robert-Houdin's act involved bandaging his son's eyes, then holding up items borrowed from members of the audience; though the boy couldn't possibly see them, he described the items with perfect accuracy.

Nicholas Ehrlich watched them perform a dozen times, at least, before it dawned on him that they were using some sort of verbal code. Naturally, he couldn't ask Robert-Houdin to reveal his professional secrets. But after observing the act closely for several more weeks, Nicholas began to grasp the basics of the system.

It took him another three years to devise a code of his own that was complete enough and subtle enough to fool an audience, and then to refine it so that it would work without fail. The first thing he did was to reinvent the alphabet—or, rather, rearrange it, so that each letter stood for a totally different letter. Here's the substitute alphabet in its entirety:

(normal alphabet)

A B C D E F G H I J K L M N O P Q R S T U V W X Y

H T S G F E A I B L U C O D V J W M N P K Y R Z Q

(substitute letters)

The letter *Z* doesn't come up often; when it does, it's conveyed simply by a cough or clearing of the throat. The numbers 0 through 10 are indicated not by letters but by words:

0	1	2	3	4	5	6	7	8	9	10
Come	Quickly	Be	Can	Do	Will	What	Please	Are	Now	Tell

Let me show you, now, how the system works in actual practice. Don't worry; when Mr. Ehrlich said that he didn't want anyone eavesdropping, he didn't mean us. We are privileged and may spy on him with complete abandon.

As Joseph sits in a straight-backed chair, facing the wall, his father says, "To give you a challenge, I've collected a number of new items, ones with which you are not so familiar." He turns to address an invisible crowd of spectators, which is represented by the bed, and breaks into a thick and reasonably accurate Russian accent: "Gud ivining, lahdeez and gantlemun." (Since dialect quickly becomes tiresome—even maddening—I will ask you from here on to imagine that, each time he speaks to the bed/audience, it is in this same accent—and, of course, in that rough, ruined voice of his.)

"I am Professor Nikolai, and this is my son, Yosef." He drops the accent and says, over his shoulder to Yosef, "I shall have to come up with a good Russian-sounding last name, one that's easy for the public to remember—and pronounce."

From the small adjacent room comes Carolina Ehrlich's plaintive voice. "Must you do that again tonight? My head is throbbing."

"Sorry, my dear. Did you take the powders the doctor gave you?"

"Of course I did."

"Good. We'll speak in the most dulcet tones, I promise." He turns back to the bed/audience. "You are about to witness an astounding—no, mystifying sounds better, doesn't it?—a *mystifying* display of a phenomenon known in scientific circles as clairvoyance. Those of you who are not scientists may call it mind reading, or second sight. Before we begin, I ask you to please dig into your pockets or handbags and select some small personal item—it may be anything you wish—and convey it to me. At the end of the evening, I will take them all to a pawnbroker and get what I can for them. I am only joking, ladies and gentlemen. Audience laughs—we hope. What I will do, in fact, is to hold up the items, one by one, and my son will, without the aid of his eyes—which, as you may see, are securely covered—"

"No, they're not."

"They will be. My son will proceed to describe the item down to the minutest detail." He turns to Joseph, who is still facing the wall. "How did that sound?"

"The same way it sounded the first seventy-five times. I do have a question, though. What if there's a real Russian in the audience?"

"I shall endeavor to avoid him. Now, then. The first item." He takes from his pocket a playing card, the queen of diamonds, and asks, in the Russian accent, "What sort of article is this? Can you tell me?"

(His entire first sentence is a code. It reveals that the item belongs to a particular group of ten related objects—playing cards, business cards, keys, buttonhooks, and so on. Nicholas has compiled nineteen such groups, or lists of objects; each one is indicated by a slightly different sentence: "Do you know what this is?" "Tell me what this is," and so on. It took Joseph four months to memorize them all. In the second sentence, only the first word is important. It is, you will recall, a code word for the number three—which tells Joseph that the item in question is third on the memorized list.)

"That's easy," Joseph says.

"Only if you know the code."

"It's a playing card," he says confidently.

"Good." (Here only the first letter is important: a G, remember, is really a D, which signifies that the card is a diamond.) "Which card is it?" (The letter W stands for Q, as in queen.)

"The queen of diamonds," Joseph says offhandedly.

"Applause, applause," says Nicholas as Joseph bows to the wall, bumping his head. "Just one thing. Try to make it look a bit more difficult, will you, so the audience is properly astonished?"

"Yes, all right." Joseph turns to glance longingly at the bed. "Can't I stretch out on the audience to do this?"

"I'm afraid not. You will need all your concentration for this next one. Turn away, please." His father pulls out a Confederate fifty-cent note, which was given him by a student and which is all but worthless. "Tell me what this is."

Joseph mistakenly identifies it as a fifty-dollar bill but correctly gives the serial number. They go through half a dozen other assorted objects before Nicholas finally says, "You may stretch out on the audience now. I can see you're exhausted."

Joseph sits on the bed and pulls off his boots. "How was my performance?"

"Good," says his father.

"But not good enough."

"I didn't say that."

"Only because I beat you to it."

"If we want the audience to be truly impressed, Joseph, there can be no mistakes."

"Maybe asking me to do the act with you was a mistake," says Joseph, a bit sulkily. "Why didn't you ask Mother?"

Nicholas sits next to his son. "I did, actually, some years ago," he says softly. "I thought it might be beneficial if she had something to . . . to occupy her mind. She said that I should stop wasting my time on . . . 'on such a lot of foolishness,' I believe were her exact words." He rumples Joseph's hair. "Don't worry. With a few more weeks of practice, you'll be the most convincing clairvoyant in the business."

Joseph sighs wearily and flops back on the bed. "I don't know. I've noticed four or five advertisements in the personals column of the *Intelligencer,* from people calling themselves clairvoyants. One of them—a Madame Misha, or Masha, or something like that—claims that she can read the past and the future and summon up spirits, and diagnose diseases, and I don't know what all. Do you suppose she can *really* do any of those things?"

Nicholas Ehrlich shrugs. "Perhaps," he says. "But can she read the serial number off a banknote?"

CHAPTER FOUR

When we encounter Joseph Ehrlich again, it is a Saturday, the day when Mr. Foley lets his employees go home at two o'clock. The weather is agreeable and, for a change, so is Carolina Ehrlich. To Joseph's surprise, his father is able to talk her into an outing.

They can't go far, for Carolina has an aversion to carriages, horsecars, trains, and any other sort of modern conveyance. They pack a picnic lunch and set out on foot for the racecourse, which is located in the area northwest of the White House known as Foggy Bottom. It is not foggy, of course, at this time of year or this time of day. But there is a veil of dust hanging in the air, thrown up by the hooves of the horses and by the large wheels of the drivers' carts, which are known as sulkies—an odd term, since the carts in fact look quite cheerful, painted as they are in bright colors so that the racegoers can easily pick out their favorites.

Carolina is clearly distressed by the dust and by the press of people, but it's also clear that she is doing her best to bear it as cheerfully as she can. "Will you find us a seat in the grandstand, Nicholas?" she asks, her words muffled by the handkerchief she is holding over her mouth and nose.

Her husband hesitates, looking distinctly uncomfortable at the prospect of paying fifty cents apiece for seats when they might watch from ground level for ten. But, despite their years of having to live on next to nothing, Carolina has never quite gotten the hang of being thrifty. "Of course, my dear."

"You two go ahead," says Joseph. "I'd rather find a spot near the fence." He says this so casually that his parents believe him.

The truth is, Joseph has volunteered to stay earthbound only in order to save them money. It would be much nicer to sit in the grandstand, where it's less dusty, less crowded, and easier to see the race. The most appealing thing about it, though, is the class of people who occupy it. They are nearly all well dressed, well mannered, and well heeled. They regard the horses—and the other racegoers—through opera glasses while making witty comments and extravagant wagers on the outcome of the race. Joseph would like very much to be one of them—if he could not be an Indian fighter.

But he is stuck down here among the ordinary folk— clerks, soldiers, laborers—who urge their favorite horses and drivers on with words that are not witty so much as they are loud, enthusiastic, and sometimes profane. And, since he is our protagonist, we are stuck here with him. At least we may have a decent view of the race, for Joseph is working his way through the many layers of spectators, searching for an open space along the whitewashed board fence.

He finds one, next to a hulking fellow with a belly that spills over the waistband of his trousers like bread left to rise too long. It's obvious at once why there is so much standing room here. The powerful smell that emanates from him may be familiar to you; we encountered it early on at the army slaughterhouse, near the base of the Washington Monument. This is not surprising, for our man has spent the morning there, cutting up carcasses.

We'll have to put up with him, though. We can't leave just yet, for there's someone of more interest, and more importance to our story, close by. Besides, the third heat of the race is about to begin.

A long-necked mare named Goldsmith Maid won the first two heats by several lengths, and many of those who line the fence are betting on her to do it again. Their wagers may seem paltry compared with those being tossed about in the stands, but even a dollar is a good deal to risk when it's taken ten or twelve hours of hard work to earn it.

Joseph likes to pretend that he's a gambler with plenty of money at his disposal. He mentally puts five dollars on a three-year-old gray filly named Adios. Though the odds are eight to one against her, Joseph fancies her, partly because her name calls up visions of Mexico (where *The Scalp Hunters* takes place) and partly because she's something out of the ordinary—a pacer rather than a trotter like all the other horses.

There's something else unusual about her: she's the only horse equipped with blinders—squares of leather, one for each eye, that prevent her from seeing the other horses unless they're ahead of her.

As the horses move into position, two of the sulkies collide. The drivers shout at each other and brandish their whips. A drumroll sounds from the stands; the crowd grows quiet. The drummer breaks off his roll and gives a single sharp rap—the signal for the race to start. The drivers urge their horses into a trot—or, in the case of Adios, a pace. One of them calls out "Hiii-yaa!" making Joseph imagine for a moment that it is Mr. Murray, the sad singing student.

To Joseph's delight, Adios takes the lead early on and keeps it, winning by half a length. Joseph's nonexistent five-dollar wager has paid off handsomely; he now has a nonexistent forty dollars.

Apparently he's not the only one to profit by putting money on the dark horse. Over the groans and grumbles of the losers, he hears someone shout, "Whooo-ahhh! Mother Mary!" and turns to see, several yards away, a stocky man with a red beard and a stained bowler hat, waving his fists triumphantly in the air. But it is the young girl next to him who really draws Joseph's attention.

Aside from her complexion, which is nearly as pale as the whitewashed boards, she looks almost like a younger, smaller version of Carolina Ehrlich—dark hair, dark eyes, a narrow face, a brown dress and bonnet. Then again, no; it's not his mother she reminds him of. It's his sister. This girl even appears to be about ten or eleven, the same age Margaretta would be, had she lived.

The red-bearded fellow turns this way and that, looking for the "outside man" who collects bets for the bookmakers and distributes the winnings. The way the girl clings to his sleeve puts Joseph in mind of the way a person might cling to a rock in the middle of the ocean—not out of any affection for the rock, but simply to avoid being swept away, in this case by the tide of spectators that swirls around her.

He catches the girl's eye, smiles, and nods in a friendly fashion. She ducks her head and moves in closer to her protector, who is now collecting his winnings. Joseph hears him say to the outside man, in a slight Irish brogue, "Can you wait here just one minute?" Then he crouches next to the girl and whispers something in her ear. She flinches, as though his breath smells rank, and shakes her head slightly.

He scowls and glances around, as if to see whether anyone is watching. Joseph pretends to be looking elsewhere; after a moment, he glances their way again. The red-bearded man is gripping the girl's thin arms in his large-knuckled hands and whispering something, more urgently this time. The girl squeezes her eyes shut, like someone trying not to cry. After a moment, she murmurs something in reply. It seems to satisfy the man. He rises and places another wager, betting every dollar of the money he has just won.

Joseph enviously watches the money changing hands and wonders how the man can be so profligate with something that is so hard to come by. He's either very wealthy—which doesn't seem likely, judging from his clothing and the girl's—or very foolish . . . or very confident that he will win again.

The drivers move their horses into position for the fourth heat. Feeling confident himself, Joseph places his mental bet on Adios again. He can't bring himself to be as free with his winnings as the red-bearded man; he wagers only ten imaginary dollars.

Adios takes the lead again and, for the first half mile or so, it looks as though she'll keep it. But a hundred yards from the finish line, another horse comes up alongside her. At first she's not aware of it, because of the blinders. When she finally does see the competitor pulling ahead, she panics and breaks into a gallop. This is against the rules; the driver has to pull her out of the running.

Joseph groans and smacks a fist into his palm, just as though he'd had some real stake in the outcome of the race.

Apparently the red-bearded man had his money on Adios as well. He curses, throws his bowler hat in the dirt, and kicks the fence, leaving a brown smudge on the whitewash. Flushed with anger, he crouches down and speaks to the girl. Joseph can't make out his words, but it's clear from the look on his face that they are far from pleasant. As illogical as it may seem, he appears to be blaming her for his loss.

The girl tries to back away, but he seizes her by the shoulders and shakes her roughly. Surprisingly, the girl does not flinch or protest; she only looks at him, and her look is neither pleading nor defiant, but somehow . . . indifferent, as though her mind is on something else altogether.

This seems to infuriate the man even more, and he raises a hand to strike her. Though Joseph has no right to interfere in what is clearly a family matter, he takes a step toward the man and opens his mouth to say something—he's not sure what. But there's no need, after all. With a wordless exclamation of disgust, the man releases the girl, making her stagger backward. Then he rises and begins pushing his way rudely through the crowd, knocking the dust off his hat.

For a moment, the girl doesn't move. She only stares after him, perhaps expecting him to change his mind and come back for her. When it becomes clear that he won't, a look of distress crosses her face. She lifts her skirts and hurries after him. But the sea of spectators will not part for her as it did for him. People seem not to notice her or to hear her murmurs of "Excuse me. Pardon me, please."

Joseph comes to her aid. "Stay close to me," he tells her.

Then, calling out, "Let us through, please!" and using his elbows when necessary, he clears a path for her.

On the fringes of the crowd he spots the red-bearded man conversing with another racegoer. As Joseph approaches, he hears the man say, "Tell you what. If my horse don't pay off, I'll give you double your money back. You can't go wrong—"

"Sir!" Joseph interrupts. "I believe this young lady is with you?"

The man glares at the girl, then at Joseph. "So? What business is it of yours?"

"None. But it seems to me it's *your* business to keep her safe, and not—"

"It seems to *me*," the man says, "that you're after sticking your nose in where it's not wanted." He looks around; the fellow to whom he has been trying to sell a tip—undoubtedly a worthless one—has lost interest and walked off. "And now you've made me lose a perfectly good prospect." He raises a fist. "I'd advise you to be off, lad, before I break that meddling nose of yours."

Joseph is reluctant to back down. For some reason—perhaps because she reminds him so much of his sister—he doesn't want to look bad in front of the girl. But he's also reluctant to have his nose broken, and there's no question that the man is capable of it. He's two inches taller than Joseph, and fifty pounds heavier, and his fists are the size of the cannonballs that once sat in front of the Armory, before the Armory blew up. He clearly knows something about broken noses, too, for his own shows signs of having been pounded once or twice.

"Well, I'd advise *you*," Joseph calls over his shoulder as he walks away, "to take better care of your daughter." He gives a last glance at the girl. She doesn't look his way. She is clinging to the man's sleeve.

CHAPTER FIVE

Though the residents of Washington are thankful to have been spared the full wrath of the war, no one can escape its effects. If you pick up a newspaper, there on the front page is an account of the battle of Cedar Creek, and a long list of those killed in action. You hear what you think is distant thunder, though there's not a cloud in the sky; it's the gunners at one of the forts that circle the city, keeping in practice. You can't walk four blocks without encountering at least one man who is missing an arm or a leg or worse. If you're not careful, you may be caught up in a group of carousing, drunken soldiers, or run down by a thousand head of cattle on their way to be slaughtered.

Hospitals are the most graphic reminders of the horror and the waste of war. But no matter how you may go out of your way to avoid them, you can't. There are far too many sick and injured men—fifty thousand, by some estimates—for the regular hospital to cope with, so other buildings have been pressed into service: churches, concert halls, museums, private mansions. Even in the Patent Office, bloody, bandaged bodies are strewn among the glass cases containing models of various inventions; it's as though the wounded themselves are on display, perhaps to illustrate the practical effects of such ingenious devices as the grenade and the Union Repeating Gun.

The citizens are weary of the war, of hearing about it, of discussing it. In an effort to forget it for a time, the wealthy indulge in an endless round of balls and visits known as "at homes," where the conversation is determinedly kept light and amusing. The less privileged find their distraction at the racetrack and prizefighting ring, in the theatres and music halls. The entertainers who lodge at Mrs. McKenna's all agree that they have never played to such full and enthusiastic houses.

Here, too, the conversation seldom touches on the war or on politics. These are dangerous topics—especially in the presence of Mrs. McKenna. She has made it clear that she is one hundred percent (or even more) in favor of Mr. Lincoln and his efforts to keep the Union together. In fact, before she will take in any prospective boarder, she interrogates him to see where his sympathies lie.

That's one reason she rents to so many performers. They tend to be well disposed toward the president. He is, after all, an avid theatregoer, and whenever the newspapers announce that he'll be attending a show, it sells out. Theatre folk also know that it's wise to give the audience what it wants. So if there's anyone under Mrs. McKenna's roof who is secretly secesh (that is, a Southern sympathizer), he keeps it to himself.

Joseph admires Mr. Lincoln, too. He's read several books about the president's boyhood, and how young Abe overcame poverty and the lack of an education through hard work and determination. What's more, for a brief time during the Black Hawk War, Mr. Lincoln was an Indian fighter.

Being new to the boardinghouse, Mr. Thomson, the trained dog man, isn't yet aware that straying into the realm of politics is a lot like straying into that notorious section of the city known as Murder Row. The presidential election is only weeks away, and it seems natural enough to comment, over dinner, upon Lincoln's chances of winning a second term.

"I think it may prove to be a very close race," says Mr. Thomson.

"Do you, now?" says Mrs. McKenna.

Mr. Thomson somehow manages to miss both the challenge in her voice and the signs of warning being sent his way by the other boarders. "From what I hear, there's a good deal of animosity toward the president. Any number of people have told me that they thought it was a mistake to set the Negroes free, that it'll only serve to alienate the South even more. At the same time, other folks are saying that Mr. Lincoln is actually helping out the Southern economy, by letting his cronies buy tobacco and cotton from them."

"People are fools," snaps Mrs. McKenna. "And if you believe everything they tell you, you're an even bigger one."

"I didn't say that I believed it. I only—"

"You only *repeated* it. If somebody told you that the planets were God's marbles, would you go around repeating that, too?"

"Speaking of marbles!" puts in Mick O'Boyle, the Irish comedian, in an obvious attempt to save his colleague from further humiliation. "I saw Mr. Booth perform in *The Marble Heart* several weeks ago."

Mr. Hayes, the clog dancer, lends his efforts to the rescue. "Which Booth was it? Edwin, or Wilkes, or the other one—what's-his-name?"

"Junius," puts in Nicholas Ehrlich. "He shares the appellation with his father—though the father was by far the better actor."

"Did you know him, then?" asks Fanny Thomson. "The father, I mean?"

"I should say I did. We shared the same stage more than once."

"You don't say so?" Mr. Hayes is clearly impressed. Junius Brutus Booth, who died a decade ago, is generally acknowledged to be America's first great dramatic actor (though, in fact, he was born in England).

"Yes, indeed." Nicholas begins to wax dramatic himself. "I shall never forget his portrayal of Richard the Third. It fairly made one's hair stand on end." He strikes a tragic pose. " 'Since I cannot prove a lover, I am determined to prove a villain, and hate the idle pleasures of these days.' " The lines do not have the effect he intended; his hoarse voice makes him sound less like the vengeful Duke of Gloucester than like a man on the gallows with the rope about his neck. Still, he goes on. " 'Plots have I laid, inductions dangerous, by drunken prophecies, libels, and dreams . . .' "

Unexpectedly, the other male boarders rise to their feet— not in order to applaud his rendition of the role, but out of courtesy to Carolina Ehrlich, who has chosen this moment to excuse herself from the table. His grand speech interrupted, Nicholas trails off. He clears his throat and shrugs awkwardly. "Well. I'm no Junius Brutus Booth."

"I thought it was very good," says Fanny Thomson politely.

Joseph picks at the food on his plate and avoids looking her way. He seriously doubts that his father ever actually knew or performed with the celebrated Junius Brutus Booth, and he's sure that Fanny and everyone else at the table is thinking the same thing—everyone except El Niño Eddie, who is eyeing the apple pie left behind by Carolina Ehrlich.

"Well," says Mick O'Boyle, "John Wilkes Booth can't hold a candle to his father, either, I can tell you."

"What's wrong with him?" demands Fanny. "I think he's very dashing."

"Oh, he's dashing enough, I suppose, and athletic—"

"And *extremely* handsome."

"Yes, yes, I grant you that. But don't you see, those are all just superficial things. There's no real *depth* to his acting."

"Oh, and of course you'd be the one to know," Fanny says sarcastically. "*Your* performances are so moving, so full of emotion." She hunches her back and launches into a wickedly accurate impression of Richard III as portrayed by Mick O'Boyle: "Sure, an' 'tis determined Oi am to prove Oi'm a villain. Oi belave Oi'll put a drap o' pizen in the little princes' tay."

Everyone—with the exception of Mrs. McKenna, of course—bursts into uproarious laughter. Mick O'Boyle laughs loudest of all. Fanny catches Joseph staring at her with undisguised admiration, and she winks at him. He blushes furiously and looks down at his plate again.

"Faith, will yez look at the toime!" says Mick O'Boyle in his stage accent. "Oi'm off to the thayatre to give one of me *movin'* and *emosh'nal* perfarmances."

As Joseph watches wistfully, Fanny and her father depart, too, carrying their trained dogs. Mr. Hayes and Monsieur Paul, the Modern Hercules, follow. Only the acrobatic Montoya family remains. Last night, in the Canterbury Music Hall, where they perform, a fight broke out between Union soldiers and Southern sympathizers. The damage was so extensive that the hall is closed for several days for repairs.

When his parents aren't looking, El Niño Eddie surreptitiously reaches across the table, pulls Carolina Ehrlich's dessert plate to him, and devours the apple pie in three bites. He glances at Joseph and puts a finger to his lips.

Joseph shrugs, as if to say, I won't tell, and heads upstairs. He finds his mother lying, propped up by pillows, in the bed normally occupied by him and his father. "It's so stuffy in my room," she says. "I think I'll lie here for a while, next to the window. I'm sure you and your father can practice your"—she waves a hand dismissively—"animal magnetism, or whatever it's called, in the parlor."

"It's called clairvoyance. Shall I get you your headache powders?"

"No. I'm just feeling a little faint and trembly, that's all."

Joseph picks up *The Scalp Hunters* from the bedside table. "I wish Father wouldn't try to impress the other boarders that way. It only makes him look . . . well, sort of sad, if you ask me."

"Sad?"

"Yes. I was embarrassed for him. Weren't you?"

"No."

"Then why did you leave the table?"

For a moment, he thinks she didn't hear him. Then she sighs and says, "It was something in the speech your father was reciting. It made me think of . . . of your sister."

Joseph frowns thoughtfully. "I don't remember what he said."

"It doesn't matter. No doubt I overreacted. Go on and read your book, now."

Joseph hesitates, fiddling with the silk ribbon that marks his place in the book. "At the race the other day, I . . . I saw a girl who reminded me of her."

Carolina Ehrlich nods and says, in a voice that wavers a little, "That's why I prefer not to go out, you see. Each time I do, I spot someone I would *swear* is Margaretta. It's only an illusion, of course, and it lasts no more than an instant." She puts a hand to her cheek and wipes away a tear. "But the pain is quite real, and lasts longer."

As Joseph prepares to settle into the armchair in the parlor, his father appears at the top of the stairs. "Are you ready?" Nicholas Ehrlich asks.

"I was just about to read. I thought you were giving a lesson to Mr. Murray."

"No." Nicholas holds up a folded sheet of paper. "Mr. Murray sent a message. He's decided not to pursue a career in opera after all."

"Well, that's no great loss. What career is he going to pursue?"

"Believe it or not, he's enlisted in the army."

"I don't believe it."

"Nonetheless, it's true." He tosses the note onto the marble-topped table. "So. That's a dollar per week we shall have to learn to do without." He sinks into the other armchair. "It's my own fault, I suppose. I should have flattered him more, instead of always insisting that he try harder." He glances at his son. "I suppose you'll be quitting on me, next."

"I hadn't planned to," Joseph says. "I have to say, though, I could stand a little flattery now and then."

Nicholas Ehrlich smiles. "I shall do my best." He jingles some objects in the pocket of his jacket. "I've collected a new set of mystifying items."

"We'll have to work out here; Mother's taken over our bedroom."

"Oh. That's unfortunate."

"Why? It's not as if someone's going to spy on us and steal our code."

Nicholas laughs. "You think not? You don't know performers as I do, Joseph. It's a sort of game with them, trying to learn one another's professional secrets. I suppose we'll be safe enough, though. The Montoyas have gone out, so there's no one here except us and Mrs. McKenna."

Joseph turns the armchair to the wall, Nicholas takes out the first item—a pocket watch—and they begin. "What is this?"

"A watch."

"Be more specific."

"A silver watch."

"Gentleman's or lady's? Be quick, now."

"A gentleman's."

"Can you tell me the manufacturer?"

"The American— No, the *Elgin* Watch Company."

"What time does it say?"

Joseph has never been asked this before. "I don't know!"

"I'm not finished. Tell me the time, please. Do you see it? Come, come."

"Ten-forty."

"Good."

Joseph glances over his shoulder anxiously. "Is that another clue?"

"No, it's a compliment."

"Oh. Thank you. It wasn't good enough, though—my

performance, I mean. Give me another one." He manages to identify, without a single mistake, an oriental fan, a box of matches, and a hymnal. He's working on naming the exact hymn his father has opened up to when he hears, from the vicinity of the stairwell, a noise that sounds suspiciously like someone trying unsuccessfully to stifle a sneeze.

CHAPTER SIX

One of the most useful devices novelists have at their disposal is omniscience—the ability to see and hear everything that goes on anywhere in the story, including things of which the main characters are totally unaware.

Nicholas Ehrlich believes that the Montoya family has gone out for the evening. But I can tell you that, in fact, it was only the mother and father. El Niño Eddie has stayed behind. He is suffering from an upset stomach.

There's something else that neither the Ehrlichs nor the Montoyas are aware of: El Niño Eddie is a spy. Or at least he imagines himself to be one. To Joseph Ehrlich, Eddie's life as an acrobat may appear daring and glamorous, but to Eddie it seems quite ordinary. The desire to be something we're not is part of human nature, and what Eddie desires is to be a secret agent, like those whose exploits behind enemy lines are recounted in the popular periodical *Frank Leslie's Illustrated.*

He practices on the other boarders, and he has discovered some things that are, if not exactly crucial to the war effort, still quite interesting. He has learned that Mr. Hayes wears lifts in his shoes to make himself taller; that Fanny Thomson occasionally filches scraps of ham from the smokehouse for Hector and Carlo, the trained dogs; that Monsieur Paul suffers from chronic back pain and takes laudanum for it; that, unlikely as it may seem, Mrs. McKenna has a suitor—a fish merchant with whom she sometimes takes a stroll, under the guise of going to the market.

And now he has discovered what Nicholas and Joseph Ehrlich are up to. For, as you've no doubt guessed, it's he who is hiding in the stairwell. He has also discovered that he is allergic to the dog hair that has collected there and been overlooked by the cleaning lady.

Hoping that his muffled sneeze will be overlooked, too, Eddie attempts to make a silent but hasty retreat. It's too late. Joseph Ehrlich and his father appear at the head of the stairs. "What are you doing there?" Joseph demands.

For an aspiring spy, Eddie is not very good at lying. "Nothing," he says. He *is* good at looking innocent, but not good enough to fool Joseph's father.

"How long have you been listening to us?" asks Nicholas Ehrlich.

"Not long," says Eddie. "Only a minute or so." In fact, he's been eavesdropping almost since they began. As he notices the anxious looks on their faces, it occurs to Eddie that maybe he's taking the wrong approach, being so defensive. Obviously they're worried about how much he knows. He doesn't really know much, only that they're rehearsing some sort of mind-reading act. But if they *think* he knows more, he might be able to use it to his advantage. They may even be willing to pay him to keep quiet.

He sighs, as though he's given up. "All right. I've been listening ever since you started."

"Then you've deduced what it is we're doing," says Nicholas.

"Of course. I'm not stupid."

Joseph says, "You won't tell anyone, will you?"

"That depends."

"On what?"

"On whether you make it worth my while not to."

Nicholas laughs. "I believe he's trying to black-mail us, Joseph."

"Black-mail?" says Eddie innocently.

Nicholas shakes his head and sighs, as though he pities the boy. "Ah, Eduardo." He sits on the step next to Eddie and puts a hand on his shoulder. "I'm sorry to disillusion you, my boy, but your scheme won't work. Shall I tell you why? There are two reasons. One is that we have no money. The other is that, if you breathe a word to anyone about what we're up to, I shall be forced to reveal to the other boarders what *you've* been up to."

"What— What do you mean?"

"Come now, Eduardo," says Nicholas reproachfully. "You said you were not stupid. You know precisely what I mean— the way you've been skulking about, peeping through key-holes and eavesdropping on private conversations. I suspect that Monsieur Paul will be especially . . . *disappointed* to hear that you've been spying on him. I know that I, for one, would not care to incur the wrath of someone so large. And muscular."

Eddie swallows hard as he considers what it would mean to make an enemy of the Modern Hercules. His stomach, which had been improving, begins to hurt again. "All right," he says weakly. "I won't tell anyone, I promise." As Eddie starts to slip guiltily away, something occurs to him, and he turns back. "Just one thing. How did you know?"

Nicholas gives him a look of surprise. "Why, isn't it obvious?" he says. "I read your mind."

As he and Joseph return to their rehearsal, Joseph says softly, "How *did* you know?"

"I didn't," admits Nicholas. "I just assumed that, if he was spying on us, he was very likely doing the same to the other boarders."

Though the Ehrlichs are now aware of El Niño Eddie's skulking tendencies, there's one more thing they don't know about him: he's not very good at keeping promises.

The notion that one person might be able to read another's thoughts, like reading a book, has caught his fancy—seized it, in fact, in an iron grip. After all, mind reading would be the ultimate form of spying. The next day he casually asks his father and mother whether they have ever shared a bill with a mentalist or clairvoyant. In the ensuing discussion, without quite meaning to, Eddie brings up the Ehrlichs.

That evening, as Joseph and his father are rehearsing in their room, there is a knock on the door. Joseph delays answering it until Nicholas has had time to put away all their paraphernalia. Their visitor, he discovers, is Eddie's father. "I hope I am not interrupting," says Mr. Montoya.

"No, no, of course not," says Nicholas. "Come in, please; sit down."

"Thank you." Though Mr. Montoya sits in the most comfortable armchair, he looks rather uncomfortable. He clears his throat. "I am not the sort to pry into other people's business, Mr. Ehrlich, but Eduardo seems to think that you are working on an act—one that involves mind reading."

Nicholas gives him a look of surprise that's quite convincing. "Really? I wonder why he would think that?"

"Well," says Mr. Montoya, with an apologetic laugh, "my son has a vivid imagination." He rises from his chair. "I'm sorry to have bothered you, then. I meant only to be of assistance."

"Assistance? In what way?"

"Oh, it's just that the owner of the National Theatre told me that he is searching for something new and different to put on his program—something besides the usual singers and comedians and"—he grins wryly—"and acrobats. I thought a mind-reading act would appeal to him. No one has done anything of that sort here, at least not recently."

"The National Theatre, eh?" Nicholas casts a meaningful glance at his son. Joseph answers it with a look of alarm, for he knows what his father is thinking. Just as Mr. Montoya is about to close the door behind him, Nicholas yanks it open again, nearly pulling the man off his feet. "Would you mind staying a little longer, sir? There's something we'd like to discuss."

You can be thankful once again for the ability to take a giant step forward in time. It means we don't have to spend the next few days with Joseph. Frankly, he is not very good company. He is, in fact, little more than a bundle of worries and jangled nerves.

Like the prospect of fighting Indians, the notion of being an entertainer sounded so attractive and exciting in the abstract. But then Mr. Montoya introduced them to Mr. Grover, the owner of the National Theatre. They did fifteen minutes or so of mind reading for him and signed a contract, and now the whole thing is no longer abstract.

Now, on the front page of *The Opera Glass*, a periodical "Devoted to General Information, Music, and the Drama," there is a sizable advertisement declaring that, at Grover's National on Monday night, Professor Godunov and Son, Mentalists, will perform mystifying feats of clairvoyance and eyeless seeing. Their astounding act, it says, has been applauded and acclaimed by all who have witnessed it. It doesn't bother to mention that the number of people who have witnessed it amounts to two—Mr. Grover and El Niño Eddie.

Professor Godunov and Son are, of course, none other than the Ehrlichs. They have been practicing madly for sev-

eral days, eight and ten hours at a stretch, in an effort to prepare for their first public performance. During the first of
these marathon rehearsals, after mistakenly identifying a
rosary as a tobacco box, Joseph wailed, in a fit of despair,
"We'll never be ready in time! I'm just not good enough!"

"If you tell yourself that you are not good enough,"
Nicholas Ehrlich said patiently, "you never will be."

"I'm not telling *myself*! I'm telling *you*! I'm not good
enough!" To Joseph's surprise, a slow smile spread across his
father's face. "What?" he demanded irritably.

"I know how we can be certain that we're *both* good
enough."

"How?"

"We'll make it our new name." He gestured grandly, as
though at a banner where the words were inscribed, illuminated by gaslight. "Professor Godunov and Son!"

Joseph has not indulged in any outbursts since then;
there's no time for it. There's time only to rehearse, to eat—
very sparingly, for his stomach seems knotted up—and to
sleep, very fitfully. He has sent a message to the China and
Lamp Store informing Mr. Foley that he's ill, which is only a
slight exaggeration. For the first time, he has an inkling of
how his mother must feel—as though the world outside her
room is just too complicated for her to cope with, and moving too fast for her to keep up.

The nearer they get to opening night, the more anxious he
becomes. If they were performing at one of the music halls,
he would still fret, but not quite so much. The audiences

there are made up mainly of ordinary working folk who ask only to be entertained. Though he's never seen a show at the National, the other performers—he can say the *other* performers, since, for better or worse, he's one of them now—the other performers have told him that the audiences it attracts are more difficult to please . . . and more difficult to fool.

On a typical night, a casual glance around the theatre will reveal a dozen congressmen, a wide selection of generals, and one or two members of the president's cabinet. And anyone who attends shows there regularly is sure to be rewarded sooner or later with a glimpse of Mr. and Mrs. Lincoln sitting in the shadowy sanctum of the presidential box.

At a music hall, Joseph and his father would have shared the program with the likes of Mr. Heaney, the Tattooed Man; the Kentucky Giant, who stands just under eight feet tall; and Mr. Herrio Nano, who impersonates, among other things, a baboon, a sloth, and a fly.

At the National they are to be sandwiched in between a performance of the dramatic poem *Faust and Marguerite* and a recital by Ada Tesman, popular singer of opera arias, like a thin ribbon of icing between the layers of a cake.

Though they don't arrive at the theatre until halfway through *Faust and Marguerite,* the wait backstage seems hours long to Joseph. To his surprise, with the exception of Miss Tesman, who seems a bit full of herself, the performers here are every bit as friendly and down-to-earth as those at Mrs. McKenna's. What's even more surprising is that his father appears to be acquainted with several of them.

"If it isn't old Nick!" A man in hideous purple makeup approaches and shakes his hand. "Did you ever get your voice back?"

"Not enough to permit me to sing or to do an entire play," says Nicholas. "Joseph and I have a mind-reading act."

"*You're* Professor Godunov?" The actor brandishes a playbill. "It says here that you're an exiled Russian nobleman!"

"Yes, and it says that you're 'a creature of Mephistopheles.' "

"True." The man turns to Joseph. "So, is this your real son, or just a pretend one? He looks terrified. I didn't realize my makeup was *that* scary."

"It's not you I'm afraid of," says Joseph.

"Ah," says the man. "Your first time onstage, is it?" He pulls a flask from inside his costume and holds it out to Joseph. "Have a pull of that; it'll help."

Before the boy can take the flask, his father snatches it. "No!" he says, in a tone that is unexpectedly abrupt, even angry. "There'll be none of that."

"Sorry, Nick. I forgot." The actor puts the flask away. "Well, I'm due to pop up out of hell any moment now. Break a leg, Professor Godunov and Son!" He scrambles down a set of stairs and out of sight.

"Why would he want us to break a leg?" asks Joseph.

"It's just something actors say to one another. You never wish someone good luck. It's bad luck."

"That makes perfect sense," says Joseph. "Where do you know him from?"

"We did a play together, many years ago. The Scottish play, I believe it was."

"What Scottish play?"

"The one by Shakespeare."

"You mean *Mac*—" Joseph is startled to find his father's hand clamped firmly over his mouth. When it's removed, he says, "Ow. What did you do that for?"

"You never say the name of the Scottish play backstage. It's bad luck."

"Oh. Is there anything else I should know?"

"Not that I can think of. Well, yes, there is one thing."

"What's that?"

"It's time for us to go on."

CHAPTER SEVEN

The winter that Joseph was nine and his sister was five, the family was living in Philadelphia. Margaretta loved nothing better than to go for walks with her brother along the riverfront to watch the ships come and go. She always brought along her favorite toy, a stuffed monkey, so he could see the ships, too. She called the monkey Arliss; it sounded better than his real name, which was Earless (for she had chewed off his ears).

One particularly nasty December day, she dropped Arliss—by accident, of course—into the river. Margaretta was inconsolable. There was nothing Joseph could do but jump in and rescue the monkey.

It took a great deal of willpower to enter that icy river. It takes every bit as much to force himself onto the gaslit stage of the National Theatre. He is convinced that the audience will laugh at them—well, perhaps not right out loud; they may be too polite for that. But he imagines the generals and congressmen nudging one another and whispering behind their hands, "Professor Godunov and Son, indeed! It's only that ordinary boy who works at Foley's china shop and his father, who pretends to give voice lessons even though he hardly has a voice himself."

Nicholas Ehrlich appears to have no qualms at all. He strides confidently to the apron of the stage and launches into his faux-Russian accent, straining his damaged vocal cords so that he can be heard. After introducing himself and his son, Yosef, he says, "May I ask for a volunteer from the audience?" He points to a portly man with slicked-down hair. "You, sir, come up, please."

While the man makes his way onto the stage, Nicholas retrieves a chair from the wings, places it downstage center, near the gas footlights, and places Joseph—who is nearly as rigid as the chair—in it. Then he takes from an inside pocket of his worn, rented dress coat a black cloth and hands it to the volunteer. "Will you please cover your eyes with that?"

Grinning foolishly, the man obliges. "Can you see anything?"

"No," the man says.

"Nothing at all?"

"No."

"Good. Can you tell me what object I am holding in my hand?" He pulls a marionette of a Hawaiian hula dancer from his pocket and makes it dance, drawing a laugh from the audience.

The man hesitates a moment, baffled. "No," he says. More laughter.

"Only joking," says Nicholas. "Will you please remove the cloth and tie it around my son's eyes? Not too tightly. Thank you. You may be seated." The man gets a round of applause; he makes a bow that is severely limited by the size of his stomach and returns to his seat.

Curiously enough, now that Joseph's eyes are blindfolded, he begins to relax a little. The cloth seems to have an effect similar to that of the blinders worn by Adios, the pacing horse. Since Joseph can no longer see the audience, he feels apart from them somehow, distanced from them. He can almost fool himself into thinking that it's just him and his father, practicing in their room at Mrs. McKenna's. Almost.

It helps that the audience has grown so quiet; they must, in order to make out Professor Godunov's words. He has descended from the stage, now, and is walking up the aisle, collecting items that Yosef will attempt to describe without seeing them.

Joseph's throat has gone so dry that he's certain, when he speaks, he'll sound like his father on a bad day. It's a pity he can't lick his palms, or his forehead; there's plenty of moisture there. He suddenly becomes aware that Nicholas has given him his first clue and that he's not entirely sure what it was. It may have been "What is this?" Or perhaps not. He can't ask his father to repeat it; that might tip the audience off. Besides, Nicholas is giving him the next clue: "Please tell me the item."

Please means the number seven, and number seven on the "What is it?" list is a ring. Joseph swallows hard and croaks uncertainly, "A ring?"

A smattering of applause tells him he's guessed right. Joseph has difficulty concealing his relief.

"Let me ask you what it is made of."

Let means two, and number two on the list of metals is: "Silver."

"On the inside is a name. How is it spelled, may I ask? Quickly."

"M-A-R-Y."

"Madam," says Nicholas to the ring's owner, "is your name Mary?"

"No, it's not," says the woman. There is a murmur of disappointment from the audience, along with a few chuckles of satisfaction from those who were just waiting for Joseph to slip up. His heart sinks. But then the woman adds, "Mary was my mother's name. It was her ring." More applause, very enthusiastic this time. Joseph holds back a grin.

He proceeds to identify a spool of red thread, a pair of tweezers, a throat lozenge, and a tuning fork. It's clear from the audience's response, which includes frequent "Oh!"'s and "Ah!"'s, that they are, by and large, properly mystified and astonished. But as you no doubt know, there is a trouble-maker in every crowd. In this case, it's a rough-looking individual sitting in the front row of the first balcony, which is called the dress circle, and he makes his voice heard now.

"Here, how do we know that the boy can't see through that blindfold?"

Nicholas Ehrlich spreads his hands, palms up. "Sir, you saw our volunteer test it, did you not?"

"Maybe he's an accomplice of yours," says the skeptic.

Nicholas has anticipated this. "Very well. What if Yosef were to turn his back to the audience? Would that convince you?"

"I suppose so," says the skeptic grudgingly.

"Yosef, would you please face upstage?" Joseph does so. Nicholas calls to the skeptic, "Would you like to contribute the next item, sir?"

"Yes, I would." The man fishes in the pocket of his jacket and tosses something down to Nicholas. "Let's see him guess *that!*" he says, rather nastily.

Nicholas gingerly holds up the object. There is a chorus of puzzled murmurs from the audience; then the spectators nearest to Nicholas give a collective gasp as they realize what it is—a shrunken human head. The skeptic, you see, is an importer of rubber from South America, and one of his representatives there recently sent him the head, which he carries around as a conversation piece. It makes for some rather macabre conversations.

Needless to say, *shrunken head* does not appear on any of the nineteen lists compiled by Nicholas Ehrlich. He needs to make Joseph aware of that fact. "Here is something we don't see often," he says. "Not often at all. In fact, never. My goodness." He calls to Joseph, "Kindly tell me what it is I'm holding. Do you know? Use your powers of concentration." He pauses a moment, as if waiting for an answer, then goes on, a hint of desperation in his voice. "I ask you once again what this object is. For heaven's sake, Yosef. Have you fallen asleep up there? Give me an answer."

There is another long pause. The audience is utterly still and silent, as though every member of it is holding his or her breath. "Is it . . . ?" Joseph hesitates. "Can it be a . . . a shrunken head?"

"Absolutely correct!" cries Nicholas, his voice breaking. "Take a bow!" The theatre fills with applause, cheers, whistles. Nicholas tosses the grotesque South American souvenir to its abashed owner, who seems to have shrunken a bit himself, and gleefully quotes a line from King Lear: " 'Methinks he seems no bigger than his head!' " The audience responds with peals of laughter.

Joseph laughs, too. Well, he thinks, that's one thing about performing for sophisticated theatregoers: they know their Shakespeare. Apparently they also know a good performance when they see one. The Ehrlichs attempt to exit, but the audience won't let them go. They must take three more bows before they can escape.

Leonard Grover, a small, dapper man, is waiting backstage. He doesn't look particularly pleased. "Gentlemen," he says, "I'm going to have to tear up your contract."

Joseph gapes at him. "Tear it up? They loved us!"

"Of course they did," says Mr. Grover soberly. "That's why we need a new contract. What would you say to a run of four weeks, at a hundred dollars a week?"

Joseph goes on staring at him, even more dumbfounded. Incredibly, Nicholas Ehrlich is shaking his head. "I'd say that's not enough. There are two of us, remember. Two hundred a week sounds more reasonable."

Mr. Grover looks outraged. Joseph is certain that he'll withdraw the offer altogether. Instead, he says, "A hundred and fifty."

"Very well," says Nicholas. "But if we're held over, we'll want two hundred."

"Agreed." The men shake hands, and Mr. Grover walks off.

"He might at least have told us we were good," says Joseph.

Nicholas smiles. "I believe he just did."

"Oh." Suddenly the significance of the deal hits Joseph. "A hundred and fifty a *week*?" he exclaims. "That's more than ten *times* what I make at Foley's!"

"Just remember, it's for only four weeks."

But Joseph is too overcome by all the applause and all the

talk of money to listen. Whatever doubts he once had about the success of the act have vanished. "Oh, he'll keep us on longer than that! He'll have to! We were a sensation! Although . . ." Joseph pauses and grimaces. "For a while there I had some serious doubts. When you said"—he mimics his father's strangled voice and Russian accent—" 'here is something we don't see very often,' my heart nearly stopped. And then when you started giving me the clues, I really panicked. *S-H-R-U-N-K?* I thought it must be a stuffed skunk, and you were spelling it wrong. But I decided to trust you."

"I am gratified that you did. By the way, though I may have sounded anxious, I wasn't. That was for the benefit of the audience. It's essential that we trust one another. We may encounter even stranger objects before we're through."

In the world of the theatre, news of a smashing success or an abject failure travels quickly. When they reach Mrs. McKenna's, they are greeted by the other boarders with huzzahs and heartfelt congratulations that seem to Joseph to bear no hint of envy. It is as though they are being welcomed into some secret society, one that requires its members to undergo a grueling ordeal, such as the one Joseph has read about in which certain Indian tribes pierce their flesh with wooden pins and then are hung up by ropes attached to the pins.

Mr. Thomson produces a bottle of whiskey, thus risking the wrath of Mrs. McKenna, who has forbidden the presence of liquor in her home, except for medicinal purposes. But

Mrs. McKenna is not here; she is, in fact, taking a stroll with her fish merchant. To El Niño Eddie's delight, he is given the task of keeping an eye out for her return, which seems to him very much like spying.

When the bottle is passed to Nicholas, he upends it, but Joseph notices that he does not swallow.

"I hope Grover had the good sense to put you under contract," says Mick O'Boyle.

Nicholas nods. "Four weeks."

"Four weeks!" echoes the Modern Hercules. "Good for you, Ehrlich!" He pounds Nicholas on the back so heartily that Nicholas threatens to topple over.

Fanny Thomson makes her way over to Joseph and, to his astonishment, leans in and plants a kiss lightly on his cheek. "Congratulations, Joseph. I hear you were marvelous." She smells of whiskey, mingled with perfume. Joseph feels lightheaded again.

At that moment, El Niño Eddie races into the parlor. "She's coming! She's coming!" The bottle of whiskey disappears. The boarders disperse. Wearily, Nicholas and his son climb the stairs to their room, to find Carolina Ehrlich propped up in their bed, reading a rather florid romance titled *Bianca*.

Her husband bends down to give her a kiss, but she makes a face and pulls away. "Nicholas, have you been *drinking*?"

"Not really. I only pantomimed it, as it were, so as not to offend the others. We were having a bit of a celebration."

Carolina, who rarely displays anything approaching

enthusiasm or interest, sits up in bed, her hand at her throat. "A celebration?" she says. "Has the South surrendered?"

Nicholas laughs weakly. "No, my dear. Nothing quite so dramatic, I'm afraid."

Joseph waits impatiently for him to go on, to tell her what a sensation they were. When he shows no sign of doing so, Joseph takes over. "Mother, you should have been there! The audience was crazy for us! Mr. Grover has promised us a four-week run, at a hundred and fifty dollars a week!"

Carolina does not congratulate them. Nor does she ask for all the details of their triumph. She merely looks bewildered, the way she always does when such crass subjects as work and money are discussed. She has always felt that these matters are the province of men, and that a well-bred woman should not concern herself with them.

"Don't you see what this means?" says Joseph. "It means we can move out of the boardinghouse and into a real hotel, one with running water and an indoor toilet!"

"Oh, my," says his mother. After a moment, she adds, "Do we have to?"

CHAPTER EIGHT

Perhaps you imagined that Carolina Ehrlich, who clearly considers herself a woman of taste and refinement, would jump at the chance to leave the humble boardinghouse and its tiresome, talkative tenants behind. Not so. For all its shortcomings, Mrs. McKenna's house has one great advantage—for Carolina, anyway—over any other lodging place: it's familiar. Though she sometimes finds her little room cheerless and confining, the very closeness of it also makes her feel safe. The world, with its wars, its clattering trains and lumbering horsecars, its constant change, its dismaying decline in morals and manners, is a daunting and dangerous place. A person needs a refuge, a retreat, and this, however unsatisfactory it may be, has become hers.

Her fears of the new and unfamiliar may be exaggerated, but they are not entirely unreasonable or unfounded. The fact is, the world of the mid-1800s is progressing (or, some would say, deteriorating) at an unprecedented rate. In a single decade, it has seen the advent of the electric lightbulb, the elevator, the storage battery, and the internal combustion engine. The first oil well has been drilled. A steamer has crossed the Atlantic Ocean in nine days. A railroad is under construction that will span the continent. The population of the United States has soared to thirty-two million (and it seems to Carolina as if half of them live in Washington). Scientists have measured the speed of light.

These things do not seem threatening to Joseph, of course. He resents the fact that his mother won't let them move to better lodgings now that they can afford it. Nicholas swore that, when they became famous, everything would change, yet it looks as though nothing will be changing anytime soon. They'll still be living at Mrs. McKenna's, not at the best hotels, and still dining on beans and potatoes, not capons and capers. And he still must go to work at Foley's China and Lamp Store in the morning.

He didn't feel it would be fair to Mr. Foley if he suddenly quit, so he's made up his mind to stay on until a replacement can be found. The moment he steps into the shop, Mr. Foley cries out, "Aha! Mr. Ehrlich! Feeling better, I presume?"

"Yes. Much better. Thank you."

Mr. Foley is one of those heavyset men who does not seem to realize that he is heavyset. He insists on wearing jackets and vests that are too small for him and seems perpetually on the verge of bursting out of them. Even his pointed Vandyke beard seems as though it belongs on a smaller man, or at least one with a smaller face. "I thought you might be, considering you were able to make it to the National Theatre last night."

"You—you were there?"

"Indeed I was! Indeed I was!" After so many years of talking to customers, who can be a rather thickheaded lot, Mr. Foley has fallen into the irritating habit of saying things twice. "You wouldn't have seen me, of course, considering that I was near the rear of the family circle, in the twenty-five-cent seats—and considering that you had a blindfold over your eyes. You did look a bit ill when you first came on, I must say, decidedly ill. But it was hardly the sort of illness I had imagined, from your note."

"I know. I'm sorry. I only—"

"Sorry? Sorry? No reason to be, no reason to be! Of course you needed time off to prepare for your opening night! Perfectly understandable, perfectly understandable."

Joseph is taken aback by his employer's suddenly solicitous manner. Ordinarily he says no more to Joseph than is necessary, and his tone is no more civil than necessary. Joseph can't help suspecting that this is a trick of some sort. Perhaps there's an important customer in the store somewhere, and Mr. Foley is trying to impress her.

But no customer appears, and yet Mr. Foley keeps it up. "I never suspected you of having such talents hidden away, my boy, never suspected it. You and your father had the audience spellbound, literally spellbound. I wish you could have seen the looks on their faces—but of course you couldn't, considering the blindfold." He pauses, then adds slyly, "Or *could* you?"

He leans in close to Joseph, as if someone might overhear—though we've established that there's no one in the store but them. "Frankly, I'm still wondering whether there was a hole in that cloth somewhere, that's what I'm wondering. I mean, certain members of the audience may have believed that you were using second sight or whatever you want to call it, but I'm a practical man, Mr. Ehrlich, a man of business, and I've learned that, no matter how *mystifying* a thing might seem, there's always a practical explanation behind it, a practical explanation."

He leans in even closer. "Tell the truth, now," he whispers. "There was a trick of some kind involved, wasn't there? Tell the truth, now."

Joseph's father has warned him about this very thing. He just wasn't expecting it to happen so soon. "As the act becomes better known," Nicholas said, "you will encounter people who will attempt to flatter you, or bribe you, or trick you into revealing the secrets of our art. Some will be fellow performers, hoping to duplicate our success. Others, like our skeptical friend last night, will simply resent the fact that you can do something they can't."

Mr. Foley belongs in the latter category. Fortunately, Nicholas has also given his son some suggestions on how to reply. "I'll be happy to teach you how it's done," Joseph says.

"Will you?" says Mr. Foley.

"If you're willing to practice two or three hours a night for the next two years."

Mr. Foley draws back. "It's that hard to learn?"

"Have you ever tried to read someone's mind?"

"Only my wife's," says Mr. Foley mournfully. "You're right; it's hard. It's very hard."

The bell over the door jingles, and two young women of perhaps seventeen or eighteen enter the shop. In keeping with the fashion of the day, the waistlines of their dresses are cinched tight, and their skirts bulge with layer upon layer of crinolines. The resulting shape puts Joseph in mind of the drawstring bags full of money that he deposits in the bank at the end of each week.

Mr. Foley hastens to their side, as Joseph knew he would. Any customer who is relatively young and reasonably attractive—and, of course, female—can count on being waited upon by the proprietor himself; all others must be content with Joseph.

The ladies look around at the china and the lamps as though they expected something else altogether, perhaps an ice-cream parlor or a millinery. The gaze of the small, blonde one lights upon Joseph, and her blue eyes, which have been squinting nearsightedly, suddenly go wide. She seizes her companion's arm and, under cover of one gloved hand, urgently whispers something.

Her friend glances toward Joseph. So does Mr. Foley. Feeling awkward, Joseph picks up a feather duster and applies it briskly to the glass shade of a coal oil lamp—too briskly. He very nearly sends the whole thing crashing to the floor. When he looks up again, the young women are headed his way. The taller of the two appears to be more or less dragging the other one along, against her will.

"May I— May I help you, ladies?" asks Joseph.

"Yes," says the taller one. "My friend wants to know whether you're the mind reader she saw at the theatre last night."

"I didn't want to bother you," says her blushing friend, "but she wouldn't believe me. You are him, aren't you?"

Joseph is so surprised that he can't come up with a sensible reply. He does manage to nod.

"I told you so!" says the blonde young woman. She moves in on Joseph and says, breathlessly, "Can you tell me what I have in my reticule?" Though this may suggest to you that she has gotten something in her eye, a reticule is in fact a sort of handbag, often made of netting.

Joseph realizes then that admitting his identity may have

been a mistake. His father has failed to prepare him for this. "I— I'm sorry, ladies," he stammers. "I can't— I can't concentrate properly unless the conditions are right."

"Oh, please," says the young woman. "You were *so* impressive last night. Won't you give it a try?"

"I'm sorry," Joseph mumbles.

Indignant at being rebuffed, the young woman turns on her heel and sweeps out of the shop, her billowing skirts displacing a china plate, which shatters on the floor. "Mind reader, indeed," says her friend, and then she exits, too.

Joseph stares after them, openmouthed. It's not their hostile reaction that has him dumbfounded; he's used to that. Hardly a day goes by that he doesn't get at last one irate customer. The astonishing thing is that they actually recognized him. They even said he was *impressive*. No one has ever told him that before, not even his own parents, let alone an attractive young woman. A pleasant, slightly dizzy feeling comes over him, not unlike the feeling he got last night, being kissed on the cheek by Fanny Thomson.

He has little chance to savor it. "Don't stand there gaping," says the practical Mr. Foley. "Get a broom and sweep up that broken plate."

When word gets around that Yosef the mentalist is working at the China and Lamp Store, more and more people begin stopping by, sometimes wanting to test his mental powers and sometimes, apparently, just wanting to get a look at him without the blindfold. At first Mr. Foley is delighted that the boy is attracting so many customers. But eventually it dawns on him that very few of them are actually buying anything, and that, as is inevitable in china shops, a number of them are actually breaking things. Besides, if the truth be known, he secretly resents the fact that his clerk is getting so much attention.

Once the intial shock has worn off, Joseph begins to relish his new notoriety. After upsetting several more admirers with his inability to tell them what's on their minds or in their reticules, he comes up with a reply that seems to satisfy them. "I'm sorry," he says, "but I have to turn off my mental power when I'm not performing. I can't leave it on all the time, you know, otherwise I'd be constantly reading the thoughts of everyone around me, and think how maddening that would be for me—and how embarrassing for them."

After a moment, in which they consider all the secret thoughts they would not want revealed, they usually blush a little and say, "Oh. Yes. I see."

Mr. Foley puts up with the situation for a week or two, and then, being a practical man, a man of business, he asks Joseph to leave. This abrupt dismissal hurts Joseph's feelings. He had felt he was doing the man a favor by staying on, and this is the thanks he gets? "All right," he says stiffly. "You never paid me what I was worth, anyway."

Now, you may be thinking, That doesn't sound like Joseph. He's always been so unassuming, so polite. And you're right. But ever since he and his father began making so much money and all those young women began making a fuss over him, he has not been his old self.

At first, the changes in his behavior were not all that pronounced, and since he was at the China and Lamp Store most of the time, his parents and the other boarders either failed to notice them or overlooked them. But now that Joseph is home all day long, his new, slightly obnoxious attitude is hard to miss.

El Niño Eddie, being such a dedicated observer of his fellow lodgers, is the first to comment upon it. He has noticed that Joseph is reading a new book, *The Spy* by James Fenimore Cooper. Naturally, the title grabs his interest, and he begs Joseph to read it to him.

"Why don't you wait until I'm done with it?" says Joseph. "Then you can read it for yourself."

Eddie hangs his head. "I'm not very good with reading or writing. We've moved around so much, I never got much schooling."

Joseph can sympathize with that. "All right. I don't think you'll like it much, though."

"If it's about spies, I will," says Eddie eagerly. But after only a few pages of Cooper's dry and convoluted prose, the boy's enthusiasm wanes. "It's not very exciting, is it?"

Joseph is inclined to agree, but he doesn't want to sound as though he doesn't appreciate Cooper, who is considered one of the country's foremost novelists. "It's literature," he says. "It's not supposed to be exciting."

"I know what!" says Eddie. "Why don't you teach me how to read minds, instead?"

"No," says Joseph abruptly and, in fact, a bit rudely.

"Why not?"

Joseph doesn't reply right away. He's trying to come up with a reason that sounds less selfish and petty than the real one, which is that mind reading is the only skill he's ever had, the only thing that has ever made him feel in any way special, and he doesn't want to share it. "It's a professional secret," he says finally.

"I won't tell anyone, I promise."

"Oh, yes, we know how good you are at keeping promises. Besides," Joseph adds, rather haughtily, "it's not something that just anyone can learn. It requires a high degree of mental acuity"—he's quoting now from Professor Godunov's spiel—"and formidable powers of concentration."

"Oh," says Eddie. "Well, I guess that would explain why you've gotten such a swelled head."

The more celebrated Professor Godunov and Son become, the more self-important Joseph becomes, and the more he finds fault with the rather humble nature of their life outside the theatre. He criticizes Mrs. McKenna's cooking (not to her face, of course). He grumbles about having to share a bed. He even makes several rather disparaging comments about the other boarders and their skills, to the effect that, though they may be good enough for music halls, it takes a special breed of performer to impress the audiences at a *real* theatre.

It's as though the boy has begun to believe the grandiose claims about their act in general, and about him in particular, that appear in the National's newspaper advertisements. The latest, which Joseph has hung on the wall of their bedroom, reads:

The entire city is agog over the unprecedented and unparalleled mental prowess and dexterity displayed nightly by

PROFESSOR GODUNOV AND SON
PROFESSOR GODUNOV AND SON
PROFESSOR GODUNOV AND SON

When the brilliant but <u>modest</u> Yosef begins, without the aid of his eyesight, to describe their personal possessions, no matter how arcane or bizarre, and to read their innermost thoughts, the spectators are at once struck dumb with

AWE! ASTONISHMENT! SHEER DISBELIEF!

The management assures all members of the audience that the Professor and his amazing prodigy are careful to reveal nothing which might prove embarrassing or detrimental in any way.

His father has pointedly underlined the word *modest,* but Joseph seems not to have noticed. Nicholas has seen this sort of affliction strike other performers, this exaggerated sense of self-importance brought on by a sudden and unaccustomed exposure to money, attention, and acclaim. As he recalls, the youngest of the Booth boys, Wilkes, had a particularly nasty case of it—though from all accounts he has largely recovered.

Nicholas foolishly imagined that Joseph, who has a long history of being levelheaded, agreeable, and ordinary, would be immune. Instead, it seems to have hit him even harder than it would someone who was already accustomed, to some extent, to excelling and being praised. It puts Nicholas in mind of the way a person who has escaped the chicken pox as a child will, at a more advanced age, be positively prostrated by it.

Even Carolina has begun to comment on Joseph's uncharacteristic behavior. She has never paid a good deal of attention to her son. He didn't seem to require it. No matter what the family's circumstances (and at times they have been downright dismal), Joseph has always remained cheerful and uncomplaining.

Besides, he's a male. She always found it easier to relate to her daughter, even though Margaretta was as changeable as the weather. There were days, sometimes several of them together, when she was stubborn, moody, and demanding. But then another emotional front would move in, and she became so sunny, charming, and endearing that it was easy to forget the dark days.

You might expect that, after her daughter died, Carolina would turn her attention to her surviving child. But Margaretta proved stubborn even in death. She had such a firm hold on her mother's affection that it was buried with her.

Yet, as oblivious as Carolina ordinarily is toward her son, she is aware that the boy has lately become strangely distracted, impatient, self-absorbed. She doesn't see the connection, however, between his behavior and his sudden success. She feels he simply has too much time on his hands. "Perhaps he should go back to school," she says to Nicholas one morning while Joseph is at the lending library. "It would be better than having him sit around all day, reading novels."

Nicholas does not bother to point out that this is the very way she spends her days. "Actually," he says, "I've been thinking the same thing. Aside from the obvious benefit of furthering his education, it would do him good to be around boys his age for a change. It might bring him back to earth."

That afternoon he broaches the subject to his son. Joseph is not very receptive to the idea. "Why would I want to go back to school? I'm already making twice as much in a week as my old schoolmaster made in a month."

"But who knows how long that will last? Besides, you may not want to be a performer all your life."

"That's a funny thing for you to say. It's how you've spent *your* life."

"Yes," says Nicholas. "And look where it's gotten me."

Joseph shakes his head and gives a humorless laugh. "You're the one who talked me into doing this act, and now you're telling me I should do something else?"

"I'm only saying that you should consider other possibilities."

"*What* other possibilities? I've never been any good at
anything except this."

Nicholas sighs. "Well," he says, "if you intend to *stay*
good at it, I suggest we spend some time rehearsing."

"All right, all right," says Joseph, long-sufferingly. He had
assumed that, once they had the act perfected, they wouldn't
need to continue working on it endlessly. But it seems as
though even perfection isn't good enough for Nicholas. If he
had his way, they would still be practicing several hours each
day. Joseph would prefer a less demanding schedule—say, an
hour a week. They've arrived at a compromise: one hour
each afternoon, which Nicholas does his best to stretch out to
an hour and a half.

Though Joseph doesn't enjoy rehearsals, he does relish the
time they spend at the theatre, and if he could, he would
stretch it out somehow. For a brief time each evening, he
leaves his old, ordinary self behind and becomes the brilliant
but modest (well, *relatively* modest) Yosef, possessor of
unparalleled mental prowess and dexterity, applauded by
audiences and accepted by some of the country's most tal-
ented actors and singers as one of their own.

Though these celebrated performers that Joseph mingles
with backstage are an interesting lot, there's little point in my
introducing them to you. They won't be playing a significant
part—or, in fact, any part at all—in the rest of the story. You

see, Joseph and his father are almost done with their engagement at the National. They are about to move on and to encounter another set of characters who are even more interesting, and who *do* have large and influential roles, not only in deciding the direction our story will take, but also in determining the course of history.

CHAPTER NINE

At the beginning of our journey, I asked you to think of me as a guide, an interpreter. But I'm also like the driver of one of those sulkies you saw at the racetrack, pulling you this way or that, to keep you headed in the right direction. I've given you the novelistic equivalent of blinders, too, so you're not distracted by irrelevant and inconsequential things.

But in keeping our gaze fixed so firmly ahead, on Joseph and his changing fortunes, we have missed some relevant and consequential things along the way, so let's turn and look over our shoulders for a moment.

Since everyone is so thoroughly sick of the war, you might expect that they would favor Mr. Lincoln's opponent, George McClellan. Even though he was formerly general in chief of the Union armies, General McClellan promised that, if elected, he would end the conflict at once and restore peace. Unfortunately, he also promised to restore slavery to the South.

Though Mr. Lincoln has done some unpopular things—

such as refusing to exchange Rebel prisoners for Union soldiers captured by the South—he is widely respected and admired among the common people, including the troops who are fighting the war. In November's election, he received half a million more popular votes than General McClellan and ten times as many electoral votes.

But with presidential elections, as with horse races, the only people who are happy with the outcome are those who were backing the winner. In Washington—which, after all, lies south of the Mason-Dixon line—there is a large contingent of citizens who consider themselves Southerners. Many of them, including Mrs. Lincoln, have relatives in the Confederate army. And not a few of them would rather see Mr. Lincoln dead than see him run the country for four more years.

In the last week of their engagement at the National, Professor Godunov and Son are very nearly duped into serving as spokesmen for the secessionists. When Nicholas asks for items from the audience, a man with bushy side-whiskers hands him a campaign button that bears a picture of the president. Without looking closely at it, Nicholas asks his son, "What am I holding, please? Now, concentrate. What is it?"

Joseph really does have to concentrate. Because he's been so reluctant to practice, his command of the code has begun to slip a little. List number nine, third item on the list . . . a button. There's also a list of different sorts of buttons, and number six on it is: "A campaign button."

Nicholas glances at the button again and notices for the first time that Mr. Lincoln's likeness has been altered. He appears to have dark skin, a broad nose, and thick lips. Atop his head is a crown, and above that is the slogan ABRAHAM AFRICANUS THE FIRST. Nicholas has seen these buttons before. They are designed and distributed not by the president's supporters but by his enemies, who accuse Mr. Lincoln of having African ancestry—which, they say, would explain why he loves Negroes so much.

"Very good, Yosef, thank you," he says, and pockets the button.

"Hey, Professor!" calls the man with the side-whiskers. "I want that back!"

"Of course," says Nicholas. "Right after the show." He knows audiences, and he can tell that they're curious about the button. If he tries to return it now, someone will want a look at it, and then tempers will flare, and they'll have a brawl on their hands. Before the man can protest, Nicholas holds up a carrot given him by a sour-faced woman—in a deliberate effort to confound them, no doubt. "So!" he says. "Have you any idea what this next item is, may I ask? Very unusual. Please concentrate."

"A carrot."

"Very good," says Nicholas. "Now, a really difficult question. What *color* is it?" The audience laughs. The crisis is over.

The act has become so popular that nearly every night, as they are leaving the building, they find half a dozen or more audience members waiting outside the stage door, hoping to talk with them, or simply holding out playbills to be signed. Many of them, Joseph has noted with satisfaction, are young women, about the age of the ones who approached him at Foley's China and Lamp Store.

Unfortunately, like those two, some of these admirers also want to put his mind-reading abilities to the test. Fortunately, he's now learned how to say no a bit more gracefully.

Tonight the stage-door group is smaller than usual, which is not really surprising, since it's nearly the middle of December and there's a chilly breeze off the river. There are no attractive young ladies, either, only two middle-aged mothers and their daughters, who are perhaps ten or eleven. One of the girls mutely holds out her playbill to be autographed. Joseph carefully writes his name—his stage name, not his real one—in a rather ornate script that he's been practicing, then passes the playbill to his father.

"Oh, no, that's all right," says the girl's mother quickly. "She only wanted *yours*." Nicholas smiles faintly and hands her the playbill. "Do you have a *carte de visite*?" the woman asks Joseph.

"No, I'm sorry," Joseph says. In fact, he has no idea what a *carte de visite* is.

"Oh, well." The mother hands the playbill to her daughter. "Say thank you."

"'k you," murmurs the girl, and gives a small curtsy.

Joseph turns to the other girl. "Would you like me to sign yours, too?"

"No, thank you," she says, in a very businesslike fashion. She holds out one hand, which is closed tightly around some object. "I'd like you to tell me what I'm holding in my hand, please."

"I'm sorry," Joseph says. "As you can imagine, it's a great strain, using my mental powers. I'm all worn-out."

"Oh," says the girl, obviously disappointed.

"Please come back and see us again, though."

"How much longer will you be performing here?" asks the mother.

"I— I'm not sure." Joseph turns to his father. "Do you think they're going to extend our contract?"

"We'll see," says Nicholas.

The admirers start to leave, but the second girl turns back and holds out her hand again, open this time. "It was just a thimble, see? That's easy."

As they head up the alley that leads to the Avenue, Nicholas says, "You've gotten very adept at that."

"What?"

"Fending off the ones who want you to read their minds."

"Somehow it doesn't sound as if you're praising me."

"I'm not."

"What am I supposed to do? Tell them it's all just a trick?" Nicholas shrugs. "That's what it is."

"They don't know that. They think I have some kind of special mental power. I don't want to spoil it for them."

"For them? Or for yourself?"

"All right, I admit it, I like having them think I have special powers. What's wrong with that? A person gets tired of being just ordinary. You know what I think? I think you're just jealous." Joseph meant this mainly as a joke, but it comes out sounding rather spiteful.

"Jealous?"

"Well, they didn't ask for *your* autograph, did they?"

"I don't mind. I've signed my share."

Joseph laughs skeptically. "Don't tell me. It was when you were appearing alongside the great Junius Brutus Booth."

"No, no one even noticed me then. They all wanted Mr. Booth's autograph, preferably on his *carte de visite*."

"What's that?"

"An inexpensive calling card, usually with the person's picture on it. Apparently some people like to collect them. In the portrait that appeared on his card, Mr. Booth looked very noble and tragic, when in fact he was merely very drunk."

"Do you think we should get some cards made up?"

"Perhaps eventually."

Across Fourteenth Street from the theatre lies one of the tallest and—aside from the White House and the Capitol, of course—one of the most imposing buildings in the city: the six-story brick edifice of Willard's Hotel. Joseph pauses to gaze longingly at the lighted windows. "You said that, if the act was a success, we'd stay in the finest hotels."

"That was mainly a way of motivating you. But who knows—if we continue to have lucrative engagements, perhaps we shall. Of course, we'd have to talk your mother into it."

"*If* we continue, you said. Isn't Mr. Grover going to keep us on?"

"I'm afraid not."

"Why? He said himself we're one of the most popular acts he's ever had!"

"I'll tell you why, but only if we can keep moving while I do it. It's too brisk a night to stand in one place for long." Nicholas strides off down E Street. By the time Joseph catches up with him, they're at the corner of Tenth, and he can see off to his left another impressive building that makes him pause and stare.

Ford's Theatre opened only a little over a year ago but is already considered, both by performers and by Washington society, to be the city's preeminent theatre. The performance of *Uncle Tom and His Cabin* must be about to let out, for elegant and expensive carriages line both sides of the street, plus a few hackneys, or hired cabs. The drivers stand about stamping their cold feet, chatting and appraising one another's rigs.

A shiver goes up Joseph's spine—less from the cold, perhaps, than from the sight of the brightly lighted theatre with its gaily painted trim, which somehow stirs him. He hurries to catch up with Nicholas again. "I wish we were performing at Ford's," he says. "Then we'd really be famous. Do you suppose Mr. Lincoln is in the audience?"

"It would not surprise me. I understand that Maggie Mitchell is one of his favorite actresses."

"I wonder why he's never come to see our act," Joseph says, sounding a bit resentful.

"I suspect he was occupied with more important matters," says his father. "Such as winning the election, for example."

"And now he won't have a chance to see us. Why is Mr. Grover letting us go?"

"For two reasons, according to him. One is that, for the next several weeks, he's going to be presenting a special holiday show consisting mostly of musical numbers, plus a new play—something about Christmas on the battlefield, with Rebels and Yankees putting aside their guns and sharing a keg of rum and singing Christmas carols. It sounds horribly maudlin."

"What's the other reason?"

"He feels that everyone in Washington who wants to see our act has seen it by now—perhaps several times—and that, if we expect to go on attracting an audience, we shall have to give them something new."

"Something *new*? It took us two years to work up what we've got!"

"Well, not a completely new act per se, just some . . . some 'fresh routines,' is the way he put it. I believe that's an oxymoron. How can something that's routine be fresh?"

"Does he know how long it takes to work up a 'fresh routine'?"

"Probably not. But he does know the theatre business. We would do well to take his advice."

Joseph grimaces. "I hope you don't expect me to start working eight or nine hours a day again, learning some new mind-reading technique."

"Of course not," says Nicholas. "Five or six should be sufficient."

Though Joseph may say unflattering things about the quality of Mrs. McKenna's cooking behind her back, he can't justifiably complain about the quantity. Knowing that her boarders are invariably famished after a performance, she has taken to setting out a cold second supper for them—nothing fancy, just pork and beans, boiled eggs, corn bread, crackers, a tin or two of Underwood Deviled Ham, that sort of thing. It is wartime, after all, and supplies are limited. It would seem a sumptuous spread, of course, to those families in the deep South whose homes are at this moment being pillaged and torched by General Sherman's troops, and who will have to survive on wild game and wild greens—if they survive at all.

While most of the music halls lie within a few blocks of the boardinghouse, it's a long walk here from the National Theatre, so Joseph and his father are always the last to return. The other performers have already eaten and retired to their rooms. They were considerate enough to leave a little of everything for the Ehrlichs (everything, that is, except the apple pie. It's easy enough to guess who finished that off).

There are two newcomers at the table, however, filling their plates with beans and corn bread. One is a stocky man with a beard and hair the color of new rust; the other is a slight, black-haired girl of ten or so, with dark eyes set in a thin, pale face.

CHAPTER TEN

At first, Joseph is baffled by their presence here. Has the man come to find him, to break his meddling nose after all, and decided that, while he's waiting, he'll add insult to injury by eating Joseph's supper? Or has he regretted his rashness, now that Joseph is so famous, and come to apologize?

Neither, it seems. When the red-bearded man glances up at him, he shows no sign of even recognizing Joseph, either as Yosef the mentalist or as the boy he threatened at the racetrack several months ago. He simply gives the Ehrlichs a cursory nod, then goes on piling the food on his plate, as if determined to take all he can before they get a chance at it.

The girl meets Joseph's gaze for no more than a second before she drops her head and sidles in closer to her protector, but there's something in the look that tells him she does recognize him. He's struck once again by her resemblance to Margaretta, and even though he knows it's irrational and impossible, for a dizzying moment he wonders whether his sister could have somehow survived—been buried alive, perhaps, as in Edgar Allan Poe's story "The Premature Burial," and then rescued.

He turns to his father, to see how he is reacting. Nicholas

doesn't seem to have noticed the girl's likeness to his dead daughter. Nor does he seem disconcerted at finding two total strangers in the kitchen of the boardinghouse sharing what little is left of the food. "Good evening to you, sir," he says cordially. "And to the young lady. I expect you must be the new boarders that Mrs. McKenna mentioned to me this morning. I am Nicholas Ehrlich, and this is my son, Joseph. Welcome." He holds out a hand to the red-bearded man, who has to put down the corn bread he's been devouring and dust the crumbs from his fingers in order to shake hands, and who doesn't seem happy about it. "And your name is?" Nicholas prompts him.

The man swallows the dry corn bread with some difficulty and mumbles, "Nolan. Patrick Nolan."

"A pleasure to meet you, Mr. Nolan." Nicholas turns to the girl, who has, incongruously, chosen to put her small frame in the huge, heavy chair constructed especially for the Modern Hercules. She looks lost in it. "And this, I presume, is your daughter?"

"Niece," the man says.

When it becomes apparent that this is all he's prepared to say, Nicholas speaks to the girl. "May I ask your name, my dear?"

The girl darts a look at her uncle, as if to ask his permission, then replies, so softly that Joseph can barely make it out, "Cassandra."

"A lovely name," says his father, "and one with an illustrious history." He suddenly throws one arm upward in a dra-

matic gesture and declaims, at the top of his ruined voice,
" 'Cry, Trojans, cry! Lend me ten thousand eyes, and I will
fill them with prophetic tears!' " Startled by the outburst, the
girl very nearly drops her plate of food. *"Troilus and Cres-
sida,"* says Nicholas. "Act Two. Have you seen the play?"
The girl, who is eyeing Nicholas warily as though wondering
what he might do next, shakes her head. "Well, there's a
woman in it named Cassandra, a prophetess. She tries to
warn the Trojans that, if they do not release the captive
Helen, the city of Troy will be burned to the ground by their
enemies, the Greeks. But no one will listen to her. They dismiss her dire predictions as merely the ravings of a mad-
woman."

Joseph has turned his attention to the food, anxious to get
his share of it before Patrick Nolan decides he wants seconds.
Still, he notices that, in the course of his father's brief speech,
the girl's thin face has lost some of its closed and guarded
look, and a hint of curiosity has crept in. "Does she ever convince them?" the girl asks.

As Nicholas is about to reply, Patrick Nolan growls, "Let
the child eat."

"Yes, of course," says Nicholas, a bit stiffly. "Your uncle is
right, you must have your supper now." He bends closer to
the girl and adds in a low voice, "I'll tell you more about the
play another time."

One corner of her mouth turns up tentatively, as if she's
tempted to smile but can't quite remember how. Then she
lifts the plate up under her chin and begins spooning in the

beans rather mechanically, as though motivated less by hunger than by a sense of duty.

As Nicholas helps himself to the food, he makes another attempt to engage Patrick Nolan in conversation, though it's clear from the man's sullen expression that the cause is doomed to fail. "Are you a performer of some sort, Mr. Nolan?"

"No," says Nolan.

"Oh. I thought perhaps you were, since so many of Mrs. McKenna's boarders tend to be actors, comedians, acrobats, and the like. How do you make your living, if I may ask?"

"A little of this, a little of that." This seems to be all he has to say on the matter. But then, unexpectedly, he volunteers something more. "I used to be a prizefighter."

"A prizefighter?" says Joseph. "Really?" He's never seen a legitimate bout of bare-knuckle boxing, only a few street fights between soldiers, which usually feature little in the way of actual fisticuffs and a good deal in the way of kicking, biting, and gouging. (You might think that soldiers would get their fill of fighting on the battlefield. But they've been taught that the only way the differences between North and South can be settled is through violent means, so perhaps it's not surprising that they would try to settle their personal problems the same way.) Joseph waits eagerly for Patrick Nolan to tell them more about his boxing career, but of course he does not.

"Well," says Nicholas, "I suppose prizefighting could be

considered a species of performing." Still nothing from Nolan.

"We're performers ourselves," Joseph offers. "You've probably heard of us—Professor Godunov and Son?"

"No," says the man, practically elbowing Joseph aside in order to take the last of the baked beans.

As Joseph and his father head upstairs, Nicholas says contemptuously, and almost loudly enough for Patrick Nolan to hear, "A prizefighter? It's no wonder he can't put two words together to form a sentence. No doubt all that pummeling has knocked something loose in his brain."

When they enter the bedroom, they find Carolina Ehrlich perched on the edge of the armchair, as though she's been anxiously awaiting their return. "Did you see her?" she asks breathlessly.

"See whom?" says Nicholas.

"The girl. The new boarder."

"Her name is Cassandra."

"Didn't you notice how much she looks like Margaretta?"

Nicholas considers this. "In a superficial way, I suppose. Margaretta was a good deal younger."

"But she'd be just the age of this girl, if she'd—" Carolina breaks off and slumps back in the chair, panting, as though there's not enough air in the room to fill her lungs.

Nicholas takes her hand and rubs it briskly between his own. "Calm yourself, my dear. However much she might resemble Margaretta, there's no significance in it. There are dozens of girls who look very similar. You know very well that each time we go out, you see at least one."

"But none of them is living in the same house with us, eating at the same table, constantly reminding me . . ." She clutches her husband's hand. "I've changed my mind. I would like to move to a hotel after all. You said we could afford it."

"That was before Mr. Grover decided not to renew our contract."

"To another boardinghouse, then?"

"That's a possibility. We're paid up here until the end of December, but perhaps then."

When Carolina has retired to the little adjoining room, Joseph says hopefully, "You know, maybe we should move sooner than that, if it's going to upset Mother so much."

"Oh, let's give her a week or so to get accustomed to the girl, and to realize that she's nothing like your sister. Margaretta was never remotely shy or reticent about talking, even to strangers—or about eating, for that matter." He smiles and shakes his head. "Do you remember our first visit to an ice-cream parlor? You were perhaps five or so, and she couldn't have been more than a year old. I gave her a small taste of strawberry ice cream from my spoon, and she was instantly transformed into an ice-cream fanatic. I would feed her a bite, and ten seconds later she was demanding another. 'I ceem!' she said. 'I ceem!' They were the first words she ever spoke—but certainly not the last."

"What did I do?" Joseph asks.

"At the ice-cream parlor? I don't recall. Sat there quietly, no doubt, as you always did."

"No doubt," says Joseph. "Count on me to be perfectly ordinary and unremarkable." He removes his shoes and places them at the foot of the bed. "She really does look a lot like Margaretta, you know." He laughs awkwardly. "For a second, downstairs, I found myself wondering whether it might be possible that . . . that she wasn't dead after all."

Nicholas places a hand on his son's shoulder. "I miss her as much as you do, Joseph, as much as your mother does, but it's a fact, and we must learn to live with it."

"Of course, I know. It's just that . . ."

"What?"

"It's just that she seems to still be with us, in spirit or something, as if she's . . . as if she's haunting us, as if she won't let go."

For several days, Carolina Ehrlich refuses to go downstairs for any reason, even for meals. It's not really much of a departure from her usual behavior, for she has always eaten so little and excused herself from the table so early that it was almost as if she'd never been there at all. Twice a day Nicholas carries a plate of bread and butter or cheese and crackers up to her, but she barely touches it. Bodily functions (a subject that is of course not discussed in polite company, but we need not be constrained by the manners of the time; we're only visiting) are no particular problem; she has never felt comfortable traveling to the privy in the backyard, anyway, preferring to use the chamber pot in the privacy of her room.

Nicholas has been giving a great deal of thought to how they can change and improve the mind-reading act, and he has hit upon something he thinks will work. The best way to explain it to you, I think, is to let you observe as he explains it to Joseph.

You will notice that Joseph does not appear to be very receptive. He sits in the armchair with his arms crossed and a skeptical, impatient expression on his face. Nicholas chooses to ignore his son's uncooperative attitude.

"You won't be required to memorize anything for this new technique," he assures Joseph, who mutters something that sounds like "Thank heaven for small favors." "But," Nicholas goes on, "it will demand considerable practice on both our parts if it's to work properly." He picks up a slate and a piece of chalk. "I will ask some member of the audience to think of a word or a name—something relatively short—and they will print it on the slate in large letters so that the audience can see it clearly. You will, of course, be blindfolded—"

"Of course," says Joseph wryly.

"Perhaps we'll even cover your head with a hood."

This is too much for Joseph. "Oh, no, we won't! It's hot enough in front of those footlights as it is; with a hood on, I'd suffocate."

"All right, a pair of opaque spectacles, then. I will convey the first letter of the word to you in the usual fashion. Let us say the word the audience gives us is . . ." He pauses.

"Scalp," offers Joseph. He has been wishing lately that he

had held on to Captain Mayne Reid's Thrilling Tale of Adventure and Romance in Northern Mexico. The Fenimore Cooper novel has proven to be slow going.

"All right." Nicholas prints *SCALP* on the slate. "Now, what is the first letter?"

"I already know."

"Well, pretend you don't."

Joseph sighs. "It's an *S*."

"Very good. Now, here's the difficult part—that's not a clue, by the way—the part that's going to require all the practice. As soon as you've said the letter, you begin counting: one elephant, two elephant, three elephant, and so forth."

Joseph snickers. "We're counting *elephants*?"

"It's merely a way of timing the seconds that pass as accurately as possible. It could just as well be coconuts or . . ."

"Or Indians."

"Exactly. I will be counting at the same speed—theoretically, anyway. When I say 'Yes,' and write the letter on the slate, you stop counting. The number of seconds that has elapsed will tell you the next letter. One second is *A*, two is *B*, et cetera."

"What if the next letter is *Z*? You can't possibly let twenty-six seconds elapse. The audience will get restless."

Nicholas smiles patiently. "I've thought of that. If it is a *Z*, I'll let two seconds elapse, then I'll say, 'Correct,' rather than 'Yes.' You will begin counting again, until I prompt you by saying, 'Next letter, please?'—six seconds, in this case. Two and six make twenty-six."

"It's a good thing you're doing a mind-reading act," says Joseph, "and not teaching school." He uncrosses his arms and leans forward in the chair, growing interested now in spite of himself. "Let's try it with a word I don't already know."

Nicholas erases SCALP and, after a moment's thought, replaces it with MODEST. "Oh, this is going to be difficult for you."

"We'll see," says Joseph. "The first letter is an M." He counts only one elephant before his father says, "Correct" and writes an M on the slate. Joseph begins counting again: one elephant, two elephant, three elephant, four elephant, five elephant—

"Next letter, please," says his father.

"The next letter is an O." One elephant, two elephant, three elephant, four elephant—

"Yes."

"The next letter is a D." One elephant, two elephant, three elephant, four elephant, five elephant, six elephant—

"Yes."

"And the next letter is . . . an F? M-O-D-F? That can't be right."

"It's supposed to be an E. We must have been counting at different speeds. You see why we need to practice extensively. Perhaps it would help if we used a metronome, as piano students do."

"What was the word?" Joseph asks. Nicholas turns the slate toward him. "Modest. Are you trying tell me something?"

Nicholas suppresses a smile. "Not at all." He goes into his stage accent. "In fact it is not pronounced *mah*-dest, but moh-*dest*, and it is the first name of a Russian composer, Mussorgsky." (Oddly enough, though Nicholas is not aware of it, in five years Modest Mussorgsky will write a celebrated opera called *Boris Godunov*—which is not about a mind-reading act, but about a ruthless Russian czar.) "So. Shall we practice counting elephants?"

"I'd rather not," says Joseph, and lets his father fret for just a moment before adding, "I prefer to count Indians."

CHAPTER ELEVEN

As it turns out, the extreme measures Carolina Ehrlich is taking to avoid Cassandra are largely unnecessary. The girl and her uncle are nearly always either in their room or out somewhere—no one seems to know where, though of course there is no shortage of speculation among the other boarders. More often than not, Patrick Nolan and his niece fail to show up at mealtimes.

For people who are not performers, they keep an unusual schedule. It's difficult to keep track of them, they come and go so silently, even secretively. But it appears to Joseph that they spend most mornings confined to their room, leave shortly after the noon meal—or sometimes before—and often do not return until quite late in the evening. Several times they've come home well after eleven, the hour at which

Mrs. McKenna locks all the doors. Joseph has heard Patrick Nolan rapping on the window of his fellow Irishman, Mick O'Boyle—who rooms on the ground floor—and asking to be let in.

Other times, Joseph notices Nolan slipping out of the house alone. Ordinarily he's gone only a few hours, during which time Cassandra stays shut up in her room. But one afternoon he leaves and does not return. Mrs. McKenna is outraged. When he still has not shown up by dinnertime the following day, she pounds on the door of their room and insists that Cassandra come out and eat something, at least.

"Did your uncle say where he was going?" she asks the girl. (I could tell you, of course, exactly where Patrick Nolan is and what he's doing—omniscience, remember?—but sometimes I must withhold such information from you to avoid spoiling the story, and this is one of those times.)

Cassandra shakes her head. "He never tells me."

"He's done this before?" says Nicholas Ehrlich. "Gone off and left you on your own?"

She nods.

"He told me he's been looking for work," puts in Mick O'Boyle. "Could be he's found something."

Mrs. McKenna gives a derisive grunt. "Looking for trouble, more likely. I should have known he was that sort. I should have known better than to rent him a room. I only did it for the girl's sake," she says, ignoring the fact that Cassandra is sitting right next to her. "I felt sorry for her, poor thing. He said he was planning to send her to school, not leave her here by herself."

"I don't mind," says Cassandra. "I read books."

Joseph is almost startled to hear her speak so many words all at once. Perhaps it was only the presence of her uncle that made her so tongue-tied before. "What sort of books?" he asks.

She lowers her eyes, as though this is too personal a question, but then she replies, "Novels, mostly."

"Oh, Lord," says Mrs. McKenna. "If you was in school, you could be learning something wholesome and worthwhile, instead of filling your head with that rubbish."

Unexpectedly, Cassandra's pale cheeks flush with indignation. "It's not rubbish," she says. "And I can't go to school."

"You could if your uncle could manage to hold down a job. Isn't that just what you'd expect from an Irishman? And I should know, for I was married to one. Nothing against you, Mr. O'Boyle," she hastily adds. "You've always paid your rent right on time. The exception that proves the rule, I guess."

Like Carolina Ehrlich—though for different reasons, as you will see—Cassandra is uncomfortable in large groups of people (and she considers more than two a large group), so she excuses herself from the table at the first opportunity. She doesn't retreat to her room, though. The window there opens onto a narrow alley, and the dim light makes it difficult to read. Instead she retrieves her book and settles into the sunny window seat in the parlor—a room that's generally deserted in the daytime.

This is where Joseph finds her, several hours later. He's not actually looking for her; he's on his way to the People's Circulating Library, to return *The Spy* and check out something more rousing, and he spots her as he's passing by the parlor. She's so absorbed in her book that she doesn't notice his presence until he sits next to her. She glances up at him with that wary, almost fearful look of hers.

"I was just wondering what you were reading," says Joseph. "Can I see?" She lifts the book from her lap and shows him the cover. "*Nicholas Nickleby* by Charles Dickens. I've never read one of his books. Is he any good?"

"I think so." She tilts her head to get a look at the book he's holding. "Is yours any good?"

Joseph wrinkles his nose. "Not very. It's kind of long-winded. I'm going to the lending library. Would you like to come along?"

"A library?" It's clear from the way her face brightens that she finds the prospect appealing. But then she winces slightly and says, "No, thank you. I'm not very good in crowds."

"Oh. Neither is my mother. She has me get books for her. I could check out something for you, too, if you tell me what."

"I don't know what they have."

"Isn't that where you got your book?"

She lowers her eyes. "No. It was my father's."

"I'm sorry. Did he— Did he die in the war?"

Cassandra nods her head ever so slightly. "Do you suppose they have any Dickens?"

"I'm sure they do. Which books of his have you already read?"

"Only this one," she says. "Four times."

Joseph laughs. "I'll bring you something new, then."

"That would be very kind of you." Joseph turns to go, but she calls him back. "Do you . . . do you mind if I ask you something, please?"

"No, I don't mind." Now that she has his attention, she seems reluctant to speak. Joseph sits on the window seat again. "What is it?"

"You . . . you said that you and your father are Professor Godunov and Son."

Joseph smiles knowingly. "Don't tell me. You want my autograph."

"Well . . . no," she replies. "I saw an advertisement in the newspaper. It said that you're a . . . a mind reader."

"That's right." Joseph isn't smiling now; he's a little put out that she didn't want him to sign something. "Oh, I see. You want to put my powers to the test, is that it? You want me to tell you what word you're thinking of, or what's in your pocket."

"No!" she protests. "I only— I was only wondering . . . Do they . . . do they pay you for it?"

"Of course. I wouldn't do it if they didn't."

"But doesn't it . . . don't you find that it . . . affects your ability? Taking money for it?"

"No. Why should it?"

"I don't know. I just— I mean, it's a . . . it's a *gift*, and it doesn't seem right somehow, using it to make money."

Joseph would like to tell her how long and hard he's worked to develop what she calls a gift, but he doesn't want to disillusion her. Let her think that it's something you're just born with. "Artists have a gift, too," he says, "but you don't see them giving away their paintings." He gestures at the books they're holding. "Authors have a gift for telling stories, but I'm fairly sure they expect to get paid for it. Why should clairvoyants be any different? Some of them even advertise their services in the personals column."

"I know. I've seen them. And my uncle—" She breaks off, as though the very thought of her uncle has made her tongue-tied again. Then she sighs and says, "I wish I could see you perform sometime."

"I'm afraid you'll have to wait awhile. Right now we're what performers call 'between engagements.' "

"Oh. Well, don't worry. Something else will turn up, very soon." The earnest way in which she says this makes it sound like more than just a bit of blithe reassurance. It sounds as though she knows it for a fact.

After two full days of being absent and unaccounted for, Patrick Nolan finally turns up again, looking grimy and exhausted and smelling of horses, even though he's said himself that he doesn't own one. As Mick O'Boyle would say, he needs washing like a Wicklow sheep.

Mrs. McKenna wastes no time in letting him know that, if

such a thing ever happens again, he and his niece will be asked to leave, no matter how sorry she may feel for "the poor thing," as she calls Cassandra—she has never thought to ask the poor thing's name.

Patrick Nolan reacts in his usual sullen fashion. He makes no attempt to apologize or to explain, beyond saying, "I was working."

"Good," says the landlady. "Then you'll be able to send the poor thing to school, instead of leaving her here for me to take care of."

"Was she after making trouble for you?" demands Nolan angrily. "I've told her to stay in the room and not go bothering anyone."

"Of course she didn't make any trouble. She wouldn't even have come out to eat if I hadn't forced her to. It's not right, that's all, leaving a girl that age all alone for two whole days."

"Ahh, it's used to it, she is. She doesn't much fancy being around other people." From the pocket of his trousers he takes a handful of crumpled banknotes, selects two fifty-dollar bills, and hands them to her. "There's two months' rent, in advance."

When so much money changes hands, it tends to change attitudes as well. Though it would be difficult to tell from her face, which seems to be permanently fixed in an expression of disapproval, Mrs. McKenna is suddenly more well disposed toward her new boarder—so much so that when, several days later, he tells her (as you might guess, he's not very good at asking) that he would like to entertain guests in the parlor from time to time, she readily gives her permission.

She's assuming, of course, that by "guests" he means friends. But the truth is, Patrick Nolan has no friends, at least not as you and I understand the term. The people he will be receiving in the parlor will be more in the nature of clients than guests, and his primary purpose will not be to entertain them. In fact, they will not be coming to see *him* at all. They will be lured there by an advertisement in the personals column of the *Evening Star* that reads:

MADEMOISELLE DELPHINE, THE CHILD ORACLE, natural clairvoyant, offers advice on the Past, Present, and Future at Mrs. McKenna's boardinghouse, 2nd and F Streets. From an early age she has shown an extraordinary ability to anticipate events, to read character, to diagnose physical ailments, and to commune with the spirit world. She can be consulted nightly, 6 to 9 P.M.

CHAPTER TWELVE

On the same day that the first client comes to seek advice from Mademoiselle Delphine, the Child Oracle, Joseph and his father also have a visitor, Mr. Henry Clay Ford, who books the plays and the performers for his brother's theatre—the very theatre whose elegant gaslit facade gave Joseph chills several weeks ago.

Like Mr. Grover at the National, Henry Clay Ford is always on the lookout for something new and unusual to offer his audience, and he does much of his looking in other theatres and music halls. He's been following the fortunes of Professor Godunov and Son for some time now, and more than once has gone to see them perform. He found their mind-reading routine impressive but rather limited, and he's been waiting to see whether they will keep on in the same vein or whether they will find some way to expand and improve it.

That's the purpose of his visit today—to learn what, if anything, they've added to the act. Fortunately for Joseph and his father, they've been working very diligently on their new technique, counting their Indians in time with a ticking metronome to make certain they count at the same speed.

They've also been experimenting with another trick, one that Nicholas saw performed, not very successfully, many years ago. He means to perfect it. In theory, the routine will work like this: an audience member will tell Professor Godunov, in a whisper, to have his son perform a particular action—take off his jacket, turn in a circle, wave his arms, or something similar. Using the existing verbal code, the professor will convey the instructions to Yosef, who will then carry them out. In order for it to work, of course, Nicholas will have to make up a new set of lists—not of objects, this time, but of physical actions.

When Nicholas proposed this addition to the act, Joseph was not happy. "It'll make me feel like a trained monkey," he protested.

But it's clear that any objections on his part will be in vain, for Mr. Henry Clay Ford is enthusiastic about the new routine. "Here's another possibility," he says. "The swells who sit in the orchestra section may pretend to be well-bred and dignified, but the fact is, they love it if they can get in on the act somehow. Suppose they ask your son to do things to *them*—remove their spectacles, tie their handkerchiefs in knots, dance with them, that kind of thing."

Joseph gives a groan that is almost audible. His father, however, seems perfectly amenable to the suggestion. "I'm sure that would be feasible. The number of things they can conceivably ask him to do is rather limited, after all, and if they choose something that might prove embarrassing, or something that is not on our lists, I can steer them in a new direction with relative ease."

When Mr. Ford offers them a five-week run at $250 per week, Joseph suddenly begins to see some merit in the idea. Still, he's not exactly thrilled with it, and as soon as their visitor is gone, he lets his father know. "Why did you have to bring up the new routine? I told you I didn't want to do it."

"I've dealt with a good many theatre managers, Joseph, and I don't need to be clairvoyant to read their minds. If all we'd had to offer was describing objects and spelling out words, he would have thanked us for our time and departed, and that would have been the end of it. Instead, we'll be playing five weeks at Ford's Theatre, before the most distinguished audience in Washington."

"And the most critical," says Joseph gloomily. "Speaking of critical, I didn't like him telling us how we ought to do our act."

"I'm afraid that's one of the realities of being an entertainer. You have to learn to be open to suggestions, sometimes ones you don't particularly like. Besides, isn't it better to dance with the ladies in the audience and knot up their handkerchiefs than to be up on the stage by yourself, waving your arms and turning in circles, like a trained monkey?"

Joseph sighs. "I suppose so. Either way, though, all I'm doing is performing tricks."

As Mr. Henry Clay Ford is leaving the boardinghouse, he encounters a tall, angular-looking woman with a conspicuous nose and an even more conspicuous fur hat—perhaps chosen deliberately to draw attention away from her nose. In one gloved hand she holds an advertisement cut from a newspaper. "Excuse me, sir," she says. "Is this Mrs. McKenna's boardinghouse?"

"Yes, it is." Mr. Ford tips his fashionable beige top hat to her and goes on his way.

Hesitantly, the woman approaches the front door and gives the knocker a tentative tap. When Mrs. McKenna appears, the woman asks, "Is this where I find"—she glances at the paper—"Mademoiselle Delphine?"

"Mademoiselle Who?"

"Delphine?"

"There's no Mademoiselle Delphine here, nor any sort of French person at all," says Mrs. McKenna, in a voice loud enough to reach the ears of Patrick Nolan, who emerges at once from his room.

"It's my niece she's wanting," he says.

"Oh. Well, I'm afraid you can't entertain anyone in the front parlor."

Nolan scowls. "You said it would be all right."

"I know, but I've got the sewing circle there tonight. You'll have to use the upstairs parlor."

As it happens, Joseph is in the upstairs parlor, finishing up *The Scalp Hunters.* He is, in fact, in the middle of the book's most riveting scene, which has the protagonist locked in a death struggle with an Indian on the edge of a cliff: "His sinewy fingers were across my throat. They clasped me tightly around the trachea, stopping my breath. He was strangling me. I grew weak and nerveless. I could resist no longer."

"You'll have to leave!" cries the Indian. Joseph raises his head from the book like someone waking from a dream. No, it's not the Indian after all. It's the Irishman, along with his niece and an unfamiliar woman with a prominent nose. "We need this room," says Patrick Nolan.

"Oh." Joseph unfolds himself reluctantly from the arm-chair.

"I'm sorry," says the unfamiliar woman.

"It's all right." As he passes her on the way to his room, he notices that she's staring at him.

"Pardon me," she says, "but didn't I see you perform at the National Theatre?"

"You may have."

"You're the mind reader, aren't you?"

"Yes, I am."

"Are you related to Mademoiselle Delphine?" the woman says. Joseph is about to ask who she means, but then she gestures toward Cassandra.

He is taken aback. Has she noticed some family resemblance, too? "Why do you ask?"

"Oh, I've read that such things run in families, that's all."

"No," says Joseph, "we're not related." He gives Cassandra a puzzled glance, as though to ask, Why did she call you Mademoiselle Delphine? The girl lowers her eyes.

"Imagine," says the woman. "Two mind readers in one house." She giggles nervously. "It must be hard for the other boarders to keep their thoughts to themselves."

"Can we get started, now?" says Patrick Nolan.

Joseph retreats to his room. But he can't seem to get back into his book. He's too curious about what's going on out in the parlor. Quietly he moves to the door and puts one eye to the keyhole. All he can see is the tall woman, who is seated awkwardly in the armchair he has just vacated. He can hear some of what's being said, but not all of it.

Luckily we're not reduced to peering through keyholes. Patrick Nolan can't evict us from the parlor; we'll stay right in the thick of things. Notice how uncomfortable the tall woman looks. It is her first experience with a clairvoyant—if you don't count the night she saw Professor Godunov and Son at the National—and she doesn't know what to expect. Certainly she didn't expect Mademoiselle Delphine to be ten or eleven years old; it makes her wonder whether the girl can possibly be any good at mind reading.

Cassandra is even more ill at ease. She doesn't know what to expect, either. This is her first attempt to offer "advice on the Past, Present, and Future" to anyone other than her uncle, and he is never satisfied with anything she tells him. There's no reason to believe that this woman will be any more receptive.

Though Patrick Nolan is not particularly intelligent (as Nicholas has said, prizefighting is hard on the brain), he's smart enough to know that he's not good with people, so he keeps his mouth shut and lets his niece do things her own way (though only up to a point, as you will see).

"What do you want to ask me?" says Cassandra softly.

The woman clears her throat. "I was wondering if you could tell me what's wrong with my daughter, Lucille. She's been . . . she's been ill."

"Do you have anything that belongs to her? That makes it easier."

"Yes." The woman digs into her reticule and hands Cassandra a mother-of-pearl comb that holds a few blonde hairs. "She's always leaving things lying around."

Cassandra holds the comb between her hands and closes her eyes. After only a few seconds, she opens her eyes again and gives the woman a reproachful look. "Your daughter is dead, isn't she? I believe she worked in the Armory. Did she die in the explosion?"

The woman draws back, startled, her face suddenly pale. Then she recovers and nods silently.

"You were testing me," says Cassandra.

Abashed, the woman nods again. Though Joseph couldn't hear or see everything that happened, he caught most of it, and he's impressed. How could Cassandra know about the daughter and how she died? Could Patrick Nolan have talked to the woman ahead of time, and then conveyed the information to his niece through some sort of code, like the one Joseph and his father use? That must be it. What other explanation could there be?

"I wanted to be sure that you were . . . legitimate," the woman is saying.

"Are you satisfied?"

"Yes."

"What did you really want to ask about?"

"About my fiancé. We've known each other for only a few months, you see. I would like to be sure that we are . . . well, compatible. I don't have anything that belongs to him— No, wait. I have his calling card. Will that help?"

"I don't know." Cassandra returns the daughter's comb, takes the calling card, and holds it between her palms, her eyes closed. After a long pause, she says, in a voice that is curiously devoid of inflection or emotion, "No. I don't think you can trust him. I believe he's only interested in you because of your inheritance."

The woman stares at Cassandra, her face a picture of shock and indignation. "What a thing to say!"

Cassandra seems bewildered by her reaction. "You do have an inheritance, don't you?"

"Well, yes, but— But I can't believe that— He wouldn't—" She gets abruptly to her feet and snatches the card from Cassandra. "How much do I owe you?" she asks coldly.

"I don't ask for a fee. You can leave a donation if you want."

"Well, I don't." She turns to Patrick Nolan. "There's no need to see me out," she says, and hurries down the stairs.

The moment she's gone, Patrick Nolan descends on his niece. "No fee?" he says, and Joseph has no trouble at all hearing him. "What do you mean, no fee? I said you were to charge a dollar! We ain't running a charity!"

"I told her she could give a donation."

"Why should she, after you insulted her and her damned fee-an-see?"

"I only told her the truth."

"These people don't want the truth! They want to hear *good* things! They want to be flattered!"

"Are you asking me to make something up? *Any*one could do that."

"You don't have to make anything up. Just tell them the good things, that's all. If you see something they ain't going to like, keep your mouth shut about it."

Cassandra puts her hands to her head. "I'll try. I—I can't think right, with you sitting there watching me. It's like trying to think with a sword hanging over your head."

"I've divil a sword," he says, "but I've got a fist, and you're going to feel it if you don't watch your mouth."

She looks at his upraised hand with total indifference. "Go ahead," she says. "Maybe it'll knock something loose in my brain. Maybe I'll stop having visions and hearing voices, and just be an ordinary person." She sinks her head in her hands again.

"Mr. Nolan?" comes the landlady's voice from downstairs. "You have another visitor."

Cassandra whispers to her uncle, "Can you please just send her up alone? I'll charge her a dollar, I promise."

Patrick Nolan considers this, then grudgingly lowers his fist. "You'd better," he growls.

CHAPTER THIRTEEN

Joseph misses much of the exchange between Cassandra and her uncle because, halfway through it, his mother emerges from her room and, seeing him crouching at the keyhole, demands, "What in heaven's name are you doing?"

"Sssh!" says Joseph. "They'll hear you!"

"Who?"

"Paddy Nolan and his niece."

"You're *spying* on them?"

"I wouldn't have put it that way. Let's say I'm scouting the competition."

"What do you mean?"

"I think they're doing some sort of clairvoyant readings. She's calling herself Mademoiselle Delphine."

"Clairvoyant readings? Like what you and your father do?"

"Not exactly. She told a woman that her daughter is dead—which is apparently true—and that her fiancé is a cad—which apparently *isn't* true."

Carolina Ehrlich sighs and sinks down on the bed. "I thought I might go downstairs for a cup of tea and a small sandwich, but not if I have to run the gauntlet to do it."

"It's hardly a gauntlet."

"You know what I mean."

"Yes, I know. But if you could just bring yourself to talk to Cassandra a little, you'd see that she's nothing like Margaretta. She doesn't even look that much like her, not really."

"Perhaps you've forgotten what your sister looked like." Her words sound like an accusation.

"No," says Joseph. "I haven't forgotten. Sometimes . . . sometimes I dream about her."

"Do you? What sort of dreams?"

"Happy ones, mostly."

"You're fortunate, then. I wish mine were." She rises and listens at the door. "I wonder whether they're still out there." Crouching, she puts an eye to the keyhole.

"Mother!" whispers Joseph, in mock dismay. "You're not going to *spy* on them!"

She ignores him and peers into the parlor. A new client is sitting in the armchair, now, a ruddy-faced woman in a worn woolen cloak. Cassandra herself is not visible through the keyhole, but Carolina can hear her voice, faintly. "How can I help you?"

"In your advertisement," says the ruddy-faced woman, "you say that you can commune with the spirit world. Is that so?"

"I see things," says Cassandra softly, as though she's ashamed of the fact, "and I hear voices. I'm never quite sure where they come from."

"Is there any way you could . . . commune with my husband? He was killed in the fighting a year ago January."

"I can try. Do you have anything that belonged to him?"

"All I have with me is a locket with his picture and a snippet of his hair. Will that do?"

"We'll see." Cassandra holds the locket between her hands for several minutes, a look of intense concentration on her thin face, before she speaks. "I'm having trouble . . . I'm getting more than one . . . Your husband's name is . . . Samuel?"

"Yes! Is he speaking to you? Is he here? Sam?"

"Be quiet, please," says Cassandra, a bit irritably. After another minute or two of silence, she speaks again. "Is there . . . is there someone in your family named . . . Margaret?"

The woman shakes her head and then, realizing that Cassandra's eyes are closed, says softly, "No."

"I wonder why I'm . . . All right. I'm concentrating on Samuel. I see . . . There's something about . . . about money." The woman leans forward eagerly in her chair. "It's hidden somewhere," says Cassandra. "The parlor . . . Do you have a picture in your parlor with . . . it looks like snow . . . and children?"

The woman gasps. "Yes! It's an engraving of little boys sledding!"

"Is one of them . . . has one of them had an accident, perhaps, and hurt himself?"

The woman thinks about this, then shakes her head again. "No. They're all very happy."

"That's curious . . . There's definitely something about a child . . . Marietta, could it be?"

"I'm sorry. I don't know anyone named Marietta or Margaret."

Cassandra opens her eyes and sighs deeply, like someone who has just completed a trying task. "You may want to look behind the engraving. I think your husband hid some money there."

"I will!" The woman rises from the chair and clasps Cassandra's hand. "Thank you. But how did you know? How did you know I was going to ask him about money?"

Cassandra shrugs. "I can't tell you how. I just . . . I just know."

"This means so much to me and my son. He's only two,

and I can't leave him to go to work, and we've barely had enough to buy food, or coal for the—" She breaks off, as if something has just occurred to her. "I'm sorry. I suppose you'll want something for your services. I never thought. I was so desperate . . ."

"A dollar," Cassandra murmurs reluctantly. "But you don't need to pay me unless you find the money."

Joseph has not heard or seen any of this, for his mother has taken over his role of spy. She hasn't stirred from her station at the keyhole for five minutes at least. When she finally does back away, she has a dazed look on her face. "What's wrong?" Joseph asks. "Are you feeling faint? Do you need to lie down?"

"No," Carolina replies. She's still staring at the door. "The girl . . . Cassandra, is it? I heard her say something about a child named Marietta, or Margaret." She turns to look at Joseph; her eyes wide. "You don't suppose—" She puts a hand to her throat. "You don't suppose she could have meant Margaretta?"

"How would she know anything about Margaretta? I've never mentioned it to her, and I'm sure Father hasn't either."

"How did she know that woman's husband was named Samuel? How did she know there was money hidden behind a picture in the parlor?"

"Calm down, Mother." Joseph guides her to the bed and makes her sit. "I think maybe Patrick Nolan is getting information out of these people and then passing it on to Cassandra somehow."

"But he wasn't out there! Besides, the woman didn't *know* there was money behind the picture, so how could she tell him?" Carolina puts a hand on her son's arm. "Joseph, please, just ask her for me. Ask her if it was Margaretta."

Joseph sighs. "All right, I'll ask her. But don't expect anything. I'm sure it's all just an act. Maybe she misunderstood her uncle's message. That's happened with Father and me." When Joseph steps out of the bedroom, he finds Cassandra still sitting on the sofa, staring into space, as though waiting for something. "How did it go?" he asks.

She turns to him, blinking her eyes as though they need to adjust to a different light. "How did what go?"

"The clairvoyant reading, or whatever you call it."

"How do you know we weren't just visiting?"

Joseph taps the side of his head. "Aha. You forget, I'm a mind reader, too."

She smiles faintly. "It went all right, I suppose. I got some messages I didn't quite understand."

So, it's just as he thought—it's an act, a routine they haven't quite perfected yet.

"I kept getting something about a child named Margaret, or something like that, anyway. I don't think that's quite it. You know how muddled and confusing messages can be sometimes. I think she was hurt in an accident, or maybe killed. I seem to see her falling. I think she's inside something that's moving—a wagon, or a train car, or . . ."

Joseph stares at her. There's a strange prickling sensation

at the nape of his neck, and his chest seems constricted somehow. He swallows hard and says, "A horsecar?"

Cassandra frowns thoughtfully. "I'm not sure. It could be." She glances at him curiously. "Did you see it, too?"

"No," he says. "That's how my sister died. She and my mother were riding, standing up, on a horse-drawn omnibus, and a drunken soldier decided it would be great fun to jam on the hand brake and see what happened." He has to pause a moment and take a deep breath before he can continue. "What happened was, it jolted to a stop and my sister was flung forward. She struck her head on one of the seats."

Tears well up in Cassandra's dark eyes. "Oh, how awful. How old was she?"

"It was her seventh birthday. They were going to the store to buy her a present."

"What was her name?"

"Margaretta."

"Yes," says Cassandra. "That's it. Margaretta."

There is a long stretch of silence. Then Joseph hears the door to their bedroom open, and hears a rustle of crinolines. He turns to see his mother standing in the doorway. For the first time since Cassandra arrived at the boardinghouse, Carolina Ehrlich addresses her. "Did my daughter . . . speak to you?" she says. It sounds almost like an accusation.

"Not exactly," Cassandra replies. "It's not like that. Mostly I just see images. Sometimes there are words, but I don't really hear them so much as sort of . . . sense them. I don't know how to describe it."

"And did you sense anything else, other than what you've said?"

"Yes." Cassandra looks down at her hands, which are twisting the fabric of her dress. "I think that you feel guilty about her death. But you shouldn't. It wasn't your fault."

Carolina stares at the girl for a moment. Then she says, rather acidly, "These *messages* you say you receive—are they ever wrong?"

"Sometimes."

"Well," says Carolina, "this is one of those times." She retreats into the room and closes the door.

"What does she mean?" asks Cassandra.

"I think she's always felt responsible somehow, as if she should have been able to prevent it."

"But that's foolish. It was an accident."

Their conversation is interrupted by the sound of heavy footsteps ascending the stairs. "My uncle," says Cassandra grimly. "He'll want the dollar I was supposed to collect."

Joseph digs into his trousers, comes up with two silver half-dollars—he actually has a little pocket money these days—and presses them into the girl's hand just as Patrick Nolan appears at the top of the stairs. "You must have given that last customer a better reading," says the Irishman. "She was smiling. I hope she paid you." Cassandra holds out the coins. "Good." He glances at Joseph. "Are you planning to consult Mademoiselle Delphine?" The French words sound out of place in his mouth.

"No," says Joseph. "We were just talking."

"Mr. Ehrlich is a clairvoyant, too," offers Cassandra.

Nolan eyes him more closely, as though considering whether or not he looks clairvoyant. "Is that so? What do you charge?"

"I don't do personal readings. My father and I perform in theatres." He adds, rather smugly, "In two weeks, we open at Ford's Theatre."

Nolan doesn't seem particularly impressed. His niece, however, responds with something like delight—an emotion Joseph has never seen her display before. "Oh, you got a new engagement! I knew you would!"

Until this moment, Joseph had forgotten Cassandra's prediction, made with such complete confidence, that something else would turn up very soon. In a teasing tone he says, "Don't tell me you can see into the future, too."

She shrugs modestly. "Sometimes," she says.

Nearly every night, at least one new person comes by to seek advice from Mademoiselle Delphine. Joseph would like to listen in. Though Cassandra's ability certainly seems real, he can't quite accept that possibility. He prefers to believe that it's all an act and that, if he could watch her enough times, he could figure out how it works. But that's out of the question, for she now receives her clients in the downstairs parlor. (El Niño Eddie, accomplished spy that he is, could probably manage to eavesdrop on her, but he and his family perform during the same hours that Cassandra does.)

At least Joseph has the upstairs parlor to himself. He has gotten through *The Scalp Hunters* at last and gone on to something called *Scar Chief, the Wild Halfbreed,* which he's not enjoying very much. The plot is predictable, and the writing is so clumsy and overwrought that it makes Captain Mayne Reid's style sound like Shakespeare. But even if it were the world's most compelling book, he'd have trouble concentrating on it. Their opening at Ford's is only a week away, and the prospect weighs heavily on his mind.

As he is reading the same passage in the book for the third time, he feels someone watching him and turns his head to see Cassandra standing at the top of the stairs. "I didn't want to interrupt you," she says. "I hate it when people interrupt me in the middle of a good part."

Joseph puts the book aside. "I don't think there are any good parts in this one. Do you need to use the room again?"

"No. I just wanted to give you this." She hands Joseph a dollar bill. "The woman from last week came back and paid me."

"So the money was right where you said it would be?" asks Joseph.

Cassandra gives him a puzzled look. "How did you know about that?"

He can hardly admit that his mother was spying on the proceedings. "You told me, don't you remember?"

"No. But then I often forget things. Sometimes the things

that are going on around me get mixed up with the things that are going on inside my head, so I'm not sure which is which. Does that ever happen to you?"

Here's something else he can't very well admit—that the only messages he ever gets are the ones his father feeds him. "Sort of," he says, and changes the subject. "You said you knew that we were going to get another job performing soon; did you happen to see anything about whether or not we were going to be a success?"

"Don't worry," says Cassandra. "You'll do fine."

This time, however, her words don't carry as much conviction. She doesn't sound as though she's making an actual prediction so much as just offering encouragement, the way all the other entertainers at the boardinghouse have done. It's kind of them, but Joseph doesn't want kindness. He wants reassurance.

He considers himself a seasoned performer now, one who knows how to read an audience, one who can confidently handle any problem or predicament that might arise. Why, then, does he have this nagging fear that they won't be good enough for the audience at Ford's, that the theatregoers there will be expecting something more, something really extraordinary, and all Professor Godunov and Son will be able to give them is a half hour's worth of tricks and illusions?

Even the humble entertainers who work the music halls can boast that what they do is genuine. When the Modern Hercules holds back a team of horses with his teeth, it's no illusion. Though El Niño Eddie may trick the audience into thinking he's lost his balance on the high wire, it requires real agility and skill to pull it off. What sort of special ability does Joseph have, aside from a good memory?

Like Joseph, all we novelists have to offer is a series of tricks and illusions. But at least we have more of them. Theoretically, we even have the ability to speak to our characters, to warn them of danger or let them know that things will turn out all right.

So, if I wished, I could reassure Joseph that his opening night will go well. But if our characters learned ahead of time what is in store for them, they would lose all their motivation. "What's the use of trying," they would say, "when I already know how things are going to turn out?" We must give them the illusion, at least, of having free will, of being able to determine their own fates.

Besides, if I revealed to them what lies ahead, you would overhear, and you would be no happier about it than the characters would be. "What's the use of reading on," you would say, "when I already know how things are going to turn out?"

CHAPTER FOURTEEN

Well, I've carelessly given away the fact that the Ehrlichs' first appearance at Ford's will be successful. I hope you'll forgive me. Since you now know that, there's not much point in showing you how dreadfully nervous Joseph is as he and his father wait backstage, or telling you what outrageous objects the audience wants him to identify (I will just tell you that one of them is a rather naughty postcard from Paris, which Nicholas immediately returns to its owner), or what arcane words they ask him to spell, or what unlikely tasks they ask him to perform (though I can't resist mentioning the elderly lady who instructs him to autograph her shoe).

Let's just skip all that and join them after the show, when the applause is ringing in their ears, and when a certain person of some importance, who has just exited from one of the private boxes on the second level, is on his way down to see them. I doubt that you will recognize his name: Ward Hill Lamon. He probably won't look familiar to you, either, since his picture does not appear in many American history textbooks. Nevertheless, he is a man worth knowing, both on his own merits and because of the company he keeps.

If I were Captain Mayne Reid, I would compare Ward Hill Lamon, with his massive build, his long brown locks, and his drooping mustache, to some fierce barbarian warrior of a thousand years ago. But, though his appearance may invite such comparisons, he's neither very barbarous nor very fierce. He is, in fact, the United States marshal for the District of Columbia, and he's come backstage to congratulate the Ehrlichs on their triumph.

They are already surrounded by well-wishers but— whether it's because of his formidable appearance or his equally formidable reputation—when Ward Hill Lamon approaches, they quickly disperse. "Gentlemen," says

Lamon, in a deep voice that would not sound out of place delivering lines onstage in some tragedy. "I was very impressed with your performance." He takes Nicholas's hand, then Joseph's, in a grip that threatens to break several small bones. Before either of the Ehrlichs can thank him, he goes on. "So were the president and the first lady. They'd appreciate it if you would stop by their box before you leave."

"The president of what?" says Joseph, thinking that perhaps there's an Association of Mentalists whose chief officer wants to commend them.

Lamon laughs. "Well, it's certainly not Jeff Davis." (He's referring, of course, to the president of the Confederacy.)

"I believe he means Mr. Lincoln," says Nicholas.

"Oh." Suddenly Joseph feels dizzy, as though he's been standing next to a gas lamp that was turned on but not lighted. "He—he wants to see *us*?"

"Would it be better if I sent you a mental message?" says Lamon. "You seem to be having a little trouble understanding the spoken word."

"No, it's just—I'm just— Should we go there *now*, or—?"

"I'll escort you. Otherwise, they might not let you in."

Aside from passing through the audience, the only way to reach the presidential box is to exit through the stage door, walk up the narrow alley that separates Ford's Theatre from Taltavul's Star Saloon, go through the front entrance of the theatre, climb the stairs to the mezzanine, circle around behind the area known as the dress circle, and pass through a white door into a sort of vestibule, where there are two more doors, marked with the numbers 7 and 8.

Ordinarily, each of these doors leads to a separate box, but when Mr. and Mrs. Lincoln attend the theatre, the partition between the two boxes is removed, converting them into a single, larger room. Outside the first door they encounter John Parker, a police officer in plain (and rather rumpled) clothing, whose job it is to protect the president. He greets Mr. Lamon and lets them pass. Inside the vestibule sits the president's messenger, a boy about Joseph's age, who is addressed as Charlie by Mr. Lamon.

Considering the number of people, even here in Washington, who would like to see Abraham Lincoln dead, or at least a prisoner of the Confederacy, it is startling to realize that this is the extent of his bodyguard—one disheveled policeman and one unarmed boy. Of course there is also Mr. Lamon, but he has not been standing guard, keeping an eye out for potential assassins or abductors; he has been inside the president's box, watching the show.

After several attempts were made on Mr. Lincoln's life—including one that was very nearly successful—his advisers convinced him that he must surround himself with soldiers each time he goes out. But the president refuses to drag them with him to the theatre. He goes there, he says, to forget about soldiers and fighting for a while.

Mr. Lamon enters the box without knocking. Mr. Lincoln is seated in a rocking chair, holding the hand of his wife, who, thanks to her voluminous skirts, occupies most of a small sofa. Though readers generally expect the author to provide at least a cursory description of his characters, in this case I hardly think it's necessary. Mr. Lincoln's rugged face has been impressed indelibly in our minds by photographs and five-dollar bills, and you have no doubt seen enough pictures of Mary Todd Lincoln to know that she is rather plain-looking and a bit on the plump side.

You may not have expected Mr. Lincoln to look so gaunt and haggard. Though he hasn't had to face death daily on the battlefield—for the politicians who are so ready to declare wars never actually fight them, of course—or lost a limb, or wasted away from dysentery in some prison camp, the endless conflict has taken its toll on him. He has lost his appetite. He has trouble sleeping; he is plagued nightly by dreams of death and disaster, including some in which he looks upon his own lifeless body. He does not dismiss these as (to use a popular term of the time) mere fudge. He believes they may be premonitions, warnings of things to come.

He has said nothing to his wife about his visions. Like Carolina Ehrlich and so many others, Mary Todd Lincoln suffers from a weakness of the nerves—or neurasthenia, as some doctors have begun calling the condition. She is also a firm believer in the significance of the supernatural, and if she knew about Mr. Lincoln's dreams, she would fret so that it might be harmful to her health.

When Ward Lamon introduces the two performers, Mr. Lincoln turns his chair around to face them. "I hope you'll pardon me for not getting up, gentlemen. My back has been bothering me lately." Though Joseph is too intimidated to step forward and shake the great man's hand, his father doesn't hesitate. "I'm guessing that Professor Godunov is what they call a stage name."

"You guess correctly," says Nicholas. "In real life, my name is Nicholas Ehrlich, and this is my son, Joseph."

"And this is Mrs. Lincoln. She was quite taken with your mind-reading act."

Nicholas bows to the first lady. "I am happy that our performance pleased you, madam—and I'm certain that, if my son could speak, he would say the same."

" 'Silence is the perfectest herald of joy,' " says the president. " 'I were but little happy, if I could say how much.' "

Nicholas looks at him in surprise. "*Much Ado About Nothing.* I didn't realize you were a Shakespeare enthusiast."

Mr. Lincoln gives a high-pitched laugh. "Contrary to what my political rivals would have you believe, I'm not an uneducated ape."

"I didn't suppose you were," says Nicholas. But the truth is, that description closely matches the opinion he has held of the president up until now. Though Mr. Lincoln's speech can take a rustic turn now and again—he pronounces *uneducated* as *uneddicated* and occasionally drops the final *g* from such words as *getting* and *bothering*—he's obviously intelligent and perceptive. Anyone who appreciates both Shakespeare and Professor Godunov and Son could hardly be otherwise.

While Nicholas and the president share views on Shake-speare, Mrs. Lincoln beckons to Joseph. "May I speak with you, young man?"

He emerges from the shadow of Ward Hill Lamon and approaches the sofa. "Of course."

"Are you by any chance a medium?"

Joseph is taken aback. What possible reason could she have to ask about his clothing size? Seeing his confusion, she rephrases the question. "Are you able to communicate with the spirit world?"

"Oh." He's still uncertain how to respond. Mademoiselle Delphine advertises that she can talk with the dead. So does the woman known as Madame Masha. Is it something that's expected from clairvoyants, then? If he says he can't, will that brand him as a fake? "I'm not sure," he says. "I've never tried."

"Well, you should. From time to time, I host a séance at the White House, with Mr. Colchester as the medium. Perhaps you could attend the next one, and try your hand at it."

The gaslights that line the walls of the auditorium dim three times—they are all controlled by a single valve beneath the stage—signaling that the next act, a farce called *O'Flannigan at the Fair,* is about to begin. The president thanks them for coming and expresses the hope that he will catch their act again, and then Mr. Lamon ushers them out.

Joseph is still feeling somewhat dazed by the encounter. As they hurry home through the chilly night, he says, "Can you believe that we were praised by the president of the United States?"

"Not exactly," says Nicholas.

"What do you mean?"

"Well, he never actually said that *he* was impressed with the act, only that Mrs. Lincoln was."

"Oh. Still, he was very cordial to us, wasn't he?"

"Yes, he was. Frankly, I was surprised at how much I liked the man. It's fortunate that I didn't meet him sooner; I might have been tempted to vote for him."

"You mean you *didn't?*" says Joseph incredulously.

Nicholas shakes his head.

"Not even the first time?"

"No. You won't tell Mrs. McKenna, will you?"

"Why didn't you vote for him?"

"I feared that he would get us into a war. I was right."

"What should he have done? Let the South secede? Told them it was perfectly all right to own slaves?"

"I don't know," Nicholas admits. "That's why I'm not president. But it seems to me that nearly any alternative would be preferable to *that*." He points across the street, where a wagon is pulled up before the entrance to the Patent Office. It isn't until Joseph hears the groans of pain and the pitiful pleas for water, or morphine, or anything to relieve their misery, that he realizes the wagon is filled with bloody, bandaged men. He lowers his gaze to the dirt street before him.

"Don't turn away," says Nicholas. "Take a good look at them."

"I don't want to."

"Of course you don't. No one wants to. That's why they wait until after dark to bring them in." The two of them walk on in silence for a time, then Nicholas says, in a lighter tone, "I noticed you and Mrs. Lincoln having a little chat. What did she say?"

"She invited me to the White House," says Joseph.

"Did she?"

"Well, sort of. She said that the next time she held a séance, I should come by and try communicating with the spirit world."

Nicholas laughs. "I had heard she was an ardent advocate of spiritualism. They say she's made a number of attempts to contact her son Willie, who died of typhoid several years ago."

"Do you suppose . . ." says Joseph. "Do you suppose there really are people who can do that? Speak with the dead?"

"I hope so," replies his father. "Perhaps the president will contact a few men out of those hundreds of thousands who have died fighting his war. Perhaps he'll ask them whether they think it was worth giving their lives for."

CHAPTER FIFTEEN

Ford's Theatre is four blocks nearer to the boardinghouse than the National Theatre, so Joseph and his father arrive not long after the other entertainers, while there is still plenty of food left on the buffet (no thanks to Patrick Nolan, who is doing his best to make certain there will be no leftovers).

Once again, word of their success has somehow preceded them. The other boarders are even aware that the Ehrlichs were summoned to the presidential box. Mick O'Boyle says to Joseph, "Did Mrs. Lincoln want you to summon up her dead son?"

"Well, no," replies Joseph. "But she did ask whether I could communicate with the spirit world."

"I knew it! She's surely given every clairvoyant in Washington a try by now—except maybe Mademoiselle Delphine, here. She hasn't been to see yourself yet, has she?" He addresses this to Cassandra, who wordlessly shakes her head.

"And she won't, neither," growls Patrick Nolan, "if she knows what's good for her."

"Oh?" says Mr. Hayes, the clog dancer. "You have some grudge against Mrs. Lincoln?"

Chewing on a slice of ham, Nolan looks warily around him, as though calculating whether it's safe to speak freely in this company. Since Mrs. McKenna, that outspoken champion of the president, is absent, he decides to chance it. "I've the same grudge again her as I had again Prince Albert." He's referring to the late husband of Queen Victoria of England.

"Meaning what?" says Mr. Hayes.

"Meaning that she's married to a tyrant."

Mr. Montoya gives him a startled look. "A tyrant? That is strong language, sir."

"Hasn't he tried by force to keep the South part of the Union, again their will? Ain't it the very same thing the English have been after doing to Ireland for six hundred years?"

"I don't think you can compare the two," says Mr. Hayes.

"I can, and I will. Hasn't he stolen their lands from them, just as the English stole lands from the Irish? Aren't the people in the South starving, just as my mother and father did during the Great Famine?"

"Maybe you should send them that ham you're making such short work of," says a harsh voice from the doorway of the kitchen. Due to the cold, Mrs. McKenna has returned early from her nightly stroll with her beau, the fish merchant. "Or maybe you should just go down there yourself, since you sympathize with them so much."

Nolan's sullen face goes red, as though a bit of food has gone down the wrong way. What he's actually having trouble swallowing, of course, is Mrs. McKenna's remarks. It is all he can do to keep himself from making some angry rejoinder. But he knows that, if he does, his days as a boarder here are numbered. He and Cassandra have been asked to leave their lodgings twice already in the past six months, after just such an exchange, and he's not eager to be out on the street in this weather, searching for a new place to stay. So he opens his mouth only to stuff it with food, and contents himself with sending murderous glances Mrs. McKenna's way.

As usual, it's up to Mick O'Boyle to salvage the conversation. "Have you heard what's happened to Nicholas and his son?" he says to Mrs. McKenna. "Mr. Lincoln has asked them to be his new advisers. It'll be their job to read General Lee's mind and find out what his next move will be."

"Can you do that?" an earnest voice asks Joseph. To everyone's surprise, it's Cassandra who has spoken. "I've never been able to."

Before Joseph or his father can reply, Patrick Nolan has one of his niece's thin arms in his grip and is urging her out of the room. "It's time you were in bed." His tone of voice suggests that he is less concerned about how much rest she gets than he is about keeping her quiet.

When they are gone, Mick O'Boyle says, "Isn't he a louty rascal, though? It's the likes of him that gives Irishmen a bad name."

"What else did he have to say against Mr. Lincoln?" asks Mrs. McKenna.

The performers glance at one another, reluctant to speak ill of a fellow boarder, even if he is a louty rascal. El Niño Eddie has no such reservations. From the day Patrick Nolan arrived, the boy has regarded him as a threat, a competitor for the limited supply of apple pie and mashed potatoes and other delicacies. "He called the president a tyrant," says Eddie.

Mrs. McKenna, who has been cutting the last of the ham from the bone, stops and raises the knife, as though she is contemplating making an Irish stew instead. "If Mr. Lincoln really was a tyrant," she says, "Mr. Nolan wouldn't feel so free to call him one. He'd be arrested as a traitor and thrown in prison."

"He's done more than just call Mr. Lincoln names," says El Niño Eddie softly. He has been keeping a close eye on Nolan lately, hoping to uncover some bit of incriminating information he can use against the man. Just yesterday he succeeded, and he has been waiting for the right moment to reveal it.

"What do you mean?" asks his mother.

"I overheard him talking to a man in the parlor yesterday. I was looking for something behind the sofa, and when they came in I just stayed there and didn't make a sound. I didn't want them to think I was spying on them." Which, of course, is exactly what he *was* doing.

"What did they say?" asks Mrs. McKenna in a conspiratorial voice.

"The visitor said 'I understand you've had some experience as a blockhead runner,' or something like that."

Under other circumstances, Eddie's error would be amusing. But no one even smiles. "A block*ade* runner," says Nicholas. "They smuggle goods and information into the South."

"Anyway, the visitor had a letter from a captured Rebel officer, and he wanted somebody to deliver it to his family."

"Did Nolan agree to do it?" asks Mick O'Boyle.

Eddie shakes his head. "He said he had done some blockade running, but he couldn't anymore, because his blank landlady—he didn't say *blank;* he used a curse word—wouldn't let him leave his niece all alone."

Ordinarily, Mrs. McKenna's expression is that of a person

who's been chewing something sour; she appears now to have bitten into something unbearably bitter. She strides across the dining room and into the hallway and pounds on the door of Nolan's room with the hilt of the butcher knife. "Mr. Nolan!" she shouts.

He yanks open the door. The scowl on his face subtly changes character as he spots the knife in her hand. "What do you want?"

"I want you out of here by noon tomorrow!"

"I gave you two months' rent!" he protests.

"You'll get half of it back, which is more than you deserve."

Nolan's massive hands curl into fists. For a moment, Joseph fears that he will seize one of Mrs. McKenna's arms—which, though hardly frail, are no match for his—wrest the knife from her grasp, and use it on her. Instead, he pushes past her, snatches his Inverness overcoat from a hook in the hallway, and storms out the front door.

Later that evening, as Joseph is curled up in the armchair in the upstairs parlor, reading *Scar Chief, the Wild Halfbreed* for want of anything better, he again looks up to find Cassandra standing silently at the head of the stairs. This time she has clasped in her arms the two books—*Great Expectations* and *The Old Curiosity Shop*, both by Mr. Dickens—that he brought her from the lending library. "I'd better give these back to you if we're leaving tomorrow."

"They're not due for a week yet, and even then I can renew them. Why don't you take them with you?"

"Something could happen to them. I don't know . . . I don't know where we'll be."

"You think you'll stay in Washington, though?"

"Probably. My uncle is always saying that he likes to be where the money is."

"Then surely he'll get another room for you somewhere."

"They're hard to find. Sometimes we just stay in lodging houses."

"Lodging houses?"

"They're sort of like hotels, only dirtier, and with a lot of people in each room." She shudders. "I don't like them."

"I'm not surprised. I don't imagine they attract the best class of customers."

"I don't mind that so much. It's just that, with all those other people around . . . my head gets so full of thoughts and images and feelings, I'm afraid it might burst. I can't shut them out. Do you know what I mean?"

Since it seems unlikely that he will ever see her again, Joseph should be able to tell her the truth—that his so-called mental powers are nothing but an illusion. But he can't bring himself to admit it. Besides, in a way he *does* know what she means. Sometimes, when he's going over all those lists of items for the act, making sure he hasn't forgotten them, his brain feels much the same way she describes. "Yes," he says.

"I thought you would."

"I also know what it's like to always be moving on to someplace new. We've done it more times than I can count."

She nods glumly and hands over the books. "I was wondering . . . ," she begins, and then she hesitates, suddenly overcome by shyness.

"What?"

"Well, if we do find another place . . . do you suppose you could . . . come and visit me sometimes? You're the only one I can talk to. You're the only one that understands."

Joseph is touched by her request. He can't refuse, of course, any more than he could refuse to rescue Margaretta's stuffed monkey from the icy river. He assures her that, if she will let him know when they've settled somewhere, he will come to see her. But even before the promise is out of his mouth, he has begun to regret it.

She clearly regards him as a friend only because she imagines that he possesses—or is possessed by—the same strange skill (or power, or insight, or whatever it is) that she has displayed. If they keep on seeing each other, she'll very quickly discover that the only power he has is the power to dupe audiences, and he couldn't even do that if they weren't, by and large, willing to be duped.

Readers are the same way. You know very well that the stories we novelists tell you are pure invention. But there is an unspoken agreement between author and reader: If we tell our tales in a compelling way and don't challenge your credibility too much, you agree to believe them.

I am doing my best to hold up my end of the bargain. It's not easy when you're dealing with such matters as clairvoyance, which may be difficult for some readers to accept. Let me assure you that there really are individuals like Cassandra, who receive mental or emotional messages of some sort from other people and from objects.

You may wonder why I haven't let you in on what's happening inside Cassandra's head, as I have with some of the other characters. Trust me; it's best if I don't. Her mind is a confusing and, frankly, a rather scary place. Venturing into it would be like taking you into those undesirable parts of the city I told you about.

She is constantly besieged by thoughts and feelings that aren't her own. Over time she has learned to block them out to some extent, the way a race driver limits his horse's vision with blinders, or the way you may sometimes try to block out the sounds around you by putting your fingers in your ears. But, just as the loudest sounds can still get through, the strongest, most disturbing images and emotions still make their way into Cassandra's mind.

So we will stay mainly with Joseph and his thoughts— which are, as you know, quite ordinary for the most part. He is, however, showing some signs of growing less ordinary. As soon as Cassandra returns to her room, he resumes reading *Scar Chief.* But after only a few paragraphs of purple prose, he sighs and puts the book down. Then, very tentatively, like someone stepping onto a high wire for the first time, he picks up Mr. Dickens's novel *The Old Curiosity Shop* (which is shorter than *Great Expectations*), opens it to the first page, and begins to read.

He will perhaps be disappointed to find that it contains not a single Indian or Indian fighter. It does have other merits, however, such as memorable characters and an engaging, witty style. Curiously enough, Mr. Dickens's story, like ours, features an unfortunate orphan girl who is being raised by an irresponsible relative.

Cassandra's irresponsible relative does not return to the boardinghouse at all that night. He still has not shown up by the time Joseph and his father leave for Ford's Theatre the next evening. "Do you think he could have abandoned her and gone off to join the Southern cause?" asks Joseph.

"I very much doubt it," replies Nicholas. "Despite his claim to have been a boxer, he strikes me as more of a schemer than a fighter."

Nicholas is right. There's not enough money, or anything else, in the South to suit Patrick Nolan. When the Ehrlichs come home after the show, they find that he has been there and gone again, taking Cassandra with him.

"Has he found them another place to stay?" Joseph asks Mrs. McKenna.

"He didn't say," replies the landlady. "I hope so, for the poor thing's sake." She shakes her head thoughtfully. "Since they left, no less than three people have come by asking for Mademoiselle Delphine. You know what I think? I think they're all part of a conspiracy to overthrow the government or some such thing. I expect that 'Mademoiselle Delphine' is their password."

The following evening, as Professor Godunov and Son are leaving the house, they encounter the woman with the prominent nose and fur hat—the same one who grew so indignant when Cassandra suggested that her fiancé was only after her money. "Is Mademoiselle Delphine receiving clients, do you know?" she asks them.

"I'm afraid she's no longer rooming here," says Nicholas.

"Oh. That's unfortunate. Do you have any idea where I might reach her?"

"Not really," says Joseph. "But I may be hearing from her soon."

"If you should"—the woman takes a calling card from her bag—"would you be so kind as to give her this?" She takes out a reservoir pen—the ancestor of today's fountain pen—and writes something on the back of the card, then hands it to Joseph.

After the woman is gone, and before he tucks the card away in his vest pocket, Joseph can't resist glancing at the message on the back. It says: "Your prediction was quite correct. Thank you."

CHAPTER SIXTEEN

Joseph almost hopes that he won't hear from Cassandra. If they don't see each other again, she will never have to know that his purported ability to read minds is only a sham. But when weeks go by and there is no word from her, he begins to wonder what's become of her and to worry about her welfare. He wishes that he really could read other people's thoughts; perhaps he and Cassandra could send mental messages back and forth—something like a telegraph, but without wires. (Such a device doesn't exist, of course. But if Joseph also had powers of precognition, he would know that, in about thirty years, Mr. Marconi will invent a wireless telegraph.)

Thinking about telegraphs and messages gives him an idea. Oddly enough, it's an idea for improving the mind-reading act. Though Joseph may bemoan the fact that he and his father are only pretending to be mental wizards, the fact remains that they are making quite a good living at it, so he has no intention of giving it up just yet.

Knowing what a perfectionist his father is, Joseph takes a week or so to work the potential flaws out of his plan before he brings it up, and even then he's a bit apprehensive. To his surprise, Nicholas is enthusiastic about it.

Though they're nearing the end of their five-week run at Ford's, the manager of the Front Street Theatre in Baltimore has caught their act and offered them a two-week engagement. Since theatregoers there tend to be less sophisticated than those in Washington—the audiences are made up largely of working-class immigrants—Nicholas sees this as an ideal opportunity to try out a new technique.

The one Joseph has in mind involves a miniature telegraph key concealed beneath the carpet of the theatre. Wires will run from it to a battery in the orchestra pit, then up through the floor of the stage, where they will connect to a brass plate. Another telegraph key will be hidden inside the upholstered chair where Joseph sits; its wires will run down the leg of the chair and connect to a second brass plate. When this plate is placed atop the one in the floor, it will complete the electrical circuit. Nicholas will operate the first key surreptitiously with his foot—one click for the letter *A*, two for *B*, and so on—and the second key will convey the clicks to Joseph.

Professor Godunov and Son leave for Baltimore a week before they open, in order to set up the apparatus and make sure it's working properly. Carolina Ehrlich stays behind—partly because she dislikes travel and unfamiliar places, partly because Baltimore is rumored to be in a state of unrest. According to a new boarder, there are frequent clashes in the streets between the city's many secessionists and the Union soldiers who are stationed there.

The only trouble Joseph and his father encounter is the telegraph wire detaching itself from the battery, and they're such veteran performers now that it doesn't faze them. They return to Mrs. McKenna's in mid-March, safe and sound and nearly four hundred dollars richer.

There's actually been more unrest in Washington than in Baltimore, thanks to the inauguration. Most of those who would rather see Mr. Lincoln in a coffin than in the White House have the good sense to keep their opinion to themselves, but a few are determined to express their displeasure. In spite of the mounted soldiers who patrolled the streets on the night before the inauguration, several abolitionists distributing antislavery pamphlets were attacked and severely beaten, as were several others whose only offense was to wear a pro-Lincoln button. And, though the inauguration platform was surrounded by police, a would-be assassin managed to break through and get within several yards of the president before he was subdued.

Something else happened while Joseph and his father were gone that is of far less consequence to the world at large, but of greater consequence to our story. Two letters were delivered to the boardinghouse. One is from Mr. Henry Clay Ford, offering Professor Godunov and Son another two-week engagement. The other is addressed to Joseph. It is, as you have no doubt guessed, from Cassandra. The message is not written but printed, in the sort of large, careful letters made by students who are still unsure of their skills.

DEAR JOSEPH,

I AM LODGING NOW AT MRS. SURRATT'S

BOARDINGHOUSE, 541 H STREET. I SHARE A ROOM

WITH A PLEASANT YOUNG WOMAN, MISS HONORA

FITZPATRICK, WHO IS TUTORING ME. I HOPE THAT

YOU WILL FIND IT CONVENIENT TO CALL UPON ME

VERY SOON.

YOURS SINCERELY,

CASSANDRA QUINN

(If you are the sort who pays attention to small details, you may have noticed that Cassandra's last name is different from her uncle's. That's not a mistake. Patrick Nolan is the brother of Cassandra's mother, who was Kathleen Nolan before she married Daniel Quinn. What you didn't notice—

because it can't very well be shown here—is that Cassandra originally closed with the phrase YOUR FRIEND but then erased it, feeling it was too presumptuous.)

The letter is dated March 2—over a week ago. Joseph locates the calling card given him by the woman with the prominent nose and sets out for Mrs. Surratt's that very afternoon. The boardinghouse lies only four or five blocks northwest of Mrs. McKenna's. It is quite a substantial building, three and a half stories high and built of brick that has been painted gray.

Joseph has to climb a set of stairs to reach the main entry, which is on the second floor. His knock is answered by a young man of twenty or so (though he looks and acts much younger) with weak eyes that are in need of glasses, disheveled black hair that is in need of cutting, a sallow complexion that is in need of sunshine, a pathetic attempt at a mustache that is in need of a good deal more hair, and a severely receding chin for which there is, unfortunately, no remedy.

His name is Davy Herold, and he has no real business answering the door. He is neither a relative of Mrs. Surratt's nor one of her boarders, only an occasional visitor. He likes to consider himself a part of the household, though, and to strengthen that illusion he takes it upon himself to welcome other visitors and to sit down, uninvited, to meals. Mrs. Surratt tolerates this, partly because she feels sorry for the boy, and partly because of the company he keeps.

As unlikely as it seems, Davy is a frequent companion of the celebrated actor John Wilkes Booth. In fact, as Joseph discovers when he enters the boardinghouse, Mr. Booth is at this very moment sitting—or rather lounging—on the sofa in the front parlor, sipping brandy and conversing in low tones with Mrs. Surratt's son, John—Jack, to his friends—a slender fellow with a sharp, shrewd-looking face. Jack is about the same age as Davy Herold, but he actually looks like a man in his twenties, and not like a boy of sixteen or seventeen, as Davy does.

Joseph has never seen Davy Herold or Jack Surratt before, but he recognizes Mr. Booth at once, for he's encountered the man's likeness dozens of times. In most theatres, there is an area backstage known as the green room, where the actors and other entertainers may relax—if they're able to—before and after their performances. On the walls are playbills from previous productions, plus signed photographic prints of noted performers who have appeared there.

Wilkes Booth (he generally dispenses with the "John") is a favorite with the audience—and with the other actors—at all three theatres where Professor Godunov and Son have performed. In fact, near the end of January, when the Ehrlichs were at Ford's, Mr. Booth was at the National, playing Romeo to Miss Avonia Jones's Juliet, and to great acclaim.

I won't waste your time with a lengthy description of the man. Like Joseph, you've seen his portrait enough times to know that he is as different from his friend Davy Herold as it is possible to be—fine featured, well mannered, impeccably groomed, tastefully dressed in a gray frock coat with velvet lapels and a silk cravat with a diamond stickpin.

To Joseph's astonishment, the famous actor recognizes him, too. When Davy Herold hollers up the stairwell, "Miss Fitzpatrick! There's a visitor here!" it calls Mr. Booth's attention to the hallway where Joseph is standing. "Say, aren't you the mind-reading boy?" he says. "What's your name— Godunov?"

Joseph is very nearly struck dumb. "Yes, sir," he manages to say.

"I caught your act last week in Baltimore. I meant to come backstage and congratulate you, but I was waylaid by a group of female admirers clamoring for my *carte de visite.* Well, you know how it is." His voice, which is hoarse from bronchitis, puts Joseph in mind of Nicholas Ehrlich's rasping, ruined voice.

"I'm sure I don't have one-tenth the number of admirers you have, sir."

"Oh, you will, my boy, you will," says Mr. Booth. "Every woman wants a man who can read her mind." Jack Surratt laughs appreciatively. Mr. Booth takes a sip of the brandy to ease his throat, and says, "Do you have another engagement lined up?"

"Yes, two weeks at Ford's Theatre."

"You don't say? I'm playing there myself next week, in *The Apostate*"—he pauses and, turning his head, coughs discreetly into a lace-edged handkerchief—"provided, of course, that I can shake this bout of bronchitis. It's been plaguing me for weeks. Perhaps we'll be sharing a bill, eh?"

"It would be an honor, sir."

Mr. Booth inclines his head in a slight bow. "The feeling is mutual, sir."

Miss Honora Fitzpatrick, in response to Davy Herold's rather rude summons, is now descending the stairs, the rear of her hoop skirts skipping down the steps behind her. The young women who appear in the novels of Captain Mayne Reid and his ilk are invariably so graceful, beautiful, and pure that the author feels compelled to devote whole paragraphs or even pages to describing them, in an effort to do them justice. It would be difficult to find that much to say about Honora Fitzpatrick. Still, she does deserve a sentence or two.

Though she makes a pleasant enough impression, she is neither particularly graceful nor noticeably beautiful. She is, like Joseph, really rather ordinary-looking, with unremarkable hazel eyes and hair that is nearly the same shade of brown as her dress and arranged in the usual way—that is, parted in the middle and pulled back into a chignon, a sort of knot at the nape of the neck.

Her most appealing feature (aside from her intelligence, of which we'll hear more later) is her slightly sarcastic smile, but it's not in evidence just now. She looks, in fact, rather perplexed. She regards Joseph briefly, then turns to Davy Herold. "You said I had a visitor?"

Curiously enough, her appearance has caused a profound

reaction in Davy. You get the feeling that, if he could write a novel, he would have several paragraphs worth of praise for her, at least. But he's no writer—and not much of a speaker, for that matter. "Well," he says haltingly, "the truth is, he ain't here to see you so much as to see the other girl."

"Then why didn't you call her?"

"I—I couldn't remember her name."

Miss Fitzpatrick makes a clucking noise with her tongue and shakes her head, as though Davy is a pupil who has neglected to learn the day's lesson. He looks like one, too, the way he ducks his head and shifts about uncomfortably. Miss Fitzpatrick turns to the visitor. "You must be Mr. Ehrlich, then. Cassandra said you might be coming by. I believe she expected you much sooner than this."

"I know," says Joseph apologetically. "I was in Baltimore." He, too, feels as though he's being reprimanded. This is not unusual, for Miss Fitzpatrick—when she can find work—is a teacher and, even though she is only eighteen herself, she has a habit of treating everyone under the age of thirty or so as if they were her students.

Well, not everyone. As she moves forward to greet Joseph, Mr. Booth catches sight of her through the doorway of the parlor. "Good afternoon, Miss Fitzpatrick," he says, raising his brandy glass as though in a toast to her.

Her demeanor changes abruptly from that of a self-possessed teacher to that of a starstruck girl, like those who sometimes wait for Joseph outside the stage door. Her face takes on a rosy tint that is quite becoming. "Good afternoon, sir," she says, in little more than a whisper. Then she swiftly sweeps off up the stairs, leaving Joseph and Davy staring after her, one in surprise and one in admiration.

"Shall I follow her?" asks Joseph.

"Yes, go ahead. Their room's two flights up. The attic, we call it." The way he says this makes it sound as if he has some claim on the building. As Joseph starts up the stairs, Davy puts a hand on his arm and says softly, "You know, the real reason I called her down here is just because I wanted to see her a little. It seems as if she spends most of the time shut up in her room, reading books." He gazes longingly after her, even though she's no longer in sight. "Ain't she a peach, though?"

Due to the slope of the roof, the two rooms on the fourth floor are quite small, and there is no space for a real parlor, only a couple of chairs and a tiny wooden table on the landing at the top of the stairs. Joseph finds Cassandra sitting here, looking better fed and better clothed than when he last saw her, but with the same somber expression as always—though it brightens a little when she sees him. "I knew you'd come," she says.

He takes a seat in the other chair. "I'd have stopped by sooner, but we were performing in Baltimore."

"I thought so. Did the theatre you were in have a picture of someone on a horse?"

"Yes. On the curtain. I think it was supposed to be George Washington."

She nods. "I saw it."

"When?"

"A few days ago."

"Oh. You mean . . . in your mind," Joseph says. He was hoping to avoid the subject of clairvoyance.

"Of course. Did the audience like you?"

"They seemed to." He searches for a way to steer the conversation away from himself and comes up with the business card given him by the woman with the conspicuous nose. "One of your clients asked me to give you this." Cassandra reads the message written on the back ("Your prediction was quite correct. Thank you.") and merely nods, as if it's just what she expected. Joseph says, "Are you still doing readings?"

Cassandra looks about rather furtively, as though afraid someone might overhear. Then she shakes her head and says softly, "My uncle says he's given up on using my gift as a way to make money. He says it's not reliable, and he can do better without me."

"He hasn't abandoned you, has he?"

"No. I don't see him very often, but he pays Honora to take care of me. I don't know where he gets the money. He says he's found a regular job, but I'm not sure I believe him." She leans in to Joseph and says, in an even lower voice, "I think maybe he's started smuggling supplies and things to the South again. I don't want Honora to know. She might hold it against me. Her father is a sergeant in the Union Army." She glances toward the door of their room, which is slightly ajar, then pulls her chair closer to Joseph's. "I haven't told her about my gift, either."

"Why not?"

"I . . . I don't want her to see me as different. I want her to think I'm just . . . ordinary."

"You should be glad you're not," says Joseph. "There are enough ordinary people in the world already."

"I know. My mother told me, just before she died, that the second sight is a gift from God, and that I should be proud of it, and make use of it. But I don't feel proud of it. I feel . . . I feel sad and ashamed. So many of the things I see are bad things, things I don't *want* to see. Maybe there's something wrong with me. Isn't there some way you can block those things out, and just let the good ones through?"

Joseph thinks about the wagon full of wounded soldiers, about how he tried to look away, to ignore them, and how his father said that people needed to see them, to be reminded of what terrible things can happen in the name of a noble cause. "I don't think so," he says. "I think good and bad are so mixed up together that you can't sort them out."

"Then I'd rather not see anything at all." Cassandra sighs. "I guess I don't have that choice, though, do I?" Joseph doesn't reply, for he knows nothing about it. He notices that her fingers are working nervously, twisting the fabric of her dress. She takes a deep breath and says, "There's something I need to tell you. I haven't told anyone else. It's something I saw, something bad that's going to happen."

Assuming that it must involve him or his family, Joseph asks anxiously, "Who do you see it happening to?"

Cassandra raises her eyes, but they don't quite meet his. They seem fixed on something far away. "To Mr. Lincoln," she says.

CHAPTER SEVENTEEN

Joseph isn't certain how seriously he should take Cassandra's warning. It's clear from the worried, almost frightened look on her face that she takes it very seriously. And it's true that in several other cases, the visions she's had—of Margaretta's accident, of the money behind the picture, of the fiancé's real motives—have been uncannily accurate. But this is something different. This time she's not picking up thoughts or feelings from the past, or from the spirit world, or from some object. She is apparently looking into the future.

"What do you see?" asks Joseph. "An assassination attempt?"

"Not exactly." After glancing again at the door of the room, she pulls a crumpled piece of paper from her pocket. "I wrote down the things that came into my head so I wouldn't forget. There was a gun, but I couldn't see who was holding it. I don't think they were going to shoot him with it. I got the feeling they were tying him up, or maybe putting a gag in his mouth. There was something about *soldiers*—I didn't actually see any soldiers, just the word. I saw some other words, too, something like 'The water is still,' or 'The water is deep.' "

"Did you get any sense of where this was taking place, or when?"

She shakes her head. "I don't know how it is with you, but I have a really hard time with . . . well, with *time*. Sometimes I get sort of a sense, though, of whether things are far off in the future, or whether they're going to happen soon, and I think this is going to be soon—maybe within a few days. I couldn't quite picture where they were. I know it wasn't inside a building. I got a feeling of movement, like I did when I saw your sister's accident, so I think maybe they were inside a carriage or on a train."

Joseph takes the paper from her hand and stares thoughtfully at the large letters she's printed on it: GUN. TIED UP? SOLDIERS. WATER IS STILL, DEEP. CARRIAGE? TRAIN? "It sounds to me like they're kidnapping him." He turns his gaze on Cassandra. "When you see something like this, does it usually come true?"

She nods and then says, in a faint, faltering voice, "I saw . . . I saw that my mother was going to die of a fever, before she ever got sick." Cassandra has to pause and take a deep, ragged breath before she can go on. "I saw the explosion at the Armory, the day before it happened. I wanted to tell someone, but my uncle wouldn't let me. He said . . . he said it served them right, since they were making ammunition for the Union soldiers to kill Confederates with."

"Good Lord," says Joseph softly. He looks down at the

paper again. "We need to tell somebody about this, Cassandra."

"I know. I just didn't want anybody here to find out. They don't know about the gift. They think I'm just a normal girl."

"Have you said anything about it to your uncle?"

"No. He hates Mr. Lincoln. He wouldn't do anything to try and stop the kidnappers. He'd probably *help* them."

"We could talk to my father. He'd know what to do."

Cassandra is clearly uncomfortable with this idea, too. "He might tell my uncle. Unless . . ." She gives a small but rather sly smile. "You wouldn't have to say that it was *me* who had the vision. You could tell him it was you."

Joseph winces slightly. "I don't think so. I never see things that are going to happen, not like this." He gives the matter another minute's thought. "It's just possible," he says, finally, "that we could talk to Mr. Lincoln himself, or to Mrs. Lincoln, at least. I've met them, you know. They came to one of our performances. Mrs. Lincoln even invited me to the White House. She's a great believer in clairvoyance and such things."

"Do you really think they'd listen to us?"

"It's worth a try. It's better than doing nothing. And if you're sure this is going to happen soon, we'd better not waste any time."

"I'm never really sure of anything I see, until it happens . . . or until it doesn't."

"I've been wondering," says Joseph. "That day when I saw

you at the racecourse—were you predicting the winners for your uncle?"

Cassandra shrugs her thin shoulders. "I was trying. Sometimes I got them right, and sometimes I didn't. It's so hard to concentrate when I'm in a crowd like that. I don't know how you can see anything at all, in a whole theatre full of people."

Joseph is at a loss for a reply. Luckily for him, at that moment the door to the room opens and Miss Fitzpatrick emerges. "Pardon me," she says briskly. "I wanted to remind Cassandra that she has not done her arithmetic yet."

"Oh." Joseph exchanges a quick glance with Cassandra. "Well . . . could she possibly do it later? We were just on our way out. For, ah, for ice cream." He's not quite sure where that came from. Perhaps it was Cassandra's resemblance to his sister that brought it to mind; as you will recall, Margaretta was a frozen-dessert fanatic.

"I love ice cream," says Cassandra, without much conviction. The truth is, she's never tasted it.

"Far more than you love arithmetic, I'm sure," says Miss Fitzpatrick. "But I believe that, in the long run, you will find mathematics more useful." She sounds so old and stodgy, I feel it necessary to remind you that she is, in fact, only three years older than Joseph.

"How about if we combine the two?" Joseph suggests. "She can count the number of spoonfuls in a dish of strawberry ice, and divide it by the number of minutes it takes her to eat it."

"And who will tell her whether or not her answer is correct? You?"

"I'm a pretty fair hand at mathematics," says Joseph. "I used to do the accounts for Foley's China and Lamp Store."

"Did you? Then no doubt you can tell me how to determine the area of a triangle." Before Joseph can begin to reply that he doesn't know, she goes on. "What is the Pythagorean theorem? If four times x, plus three minus eight, equals nineteen, what is the value of x?"

Joseph laughs. "Are you teaching that to Cassandra?"

"Not yet," says Miss Fitzpatrick. "Give us a few months." She glances at Cassandra, who is waiting patiently for her fate to be decided, and sighs. "I suppose it won't hurt to postpone your lessons for an hour or so."

"We may be a little longer than that," says Joseph.

"Don't worry. I'll keep you on schedule."

"I—I didn't imagine you'd want to come with us."

"Well, I can hardly let Cassandra go traipsing off without a chaperone, can I? Besides—" She pauses, and for the first time Joseph gets a look at the appealing, sarcastic smile I mentioned earlier. "I happen to be very fond of ice cream myself."

As they are passing the parlor on their way out, Davy Herold, who is engaged in an animated conversation with Mr. Booth and Jack Surratt, spies them. He springs up at once and catches Miss Fitzpatrick at the front door. "Going out for a stroll, Miss Fitzpatrick? Would you care for some company?"

"Sit down, Davy," calls Mr. Booth. "You're behaving like

a terrier who's been cooped up in the house too long. Besides, we still have things to discuss."

With a look that could be described as hangdog, Davy returns reluctantly to his seat on the sofa. Miss Fitzpatrick sends a grateful glance in Mr. Booth's direction, then makes her exit, her face as flushed as though she were in the throes of a fever.

"Mr. Booth doesn't room here, does he?" asks Joseph.

"Oh, no. He stays at the National Hotel. He only comes by from time to time to visit with John Surratt."

"Is Mr. Surratt an actor, too?"

"Not that I'm aware of. I believe he works for an express company." Confidentially, she adds, "Honestly, I can't imagine what Mr. Booth could possibly have in common with him, or with Davy Herold."

"Politics, maybe? They say it makes strange bedfellows."

This suggestion seems to rub Miss Fitzpatrick the wrong way. "I doubt that. Frankly, I suspect John Surratt of having secessionist tendencies."

"And Mr. Booth doesn't?"

"I understand that Mr. Booth is one of Mr. Lincoln's favorite actors."

For some reason, Joseph is feeling rather resentful toward Mr. Booth. Perhaps he's just the least bit jealous of the man's fame and the number of admirers he has, or of the fact that he stays at the National Hotel and not some shabby boardinghouse. "Well, if he's such a good actor, he could just be *acting* as if he's loyal to the Union."

Miss Fitzpatrick casts him a look that might better be called a glare. Cassandra tugs at Joseph's sleeve, and when he bends down, she whispers, "Don't say anything bad about Mr. Booth. I think Honora likes him."

"I think you're right."

Cassandra beckons Joseph closer. "How are we going to go see Mr. Lincoln, with her along?"

"I'm not sure. For now, I guess we'll have to go to the ice-cream parlor."

This is the first warm day the city has seen since November, and the streets are busy. It's clear that the presence of so many people is having an effect on Cassandra. Her face looks set, tensed, as though she's holding her breath. She keeps her eyes fixed on the street before her. Under her breath she counts her steps, trying to keep her mind occupied so that perhaps it won't pick up the desperate thoughts of the banker whose bank is about to go under; the penniless widow who has overextended her credit at the grocer's and is working up the nerve to ask for more; the thief who is scanning passersby, looking for his next victim; the blind beggar, a former soldier, who is reliving the horrors of Cold Harbor in his head.

When she edges closer to Joseph, he notices how rigid she seems and guesses the cause. On an impulse, he reaches down and takes her hand in his, as he used to do with his sister. Cassandra grasps it as though it's a lifeline, as though being in physical contact with him somehow helps her to shut out everything else. Miss Fitzpatrick observes the gesture and smiles—without a hint of sarcasm, for a change.

Fortunately, the ice-cream parlor is not so busy. Though the weather is growing warmer, it's not warm enough yet to set people thinking about cold confections. Miss Fitzpatrick orders chocolate and insists upon paying for it herself, over Joseph's objections. "Why should you buy it for me?" she asks, rather loudly. "It's not as if we're courting."

"I just thought that— Well, I wasn't sure whether—"

"I have sufficient money, if that's what concerns you."

"Oh. Well. Good." Joseph turns to Cassandra. "What flavor would you like?" Pointedly, he adds, "I'll pay for it."

"What are you having?"

"Strawberry, I guess."

"That's what I'd like."

For several minutes, they sit in silence, relishing the first ice cream of the season. In Cassandra's case, of course, it's her first ice cream ever. She digs in so enthusiastically that the cold stabs her forehead with a spear of pain, and she clamps a hand to the spot. With a similar stab, Joseph recalls how many times Margaretta did the very same thing and never did learn to restrain herself. Though the memory is painful, it also makes him laugh. So much of life is like that.

Cassandra gives him a peevish look. "It's not funny. It hurts."

"I know. That was a sympathetic laugh."

" 'My feast of joy is but a dish of pain,' " says Miss Fitzpatrick.

Joseph glances at her, startled. "That's a cheerful thought."

"It's poetry."

"Oh, no," says Joseph. "Not you, too."

"What?"

"My father's always quoting somebody. Is that Tennyson, or Shakespeare?"

"Neither. It's Tichborne."

"Never heard of him."

"Perhaps you would have, if you'd stayed in school."

"Now you sound even more like my father. Besides, how do you know I'm *not* in school?"

"You said you worked at Foley's China and Lamp Store."

"I don't anymore."

"Then you're in school?"

"Well, no. I'm a performer."

"Really? An actor, you mean? Like Mr. Booth?"

"Not exactly. My father and I have a mind-reading act."

Miss Fitzpatrick laughs. "A *mind-reading* act?"

"What's wrong with that?" says Joseph indignantly.

"Nothing, I suppose." But she's smiling that sarcastic smile. "Tell me, do you really read minds, or is it just an illusion?"

Joseph hesitates, uncertain how to answer. He senses that Cassandra is watching him, waiting for him to assure Miss Fitzpatrick that it is no illusion, that he is a genuine clairvoyant. "Why don't you come and see us perform," he says at last, "and decide for yourself?"

"I'll do that," says Miss Fitzpatrick. "And, just for future reference, Chidiock Tichborne was a poet—obviously—who conspired to assassinate Queen Elizabeth in 1586, and was executed. Disemboweled, in fact," she adds, and takes a brisk bite of her chocolate ice.

"Another cheerful thought. Is this the sort of thing you're learning?" he asks Cassandra.

"Sometimes. We study a lot of different things. Honora is a good teacher."

"Thank you," says Miss Fitzpatrick. "Would you like more ice cream? *I'm* paying."

"No. It was delicious, though." Cassandra turns toward Joseph and makes a face that conveys her message as efficiently as a wireless telegraph: How can we get rid of her?

The look Joseph sends back is just as easily deciphered: I have no idea. Perhaps if he insults her somehow. "If you're such a good teacher," he says, "why aren't you teaching in a school somewhere?"

Miss Fitzpatrick isn't put off in the least. This is just the sort of blunt, tactless question she herself is accustomed to asking people. "I was," she replies, "up until a few months ago. The headmaster disapproved of some of the things I was teaching."

"Was disemboweling one of them?"

"No, I think that would have been perfectly acceptable. It was mainly the subject of Darwinism he objected to."

"Darwinism?"

"My, you have been out of school a while, haven't you? *The Origin of Species?* Natural selection? Evolution?"

"Ah," says Joseph. From reading the occasional newspaper, he does have a nodding acquaintance with the theory of evolution and the howls of protest it has drawn from organized religion.

Miss Fitzpatrick pulls a man's gold pocket watch from her reticule and opens the cover. "I'm afraid our hour is up," she says. "It's back to the attic and the mathematics."

Cassandra casts another helpless look at Joseph, who says, "Would you mind giving us a moment, Miss Fitzpatrick?"

"Of course. I'll be outside."

As her teacher walks away, Cassandra whispers, "You'll have to go see Mr. Lincoln without me."

"Can't we just take Miss Fitzpatrick with us?"

"No. You saw how she reacted when you said you were a mind reader. She's always saying that we should put our faith in science, not superstition. I don't want her to think I'm stupid, or strange, or something. Anyway, it might be better if I don't go with you. What reason does Mr. Lincoln have to believe me? He's seen you perform. He's a lot more likely to take it seriously if it comes from you."

Joseph is not so sure. Though Mrs. Lincoln may be convinced that he's clairvoyant, he has a feeling that the president is not so easily fooled. If Joseph goes to him claiming to have seen something that hasn't happened yet, Mr. Lincoln is likely to do the very same thing Miss Fitzpatrick did—laugh in his face.

CHAPTER EIGHTEEN

In the hottest months of the year, when the political life of Washington dries up and the threat of typhoid and cholera hangs in the air, the president and his family relocate to Anderson Cottage on the shady grounds of the Soldiers' Home, which sits atop a hill three miles north of the city. (Though the dwelling—also known as the Summer White House—is certainly more modest than the Executive Mansion, it's hardly what most of us would consider a cottage.)

But it's only the middle of March, and as much as he might prefer the more peaceful atmosphere of Anderson Cottage, Mr. Lincoln is bound by duty to remain within easy reach of his advisers and the members of Congress, as well as ordinary citizens who have some pressing complaint or request that only he can address.

In 1865, it's a relatively simple matter to get an audience with the president—at least compared with how complicated and time-consuming a task it will be in a hundred years or so, when our elected representatives are more interested in visiting with campaign contributors and special interest groups than with their constituents.

All you have to do is show up at the Pennsylvania Avenue entrance to the White House, present one of the president's attendants with a calling card or a message, then wait in the upstairs reception room until Mr. Lincoln summons you to his office, which he calls "the shop." During business hours—from nine in the morning until three in the afternoon—the reception room (and often the hall and the stairway as well) is almost invariably packed with petitioners of every description—office seekers, foreign diplomats, autograph collectors, inventors promoting plans for a repeating rifle or a submarine boat, soldiers hoping for a promotion, mothers who will plead with the president to bring their sons home from the war.

But it's after four now, and the place is practically deserted. There was a time when guards were posted at the gates, but Mr. Lincoln did away with that years ago. This late in the day, all that stands between the president and a visitor—or a would-be assassin, for that matter—is a single plainclothes policeman. And when Joseph passes through the gate and walks up the circular drive to the wide portico that faces the Avenue, even that lone sentinel is nowhere to be seen. (In fact, he is in the servants' anteroom, snacking on a piece of cold fried chicken.)

Joseph hesitantly climbs the stairs to the entrance and, after glancing nervously this way and that for several minutes, gets up the nerve to pull gingerly on the doorbell. The door is answered not by a servant or a bodyguard but by a lively lad of nine or ten, bouncing a rubber ball. "Hello," says the boy amiably. "Who are you?"

"Joseph Ehrlich."

"I've never heard of you. Are you here to see my father?"

"That depends on who your father is."

The boy laughs. "He's the president, silly."

"Then, yes, I am here to see him—or Mrs. Lincoln."

"My mother's at the Soldiers' Home, getting our summer cottage in order. But my father's in the Red Room. Shall I tell him you're here?"

"Yes, please. No, wait. He probably won't recognize that name. Tell him it's Yosef, of Professor Godunov and Son."

The boy's jaw drops. "You're the mind reader? Why didn't you say so? I'll get my autograph book!" Abruptly he whirls about, goes racing off across the entrance hall, and disappears.

Joseph steps warily through the open doorway and looks around—or, more accurately, stares openmouthed—at the elegant interior. To his right are two wide carpeted stairways that lead to the reception room and offices. To his left, double doors open into the lavishly decorated, cavernous East Room. Straight ahead, at the far end of the entrance hall, a large screen made of ground glass panes framed in brass separates the first family's private rooms from the more public parts of the mansion.

From somewhere beyond the screen comes the unmistakable sound of a banjo and a deep voice singing a melancholy Stephen Foster tune: " 'Tis the song, the sigh of the weary/ Hard times, hard times, come again no more/Many days you have lingered around my cabin door/Oh, hard times, come again no more."

After a few minutes Mr. Lincoln's son returns, carrying a bound autograph book, which he thrusts into Joseph's hands. Following close behind the boy is a figure three times his size. It's not the tall, gaunt frame of Mr. Lincoln, though, but the massive one of Mr. Ward Lamon, the United States marshal, whom we last saw at Ford's Theatre congratulating Professor Godunov and Son and conducting them to the presidential box. He has his banjo slung around his neck and is turning the keys to and fro in an attempt to put the strings in tune. As he approaches, he glances up at Joseph. "There are those who say that tuning a banjo is like aiming a cannon; the best you can hope for is to come close."

Joseph laughs dutifully, but it sounds hollow and half-hearted in the vast entrance hall. Mr. Lamon offers one huge hand, and he shakes it.

"To what do we owe this visit from the renowned Mr. Joseph Ehrlich?" asks the marshal.

"I'm surprised you remember my real name."

"I make it my business to remember people's names and faces. You never know when it might prove useful. I understand you're going to perform at Ford's again."

"Yes. We open there on Saturday."

"Well, I'm sure the president and Mrs. Lincoln will want to take in the show."

"So will I!" says the boy. "Mother says you were amazing! Are you here to have a séance?"

"No," says Joseph. "Actually I . . ." Joseph hesitates, reluctant to reveal to the president's son his real purpose in coming here. "Actually I was hoping to speak to Mr. Lincoln."

Mr. Lamon puts a hand on the small boy's shoulder. "Tad, why don't you go and keep your father company?"

Tad screws up his face in an expression of displeasure. "Must I? I wanted Yosef to read my mind."

"Your father needs someone to cheer him up. Go on, now."

Tad snatches his autograph book and with a quick "thank you" dashes off again.

"Is this a social call?" asks Mr. Lamon. "If so, I'm afraid you'll have to make it another time. The president has had a long day, and a sleepless night before that."

"No," says Joseph. "It's a . . . it's a matter of some importance. In fact, it may be rather urgent."

The marshal conducts Joseph to a pair of upholstered chairs in one corner of the hall and motions for him to be seated, then eases into a chair himself, taking care not to bump the banjo on the wooden arms. "I don't really want to give the president anything more to worry about just now. I assure you that whatever you have to say to him can be entrusted to me."

Joseph shifts uncomfortably in his chair. "I believe that . . . I believe that Mr. Lincoln's life may be in danger."

Mr. Lamon lets go a sharp, humorless laugh. "His life is always in danger. Are you aware of some specific threat?"

"Not exactly. I mean, I don't have any names or anything, just a . . . just a feeling."

"A *feeling*?"

Joseph wishes that he had brought Cassandra along and let

her explain it. It seemed to make sense, coming from her. He hasn't the vaguest idea what she actually experienced, what having second sight is like. "Well, it's more than a feeling. It's more like a . . . like a vision."

"A vision."

"Yes." Joseph pulls Cassandra's crumpled note from his vest pocket and consults it. He tries to put into his voice the same confident tone he uses when he's in front of an audience describing in detail, despite his blindfold, the object his father is holding. "I saw someone pointing a gun at the president, but I don't think they meant to shoot him. I think he was being tied up, and possibly gagged. They seemed to be inside some conveyance—a carriage, or a train car. I kept seeing the word *soldier,* and some other words, too, something like 'the water is deep,' or 'the water is still.' "

Mr. Lamon doesn't seem so skeptical now. He is leaning forward in his chair, listening intently. When Joseph is finished, the marshal strokes his barbarian's mustache thoughtfully. "Could it have been *Still Waters Run Deep?*"

"Maybe. Does that mean anything to you?"

"It's the title of a play. It's being performed tomorrow at the Soldiers' Home. The president was planning to attend, but I doubt that he'll be up to it."

"The Soldiers' Home? That might explain why she—why I kept seeing the word *soldier.*"

"*She?*" says Mr. Lamon.

"I beg your pardon?"

"You said *she.*"

"Did I?" For a moment, Joseph considers telling him the truth—that the vision was someone else's. But it would be a severe blow to his ego to have to admit that the only visions he's ever had came while he was asleep. Besides, if he were to bring Cassandra into this, the marshal might decide to question her, and perhaps the others at Mrs. Surratt's, and she would no longer be able to pass herself off as a normal, ordinary girl, the way she wants. "It must have been a slip of the tongue."

Mr. Lamon nods, looking skeptical again. "Go on."

"That's all there is." Joseph is about to tuck the paper back in his pocket, but Mr. Lamon reaches for it.

"May I have that?"

Joseph hands it over reluctantly, even though he knows there's no way anyone could deduce that the words on it were not printed by him.

The marshal stares at the paper. "You couldn't tell who was holding the gun?"

"No."

"You're sure the man being tied up and gagged was the president."

"Yes," replies Joseph, though of course he's not sure at all. He knows only what Cassandra has told him, and at the moment it sounds very flimsy. "You believe me, don't you?"

"Is there some reason why I shouldn't? After all, you are a clairvoyant. Aren't you?"

"Well, I— I'm a mentalist, of course. But I've never gotten a message quite like this."

Mr. Lamon nods again, then gazes evenly at Joseph for a time—so long that Joseph begins to feel distinctly ill at ease. Finally the marshal says, "I'll be frank with you, Mr. Ehrlich. Unlike Mrs. Lincoln, I am not a great believer in mesmerism and animal magnetism and spiritualism, and all those other *isms* that are in vogue at the moment. Any other day, I would probably have listened politely to you for perhaps one minute, then thanked you for coming and sent you on your way, and that would have been the end of it.

"But this morning Mr. Lincoln told me something that gave me pause. He said that, last night, he had an unusually vivid dream—he called it a vision, actually—in which he heard crying coming from the East Room." Mr. Lamon gestures toward the double doors. "He went to investigate and found a crowd of people gathered around a corpse, which was laid out for a funeral. When he asked one of the guards who the dead man was, the guard replied, 'It's the president. He was shot by an assassin.' Now, Mr. Lincoln has been the target of at least half a dozen assassination attempts, but in no case did he dream about it in advance. And now you turn up and tell me that you've had a similar vision."

"Not very similar. I don't think he was being assassinated, only abducted."

"But you're not sure. They could have been spiriting him away to some secluded spot in order to shoot him, couldn't they?"

"I suppose so. But it—it didn't feel like that."

"There you go again with the feelings, sir," says Mr.

Lamon. Though he is, as I've said, ordinarily quite good-natured, when he feels that someone is withholding something from him, he quickly loses patience. "I can't act on feelings, only on facts. Do you have any *facts*? Anything at all?"

"Well, it sounds as if he'll be ambushed on his way to the Soldiers' Home—"

"That is a conjecture, not a fact." Mr. Lamon sighs, shoves the paper in his own vest pocket, and gets to his feet. "If you have any more feelings or visions—preferably something more substantial—I trust you'll let me know. I won't tell Mr. Lincoln about this. As I said, he doesn't need something more to worry about." Joseph starts to protest, but the marshal interrupts. "However, I *will* try to discourage him from going to the Soldiers' Home tomorrow. If there really is some plan to kidnap him en route, perhaps we'll foil it."

"So you do think it's possible?"

"Of course it's possible. He'd make a good hostage, after all, for some wild-eyed Southern sympathizer who wants the Rebel prisoners released." The marshal accompanies Joseph out the door and onto the portico. "I'd strongly advise you not to mention all this to anyone else. People who go around talking about assassinations and abductions tend to attract the attention of the police. You're liable to find yourself accused of conspiracy and thrown in jail." As Joseph starts down the steps, the marshal calls after him, "Please thank her for the information."

Joseph throws him a puzzled look. "Thank who?"

Mr. Lamon smiles slightly, slyly. "You would know that better than I."

Willard's Hotel is only a block from the White House. Joseph lingers a few minutes in front of the National Theatre and gazes across Fourteenth Street at the women in bright spring dresses being helped from carriages and escorted into the hotel lobby by dapper, important-looking men and wishes for the hundredth time that he and his family were living there, or someplace like it.

If their return engagement at Ford's is successful, maybe they'll be asked to extend their run, and then his father will at last concede that they can afford lodgings more suited to their status than Mrs. McKenna's boardinghouse. Of course, it won't be easy talking Carolina Ehrlich into it; now that Cassandra is gone, she's lost what little interest she had in moving. Joseph wonders whether hypnosis would help. He has been reading about the exploits of the Swiss stage hypnotist Charles Lafontaine and considering the notion of adding something similar to their act. If he learned how to put people in a trance, he could try the technique on his mother; it might make her more agreeable.

The route Joseph follows to Mrs. McKenna's also takes him within half a block of Ford's Theatre. It occurs to him that he needs to talk with one of the stagehands there, to make sure it will be possible for Professor Godunov and Son to conceal a telegraph key under the carpet and run wires beneath the stage, as they did in Baltimore.

When they played Ford's back in February, the man in charge of such technical matters was Ned Spangler, a paunchy fellow who drank too much and engaged Nicholas Ehrlich in rambling conversations about the evils of war. There's no sign of Ned, either in the auditorium or backstage, so Joseph descends a narrow set of steps and enters the passage that leads below the stage to the prompter's box and the orchestra pit.

He has to duck to avoid bumping his head on the iron pipe that carries gas to the houselights and the footlights. Ahead of him is a burly figure holding a lantern; he appears to be examining the main shutoff valve that controls the flow of gas. "Ned?" calls Joseph.

The man spins around to face him, lifting the lantern so that it sheds light on both their faces. The glow reveals not the pale, puffy face of Ned Spangler, but the scowling visage of a man with a red beard and mustache and a crooked nose.

CHAPTER NINETEEN

Joseph takes an involuntary step backward and stifles a gasp. "Nolan! What are you doing here?"

"I was about to ask you the same thing," the man growls.

"I'm looking for Ned Spangler."

"He's upstairs, fixing a door. What do you want him for?"

"I'll discuss that with him."

"You can discuss it with me," says Nolan, "or you can be on your way."

"With you? Don't tell me you're working here."

"Is there something wrong with that? I can do a job as good as anyone—when it suits me."

"Of course you can." It's making Joseph extremely uneasy, being in such close quarters with the likes of Patrick Nolan. He certainly has no desire to discuss anything at all with the man, let alone one of the techniques that they use in their act. He is sure that Nolan wouldn't hesitate to sell the information to some rival performer. "Actually, I just stopped by to say hello to Ned. I'll come back when he's not so busy." Joseph heads back the way he came, and this time he doesn't manage to avoid the gas pipe. As he scrambles up the steps, holding his aching head, he can hear Nolan chuckling nastily, probably relishing Joseph's misfortune.

As you've no doubt noticed, life is filled with unexpected and unlikely chance encounters. Joseph is about to experience a second one, right on the heels of the first. When he emerges from the auditorium and into the lobby, he spots another familiar figure—a far less menacing one—standing by the door of the ticket office, reading a letter. At least a dozen more letters protrude from the pocket of his coat.

"Mr. Booth?" says Joseph.

The actor glances up from his letter and smiles cordially, revealing beneath his trim, dark mustache a row of white, even teeth—something of a rarity in this age when dental care is still relatively primitive. "Mr. Godunov. It's a pleasure to meet you again so soon." His voice sounds a little less rough now, thanks to the numbing effect of several glasses of brandy. "Getting familiar with the place, are you?"

Joseph is a bit irked by the implication that he's new to Ford's Theatre. "I'm quite familiar with it already," he says. "We've played here before, you know."

"Good, good. I much prefer sharing the stage with a seasoned performer like yourself. Working with novices is too nerve-racking. I'm always waiting for them to freeze up or fall apart."

Joseph's head is still paining him, and he can't help rubbing briskly at the lump that's begun to form.

"Is something wrong?" asks Mr. Booth, with concern in his voice.

"I had a little dispute with the gas pipe, that's all."

Mr. Booth laughs sympathetically. "I can't tell you how many times I've had that same dispute. The pipe always wins." He moves closer and says confidentially, "I was afraid you might have had a run-in with Mr. Nolan, instead."

"I did, but we didn't come to blows."

"He's an unpleasant chap, isn't he? I'm almost ashamed to confess that I was the one who got him hired here."

"If you don't mind my asking, how do you happen to know someone like him?"

"Through a mutual acquaintance. Jack Surratt, in fact— the fellow you saw me talking to earlier, in the parlor."

Mr. Raybold, the box office manager, enters through the street doors. "Ah, Joseph. You're back from Baltimore. I've been holding some mail for you and your father." He steps inside the ticket office and retrieves two letters addressed to

Professor Godunov and Son, in care of Ford's Theatre. Both are from young women—or at least Joseph hopes they're young—expressing a desire to meet him.

"You look pleased," says Mr. Booth. "Are they offers from theatres or from ladies?"

Joseph blushes. "Ladies." He nods at the much larger bundle of letters Mr. Booth has crammed in his pocket. "What about yours?"

"Roughly a third are from theatres; the rest are from ladies."

"Do you reply to them?"

"To the theatres, yes. To the ladies?" He shrugs. "That depends."

"On what?"

Mr. Booth gives Joseph a wink and says, in a conspiratorial tone, "On whether they enclose a photograph, and what it looks like." He folds up the letter he's been reading and pockets it, too. "Well, Mr. Godunov, it's been a pleasure, but I must be going. I have a demanding day ahead of me tomorrow." He clears his throat, which has begun bothering him again.

"Are you performing somewhere?"

"Yes. I'm doing a matinee at the Soldiers' Home." He shakes Joseph's hand firmly and walks off, whistling a refrain that sounds familiar to Joseph. It's not heard very often these days, except in the South, so it takes him a few moments to recall the words: "Oh, I wish I was in the land of cotton/Old times there are not forgotten/Look away, look away, look away/Dixie Land."

Joseph is sure that Cassandra will want to know the results of his visit to the White House, but she will have to wait. He and his father have made plans to take in a show at the Odd Fellows' Hall, where a magician who bills himself as the Fakir of Vishnu is performing. The act also features a mind-reading routine, but the technique used by the Fakir is painfully obvious. He has a member of the audience write a word on a piece of paper, then he communicates it to his attractive female assistant—who does not wear a blindfold (or very much else, for that matter)—by wiggling his right ear.

Despite the crude nature of their act—or perhaps because of it—the audience loves them. Joseph shakes his head in disbelief and whispers to his father, "I hope we're never reduced to playing music halls."

"So do I," Nicholas replies. "But if you had to choose between performing here and starving, I daresay you would perform here."

"I don't know," says Joseph. "I think I'd go back to Foley's China and Lamp Store."

Not caring to incur Miss Fitzpatrick's displeasure again by interrupting her study schedule, Joseph decides to wait until late afternoon of the following day to return to Mrs. Surratt's. He and his father spend the morning rehearsing, preparing to perform again for the demanding audiences at Ford's.

They work for three hours straight before Nicholas will consent to a short break. Joseph goes downstairs for a glass of lemonade and returns to find the distinguished Professor Godunov standing before their bedroom mirror, making a series of grotesque and foolish grimaces, like a man in the grip of palsy. "What on earth are you doing?" asks Joseph.

Nicholas twitches his cheek, arches his eyebrow, twists up his mouth. Then he turns away from the mirror, sighing a disappointed, frustrated sigh. "Trying to wriggle my ears," he says.

After lunch, Joseph takes the lending library's copy of *The Old Curiosity Shop* to the downstairs parlor, which is better lighted than the upstairs one, and settles into what was once Cassandra's favorite spot—the window seat. He had gotten only a few chapters into the book before they left for Baltimore, so he starts over from the beginning.

He has read only as far as the second page when he hears a faint voice say, "Pssst! Joseph!" Startled, he leans out of the window seat to survey the room but sees no one. He scratches his head in bafflement. Perhaps, he thinks, he's begun to hear voices, the way Cassandra does. He turns his attention back to the book but takes in no more than two sentences before he hears the voice again: "Joseph! Over here!"

This time when he looks around he spots the top half of a head, poking from around the back of the sofa. There's more to the head than merely the top half, of course; it's just that the rest is concealed behind the sofa. It's even attached to a body, belonging to our old friend El Niño Eddie.

"What on earth are you doing?" Joseph asks, for the second time that day.

"Spying!" whispers Eddie.

"On me?"

"No! On *him!*" A hand emerges and makes pointing motions in the direction of the front window.

"Who?" Joseph rises from the window seat to take a look, but El Niño Eddie hisses urgently, "Stay down!" Crouching, Joseph scurries across the room and slumps onto the sofa.

"Across the street!" Eddie whispers.

"I don't really think we need to keep our voices down," says Joseph. "If he's across the street, he can't possibly hear us."

"Take a look," Eddie says, in a more normal voice. "The fellow in the wide-awake hat. He's been there for a couple of hours, at least."

Joseph peers through the sheer curtains. Because of the wagons and carriages and pedestrians passing by, he has trouble at first singling out the man Eddie is talking about. H Street is not a particularly busy thoroughfare, but it does boast a few businesses, including a dentist's office, a boot and shoe store, and a rather distasteful enterprise run by a Mr. Seligman, who advertises himself as an Authorized Recruit and Substitute Agent.

His clients are men between the ages of twenty and forty-five who have been selected for military service by the draft, which was instituted two years ago and is so unpopular that it has sparked bloody riots in several cities. Mr. Seligman (an appropriate name, since he is in the business of selling men) maintains a long list of others who are willing, for the modest sum of two hundred dollars or so, to act as substitutes for the reluctant draftees, to fight and perhaps die in their stead.

The man Eddie has been spying on is just inside the open door of Mr. Seligman's office, sitting on a pile of what looks like newspapers or handbills. It's impossible to make out his features, obscured as they are by the newspaper he's reading and by the wide-awake hat. (This style of headwear, which is made of smooth felt and has a low crown and a wide brim, is supposedly called a wide-awake "because it has no nap." And there you have an example of 1860s humor.)

"I don't see anything very suspicious about him," says Joseph. "I imagine he's one of Mr. Seligman's customers, that's all."

"No, he's watching this house, I'm sure he is."

"Why would he do that?"

"I don't know." El Niño Eddie snickers. "Maybe it's Mrs. McKenna's beau, the fish merchant, and he's making sure she's not seeing another man."

Joseph returns to the window seat. "Well, you go ahead and keep an eye on him. I'm going back to my book."

Eddie crawls out from behind the sofa. "What are you reading?"

"*The Old Curiosity Shop.*"

"Are there any spies in it?"

"Not yet," says Joseph, and adds pointedly, "But then I'm only on page *three.*"

Eddie lets him read a sentence or two before he interrupts again. "I'm going to start reading books."

"That's good," murmurs Joseph.

"We got a job performing with the circus, so we're going to stay here a while, and my mother and father are going to let me go to school."

Joseph glances up at him. "It sounds as if you *want* to."

Eddie nods eagerly.

"Why?"

"Well, if I want to be a spy, I've got to be able to read and write really good—especially since I'll be deciphering coded messages and that sort of thing."

Joseph smiles and shakes his head. "By the time you're old enough to be a spy, Eddie, the war will be over."

Eddie shrugs. "Maybe so," he says. "But there'll always be another one."

Business must be slow at the Authorized Recruit and Substitute Agency because, when Joseph sets out for Mrs. Surratt's several hours later, the man in the wide-awake hat is still sitting there in the vestibule—waiting, presumably, for a substitute to turn up, or perhaps waiting to be one.

Joseph doesn't take the shortest route to the Surratt boardinghouse. He swings northward a few blocks instead, to Massachusetts Avenue, where he will pass a bookstore so small as to not even require a name. In its window is a display, which changes weekly, of the latest novels and poetry collections. Today it features, among other things,

Hawthorne's *The Marble Faun*, Tennyson's *Enoch Arden*, and a new translation of Victor Hugo's *Les Misérables*.

Joseph doesn't buy anything; he's too used to thinking of books as an unaffordable luxury. Besides, he enjoys merely looking at them and imagining what sorts of stories they contain. It's probably just as well; books seldom prove to be as exciting or as compelling as we imagine they will be. But of course there are also those rare volumes that affect us far more deeply and permanently than we ever expected. They are the reason we go on reading.

As Joseph leans in to the window, shading his eyes from the sun with one hand, he notices for the first time the image of something—or rather some*one*—familiar, reflected in the glass. He glances over his shoulder. The man retreats quickly into a doorway, but not so quickly that Joseph fails to recognize him. It is the man in the wide-awake hat who sat waiting so long across the street from Mrs. McKenna's. It begins to look as though what he was waiting for was Joseph.

CHAPTER TWENTY

Joseph goes on staring in the window of the bookstore for a long time, but he is no longer speculating about what the books contain. He is speculating about the man in the wide-awake hat, who he could possibly be, and what reason he could possibly have to follow Joseph—for that is clearly what he's doing. If his purpose was to speak with Joseph, or perhaps to rob him, the man could easily have overtaken him.

In the sort of adventure novel Joseph was once so fond of, it is almost a requirement that the hero be shadowed at some point by a mysterious figure, so Joseph is well versed in the methods one uses to throw a pursuer off the trail. Very casually, as though he has every intention of purchasing a volume of Hawthorne or Tennyson, he steps inside the bookstore.

"Good afternoon, sir," says the clerk, a thin, bespectacled young man about Joseph's age. "May I help you?"

"Yes," says Joseph. "You can show me where the back door is."

In adventure novels, this ruse seldom works. More often, just when it appears that the hero is home free, his adversary materializes directly in his path, cutting off all hope of escape. But the mysterious figure in our story is apparently not that resourceful. Though Joseph glances repeatedly over his shoulder, there is no sign of his shadow. Joseph congratulates himself on his cleverness, but it's somewhat premature, for he hasn't seen the last of the man in the wide-awake hat.

At the boardinghouse, Mrs. Surratt herself answers the door. She is a rather small woman with a rather large chin, but otherwise as unremarkable in her appearance as Honora Fitzpatrick. Like Miss Fitzpatrick, she is an admirer of Wilkes Booth—though, being a respectable widow in her forties, she does not let herself appear quite so flustered and tongue-tied in the presence of the dashing actor.

Curiously enough, Mr. Booth and his two companions,

Davy Herold and Jack Surratt, are here again, just as they were when Joseph last visited. They're not gathered in the parlor this time, though, but in the back bedroom on the third floor, which Joseph must pass on his way up to the attic.

The door is hanging open a few inches, and through the gap Joseph catches a glimpse of Mr. Booth striding back and forth, obviously distraught. The actor's voice is raised in anger or frustration, so that some of what he is saying reaches Joseph's ears: ". . . even more of a fool than I imagined! He can't even show up when and where he's supposed to!"

Joseph gathers that the matinee of *Still Waters Run Deep*, in which Mr. Booth was appearing, did not go well. Presumably the fool he is ranting about is one of the other actors, who perhaps failed to make his entrance on time. Curious, Joseph is about to descend a step or two in order to hear better, when the door to the bedroom slams shut. He can hear nothing now but an occasional muffled curse or exclamation.

I know what you're thinking: just because Joseph is prevented from seeing or hearing anything further, it doesn't mean that we are. We could easily insinuate ourselves into the room, and none of the men inside would be the wiser. We've done it before.

But I'm not sure we really need to. If you've studied much American history, you undoubtedly have a pretty good grasp of what Mr. Booth and his companions are up to. If so, I don't mind. Sometimes it actually helps for you to know something the main character doesn't know. You're aware, then, of just what he's up against and can anticipate the moment when it all becomes clear to him.

That moment—as you can tell by the number of pages remaining in the book—is likely to be a long way off. We'll have to be patient with Joseph. He's no detective, after all, nor is he actually a mind reader. He is merely, as I have said, a boy of ordinary intelligence. He'll require a few more pieces of the puzzle before he begins to see the picture.

Miss Fitzpatrick has gone out, so Joseph doesn't have to worry about anyone overhearing as he recounts for Cassandra the conversation he had with Marshal Ward Hill Lamon. "From what he said, it sounded as if the kidnapping was going to happen today, on the road to the Soldiers' Home. But if Mr. Lincoln didn't *go* to the Soldiers' Home, then he couldn't possibly be kidnapped on the way."

"And obviously he wasn't," says Cassandra, "or the news would be all over the city."

"But how can that be? You *foresaw* it. If you foresee something, doesn't that necessarily mean it's going to happen?"

Cassandra considers this for a moment. "I don't think so," she says. "I think maybe the things I see are what's going to take place *if* something else doesn't happen to change it." It's obvious that Joseph is having a little trouble with this concept, so she attempts to explain. "Remember when you saw my uncle and me at the racecourse?" Joseph nods. "Well, he asked me to tell him which horse was going to win. I couldn't see anything very clearly with all those people around. Imagine if a whole lot of people were talking to you all at the same time; you wouldn't be able to understand what any of them were saying. That's what it was like for me. But I did get this sort of quick glimpse of a horse winning, and the name Adios, and I told him that, and she did win, so he asked me to do it again, and I saw the same thing again. What I didn't see was how upset Adios was going to get when that other horse came up beside her. If she hadn't done that, she would have won."

"In other words, you're not actually seeing what's going to happen, you're seeing what's *probably* going to happen."

"I guess so."

"So maybe the fact that I told Mr. Lamon about the abduction is what kept it from happening?"

"I guess so." Plaintively she adds, "I really don't know exactly how this works, Joseph. All I know is that I see things and that sometimes they come true."

Joseph lightly pats one of her thin shoulders. "I know. I'm sorry."

From below them comes the sound of the front door opening and closing, and a moment later there are footsteps on the stairs. Cassandra peers over the railing. "It's Miss Fitzpatrick." Unexpectedly, a giggle escapes her. She turns to Joseph and says softly, "Mr. Herold has ambushed her."

Davy Herold's nasal voice drifts up from the third-floor landing. "You should've told me you was going out, Miss Fitzpatrick. I would've been glad to've escorted you."

"Thank you, David," replies Miss Fitzpatrick, in her schoolteacher's tone, "but I don't require an escort."

"Oh. Well, if you ever do, you just let me know—like if you would want to take in a show or something of that sort." Miss Fitzpatrick has circled around him and is heading up the stairs to the attic, but that doesn't deter Davy. "Can I carry them books for you?"

"Thank you, David, but I can manage."

"You know," he calls after her, sounding slightly desperate, "Mr. Booth is acting in a play at Ford's next week. Maybe you'd like to go."

"Yes, perhaps I shall," replies Miss Fitzpatrick over her shoulder.

"Really?" Davy says hopefully. "You'd go with me?"

"With you?" Miss Fitzpatrick looks rather ashamed of herself. She turns and says in a tone that is uncharacteristically subdued, "I'm sorry, David, I didn't realize . . . I only meant that *I* might go."

"Oh. I see. Well, maybe some other time, then." As Davy reluctantly reenters the bedroom, a few more angry words escape through the open door—"I've had enough, that's all! I want out!"—and are cut off again when the door closes.

Miss Fitzpatrick appears at the head of the stairs, lugging half a dozen substantial books. She dumps them unceremoniously on the small table next to Joseph; it threatens to collapse under the shock. "I wish the lending library were a little closer," she says, clearly out of breath but trying to conceal the fact.

"Maybe you should have taken Davy along," says Joseph. He offers her his chair, but she ignores him.

"Somehow I don't think he's much of a reader."

"To carry the books, I mean." Joseph tilts his head and reads the titles on the spines: *The Antiquity of Man*; Emerson's *Essays*; *On Heroes, Hero-Worship, and the Heroic in History*; *Lays of Ancient Rome*; *Life of Washington*; *Vanity Fair*. "I guess you're not very fond of novels."

"I enjoy a good novel," she says. "When I can find one. In fact, *Vanity Fair* is fiction. But I also enjoy history and philosophy and biography and science . . ." She waves one hand as though to indicate that she could go on indefinitely if she chose. "I don't suppose you're a reader," she says. "Aside from minds, that is."

"Oh, I've been known to pick up a book. Right now I'm reading *The Old Curiosity Shop*."

She is impressed enough to grudgingly raise one eyebrow. "Oh? Not the most profound thing Dickens has ever done, but even the worst of Dickens is preferable to the best efforts of most other writers."

"We're reading *Hard Times* aloud," puts in Cassandra.

"I thought that was a Stephen Foster song."

"Is it? Will you teach me to play it on the recorder, Miss Fitzpatrick?"

Miss Fitzpatrick does not appear very receptive to this idea. "We'll see. I hardly consider Mr. Foster one of the great composers."

"He's certainly popular, though," says Joseph. "There's a singer on the bill with us at Ford's who'll be performing all Stephen Foster songs."

"You're playing at Ford's again?" says Cassandra. "May we go watch their act, Miss Fitzpatrick?"

"We'll see," she replies, in the same dubious, slightly distasteful tone she used when speaking of Mr. Foster.

Joseph is surprised and flattered that Cassandra would be so willing, even eager, to subject herself to the strain of being surrounded by six or eight hundred other people. He wishes that his mother were that daring. So far he hasn't managed to talk her into attending a single one of their performances.

Carolina Ehrlich's reluctance, however, can be attributed to something more than just an aversion to crowded, noisy places. Though such places do grate on her fragile nerves, on a good day she can sometimes be persuaded to take a stroll or do a bit of shopping or attend a concert or lecture. Curiously enough, she seems to be put off by the mind-reading act itself. She has never even watched Nicholas and Joseph rehearse.

Joseph knows that there are people who object in principle to clairvoyants or séances or anything that smacks of the occult. But Professor Godunov and Son aren't exactly summoning up demons or consorting with the spirits of the dead; their act is all just illusion. Besides, Carolina Ehrlich has been known to dabble in the occult herself. Joseph can clearly recall her reading her friends' fortunes (yes, there was a time, before Margaretta's death, when she actually had a social life) using a deck of tarot cards.

Of course, she hasn't done that sort of thing in years. Perhaps she has come to regard it the same way she regards their act—as "a lot of foolishness."

By the time Joseph gets back to Mrs. McKenna's, everyone is sitting down to supper, including his mother. Now that Cassandra is gone, Carolina Ehrlich ventures out of her little room more often and even takes her meals—at least on those days when her nervous stomach can tolerate food—with the other boarders.

Now that Joseph is a full-fledged colleague, the other entertainers routinely allow him some time in the conversational limelight. He is tempted to tell them about Cassandra's vision and about his subsequent visit to the White House, but he decides it's best to keep it to himself, as Cassandra has asked him to, and as Marshal Lamon has warned him to.

Nor does he mention the incident with the mysterious man in the wide-awake hat. Now that he's had time to reflect on it, he has begun to suspect that he overreacted and that perhaps the figure he glimpsed so briefly in front of the bookstore was someone else altogether. We, of course, know better.

Instead, he tells them of yesterday's encounters at Ford's Theatre, with Patrick Nolan, with Mr. Booth, and with the gas pipe. "My head's still sore," he complains, rubbing at the spot. He makes no mention of the letters from female admirers; that would be too embarrassing.

"I can't believe they'd be so foolish as to hire that good-for-nothing Irishman," says Mrs. McKenna. "I know I wouldn't trust him as far as I could throw him. They'll be lucky if he don't blow up the theatre. Did he say what he's done with his niece, the poor thing?"

"I've just come from seeing her, actually. She's staying at Mrs. Surratt's, over on H Street. Nolan is paying a young woman to tutor her."

"You don't say?" exclaims Mick O'Boyle. "Could it be you've misjudged the man, Mrs. McKenna?"

The landlady sniffs doubtfully. "It's possible, I suppose. But in my experience, when a rascal like that appears to be turning over a new leaf, that's the time you've got to watch out. It usually means that, underneath it all, he's up to no good."

"What did Wilkes have to say?" asks Nicholas.

"Wilkes? Oh, Mr. Booth, you mean. Well, he said that he'd caught our act in Baltimore. Apparently he enjoyed it."

"Of course he enjoyed it. Did he remember me?"

"Remember you?" says Joseph warily, fearful that his father may be leading up to a story of how he once played Tybalt to Mr. Booth's Romeo, or some such fabrication.

"Yes. As you know, I acted alongside his father, the great Junius Brutus Booth, years ago. Of course, Wilkes was no more than a boy."

"No." Joseph cuts his father off, to save him from looking any more foolish and boastful. "He didn't mention you. He did offer to find us an engagement in Philadelphia, though."

"Not too soon, I hope," says Nicholas.

"Why? We're only doing two weeks here. Aren't we?"

Nicholas smiles broadly. "Mr. Grover informs me that his audiences are clamoring for our return. So when we complete our run at Ford's, two more weeks await us at the National."

After supper, several of the men adjourn to the front parlor to smoke cigars and trade tales of life in "the show business." The Modern Hercules transfers his specially built chair to the parlor; if he were to sit on the ordinary furniture, it might not survive.

It would probably be entertaining to listen in, but it would contribute nothing to our story. We'd do better to stick with Joseph as he climbs the stairs to the small parlor. To his surprise, his mother has not retreated to her inner sanctum, as she usually does after the evening meal. She is, instead, ensconced in one of the armchairs with a book in her hands—something called *Eva, or the Isles of Life and Death*. Joseph fetches Mr. Dickens and settles into the other armchair. If he can lose himself in a book, maybe it will keep his thoughts from dwelling anxiously on tomorrow's matinee at Ford's.

Just as he is about to mentally leave the upstairs parlor and enter the shabby, cluttered curiosity shop, his mother's voice abruptly pulls him back. "Is she still doing readings?"

Joseph blinks at her, baffled. "I beg your pardon?"

"The girl. Nolan's niece. Is she doing clairvoyant readings?"

"Her name is Cassandra. No, she's doing her best to seem

normal and ordinary. She still sees and hears things, though, without trying."

"Has she said anything more about . . . about communicating with Margaretta?"

"No. Do you want me to have her try?"

Carolina Ehrlich doesn't reply right away. At last she says softly, "Do you suppose she really can?"

Joseph scratches his head and winces as he contacts the sore spot. "I'm not exactly sure. I am sure that she has some kind of a . . . well, she calls it a *gift*. I mean, she obviously knows things that, logically, she should have no way of knowing. But I can't tell you where they come from, and I don't think she can, either."

His mother stares at the book lying in her lap, and when she speaks it's as if the words she's saying are printed there, but of course they are not. "My grandmother often saw things, the way Cassandra does. She always called her ability a gift, too, as if it were something someone could give you, something you should be happy to have, and I used to wonder why she didn't pass it on to me. Now I know that, even if she could have, she might not have wanted to."

"What do you mean?"

She glances up at him. "It's not always a gift, Joseph. Sometimes it's a curse."

"So . . . so you found out you did have it, after all?"

Her eyes go back to the book. "No," she says, with a rueful laugh. "I'm afraid I was quite ordinary."

"I know what that's like," says Joseph wryly, but she doesn't appear to hear him.

"How I longed to have some special skill or power, like my grandmother's," Carolina goes on. "I pestered her until finally she agreed to teach me how to read the tarot deck. I was never really very good at it, but good enough to amuse myself and my friends by reading fortunes."

"I remember. Why did you quit?"

"You've heard the saying 'A little knowledge is a dangerous thing'? Well, it's true." Her voice breaks. She pulls a handkerchief from her sleeve and presses it to her eyes.

"I don't understand," says Joseph. "How could reading someone's fortune be dangerous?" Her only reply is a trembling intake of breath. "Mother? Whose fortune did you read?"

She rises suddenly from the chair, sending her book tumbling to the floor, and heads for the safety of her little room.

"Mother, wait," Joseph calls after her. She pauses, gripping the handle of the bedroom door as if to support herself. "Was it Margaretta's?" he asks softly.

She hesitates, then gives a single, almost imperceptible nod.

"You saw in the cards that . . . that she was going to . . . ?" Though his mother doesn't reply, Joseph can tell from the way her body seems to sag that he's hit on it. "But surely it didn't mean anything. You said yourself you didn't have any real skill with the cards. It was a coincidence, that's all."

"Perhaps," says Carolina softly. "Or perhaps it was my punishment, for playing about with powers I was never meant to have."

CHAPTER TWENTY-ONE

The next morning, Joseph and his father, with the help of Ned Spangler, install the telegraph system they will use in the two o'clock matinee. Though they connect all the wires carefully and test the setup to be sure it's working flawlessly, halfway through the performance, as Nicholas is tapping out with his toe the word *muzhik*—there's always one smart aleck in the audience who gives them the most difficult word he can think of —the line goes dead.

Luckily they're prepared for just such an emergency. Joseph scratches his right leg—a signal that something has gone wrong—and Nicholas switches to their verbal code. The audience, who has no idea that anything is amiss, gives them such a prolonged round of applause that they're obliged to take two extra bows.

As Joseph heads beneath the stage to check on their electrical circuit, he nearly collides with Patrick Nolan, who is coming up the narrow flight of stairs. "Were you down there during our act?" Joseph asks irritably.

"I was after running the lights," replies Nolan. "What of it?"

"You didn't happen to bump into any wires, did you?"

"No." Nolan pushes past him, forcing Joseph to flatten against the wall.

Being careful to avoid the gas pipe, Joseph enters the passageway. Taking up the lantern, he inspects the storage battery that powers their telegraph system. As he suspected, one of the wires has been pulled completely free from its terminal.

He finds Nolan outside the theatre's back door, smoking a cigarette. "Mr. Nolan. It looks as if our wiring has been tampered with. You wouldn't happen to know who's responsible, would you?"

Nolan turns and squints at him through a cloud of tobacco smoke. "If I didn't know better, I might think you were accusing me."

"And if I didn't know better," says Joseph, "I might think I had a reason to."

"Why would I want to pull one of your wires loose?"

"I didn't say it was pulled loose."

Nolan flicks the cigarette away and takes a step toward him. "Don't rile me, lad, or I'm liable to pull something loose from you."

Joseph holds his ground. "What grudge do you have against us, sir?" he demands. "We've done nothing to you."

"Oh, no," Nolan said with a sneer. "You never stuck your nose in my business at the racetrack, did you? And when me and my niece were tossed out on the street, I guess you weren't all laughing up your sleeves, were you?" The Irishman clamps one heavy hand onto Joseph's forearm and gives it a painful twist.

"Patrick!" calls a voice from the alley that runs behind the theatre. Joseph turns his head to see Mr. Booth sitting atop a sleek chestnut horse. The actor swings gracefully from the saddle and leads his mount forward. "What's going on, gentlemen?"

"This young pup is accusing me of meddling with their equipment," growls Nolan.

"And of course you did no such thing," says Mr. Booth.

"No."

"I'm glad to hear it. Mr. Godunov is a friend of mine, and I wouldn't like to see him inconvenienced in any way. If there was any damage done, I trust you'll take care of it?"

Nolan sends a venomous glance in Joseph's direction, then nods sullenly.

"Good." Mr. Booth lifts the man's hand and slaps the reins into it. "Would you kindly take care of my horse as well?" The actor accompanies Joseph into the theatre, where the other stagehands are moving flats and furniture into place for *Jane Shore,* the drama that is next on the bill. "If Mr. Nolan gives you any more trouble, let me know, will you?" The rough edge on his voice suggests that he still hasn't quite shaken the bronchitis.

"Thank you," says Joseph. "I'm surprised you're here so early. You're not doing a matinee of *The Apostate,* are you?"

"No, no, I was just feeling a little restless, that's all. The rooms at the hotel are a bit too cramped and drab to suit me."

"I thought you were staying at the National Hotel."

"I am."

Joseph laughs and shakes his head incredulously. "I always imagined that the rooms there would be very grand and tastefully decorated."

"Oh, well, they're not so bad, actually. I'm just playing the temperamental *artiste*. I've stayed in far worse, I assure you. Anyway, it's not really the accommodations I object to so much as the staff. They don't have the vaguest notion of what hospitality means, not compared to the hotels in Richmond and Atlanta." He pauses, and his expression turns sober. "Compared to what they once were, I should say. I understand there's not much left of Atlanta, now that Sherman is through with it."

As they're about to enter the green room, the actors who make up the cast of *Jane Shore* file out to take their places in the wings. Mr. Booth greets them all like old friends. Close behind them comes Nicholas Ehrlich, dressed in his street clothes. "Joseph. I was beginning to wonder what had become of you."

"I was just downstairs, checking on our equipment. Somebody pulled a wire loose."

Nicholas sighs. "If this keeps up, we may have to eliminate that part of the act." He turns to Mr. Booth and extends a hand. "Hello, Wilkes. It's a pleasure to see you again."

Joseph groans inwardly. It was embarrassing enough when his father bragged about his connection to the Booth family in front of the other boarders. This is positively mortifying.

It's obvious that Mr. Booth has no idea who Nicholas is.

"You don't remember me, do you?" his father says, a patient smile on his face.

"Well, I assumed you must be Professor Godunov. I saw you and your son perform in Baltimore, but—"

Nicholas laughs. Like his speech, it sounds hoarse and strained. "That's merely a stage name, my boy. Perhaps you're more familiar with the name Nicholas Ehrlich."

Mr. Booth's perplexed look fades and he shows his perfect teeth in a delighted smile. "Nicholas!" He seizes the other man's hand again and pumps it enthusiastically. "It's no wonder I didn't recognize you! How long has it been? Ten years?"

"Closer to fifteen. My hair wasn't nearly so gray back then, and I still had my voice."

"And what a magnificent instrument it was! My father often said that he'd trade all his fame and all his fortune for a voice like yours."

Joseph is experiencing that dizzy feeling again, as though he's been standing next to a leaking gas pipe. Is it possible that the grandiose stories his father has been telling all these years are not fabrications or exaggerations after all, but the plain truth? He says to Nicholas, "You always told me that Junius Brutus Booth was the one with the magnificent voice, that it fairly made a person's hair stand on end."

Mr. Booth answers him. "Oh, it did, it did. But it was an actor's voice. Now Nicholas, here, could certainly hold his own as an actor, even against my father. But give him a song to sing, and he had no equal."

A look of profound melancholy has come over the Professor's distinguished features. For years he has been careful not to think much about that time, those days when his face and his voice and his name were nearly as well known as Mr. Booth's are today. But the wall he has built to keep out the past has crumbled, and the memories have come flooding over him, and with them the realization of how much he has lost, and how much he misses it all.

He takes a deep breath and straightens his shoulders. "Well, I'll see you this evening, Wilkes. Just now I need to have a good long rest, or I won't make it through a second performance. I'm not as young as I once was. 'Weary with toil, I haste me to my bed/The dear repose for limbs with travel tired.' "

"I know that's Shakespeare," says Mr. Booth, "but I can't for the life of me recall which play."

Nicholas manages a faint smile. "That's because it's not from a play. It's from a sonnet. Shall I wait for you, Joseph?"

"No, go ahead. I have to change." Joseph gazes after his father as Nicholas circles around behind the set, heading for the exit door on the far side of the stage. "I never realized that he used to be such a success."

"Used to be?" says Mr. Booth. "I'd say he still is."

Joseph shrugs. "We do well enough. But I doubt that we'll ever be as famous as you."

"I said nothing about fame. I was talking about success."

"Is there a difference?"

"Oh, yes. You can be quite famous without being successful, and you can be quite successful without being famous."

"I don't understand."

"Then I'll explain it to you." Mr. Booth leads him into the now empty green room, sinks into a chair, and pulls a metal flask of brandy from an inside pocket of his tweed cutaway coat. "I'd offer you a drink, but I don't imagine your father would approve." He laughs. "Although there was a time when he could match my father drink for drink—and that's saying a good deal."

"I never realized that, either," says Joseph.

"Oh? Perhaps I shouldn't have mentioned it, then. If you want to know more, you'll have to ask him." Mr. Booth takes a sip of the brandy. "We were speaking of success. When I was your age, I firmly believed that success was measured in money and the things money could buy, or by the amount of applause and acclaim you received. Correct me if I'm wrong, but I suspect you have that same notion. No need to answer; I can see it in your face."

He upends the flask again. "It's nice to have those things, I'll grant you, and having them may mean that you're famous, but it doesn't mean you're a success." He leans forward in his chair, so that his face is no more than two feet from Joseph's, and says softly, "The only way to really be successful, Joseph, is to learn what your true talent is, and then develop it to the best of your ability."

For a moment, Mr. Booth stares intently at Joseph, as if trying to see whether his words have sunk in. Then, so abruptly that it startles Joseph, he lets out a laugh, slumps back in the chair, and takes another drink. "Will you listen to me," he says. "I almost sound as though I know what I'm talking about, don't I? Well, in a way I do, but not because I'm such a shining example of success."

"Of course you are," says Joseph. "Everyone says you're one of the best actors in the—"

"Yes, yes, spare me," says Mr. Booth impatiently. "I've heard it all so many times that I could almost bring myself to believe it." He pauses for a dose of brandy. "I don't suppose you ever saw my father perform, or my brother Edwin?"

"No."

"My father was both famous *and* successful, and it looks as though Edwin will be, too. Like my father, he doesn't *act* a part. He *lives* it. He believes he *is* the person he's portraying, and he makes you believe it. I used to think that I could follow in their footsteps, but—" Mr. Booth slowly shakes his head. "Well, I give the audience a good show. I rant, I declaim, I brood, I exclaim, I sob, I make my voice tremble. I strut and bellow, as Hamlet says; I tear a passion to tatters, to very rags. I make the audience gasp and laugh and weep and . . . and applaud. But I never make them believe. It's all just an illusion, an actor's bag of tricks."

He heaves a sigh and finishes off the flask of brandy. "But who knows? I may yet manage to make a success of myself— a *true* success. You know, I think I'll give up acting altogether and become a war hero instead, or a celebrated criminal. Or perhaps I'll become president. Maybe I could actually *do* something to deserve all the fame that's been lavished upon me."

Mr. Booth gets to his feet and straightens his coat. Despite all the brandy he's downed, he seems perfectly in control of himself. "But for now, I suppose I should go and study my lines so I have something to exclaim and bellow when the time comes."

In the dressing room, Joseph slips out of his dress coat and trousers and into his everyday clothing, then sits before the mirror to remove the thin layer of makeup he has begun wearing to keep his face from looking so deathly pale in the glare of the limelight. (In a century or so, the term *in the limelight* will mean simply being the center of attention, but to Joseph a limelight is an actual piece of stage equipment that burns lime to produce a bright beam.)

The makeup, it occurs to him, is yet another trick, like the telegraph and the coded alphabet and Mr. Booth's bellowing and exclaiming. What was it the actor said about success? That the only way to achieve it was to find your true talent and develop it to the best of your ability?

Joseph wonders whether being able to fool a lot of people into thinking that he's reading their minds is his true talent. And if it's not, then what is? He's always been so ordinary; maybe he has no talent, true or otherwise. Maybe this is the best he can do. In any case, it's not such a bad fate, is it?— being paid hundreds of dollars a week and receiving flattering letters from young women and signing his name on playbills.

When he leaves the theatre through the stage door, no one is waiting outside for his autograph. There were several admirers here earlier, but Joseph tarried so long that they've given up and gone home. Disappointed, he heads for home as well.

That evening, Joseph arrives at the theatre an hour before he's due, in order to take in a bit of Mr. Booth's portrayal of Pescara in *The Apostate*. Naturally, we've come with him, so we can stand alongside him in the wings and watch.

Whatever anyone—including Mr. Booth himself—may say about his acting, one fact is undeniable: it's impossible to take your eyes off the man. He has an abundance of the quality that Dr. Franz Anton Mesmer called animal magnetism and that Mesmer's disciples believed could be used to induce a hypnotic state. And much of the audience does, indeed, appear to be mesmerized by Mr. Booth's performance.

You can't help feeling a little sorry for the other actors. Mr. Booth seems to eclipse them, somehow, and it's not just because the limelight is always on him (he is the star, after all). Animal magnetism is an appropriate term to use in describing him, because he reminds you very much of a caged animal, the way he paces nervously about the stage as though it can barely contain him, the slightly wild, slightly dangerous look in his eyes, the way he snaps and growls and hisses his lines.

But, though Mr. Booth exudes all sorts of energy, there's something missing. As Mick O'Boyle put it, there's no real *depth* to his performance. Or, to use the words of Mr. Shakespeare again (from that play whose name we dare not mention when we're standing backstage), it is full of sound and fury, signifying nothing.

Joseph, of course, doesn't see this. He thinks that Mr. Booth's acting is spectacular—which it is. I could tactfully point out to him that it's somewhat lacking in real emotion, but it would probably do no good. It's hard to tell anything to a fifteen-year-old. Besides, the audience has let loose a veritable thunderstorm of applause, combined with shouts and whistles, and it's so deafening that he would never hear me.

Compared with the sound and fury of Mr. Booth's ovation, the perfectly respectable amount of applause that Professor Godunov and Son receive seems rather pathetic to Joseph, almost insulting.

Mr. Booth presents only two performances of the play and then is off to New York. But his influence seems to linger. The reactions of the audience still feel rather halfhearted to Joseph. After several nights of this, it occurs to him that perhaps he can increase their enthusiasm by adding a little drama to the act.

In the same way that El Niño Eddie pretends to lose his footing, Joseph lets the theatregoers believe—momentarily—that he can't identify the arcane object his father is holding up, though the clues Nicholas has given him are perfectly clear, even to you (provided you consult the code we discussed in detail back in Chapter Three) and even when spoken in a pseudo-Russian accent: "Here's an interesting item.

Maybe a little difficult. *Very* difficult, perhaps. I will give you plenty of time. Focus your mind. Go ahead."

Joseph shifts about nervously, or rather mock-nervously, in his chair. "Um . . . I'm— I'm not sure . . . Could it be a . . . No, no, that's not it. I see something . . . something rather small and . . . and pointed . . . Is it . . . is it an arrowhead?"

His ploy works. The audience is practically ecstatic. Nicholas is not. When it seems as though Joseph is having problems, it makes his father more than just mock-nervous. He was seriously considering spelling the word out a second time, using the telegraph key, which is working again.

A bit grumpily he says, "And now, ladies and gentlemen, we will present Yosef with another, more arduous challenge. If one of you will please print a word on this slate, any word at all—though for the sake of brevity I would prefer a short one—Yosef will attempt to divine what the word is, and to spell it correctly."

A half-bald fellow with a pockmarked face takes the slate, prints something on it, and returns it to Nicholas. Using the "one Indian, two Indians" technique (which we've also discussed in detail), he conveys the word to Joseph, who spells it back to him: *K-I-D-N-A-P.*

CHAPTER TWENTY-TWO

As Professor Godunov and Son disappear into the wings, after having taken three bows, Joseph snatches his father's sleeve and demands, "Who was it that gave you the word *kidnap?*"

Nicholas gives him a puzzled look. "I don't know. I don't recall ever seeing him before. Why do you ask?"

Joseph hesitates. He's tempted to tell his father about Cassandra's vision and about his conversation with Ward Hill Lamon, but he decides against it. As Marshal Lamon has pointed out, it's probably not a good idea to discuss such topics as presidential abduction or assassination if there's a chance you'll be overheard.

Besides, it's been over a week since Cassandra informed him of her prediction, or precognition, or foreboding, or whatever it can be called, and it hasn't come true. Apparently she hasn't had any more like it, either, or she would surely have told him. So perhaps it was all a mistake, a false alarm.

But if that's so, if there is no conspiracy afoot to kidnap Mr. Lincoln, why would someone choose to confront him with that particular word, of all the possible words in the world? It can hardly be chalked up to sheer coincidence.

"What did he look like?" asks Joseph.

"You haven't told me why you want to know."

"I just do. What did he look like?"

"Let me see. He had a"—Nicholas raises his hands and makes the sort of motion he would make if he were shampooing the sides of his head—"a fringe of brown hair around here." He moves one hand to the top of his head and pantomimes shampooing it. "The whole crown up here was bald. He had a short, skimpy beard, and pockmarks on his cheeks. You think it was someone you know?"

Joseph shakes his head. "I just . . . I thought I recognized his voice, that's all."

"Oh?" says Nicholas. "That's odd. I don't recall him saying a single word."

Life—which is, as I've pointed out, filled with unlikely and unexpected chance encounters—is also filled with coincidences. Joseph just observed that Cassandra had seen nothing more about the kidnapping, or at least had reported nothing to him. But a few days later a message (of the written sort, not the mental sort) arrives, requesting him to kindly call upon her at his earliest convenience. (One of the things she's been learning from Miss Fitzpatrick is how to compose a polite, proper letter.) As Joseph is about to discover, she's had another vision.

The next morning Joseph is on his way out the door when he hears a familiar summons from the parlor: "Psst! Joseph!" He backs up a step and peers into the room. El Niño Eddie's head is again poking out from behind the sofa. "Be careful!" says Eddie in a stage whisper. "He's still out there!"

"Who?"

"You know! The spy!"

Joseph surveys Mr. Seligman's Authorized Recruit and Substitute Agency. "I don't see him."

"Of course not! He's hiding!"

"All right. I'll be careful, I promise." Shaking his head,

Joseph steps out onto the street. He glances around, just in case Eddie might be right, but he doesn't spot anyone wearing a wide-awake hat or in any other way looking suspicious.

Nevertheless, before he's gone very many blocks, he gets the prickly feeling that he's being followed. Maybe he's a little clairvoyant after all, or maybe it's just that El Niño Eddie's warning has spooked him. As Joseph rounds a corner, he sees an enclosed delivery wagon parked across the street. He crosses quickly and crouches down behind it. Through the small windows in the sides of the van, he can observe the far side of the street without being seen himself.

Several people pass by, but they're hardly the sort Joseph would expect to be shadowing him. Two are respectable-looking middle-aged women; one is a boy of eight or nine. Then, just when Joseph is about to dismiss the notion that he's being followed and go on his way, a man in a wide-brimmed felt hat comes around the corner.

He stops and surveys the street ahead of him, clearly searching for someone. It's just as clear that he can't spot the person he seeks, for he scowls and mutters some vile invective under his breath. He takes out a kerchief and, removing the wide-awake hat, wipes the sweat from the bald crown of his head, then pats at his perspiring face, which, even at this distance, Joseph can see is pitted with smallpox scars.

Joseph remains concealed behind the wagon until he's sure his pursuer has given up on him. He knows now that the man in the audience yesterday and the man who's been trailing him are one and the same. Unfortunately, that knowledge sheds no light at all on the more perplexing questions of who he is and what he wants.

This time when Joseph knocks on the front door at Mrs. Surratt's, it's answered by Cassandra herself. "I was just in the parlor, studying," she says, and shows him the book, *History of England in the 16th and 17th Centuries.*

"Ah," says Joseph. "That must make for fascinating reading."

Cassandra seems not to hear the sarcasm in his tone. "It *is* fascinating," she replies earnestly. "Especially the parts about Queen Elizabeth. One of her advisers had second sight, you know—or at least he claimed to."

"Oh? Did he foresee any abductions or assassinations?"

"Not yet." She glances warily in the direction of the stairs, then leads him into the parlor. "We'll have to keep our voices down. Miss Fitzpatrick doesn't like it when my studies are interrupted."

"Maybe I should have waited until this afternoon."

"No, I'm glad you came so soon." She sinks down on the sofa and says softly, "I've seen something more about Mr. Lincoln. Only it's different this time. There's still the gun, and he's still being tied up and gagged, but I don't think they're in a carriage or a train car. It's more like . . . like a parlor, actually. I saw a sofa and a chair. The room was dim, almost dark, but there was a bright light, too, like I was looking through a window at the sun." She turns her gaze, which has been focused on something far away, on Joseph. "Could it be a room in the White House?"

"I don't know," says Joseph. "I never got past the entrance hall. What about the words you mentioned before—*soldier* and *still waters?*"

Cassandra shakes her head. "I didn't see them this time. There was something else, though, something like *our nanny*. But that doesn't make any sense."

"Not a whole lot," Joseph admits. "But neither did *still waters*, until Mr. Lamon mentioned the name of the play." He ponders the matter for a minute. "If the kidnapping didn't go as planned the first time—which it obviously didn't, since Mr. Lincoln is still around—maybe they're going to try it again. Whoever *they* are. I guess you didn't see any faces. Somebody with a bald head and pockmarked cheeks, for example?"

"No," replies Cassandra. "Who looks like that?"

"Some fellow who's been following me. I wish I knew what he's up to. Isn't there some way you can aim your clairvoyance at a particular person—sort of like aiming a gun?"

The image makes Cassandra giggle. "Sometimes. But usually only if I'm holding something that belongs to the person. Why didn't *you* read his mind?"

"Because," says Joseph. "Because, to tell you the truth, I was a little scared. I thought he might be a thief, or a murderer."

To his relief, Cassandra nods understandingly. "I have trouble concentrating, too, if I'm frightened or hungry or something."

Joseph tries to convince Cassandra that, since it's her

vision, she should be the one to tell Mr. Ward Hill Lamon about it, but—like those draftees who don't wish to fight—she begs him to be her substitute. Reluctantly, he agrees. He's not sure how receptive the marshal is likely to be, after the first prediction proved false. But Mr. Lamon did say to let him know if there was anything further to report.

There have been so many rumors of assassination plots lately that Marshal Lamon, in his desire to protect the president and his family, has all but moved in with them. He's even established an office just down the hall from the president's. This is where Joseph finds him.

Joseph doesn't just walk in unannounced, of course. He gives his name to the guard downstairs, waits until Mr. Lamon calls for him, then, with some difficulty, makes his way through the tightly packed and uncooperative crowd of petitioners who are here to see Mr. Lincoln. We're lucky to be able to follow so effortlessly in his wake.

To Joseph's surprise, his report is taken quite seriously. Mr. Lamon believes that the first warning may not have been a false alarm after all. On the day of the *Still Waters Run Deep* matinee, the presidential coach *was* in fact stopped by several suspicious-looking men on the road to the Soldiers' Home. However, the president wasn't in it; he had stayed in the city for a ceremony involving a captured Confederate flag and sent his secretary instead, who wasn't worth the trouble it would have taken to kidnap him.

Mr. Lamon is puzzled by this new information, though. He jots down the details on a piece of paper and studies them. He can't imagine that the room with the chair and the sofa could represent a room of the White House. Surely no one would be so audacious as to attack the president in his own parlor. "And what about this *our nanny* business? What could that possibly mean? Tad has a nanny, of course, but she's fiercely loyal to the family. It's inconceivable that she could be involved in a plot against them."

"Maybe those weren't exactly the right words," says Joseph lamely. "Maybe it only sounded like that."

Mr. Lamon lights up a cigar and, through the cloud of blue smoke it creates, coolly studies Joseph, who is doing his best to appear cool as well. "What am I thinking?" asks the marshal at last.

"I beg your pardon?"

"You're a mind reader. Tell me what I'm thinking."

"I—I can't just turn it on and off at will," protests Joseph.

"I see." The marshal pauses and blows a perfect smoke ring. "You know, Mr. Ehrlich, I may not be a mind reader, but I do have a . . . an instinct, let's call it, that tells me when someone is lying to me. Right now it's telling me that these *visions* you describe are not really yours."

Joseph tries to come up with a sensible reply and fails.

"Now, three possibilities have occurred to me," Mr. Lamon goes on. "One is that you're making all this up, in an attempt to promote your mind-reading act. But I don't think that's the case; the act doesn't really need promoting, does it? The second is that someone else is having these visions, and you're acting as a go-between. But I'm not satisfied with that theory, either. As I told you, I'm not a great believer in fortune-tellers and clairvoyants and that sort of thing. The third possibility is that you're personally acquainted with the conspirators, and you're trying to protect them while at the same time making sure their plot doesn't succeed."

Joseph swallows hard. "I—I don't have any idea who the conspirators are, and that's the truth."

"I hope so, for your sake. Are you trying to boost your reputation as a mind reader by pretending you can see the future?"

"No."

"Then that leaves us with the second possibility, doesn't it?"

Reluctantly, Joseph nods. "But I can't tell you her name. I promised."

"Do you think *she's* involved somehow with the conspirators?"

"No. I'm certain she's not."

The marshal is silent for a time, as though he's listening to what his instincts tell him. "You know, I could have you locked up, Mr. Ehrlich, and I could undoubtedly force you to reveal the name of your source. But I don't know that I could force *her* to foretell the future—if that is what she's doing, and I have my doubts. If she should happen to see anything else, be sure to let me know." He brandishes the notes he's made. "This doesn't give me much to go on," he says drily. "A chair, a sofa, a bright light, and a nanny."

That evening, when Professor Godunov and Son arrive at Ford's, Joseph pauses to look at the playbills that are posted in front of the theatre, announcing upcoming shows. From time to time, when there's something worth seeing, he stays around after he and his father are finished and takes in the play or musical act that follows them on the bill.

This is opera week. A touring company from New York is presenting a different show each night. Tomorrow night's offering will be, according to the playbill:

THE GREAT DRAMATIC OPERA
OF GIUSEPPE VERDI

Ernani

A tragic, romantic tale of frustrated love,
abduction, and suicide, featuring the beloved arias
"Lo vedremo" and *"Ernani, involami"*

Joseph has never seen an opera, and isn't sure he wants to. But—even considering the management's tendency to describe their attractions in overblown terms—it does sound exciting. As they walk down the alley to the stage door, Joseph says casually, "Maybe I'll stay and watch the opera tomorrow."

Nicholas raises his eyebrows. "You really think you'd enjoy it?"

"I don't know. Have you ever seen one?"

"Oh, yes. I've even sung in a few."

"Did you like them?"

"Very much. Of course, it will be in Italian, you realize.

Still, you should be able to follow the plot. As operas go, *Ernani* is fairly straightforward."

Joseph halts and stares at his father. "Say that again."

"As operas go, *Ernani* is—"

"*Ernani*," Joseph repeats, under his breath. "*Ernani*." If he pronounces it just so, it sounds a good deal like *our nanny*.

CHAPTER TWENTY-THREE

Nicholas Ehrlich is no mind reader, but he's no fool, either. He's been aware for some time that something odd is going on. He's a patient man, though, and he has let his son go on evading the issue, trusting that Joseph will open up when he's ready.

Joseph is ready. All that talk about being involved with conspirators and being locked up has made him nervous. So has the fact that he's being followed. There's still plenty of time before Professor Godunov and Son are due onstage, so they sit on the steps that lead to the stage door and Joseph tells his father all the things he's been keeping to himself for the past two weeks or so.

There's no need for us to eavesdrop; we know all about it. We'll catch up with Joseph when he's finished, when his father says, "Have you considered the possibility that Cassandra is only imagining all this . . . or perhaps inventing it?"

"Why would she do that?"

"You say that Mr. Lamon accused you of making it up, as a way of promoting our act. Might that not be what she's doing—trying to enhance her reputation as a clairvoyant? What does she call herself? Mademoiselle Delphine?"

"She's not doing readings anymore. That was her uncle's idea. She doesn't even want anyone to know about her gift. I know it sounds strange, but I think somehow she's seeing things that haven't happened yet."

For most of a minute Nicholas sits silent, with a thoughtful frown on his face. Joseph wishes he actually could read his father's mind. Finally Nicholas gets to his feet. "Well, then," he says. "I'd say that what we need to do first is to find out whether the president will be attending the opera."

According to Mr. Henry Clay Ford, Mr. Lincoln (who is, surprisingly, quite fond of opera) sent word several days ago that he and the first lady would want the presidential box for *Ernani*. But apparently Mrs. Lincoln (who is *not* fond of opera) vetoed the idea, for this afternoon Mr. Ford got a message saying that they're not coming after all.

He is not happy with this news. If Mr. Lincoln won't be in the audience, all those celebrity watchers who were coming to see him rather than the show will want a refund. And if, as Joseph suspects, there is indeed a plan to kidnap the president on his way to the theatre, the conspirators will undoubtedly be even more unhappy than Mr. Ford.

In the morning, Joseph relays his suspicions to Mr. Lamon. But the warning doesn't really mean much, now that the president won't be attending the performance of *Ernani*. Apparently Cassandra was again just seeing what *would* have happened.

That evening, after Joseph has done his turn upon the stage, he takes a seat in one of the cane chairs in the mezzanine to watch the opera. But because it's performed in a foreign language, it's like trying to do the mind-reading act without knowing the secret code. He's pretty sure the story is set in either Spain or France, or maybe Norway, and has something to do with bandits, but aside from that, he's at a loss. He has no idea why the girl, whose name is apparently Donna, is being abducted by the king, whose name is apparently Don, or why the main bandit, whose name also seems to be Don, decides to stab himself to death at the end.

Fortunately, there is one aspect of the opera that requires no knowledge of Italian, or of European history or geography. The music speaks to him in some primal language that he understands intuitively, instinctively. It conjures up vague, fleeting images and stirs up unfamiliar, indefinable feelings. Though Joseph doesn't know it, of course, what he's experiencing is very much like what Cassandra experiences when her second sight is operating at full force.

Though it's quite late when Joseph returns to the boardinghouse, Nicholas Ehrlich is still up, sitting in the small parlor with an open book in his lap. "Did you enjoy the opera?" he asks.

"I enjoyed the music," says Joseph. "I couldn't really

make much sense of the story. I wish I could understand Italian."

"Oh, that's not really necessary," says Nicholas. "It's only necessary to find someone who *does* know what it's all about." He holds up the book he's been reading. It's called *Stories of the Great Operas*. "This should tell you everything you need to know about *Ernani*. I've had it packed away in my old traveling trunk for years. I had a feeling you might want it."

Joseph takes the book and settles into a chair with it. "Why didn't you give me this *before* the performance? I'd have understood things a lot better."

Nicholas shrugs. "I didn't know you were going to watch it. Besides, a man is never truly ready to learn until he can admit how little he knows."

Joseph gives him a peevish glance. "Who is that a quote from?"

"No one," says Nicholas. "I just made it up."

I could easily fill you in on the plot of *Ernani,* too, by letting you read over Joseph's shoulder, but there are too many other things you need to know, things that are essential to the plot of our story.

I hope you're not expecting some new revelation from Cassandra. She's so totally occupied with her lessons now that, to her relief, she is able to block out most of those unwanted visions and messages—all, in fact, except the very strongest ones, the ones that are not just a feeble signal, like those sent by a telegraph, but are more like lightning striking the telegraph wires.

On Monday, the third of April, as Professor Godunov and Son are beginning their two-week engagement at the National Theatre, the telegraph operator at the office of the *Evening Star* receives a message that, though it is nothing more than a series of Morse code dots and dashes, has all the impact of a lightning bolt. The newspaper hurriedly prints up a special edition with a headline in huge, bold letters that exults

GLORY!!! HAIL COLUMBIA!!! HALLELUJAH!!! RICHMOND OURS!!!

The news that the Confederate capital has fallen spreads through the city like some sort of contagion, infecting everyone with a strange delirium that causes them to desert their offices and shops and to dance in the street, where a hastily assembled brass band is belting out "Yankee Doodle," and "Columbia, Gem of the Ocean," and "Blue-Tailed Fly"—a favorite of Mr. Lincoln, who is, unfortunately not here to appreciate it. (No, he hasn't been abducted; he has merely gone to Richmond to watch his army rout the Rebels.)

Every few seconds, the music is punctuated—obliterated, in fact—by the peal of church bells, the crackle of fireworks, the roar of artillery fire from the forts that encircle the city, a blast of steam from one of the horse-drawn fire engines that come careening down the street, sending ordinary citizens scrambling to safety.

For a full week the festivities continue almost unabated. By night, the city seems almost to be on fire from all the lights. Candles burn in the windows of nearly every home. Atop the Capitol building is a fifty-foot fabric banner, illuminated from behind, bearing the message THIS IS THE LORD'S DOING; IT IS MARVELLOUS IN OUR EYES. When Joseph and his father arrive at the National Theatre on Tuesday evening, they are greeted by a display of burning gas jets that spell out the word VICTORY.

With all this hoopla going on in the streets, there's no need to pay for entertainment. The small audiences that the theatres and music halls do manage to attract have trouble hearing the dialogue and the songs over the din from outside.

Just when it seems that things are beginning to return to normal, there comes a new cause for celebration. On the ninth of April, General Robert E. Lee, commander of the Confederate Army, surrenders. After four years, almost to the day, the cruel war is over. The city erupts all over again with cannon fire and pealing bells and fireworks and steam whistles. But unlike the citizens of Washington, we will not delight in the fireworks, and we will not be stirred by the ringing bells or the rolling thunder of artillery, for we know several things that they are not yet aware of.

We know that over half a million lives were wiped out in

those four years, and that millions more were damaged beyond repair. We know that, though the war has supposedly put an end to the institution of slavery, its legacy will continue to haunt us for generations to come. And though the fighting may be over for the moment, we know that, in just thirty-three years, the country will find an excuse to wage another war, and nineteen years after that, another, and then another and yet another, in an endless succession.

But the people of 1865 know nothing of all that, and we will not tell them. Let them enjoy their brief, ignorant bliss. Watching them, though, you can't help but wonder: If the end of a war inspires in people such profound joy and relief, why in the name of God (and it is in God's name that most wars are waged) would they ever allow themselves to be led into another one?

If there actually were people plotting to abduct Mr. Lincoln and use him to negotiate the release of Confederate prisoners, they've lost their motive. All the captured soldiers on both sides—or at least those who managed to survive the inhuman conditions of the prison camps—are already on their way home (though, thanks to the destruction wreaked by guerrilla bands, many of them no longer have a home to go to).

The week leading up to Easter is traditionally a slow one in the show business, even under ordinary circumstances, and the evening performance on Good Friday is invariably the worst of all. In an attempt to lure entire families to the National on Thursday and Friday, Mr. Grover has scheduled a play—or, as he would have it, a Grand Oriental Spectacle—titled *Aladdin, or the Wonderful Lamp,* which will feature Grand Marches, Magical Illusions, Splendid Scenery, Gorgeous Dresses, and Entrancing Music. As if this were not enough to dazzle the audience, there will also be a Pyrotechnics Display, a Living Fountain of Colored Water, a reading of Major French's patriotic poem "The Flag of Sumter"—and, of course, a performance by Professor Godunov and Son.

Mr. Grover has asked them to devise a new mind-reading routine, one that will be in keeping with the Aladdin theme. Since they don't have much time, it will have to be something simple. They hit on the notion of passing Aladdin's lamp around to members of the audience, with instructions to rub the lamp and make a wish—and whisper it to Nicholas, of course, so that he can convey it in the usual fashion to Joseph, who will parrot it back.

Mr. Grover puts the Grand Oriental Spectacle first on the bill so parents may bring their young children to the show and still get them home at a reasonable hour. This means that Professor Godunov and Son won't be performing until at least nine-thirty. They can rehearse all morning and most of the afternoon, and still fit in a long rest and a leisurely supper before leaving for the theatre—theoretically, anyway.

As it turns out, Joseph will be getting very little rest, and no supper at all. That afternoon, while Nicholas is upstairs having a nap and Joseph is in the parlor reading *Stories of the Great Operas*—if he ever gets the chance to see an opera again, he wants to be prepared—there is a knock at the front door. Joseph sighs. He was just getting interested in Verdi's *Il Trovatore*, which is partly about Gypsies. Reluctantly, he rises and answers the door.

"Hello," says Cassandra. She peers past him, into the hallway. "Are you alone?"

"Yes. And so are you, it looks like. Come in." He leads her into the parlor.

"Miss Fitzpatrick is having a *siesta*. That's Spanish for 'a nap.'"

"I know. They were always taking *siestas* in *The Scalp Hunters*."

"Are you busy?"

"Not really. Just reading. I'm sorry I haven't been to see you. I can't come at night, and if I come during the day, it upsets Miss Fitzpatrick."

Cassandra smiles wanly. "It's all right. I just needed to talk to you."

"About what?"

"I—I saw something happening again."

"To Mr. Lincoln?"

She nods. "A lot of it is the same as before—the sofa, the chair, the bright light, the gun being held on him. Only this time . . . only this time the light goes out, and everything is dark, and then—" Her voice breaks.

"What?" says Joseph.

"And then," she continues, her voice a whisper, "they shoot him."

CHAPTER TWENTY-FOUR

Joseph stares at her, speechless, for a moment. Finally he says, "Are you *sure?*" He doesn't mean to question Cassandra's clairvoyant ability; she's been right too many times. But neither of her previous predictions involving Mr. Lincoln came true, and it's hard to imagine that this one will either.

Who in his right mind would pick this, of all times, to assassinate the president? What could it possibly accomplish? The war is over, and Mr. Lincoln has vowed, in a speech he delivered just two days ago, to do everything in his power to reunite the nation and rebuild the South. Is there anyone who doesn't want those things?

"You don't believe me," Cassandra says.

"It's not that. It's just that I don't see why anyone would do such a thing now."

"I can't tell you the reason. All I can tell you is what I saw."

"Is that *everything* you saw? You have no idea who, or where, or when?"

"No."

Joseph sighs. "I can't very well go to Marshal Lamon again, with nothing more than what you've told me, and expect him to believe me, or to do anything about it."

"I suppose not." Cassandra is silent for a moment, her

hands nervously twisting the fabric of her dress. "Would you if . . . if I went with you?"

Joseph stares at her. "You'd be willing to do that?"

"If it's the only way we can convince anyone."

"Well, I can't guarantee you that Mr. Lamon will be convinced, but at least he might listen. I'll go get my coat." (He's not referring to a topcoat—it is the middle of April, after all—but to the light sack coat that respectable men wear when they go out in public.)

Cassandra follows Joseph upstairs to find Carolina Ehrlich seated in the small parlor, with a book in her hands. At the sight of this girl who looks so much like Margaretta, Carolina flinches, almost as though she's been struck, and puts a hand to her throat.

"We'll just be a minute," Joseph assures her. "I'm getting my coat." He slips into the bedroom and retrieves it.

When he emerges, Carolina is saying to Cassandra, "Have you . . . have you seen anything more regarding my daughter?"

Cassandra silently shakes her head.

"Do you think that, if you tried, you could . . . speak with her, or whatever it is you do?"

"Maybe, if I had something that belonged to her, but—"

"What?"

"Well, I'm— I'm not really doing that kind of thing anymore."

"Oh. I see."

The disappointment in Carolina's voice is so obvious that Cassandra feels sorry for her. "Not for money, I mean. If you want, I suppose I could try it just . . . just as a sort of favor, for a friend."

"You consider me a friend?" says Carolina. "When you lived here, I hardly said a word to you. I did my best to avoid you."

"You did?"

"Yes. You . . . you reminded me so much of Margaretta, I couldn't bear it."

"Oh. I thought you just didn't like being around people." There is an awkward pause. "Do you want me to try and contact her, then?"

"I—I'm not sure. I need to think about it. Perhaps another day."

Mr. Ward Hill Lamon undoubtedly would listen to Joseph and Cassandra—if he were in his office. Unfortunately, he's not. In fact, he's not even in Washington. He has gone to Richmond, along with a number of other law officers, to help bring order out of the chaos that now reigns in the former Confederate capital.

Joseph and Cassandra learn all this from the president's daytime bodyguard, a plainclothes policeman named, curiously enough, Mr. Crook. "What did want to see him for?" asks Mr. Crook. "Maybe I can help."

But Mr. Lamon has specifically warned Joseph that, if he mentions abduction or assassination to the police, they're likely to take him for a conspirator. He'll have to think of something else. Luckily, Joseph has learned to think quickly.

"Oh, I . . . ah . . . I brought him some tickets for the show."

"The show?"

"At the National Theatre."

"Aha!" says the policeman. "You're the mind reader, aren't you?" Joseph bows slightly. "I thought I recognized you. I've seen your act." Mr. Crook nudges him with one elbow. "See if you can tell me what I've got in my vest pocket."

"I'm sorry," says Joseph. "I have to save my mental energy for the performance."

"Oh, come on, now. See if you can't guess. Be a sport."

"No," says Joseph, "I'm sorry."

Mr. Crook is clearly put out with him. "You could at least try."

"It's a photograph," says Cassandra quietly. "Of an actress, I think."

The policeman gives her a wide-eyed look. "How did you know that?"

Cassandra shrugs. "I just do."

"Well, you're exactly right. It's a signed picture of Miss Kate Vance. I guess mind reading runs in the family, then, does it?"

"Yes," says Joseph. "Listen, is there any chance that we could talk to Mr. Lincoln?"

The bodyguard shakes his head. "Afraid not. He and Mrs. Lincoln are just about to leave for a party out in the country somewhere. But you can catch him tomorrow evening easy enough."

"What do you mean?"

"At the theatre. He and Mrs. Lincoln are taking Tad to the show."

As they're walking back to Cassandra's boardinghouse, Joseph says, "I wish we had more information. It's hard to warn somebody about something if you don't know when it's going to happen."

"I'm sorry," says Cassandra. "I guess I should try to develop my gift so I see things better. But I don't want to see them at all."

"You said that, in your vision, it got dark. Does that mean it happens at night?"

"I . . . I think so."

"It won't be at the party they're going to, will it?"

"It definitely wasn't at a party. I didn't see a lot of other people around, or anything, and it wasn't in a big room. It was more like a small parlor, like the one upstairs at Mrs. McKenna's."

"Well, I don't think it's likely to happen there. I'll try and speak to Mr. Lincoln tomorrow night at the theatre."

"Maybe it'll help if I'm with you. I'll ask Miss Fitzpatrick to take me. She's already promised that we'd go and see you perform sometime."

Joseph isn't exactly eager for that to happen. If Cassandra has any clairvoyant ability at all—and she clearly does—it'll be obvious to her at once that Professor Godunov and Son are only faking it. Still, she's bound to figure that out sooner or later. Maybe it's best just to get it over with.

"That man thought I was your sister," says Cassandra.

"I know."

"What was she like?"

"Margaretta? Oh, she was smart and lively and funny—when she wasn't being stubborn and grumpy and spiteful."

Cassandra laughs. "She doesn't sound very much like me. Were you friends?"

With a shrug, Joseph says, "As much as any brother and sister, I suppose. Sometimes I . . ." He hesitates, not sure he wants to share this.

"What?" Cassandra prompts him.

"Well, it sounds rather stupid, since she was so much younger than me, but I was a little . . . jealous of her, I guess you'd say. Everybody paid so much attention to her."

"Your mother still seems to think more about Margaretta than she does about you."

Joseph winces, as though she's struck him in a sore spot, and nods.

"I hope I'll hear something from her," says Cassandra. "Margaretta, I mean. Maybe she'll tell your mother not to feel so guilty about her death. I tried to tell her, but she wouldn't listen."

"She seems to think it was her fault, somehow. She says she saw in advance that it was going to happen."

"The way I do, you mean?"

"Sort of, except she was using tarot cards. I guess she feels that, if she knew it was going to happen, she should have been able to prevent it."

"Maybe," says Cassandra. "Or maybe it's like she *made* it happen, like it happened *because* she saw it in the cards."

Joseph glances down at her. "Is that the way you feel?"

"Sometimes." They walk along in silence for a while, and then Cassandra says, very softly, "I wish I was your sister." At least Joseph thinks she said it. But perhaps he only imagined it. Or perhaps she said it only to herself, and the thought passed directly from her mind to his, by mental telegraph.

When they're within a block of Mrs. Surratt's, Joseph notices Cassandra glancing anxiously over her shoulder. "What's wrong?" he says.

"I don't know. I just have this feeling . . . like somebody's watching us."

Joseph turns and scans the street behind them. There are a few ordinary-looking pedestrians and a man sweeping up litter with a large broom, but no one worth worrying about. "Probably just one of my many admirers," says Joseph lightly. "They're always following me, you know."

Cassandra giggles. "Why would they follow *you?*"

"Because I'm famous."

"As famous as Mr. Booth?"

"Well, no. Not yet, anyway."

As they're heading up to the attic, Davy Herold comes thundering down the stairs and nearly bowls them over. "Beg your pardon," he mumbles, his face turned awkwardly away from them. Then he hurries on down the steps and out of the house, banging the door behind him.

"I wonder what's the matter with him," says Joseph.

When they reach the top of the stairs, they find Miss Fitzpatrick standing there, her normally pale face flushed, her normally tidy hair disheveled, her normally composed manner distinctly uncomposed. "What happened?" asks Cassandra.

"Mr. Herold attempted to kiss me," says Miss Fitzpatrick, in a tone that is less indignant than it is puzzled, as though she can't imagine what would cause Mr. Herold to do such a thing.

"What did you do?"

"I slapped his face. Perhaps I shouldn't have done that. But it's what the women in books always do in such cases."

"Not always," says Joseph, thinking of a particular scene in *The Scalp Hunters*. "Sometimes they let the men kiss them."

"Evidently you don't read the same books that I do," says Miss Fitzpatrick.

"Neither does Davy, apparently. He looked upset."

"I don't know why he should be. I've never encouraged him in any way." She turns to Cassandra. "Mr. Herold is not the only one who's upset. Why did you go out alone, without even letting me know?"

"You were asleep," replies Cassandra meekly.

"Then you should have waked me. May I ask where you've been?"

"She was with me," says Joseph. "At the ice-cream parlor."

"Mr. Nolan left her in *my* care, Mr. Ehrlich, not yours. I would appreciate it if—"

The front door bangs again, distracting her. She leans over the railing to see if perhaps Davy Herold has returned for another attempt. But Cassandra is aware of who the visitor is, even before he comes into sight on the stairs. Joseph knows, too, just from the look on her face. It's the same strained, almost frightened look she gets when some unpleasant, unwanted message intrudes upon her mind.

"Mr. Nolan," says Miss Fitzpatrick. "I thought you'd forgotten us."

"I told you I'd pay you once a month, didn't I?" He shoves several bills into her hand, then turns to his niece. He does not bother to ask about Cassandra's welfare or about her studies. He does not comment on how well dressed and well groomed she looks. Instead, he says harshly, "There's somebody watching the house."

Cassandra has no idea how to reply to this. He sounds as though he's accusing her of something, but of what?

"What does he look like?" asks Joseph—fearing, of course, that it's the man in the wide-awake hat.

"Like the law," says Nolan. "Why is he out there?"

"I don't know."

Nolan glares accusingly at his niece again. "Have you been talking to somebody you shouldn't have?"

Cassandra finds her voice, but just barely. "A-about what?"

He bends down and growls, almost in her ear, "You know well enough what I mean. The messages. The visions. What is it you've been seeing, and who is it you've been telling it to?"

"Mr. Nolan!" says Miss Fitzpatrick, in the voice she uses on unruly students. "Stop that at once! You're frightening her!"

Nolan is not intimidated by her schoolteacher's tone. "You stay out of this," he tells her. "It ain't your concern." He seizes Cassandra by the arm. "Now, I want to know what you've seen!"

"Nothing," replies Cassandra defiantly. "I've seen nothing."

"You're lying! Tell me, or by the stars of God, I'll knock it out of you!" He thrusts one massive fist in front of her face.

Joseph can stand no more. He strides forward and grabs the Irishman's sleeve. "She said she didn't see anything. Let her alone."

Nolan straightens and yanks his sleeve effortlessly from Joseph's grasp. "Didn't I warn you to stop meddling in my affairs?" So swiftly that Joseph can't even see it coming, let alone block it, he delivers a blow to Joseph's stomach that drives all the breath out of him. Gasping, the boy sinks to his knees, so stunned that he doesn't see Miss Fitzpatrick snatch up a soapstone ashtray from the table and hurl it at Nolan. Though her aim is good, the ashtray bounds more or less harmlessly off the man's broad back.

"Get out of this house, sir!" she commands, and surprisingly, Nolan obeys. Unfortunately for Joseph, his crumpled form is blocking the stairs. With one dusty boot, Nolan kicks him out of the way. As the Irishman clomps down the steps, Miss Fitzpatrick leans over the rail and flings after him the bills he gave her. "And I don't want any more of your money! I'll provide for Cassandra; there's no reason for you ever to come here again!"

She kneels next to Joseph, who has regained enough wind to let out a series of small but very expressive groans. Miss Fitzpatrick asks the same solicitous question that is universally asked in such circumstances, even though the answer is almost always painfully obvious: "Are you all right?"

"Some parts of me are," says Joseph brokenly.

Miss Fitzpatrick and Cassandra lift him into a chair. "Thank you for trying to help me," says Cassandra.

"Well, I wasn't much help, but I did try."

"What did he want from you?" Miss Fitzpatrick asks her student. "What did he think you saw?"

"I don't know," replies Cassandra.

"He said 'the messages, the visions.' What did he mean?"

Cassandra and Joseph exchange glances. "You may as well tell her," says Joseph. "She'll find out sooner or later." If these words sound familiar, it's because Joseph told himself very much the same thing not half an hour ago.

"I don't want to," says Cassandra.

"Whatever it is," says Miss Fitzpatrick (and there's not a trace of the schoolteacher in her voice), "I promise you, it won't make any difference. We'll still be friends."

Cassandra bows her head in resignation. "Let's go in the room, so no one else hears." (Though we've been deliberately avoiding them so as not to weigh the story down with too many characters, there are other boarders in the house, and Mrs. Surratt's daughter, Anna, occupies a room on this very floor.)

Like Joseph's confession to his father, nearly everything Cassandra tells her tutor is something you already know. You also know that Miss Fitzpatrick is an intelligent woman, so it won't surprise you to learn that she has not been completely oblivious to all that was going on. As Nicholas did with Joseph, she's been waiting until Cassandra felt ready to confide in her.

To Cassandra's great relief, her tutor does not scoff at the notion of second sight on the grounds that it is illogical and unscientific. As Miss Fitzpatrick herself has indicated, she is interested in all manner of things. In her wide-ranging reading, she has learned about the theories of Franz Anton Mesmer and the beliefs of the spiritualists and a number of other questionable ideas, and though she may not embrace them, she doesn't dismiss them, either. Her personal motto (or at least one of them) is: You can't be certain what you believe until you know what all the choices are.

Since Joseph is also familiar with everything Cassandra is saying, he doesn't listen very closely. Holding his ribs and clenching his teeth against the pain, he crouches down next to one of the low dormer windows that keep the room from being insufferably stuffy. He surveys the street below, searching for the man who Patrick Nolan thinks is watching the house. It takes him several minutes to spot the spy, half hidden in the shade of a cherry tree so bright with blossoms that it would not look out of place in Mr. Grover's Pyrotechnics Display. Leaning against the trunk of the tree is a large broom. So the man he took for a street sweeper was in fact trailing them.

When Cassandra has recounted the various visions she's had about the president's fate, Miss Fitzpatrick says, "Why didn't you tell your uncle all this?"

"Because," says Cassandra. "Because I'm afraid that, if there is a plan to kidnap Mr. Lincoln, or to kill him, my uncle may be part of it."

CHAPTER TWENTY-FIVE

"What makes you think your uncle might be in on the plot?" asks Joseph.

"I could feel it, just now," says Cassandra, "when he was asking me all those questions."

Though it's an unpleasant notion, Joseph has to admit that it's also a credible one. Nolan has made it clear, after all, that he has no great love for Mr. Lincoln; in fact, he called the president a tyrant. He also expressed a good deal of sympathy with the Confederate cause. According to El Niño Eddie, Nolan is even guilty of smuggling supplies into the South. If he's committed small acts of treason, perhaps he's capable of a larger one.

"If there's even a chance that this is true," says Joseph, "we'll have to tell the president. It's the only solid, specific piece of information we've got."

"I know," Cassandra replies soberly.

"Shouldn't you inform the police?" says Miss Fitzpatrick.

Joseph shakes his head. "Marshal Lamon says that if we do, they're liable to suspect us. Besides, what would we tell them? That she's been having visions? Mr. Lincoln's more likely to listen. According to Mr. Lamon, he's had visions of his own. He'll be at the theatre tomorrow night. It'd be best if Cassandra speaks to him, too."

Miss Fitzpatrick turns to her pupil. "Do you want to?"

"Yes," says Cassandra.

"Very well, then. What time should we be at the theatre?"

"You may as well come at half past seven and take in the Grand Oriental Spectacle. I'll have tickets waiting for you at the box office. Unless, of course, you prefer to pay your own way."

If the supposed street sweeper—who is, in fact, as Joseph suspected, the bald-headed, pockmarked man—wanted to go on following Joseph, he would certainly have no trouble keeping up. Thanks to Nolan's prizefighter's punch, Joseph can barely walk upright. But the spy stays beneath the cherry tree. Either he's enjoying the shade, or he is less interested in Joseph than he is in Mrs. Surratt's boardinghouse.

Joseph considers hiring a cab but decides against it, not because of the money—he has plenty of that these days—but because he would have to go several blocks to Massachusetts Avenue and wait until one comes by. He wants to go home at once and lie down.

By the time he reaches Mrs. McKenna's, the painful effort

of walking has him drenched in sweat. Unable to drag himself up the stairs, he curls up on the sofa in the parlor. After a time, he hears a soft scrabbling sound from behind the sofa. It's either a rat or . . . "Eduardo?"

There is a moment of silence, then El Niño Eddie's voice says, "Joseph?"

"Yes."

"Aw, jiminy. I thought it might be somebody interesting."

"Well, thanks very much."

Eddie crawls out from his hiding place. Ever since it proved so instrumental in getting the goods on Patrick Nolan, he's been spending a good deal of time there. Though he hasn't observed anything else quite as incriminating, he figures it's only a matter of time. "What's wrong with you?" he asks.

"I got hit in the stomach."

"By who?"

"Patrick Nolan."

"Ouch. He used to be a fighter, didn't he?"

"Apparently he still is."

"You want me to get your father?"

"Yes, please." Eddie starts for the stairs, but Joseph raises himself up and calls, "No, wait." The effort makes him groan and sink back on the sofa. "I want to ask you something first."

"What?"

"A couple of weeks ago, before Nolan left, you said you

overheard a man asking him to smuggle something into the South."

"That's right."

"Do you have any idea who the man was?"

Eddie shakes his head. "I didn't actually see him. I only heard his voice. Let me look at my notes."

Joseph laughs and then regrets it, as pain stabs him in the ribs. "You keep *notes*?"

"Of course," says Eddie, a bit haughtily. "Every good spy does." He pulls a small notebook from the pocket of his trousers and flips it open. Since Eddie has never learned to write very well, most of his "notes" are mere scribbles. He is relying mostly on his memory, which is nearly as good as Joseph's. "Let's see," he says. "He mentioned the name Jack, but that wasn't *his* name. He said something like 'Jack told me about you.' And . . . umm . . . what else? Oh, he had kind of a rough sound to his voice, like he had a sore throat or something. I heard some funny noises, too, like somebody screwing the cap off a bottle and having a drink." He glances up at Joseph. "Does that help?"

Joseph is too distracted to answer right away. He knows well enough—and so do we—who fits that description. It's hard to imagine, though, that a gentleman like Mr. Booth would be involved in such nefarious activities. Still, there's no denying that the actor is acquainted with Patrick Nolan. Booth has said himself that he was the one who got Nolan the job as a stagehand at Ford's Theatre. "Did they discuss anything besides blockade running?"

Eddie consults his "notes" again. "Well, after Nolan told him that he couldn't leave Cassandra by herself, the man said something like 'I may have a proposition for you that won't require you to leave Washington.'"

"Did he say what the proposition was?"

"No. He said he couldn't discuss it here, and to come and see him at the hotel."

The proposition Mr. Booth was referring to might have just been the job at Ford's, of course. But if that were the case, why wouldn't he simply say so? Why would he be so secretive about it? "Is that all the notes you have?"

Eddie nods and closes his notebook, then holds out his hand.

"What?" says Joseph.

"Spies always get paid for their information."

Joseph sighs, groans at the pain it causes, and gives Eddie a half-dollar. "If I ask you to go get my father now, are you going to charge me for that, too?"

"Not unless you send him a secret message," says Eddie.

To Joseph's surprise, Nicholas, who is ordinarily quite patient and understanding, doesn't show much sympathy for his son's condition. He's rather businesslike, in fact, prodding the boy's midsection with the tips of his fingers until Joseph cries out. Nicholas nods, as if this proves something, and says, matter-of-factly, "It appears that at least one of your ribs is broken. I'll get some cloth and wrap it tightly. That's about all that can be done. It will heal up in a few weeks. It's fortunate that he didn't hit you a few inches lower; he might have really injured you."

"Oh, well, it's good to know that I'm not really injured," says Joseph. "This must be fake pain I'm feeling."

Nicholas can't help smiling. "I know well enough how much it hurts. I only meant that it's not life-threatening."

"From the way you said that, I assume that you've had a broken rib?"

"Oh, yes. In fact, I'd be surprised if there are any that *haven't* been broken."

"Did you have a prizefighting career you haven't told me about?"

"Well," says Nicholas, looking a bit shamefaced, "I would hardly call it a career, and I certainly never took home any prizes, but I have done more fighting than I care to admit."

"You weren't in a war, were you?"

"No, no. There were no guns involved, only fists and feet, and occasionally teeth—and, of course, a good deal of beer and whiskey. You see, the show business was not as respectable and civilized an occupation twenty years ago as it is now. Most of the actors I worked with back then, including Junius Brutus Booth—*especially* Junius Brutus Booth—were heavy drinkers. I think perhaps it was their way of proving to the world that they were not just a lot of muliebrous milksops who dressed in tights and made pompous speeches."

"What does *muliebrous* mean?"

"Unmanly. And since it was my ambition to become a great actor, naturally I emulated them, both onstage and off. After every performance, in every town we played, we adjourned to the nearest tavern and commenced to prove how manly we were by becoming seriously besotted. As you might expect, the locals regarded us interlopers with a good deal of suspicion—resentment, even. And, as Shakespeare's porter says, 'Drink, sir, is a great provoker.' Insults were invariably exchanged, and that led to blows, and before long we would find ourselves in the middle of a full-fledged *melee*."

"What's a may-lay?"

"In ordinary terms, a brawl." Nicholas's always tenuous voice is growing strained and hoarse from so much sustained speech. "I'd better end my monologue there if I want to have anything left for tonight's performance. Do you think you'll be up to it?"

"I'll manage, as long as I don't have to laugh. Or cough. Or take a deep breath."

"It'll help if I wrap you up. Stay there."

"Believe me, I won't move until I absolutely have to."

Nicholas returns a few minutes later with a long strip of linen cut from an old bedsheet. As Joseph's ribs are bound up, he says, between the gasps and groans, "Is that how your throat got injured? In a fight?"

Nicholas gives him a sharp glance. "How did you know that?"

"It was just a guess. Why didn't you ever tell me?"

"Well, it's a rather ignominious fate, isn't it, having one's career destroyed by a blow from the elbow of a fatuitous farmhand in a drunken quarrel?—before you ask, *fatuitous* means 'stupid.' People are far more sympathetic if they believe that I lost my voice doing Lear, or that I was struck in the throat by a sword." He ties the ends of the linen bandage together so tightly that Joseph has to suppress a yell. "There. Get some rest, now. It's nearly supper time. I'll bring you in a plate of food."

"Don't bother. I wouldn't be able to keep it down. Before you go, I need to ask you something."

"Nothing that requires a long answer, I hope," says Nicholas hoarsely.

"Cassandra thinks her uncle may be in on the plot to kidnap Mr. Lincoln."

"Knowing Patrick Nolan, that wouldn't surprise me."

"Would it surprise you if Mr. Booth was involved?"

"Why? You think he might be?" When Joseph has repeated what El Niño Eddie told him, Nicholas says, "It does sound as though Wilkes has been doing some blockade running, or at least hired others to do it. Frankly, that doesn't surprise me. His sympathies have always been with the South. I've even heard him defend the institution of slavery, on the grounds that Negroes are better off under the white man's protection than they would be on their own. And he can certainly be headstrong and rash at times. But I can't imagine him being so rash as to try to abduct the president."

"Actually, Cassandra thinks it may have turned into an assassination plot."

"That's even harder to believe. Have you told all this to Mr. Lamon?"

"He's out of town. I was planning to speak to the president. He'll be at the theatre tomorrow night."

"If you want him to take you seriously, you may want to leave Booth's name out of it. I understand he's one the president's favorite actors."

You may imagine that we novelists are completely in control of our characters, that we know just what they're going to do next, that, in fact, we *tell* them what they're going to do next. But the truth is, sometimes characters—like people in real life—surprise you.

I've been telling you since the very first chapter what a perfectly ordinary boy Joseph is, but I'm beginning to think I may have overstated the case. I'm not sure that an ordinary person, after being punched in the ribs by a former prizefighter, would drag himself off to the theatre and spend an agonizing hour sitting upright in a hard chair and pretending to read minds, as Joseph now proceeds to do. An ordinary person would be more likely to just stay home.

Of course, an ordinary person probably would not have gotten punched in the ribs by a former prizefighter in the first place, because he would not have had the nerve to step in and protect Cassandra, the way Joseph did. Then again, it may be that people who seem to be quite ordinary are sometimes capable of doing extraordinary things. Let's assume that that's the case with Joseph.

If we misjudged Joseph, how can we be sure that there are

not other characters in the book who will turn out to have resources we didn't suspect them of having? Davy Herold, for instance. Based on what I've told you, you've probably written him off as rather foolish and harmless and not very bright. But perhaps I was wrong about him, too. Or perhaps I've deliberately misled you. Like our characters, we novelists can't always be trusted to do what you expect.

CHAPTER TWENTY-SIX

Though Joseph may be capable of extraordinary things, he is not the sort of hero you sometimes encounter in books, who can suffer the most brutal physical punishment over and over and keep coming back for more. After forcing himself to go onstage that evening, our hero returns to the boarding-house—in a cab, this time—collapses on his bed, and stays there until supper time the following day.

After supper, as Professor Godunov and Son are preparing to depart for the theatre, Mrs. McKenna knocks on the door of their room and announces that Joseph has a visitor. "He wouldn't tell me his name," says the landlady, "and he wouldn't come into the parlor. He insisted on waiting outside."

Joseph goes downstairs, but he doesn't go directly to the front door. With all that's been going on, there's no telling who might turn up, asking for him. He slips into the unlighted parlor and peeks through the curtains.

As far as he can see, there's no one waiting outside. Baffled and a little spooked, Joseph starts up the stairs again and meets his father coming down. "Who was it?" asks Nicholas, handing Joseph his coat.

"I have no idea. Whoever it was, he seems to have left."

But the moment they step out of the door, Joseph hears a voice call softly, "Ehrlich!" It's coming from the shadows next to the house.

"Who's there?"

"It's Davy. Davy Herold. Can I talk to you for just a minute? In private?"

"I suppose so." Joseph turns to his father. "Why don't you go on ahead. I'll catch up."

"Are you sure?" asks Nicholas.

"Yes, it's all right. Davy's harmless." You see, Joseph thinks so, too.

"Well, don't be long. We go on in an hour." His father heads off down F Street, whistling a tune that Joseph recognizes from the opera he saw. Despite the injury to his throat, Nicholas is still quite an accomplished whistler.

"Can we walk while we're talking?" asks Joseph.

"I'd rather not," replies Davy, who is still concealed in the shadows.

"Well, can you at least come out where I can see you?"

"I'd rather you'd come over here."

Hesitantly, Joseph steps into the mouth of the alley. "What's on your mind, Davy?"

"I was just wondering whether you'd give something to Miss Fitzpatrick for me."

"Why can't you give it to her yourself? Oh, I see. You're embarrassed, after what happened."

"Well, that, too. But mainly it's because they told me not to go near Mrs. Surratt's boardinghouse."

"*Who* told you?"

"Never mind that. Will you do it?"

"All right. But I don't see why—"

"I ain't allowed to say nothing more. Here." Davy comes forward, to where the light from a streetlamp barely illuminates his face, and hands Joseph a folded paper. "I hope she can read my writing. I never was much account when it come to writing and figuring." He kicks halfheartedly at a stone. "I guess if you was to ask Miss Fitzpatrick, she'd say I wasn't much account altogether."

"Oh, I don't think that's true. It seems to me she likes you well enough."

"Why would she go and hit me, then?"

"Because that's what women do in the books she reads, when men try to kiss them."

"Oh. I tried to tell her she reads too many books. I guess that proves it." He boots another stone into the street, more forcefully this time. His voice is becoming more forceful, too. "I know I ain't half as smart as she is, but that don't mean I don't have feelings. And it don't mean that I'm a shiftless good-for-nothing, either."

"I'm sure she doesn't think—"

"I know well enough what she thinks. But before I'm

done, she'll think differently, I promise you that." There's something almost menacing in the way he says this.

"What do you mean?" asks Joseph, though he has the uneasy feeling that he may already know the answer. He's begun to suspect that Davy may be caught up in the conspiracy, too. After all, why would he be warned not to go near the boardinghouse? Because it's being watched, obviously. And who is the most likely person to warn him? Patrick Nolan, obviously. "What do you mean?" he asks again.

Davy seems so agitated that, for a moment, Joseph thinks he may blurt out what he's so far only been hinting at. But then he shakes his head. "Never you mind. You'll find out soon enough, the same as she will."

"I don't need find out, Davy. I already know."

"You don't know nothing," says Davy, but there's uncertainty in his voice.

Joseph isn't exactly certain, either, but he puts on the same false air of confidence he displays when he's doing the mind-reading act. "You're wrong. Patrick Nolan told his niece the whole plan, and she told me."

Davy's jaw drops in surprise. "He oughtn't to have done that! Mr. Booth said not to say nothing to nobody!"

Joseph's heart sinks. He has been hoping that he was wrong about Mr. Booth. But clearly the actor is one of the conspirators. In fact, it sounds as though he's in charge. Despite his dismay, Joseph somehow manages to act as though he knew this all along. "You can't trust a man like

Nolan to follow orders. I can understand the likes of him plotting to shoot the president, but I can't believe you'd go along with it."

"*Shoot* the president? He—he didn't say we was going to *kill* Mr. Lincoln, did he? That ain't part of the plan. All we're supposed to do is kidnap him."

"I'm afraid the plan has changed."

"No." Davy shakes his head vehemently. "No. Mr. Booth would have told me. Look." He pulls something from his coat pocket and holds it out. It's a single-shot pistol known as a derringer. This one is larger than most, with a three-inch barrel that takes a .44 caliber ball. It has a carved wooden stock, a brass trigger guard, and a steel plate engraved with the identity of the gun's maker: DERINGER/PHILADELa.

Davy is not threatening Joseph with the pistol, only showing it to him. "Mr. Booth give me this. He's got one just like it. But he didn't put no ball in it, just a percussion cap. You can't kill nobody with a percussion cap."

"Just because he didn't load yours doesn't mean he's not going to load *his*. Besides, maybe Nolan has a gun."

"Even if he does, he ain't going to be nowhere near the president. His job is just to—"

"What?"

A sly look crosses Davy's face. "Oh, no. I ain't stupid. You're trying to get more out of me. You may know what's going to happen, all right, but I'd bet my life you don't know where it'll happen, or when."

"You *are* betting your life, Davy. But you don't have to. You can still stop this."

"No. No, I can't. If I did, then what would I be? I wouldn't be no hero, like Mr. Booth promised. I wouldn't be no brave soldier striking a blow for the Southern cause. I'd be just what Miss Fitzpatrick takes me for— a shiftless good-for-nothing who don't even have the courage to stand by his friends."

"Friends?" cries Joseph. "What sort of friend would ask you to be part of an assassination plot?" When Davy doesn't reply, Joseph tries a different tack. "Do you really think Miss Fitzpatrick will admire you for this? She won't, Davy. She'll *despise* you. Nobody will consider you a hero, or a soldier. You'll just be a traitor."

Davy's soft face hardens. He jams the derringer into his pocket and, turning, disappears in the darkness of the alley.

Joseph calls after him, "Davy, wait! Tell me when it'll be so I can warn Mr. Lincoln! Davy!" All that comes back is the sound of rapid footsteps fading away. "Blast him!" Well, at least he's certain now that there really *is* a conspiracy, and he knows who the conspirators are. He has something concrete to tell the president. Whether or not Mr. Lincoln will believe him is another matter.

Joseph still can't walk very rapidly without hurting his ribs. By the time he reaches the theatre, it's too late to visit the presidential box. It's all he can do to get into his dress clothing and apply his makeup before the orchestra strikes up the Russian music that introduces Professor Godunov and Son.

With the assassination threat uppermost in his mind, Joseph has trouble concentrating on his father's clues. For the first time since they began performing publicly, he fails to identify the object Nicholas is holding—or, rather, he identifies it incorrectly. It is not, in fact, an inkstand. It is a corkscrew.

Oddly enough, the theatregoers don't seem disappointed at all by the mistake. It merely makes them root for him to get the next one right, and when he does, the applause is even more enthusiastic than usual. Joseph makes a mental note of this phenomenon. Perhaps it's actually a good idea to make a mistake now and again, to show the audience that he's not infallible.

When it's time for Joseph to remove the blindfold, he glances up at the presidential box, which is on the second level, overlooking stage left. The interior of it is so dark, he can't make out any faces except for that of Tad, who is leaning forward in his chair, resting his chin on the railing of the box. The boy waves to him, and Joseph raises a hand in return.

As Professor Godunov and Son are taking their bows, the uninhibited son of the president shouts, "Come up and see me, Yosef!" The audience responds with laughter and another round of applause.

During the intermission, Joseph, who has wiped off his face paint but is still wearing his stage clothing, hurries up the aisle, fending off several well-wishers and autograph seekers. At the foot of the stairs that lead to the mezzanine, he finds Cassandra and Honora Fitzpatrick, who are sipping cups of the punch that Mr. Grover has provided as part of the festivities.

"I'm on my way to speak to Mr. Lincoln," he tells Cassandra. "Are you still coming with me?"

Cassandra nods and turns to her teacher. "Do you want to meet the president?"

"Not really," replies Miss Fitzpatrick. "I don't consider him *my* president, since I wasn't permitted to vote." As Joseph starts up the stairs, she calls after him, "Don't you want to know what I thought of your act?"

"Of course," says Joseph. "But I need to—"

"It was very clever," says Miss Fitzpatrick, seemingly with none of her trademark sarcasm. "Even though I knew more or less what the trick was, I couldn't help marveling at how adept your father was at phrasing the clues so they sounded like ordinary conversation. You must have practiced endlessly."

"You think we were using some sort of trick?" says Joseph innocently.

She laughs. "Oh, come, Joseph. You're not onstage now. Of course you did. I'm guessing that it involves a substitute alphabet, like the one Robert-Houdin used in his act. Did your father steal it from him, or did he invent his own code?"

"How do you know about Robert-Houdin?"

"I told you, I'm interested in a very wide range of subjects.

How long did it take the Professor to develop a code that works so flawlessly? Well, almost flawlessly," she adds, this time with just a touch of sarcasm. She's clearly referring to Joseph's blunder.

"I don't know," says Joseph peevishly. "Maybe a year or two." His ego is injured, not only by the fact that Cassandra now knows for certain that he's a fake, but also by the fact that Miss Fitzpatrick hasn't said a single word about his performance—aside from the blunder, of course. All she's done is praise his father. What rankles him even more is the sudden realization that she may be right, that perhaps Nicholas does deserve most of the credit for their success.

After all, he was the one who invented and perfected the code and patiently schooled Joseph in its use. And, though Joseph has never admitted it before, Nicholas does most of the work in the act. It can't be easy, wording the clues so that they convey the information clearly and at the same time sound perfectly natural to the ears of the audience—and doing it on the spur of the moment. All Joseph really has to do is listen carefully.

The gas lamps dim, indicating that the intermission is nearly over. "Excuse me," says Joseph. "I really need to speak to Mr. Lincoln." As he and Cassandra head upstairs, other theatregoers press around them, anxious to find their seats before the next act goes on.

Many of the audience members are anxious about other things as well—the sick child they left at home, the job they will lose now that the soldiers are returning to work, the loved one who has been reported missing in action—and their thoughts, too, press in upon Cassandra. She reaches up and tentatively takes hold of Joseph's hand.

"I liked your act," she says.

"I was afraid you might be disappointed to find out . . . you know . . . that I can't really read minds."

"I figured it out some time ago. And I was disappointed—at first, anyway. But then I started thinking about it, and I think that, in a way, you can."

"I can?"

"Yes. When I tell you things, even if they don't make much sense, you really listen to me, and you try to understand. When you do that, it's almost the same thing as reading someone's mind. I think it must be a gift, too, like second sight, because most people can't do it, or at least they *don't* do it. They pretend to listen, but they're really thinking about what they want to say, not about what you're saying. Do you know what I mean?"

Joseph is so taken aback that he can't manage to reply. He merely squeezes her hand. Though he's not altogether sure what Cassandra is trying to say, or whether it's true, it does improve his mood considerably. He's not feeling nearly so sorry for himself now, or nearly so ordinary.

We briefly met John Parker, the disheveled bodyguard, at Ford's Theatre many chapters ago, when Mr. Lamon took Joseph and his father to meet the president. We now encounter him again, just as briefly, as he nods at Joseph and lets him and Cassandra pass. The presidential box at the

National looks quite similar to the one at Ford's in its layout, and in its furnishings—an upholstered rocker and a sofa.

There is one thing different about it, however: the president is not in it.

CHAPTER TWENTY-SEVEN

The first lady is not in the box, either. Its only occupants are Tad Lincoln and a companion, a burly army major named Thomas Eckert, who has gained a small measure of fame because of an ability to break iron pokers over his knee.

Tad isn't paying much attention to the act onstage. He's been waiting eagerly to talk to Joseph, whom he knows only as Yosef Godunov, and whose mind-reading powers he doesn't doubt in the least. When Joseph and Cassandra enter the box, Tad springs from the rocking chair originally placed there for his father and beckons to them enthusiastically. "I thought you weren't going to come! I wanted to give the Professor an object for you to guess, but he was too far away. Will you guess it now?"

"Tad," says Major Eckert quietly but sternly. "Your father said you were not to badger the performers."

"I'm not badgering. I'm only asking." The boy regards Cassandra with frank curiosity. "Who's this? Is she your sister? Does she read minds, too?"

"Far better than I do," says Joseph. "This is Cassandra Quinn. Cassandra, this is Mr. Lincoln's son Tad."

Cassandra doesn't seem to hear him. Her face, which is turned toward the stage, wears an expression of rapt attention, as though she's transfixed by the Hutchinson Family's rendition of Stephen Foster's "Nelly Was a Lady." But Joseph has observed that same expression enough times to know that it's not the musicians she's so focused on. She's probably not even aware of them. Whatever she's seeing, it's not here in the theatre but in some other place, perhaps in some other time.

"Why doesn't she say anything?" asks Tad. "Can't she speak?"

Joseph bends down and says softly to Cassandra, "What is it? What do you see?"

"The bright light," she whispers. "The one I saw in the vision. It's the stage lights." She looks around the box, blinking as though the lights have blinded her. "And the rocking chair . . . And the sofa . . . It wasn't a parlor, Joseph. It was a theatre box."

"This one?" says Joseph. "Was it this one?"

She frowns in concentration. "I don't think so. It's not quite the same."

Joseph turns to Major Eckert. "Where's the president, sir? They said he was coming here tonight."

The major gives a helpless shrug. "Mrs. Lincoln decided she'd rather see the play they're doing at Ford's."

"Did they have any sort of protection? A bodyguard?"

"Mr. Parker is usually on duty, but they sent him with us. Why—"

Joseph cuts him off. "Can you come with me to Ford's, sir?"

"My orders are to stay with the boy."

"I'll come with you," says Tad staunchly.

"No, you won't," says Eckert. "Take Parker. He should be just outside."

But Mr. Parker is not just outside. He's deserted his post and taken a seat near the front of the dress circle, where he can see the stage better, but where Joseph can't see him. "Listen," Joseph says to Cassandra. "I'm going over to Ford's. You go and sit with Miss Fitzpatrick, all right?"

Cassandra nods. "What are you going to do?"

"Warn Mr. Lincoln."

As Joseph heads east on E Street, he takes out his pocket watch and, in the light of a streetlamp, checks the time. It's nearly ten. If he doesn't hurry, the show at Ford's will have let out, and he'll have missed his chance to catch the president. Holding his aching ribs, he sets a quicker pace for himself.

The play at Ford's, *Our American Cousin*, has attracted a large audience; both sides of Tenth Street are lined with hackneys and private carriages. As Joseph is about to cross the street, he catches sight of a familiar figure in a slouch hat and tweed cutaway coat, leaning against the front of the theatre, smoking a slim cigar.

Joseph halts abruptly, his heart pounding from something more than just the brisk walk. As he watches, another figure he recognizes—that of Jack Surratt—strolls past the theatre, furtively whispers something to Mr. Booth, and then moves on. "Oh, Lord!" Joseph murmurs. There are a dozen possible reasons for Mr. Booth to be at the theatre; there's only one reason why Surratt would be there.

The actor flicks his cigar into the street, then turns and heads for the theatre entrance. "Mr. Booth!" cries Joseph, his voice breaking. He steps into the street, oblivious of the carriage that is bearing down upon him until he hears the driver's shout of alarm. Joseph stumbles backward, collides with the rear wheel of a parked carriage, and doubles over, gasping, from the pain that shoots through his broken ribs.

He forces himself upright and, after a quick glance both ways, sprints across the street, up the wooden ramp, and through the main doors, just in time to get a glimpse of Mr. Booth at the top of the staircase that leads to the dress circle. There is no one to appeal to for help; the ticket office and lobby are empty. Everyone is inside, watching the show.

A burst of laughter issues from the auditorium, and for a moment Joseph feels oddly reassured. Surely he must be wrong about the assassination. Death is something that takes place on the battlefield or on Murder Row, not here, in the city's most elegant theatre, before an audience of people who are laughing, lighthearted in the knowledge that the war is finally over.

But a new jolt of pain in his side reminds him that violence can happen anywhere, that there are people who regard violence not as a last resort, but as the first. Joseph scrambles up the stairs. The white door that leads to the small vestibule outside the president's box is just closing. He staggers around the rear of the dress circle, to where the president's messenger is sitting and asks breathlessly, "Did Mr. Booth just go inside?"

"Yes," says the boy. "He said the president wanted to see him."

Joseph lunges toward the door. It won't open, even when he throws his weight against it.

"Wait a minute!" the messenger protests. "You can't—"

"Do you have a key?" Joseph demands.

"No," replies the boy. "The lock's broken. And anyway, you can't just—"

Joseph raises one foot and kicks the door as hard as he can, but still it doesn't budge. It must be barred from inside somehow. He pounds on it with his fists and shouts, "Mr. Lincoln! Mr. Lincoln!" But his words and his frantic drumming are drowned out by a sudden surge of laughter from the auditorium. Before he can renew his attack, he's seized from behind by the collar of his coat and dragged bodily away from the door.

Joseph thrashes about in an effort to free himself, or at least get a look at his captor. He has no idea whether it's a bodyguard, an irate audience member, or one of the conspirators. Neither do we. All we know is that it's a man with a bald head and a pockmarked face.

The man has hold of his right arm now and is yanking it painfully upward, behind Joseph's back. Joseph feels the man's breath on his neck and hears him say, "Stop struggling, now!" In desperation, Joseph flings his head backward. He feels it connect with his assailant's face.

The man gives an agonized cry and loosens his grip enough so that Joseph can break free. He makes a dash for the stairs and nearly tumbles down them headfirst, but somehow manages to make it to the bottom in one piece.

He bursts through the center door of the auditorium and halts, bewildered. The theatre is in nearly total darkness; both the houselights and the footlights are turned to their lowest setting. It's obvious from the chorus of murmurs that the audience is confused, too, perhaps wondering whether this is part of the show. "Everyone remain calm, please," says a voice from onstage. "We'll have the lights back on momentarily."

Joseph plunges on down the aisle, feeling his way. "Mr. President!" he shouts. "Mr. President, your life is in—" Before the words are out of his mouth, he sees a flash of light from the right-hand side of the auditorium, ten feet or so above the stage—just where the presidential box is located. In the same instant, he hears the report of a small pistol.

Joseph gives a cry of despair, but no one can hear it, for the auditorium is suddenly filled with angry shouts, terrified screams, wails of distress. From memory, Joseph manages to locate the steps at the end of the orchestra pit. He stumbles up them and across the stage, staring up at the president's box, hoping against hope that somehow Mr. Lincoln has escaped the fate that Cassandra predicted.

He can see nothing at all in the dark recesses of the box, but strangely enough there is a shadowy shape *outside* it, dangling from the bunting that is draped across the front of the box. The form drops to the stage with a barely audible thump, not five feet from Joseph. Though he can't see the man's features, Joseph recognizes the voice that rings out over the clamor of the crowd: *"Sic semper tyrannis!"* And, though he knows practically no Latin, he knows this phrase. It is the state motto of Virginia, and it may be translated as "Thus always to tyrants!"

For a moment Joseph stands frozen, uncertain what to do. Some part of him is still insisting that Mr. Booth would never shoot the president. Another part is telling him that, if he gets in the way, Mr. Booth may well shoot *him*. Then Booth turns upstage and heads for the rear door of the theatre, limping a little, and Joseph knows that, however much he once admired the man, and whatever the risk to his own life may be, he can't let the assassin escape.

Joseph catches up with him just as the actor flings open the door that leads to the alley. There's no denying now that it is Booth, for the light from a streetlamp falls on his features. Joseph grabs hold of the man's arm. Booth whirls about, a wild look on his face. His free arm sweeps upward, and the lamplight reveals something Joseph didn't notice before: Booth is clutching a bloodstained dagger in one hand.

CHAPTER TWENTY-EIGHT

Joseph cries out and flings up one arm in a feeble attempt to ward off the blade that's descending on him. But the blow never comes. Joseph's features, too, are illuminated by the streetlamp, and though Booth may be capable of killing someone he perceives as an enemy, he is not so mad as to murder a friend.

He has nothing to fear from Joseph, in any case, for at that moment the boy is again seized from behind. A powerful arm encircles his throat, nearly lifting him off the floor. Booth lowers the knife. "I'm sorry, Joseph," he says. Then he turns and limps out the door and into the alley, where two horses are saddled and waiting. There is a man standing between the horses, holding their reins.

"Davy!" calls Joseph. The arm around his neck tightens, cutting off his breath.

Booth's injured leg makes it awkward for him to mount, but he manages, and Davy follows suit. As they're turning their horses toward the mouth of the alley, another figure comes running across the stage and into Joseph's very limited field of vision. It's the bald, pockmarked man. Joseph is startled to see him; he supposed it was that man's arm that was pressing upon his throat.

The pockmarked man halts in the doorway and raises a Colt's revolver. He takes careful aim at the two fleeing riders and pulls off a shot. Davy Herold tumbles from the saddle. The man fires three more times, but apparently to no effect, for he curses and lowers the pistol. Then he turns toward Joseph and his captor, whose face is concealed in the shadows. The pockmarked man believes that Joseph is one of the conspirators and assumes that the person holding him is someone from the audience. "Don't let him get away," he says, and steps into the alley to check on Davy Herold.

But the person who seized Joseph did so only to let Booth escape, and now it's his turn to flee. "When will you learn not to meddle, boy?" he growls, then drives a heavy fist into the small of Joseph's back, stunning him. Joseph sinks to the floor of the stage, retching. Lights dance before his eyes— and not only imaginary ones, for someone has brought up the gaslights again at last. Painfully, he sits up and looks around. His attacker—who, as you have no doubt deduced, was Patrick Nolan—has disappeared.

To his surprise, so has the audience's fright and dismay. In fact, the theatregoers are beginning to break into cheers and applause, plus a few scattered boos from mavericks who are quickly silenced by their neighbors. Puzzled, Joseph shades his eyes and peers at the presidential box. Mr. Lincoln is leaning over the rail, waving reassuringly, obviously unhurt—or at least undead.

Davy Herold is not so lucky. He is sprawled in the dirt of the alley, his eyes closed, a dark stain spreading across the front of his shirt. The pockmarked man kneels next to him, holding up his head. Joseph emerges unsteadily from the theatre and shuffles over to them. "Is he . . . is he alive?"

"Yes," replies the pockmarked man, in a tone that leaves no doubt he will not be much longer.

Davy's eyes open, and with some difficulty, he focuses them on Joseph. "How's Mr. Lincoln?" he asks.

"He seems to be all right."

"Good. Good. I told you I wasn't stupid, didn't I?"

Joseph crouches beside him. "What did you do?"

Davy smiles a faint, crooked smile. "I switched pistols. Mr. Booth never even noticed. Alls he fired off was a percussion cap." He gives a weak cough; a small spray of blood issues from between his lips. Raising one limp hand, he places it on Joseph's arm. "Do you suppose . . ."

"What?"

"Do you suppose Miss Fitzpatrick will think better of me now?"

Joseph swallows hard. "I know she will."

"You'll tell her, won't you? About how I was a hero and all?"

"I'll tell her, Davy. You rest, now."

"Good idea," murmurs Davy. "I'm feeling real tired." He closes his eyes again, for the last time.

The pockmarked man gently lays Davy's head on the ground and gets to his feet. "Sorry I grabbed you earlier. I thought you were part of the plot." He nods at Davy's body. "He said you were only trying to stop it."

At last Joseph can ask the question that has been plaguing him for weeks. "Who *are* you?"

"James Clarvoe, deputy United States marshal. I've been tailing you for some time, on Marshal Lamon's orders, trying to find out who else was involved in the conspiracy."

"You were wasting your time. I had no idea who the conspirators were. I do now, of course."

"Then you can give me their names and descriptions."

No sooner has Joseph done this than the president's messenger appears in the doorway. "Mr. Lincoln would like to see you."

"He's not hurt, then?"

"Well, he does have a nasty powder burn."

As they head inside, Joseph turns back to Clarvoe. "There's one more thing I wanted to ask. Why did you come to see our act and give me the word *kidnap*?"

The deputy grins. "I thought it might scare you a little, send you running to tell your co-conspirators, and I could follow you."

Half the audience seems to have gathered outside the presidential box, and half of them are attempting to learn the president's condition from the uniformed policemen who are holding them at bay, and who know no more about it than the theatregoers do. Because Joseph is escorted by the messenger, the policemen let him through.

Mr. Lincoln is being tended by a doctor who happened to be sitting in the dress circle. A second playgoer with a medical degree is bandaging up one of the president's guests, Major Henry Rathbone. The major attempted to restrain the would-be assassin and, for his efforts, had his arm sliced to the bone by Mr. Booth's dagger. Rathbone's fiancée, Miss Clara Harris, is gripping his other arm so tightly that the doctor might have done well to employ her as a tourniquet for the injured limb. Mrs. Lincoln is reclining on the sofa with a vial of smelling salts in one hand.

The president spots Joseph at once and beckons to him. "I wanted to thank you, Mr. Ehrlich. I understand it was you who tried to warn me."

"Yes, sir. I only wish I'd succeeded."

"Well, there's no harm done." Mr. Lincoln winces as the doctor sticks carbolic dressing on the powder burn. "Not much, anyway. They tell me you also tried to capture Booth."

"I'm afraid I didn't succeed at that, either."

The president—to the dismay of his attending physician—shakes his head in bewilderment. "I can't understand what he hoped to gain by killing me. With any luck, they'll catch him alive, and he can explain it to me." He raises his sad eyes to Joseph. "I'd like you to explain something to me, too, Mr. Ehrlich. How in the world did you know he was going to do it? Did you read his mind?"

Joseph is sorely tempted to say yes. After all, if the world learns that the young mentalist from Professor Godunov and Son foresaw and helped prevent the president's murder, he and his father will become even more famous than Nicholas has always promised they would—perhaps more famous than Mr. Booth, who, even if he escapes, will never act on a stage again and who will rate only a footnote in history books, as the man who attempted to assassinate Abraham Lincoln.

But Joseph is tired of pretending. The fact is, he's not a mind reader, or a medium, or a prophet; he's merely an illusionist, an entertainer. And it may be that there's nothing wrong with that. People like to be entertained.

Besides, Cassandra has taught him what it's like to actually possess the gift of second sight, and he's just as glad that he hasn't been blessed with it. It seems to him to be more of a burden than a blessing. Perhaps it's better to be content with the more ordinary talents he does possess, and—as Mr. Booth once said—to develop them to the best of his ability.

Mr. Lincoln is still waiting for an answer. Joseph is sure that Cassandra won't want credit for foiling the assassination attempt, either. But he knows someone who will. "Actually," he says, "the person you need to thank is a boy named Eduardo Montoya. He overheard the conspirators making their plans. He wants to be a spy."

CHAPTER TWENTY-NINE

Fortunately for Joseph, the performance he and his father have just completed marks the end of their two-week engagement at the National. He desperately needs some time to relax and recover from the exhausting and sometimes excruciating events of the past few days.

He fashions a sort of bower for himself on the sofa in the

upstairs parlor, piling up pillows into a ramp on which he can recline with a minimum of pain to his bruised and broken ribs. He spends most of his waking hours there, reading and thinking, and some nights he even sleeps there so he won't keep his father awake with his restless and vain attempts to find a comfortable position.

Once he has finished *Stories of the Great Operas,* though, he finds himself severely lacking in suitable reading matter. He can't ask his father to find some for him; Nicholas has gone to Philadelphia to talk with the manager of Wignell's Company, which books acts for theatres in the Middle Atlantic states. Joseph is debating whether to drag himself down to the lending library or face the even more dismal prospect of picking up one of his mother's historical romances, when a savior arrives—two of them, actually.

"We brought you something to read," says Cassandra.

"Bless you," says Joseph. "How did you know?"

She smiles and shrugs. "I just had a feeling."

"She chose all novels," says Miss Fitzpatrick, "but I thought you might be ready for something more informative and enlightening."

Joseph examines the spines—some broad, some narrow—of the volumes she has piled on the marble-topped table: *The Communist Manifesto; History of the Conquest of Mexico; Walden, or Life in the Woods; Idylls of the King; Leaves of Grass.* Though he's a bit dubious about the entertainment value of the books—and no doubt you are, too—he dutifully thanks Miss Fitzpatrick. And so he should. If he gives the nonfiction and poetry books a chance, as I suspect he will (though perhaps only after he's read *Silas Marner* and *The Woman in White,* and the other novels that Cassandra has brought him), he'll find that they transport him, just as novels do, out of the ordinary world and into unfamiliar, unimagined territory.

"Have you heard anything about the conspirators?" he asks.

"I understand that John Surratt has fled to Canada," says Miss Fitzpatrick. With a despondent sigh, she sinks down on one of the armchairs. "Though I'm no great admirer of Mr. Lincoln, I can't imagine why anyone would want to kill him at this point, least of all . . ." She trails off, still unable to connect the dashing Mr. Booth with such a despicable deed. "I can easily imagine poor Davy getting caught up in the plan, however. He would have done nearly anything for . . ." Again she stops short of saying the actor's name.

"Anything but murder," Joseph says. "Oh. That reminds me." He reaches into a trouser pocket and comes up with a folded piece of paper, which he passes to Miss Fitzpatrick. "Davy asked me to give this to you."

Miss Fitzpatrick unfolds the missive and reads the childish block letters, which resemble those in Cassandra's messages to Joseph. She has difficulty making out the words, not because they are illegible, but because of the tears that well up in her eyes and threaten to spill onto the paper, so I will let you read it for yourself. For clarity, I have corrected Davy's unorthodox spelling.

MISS FITZPATRICK,

I KNOW YOU DON'T THINK TOO WELL OF ME AND I
CANT BLAME YOU. I HAVE NOT DONE MUCH OF
ANYTHING UP TO NOW. BY THE TIME YOU READ THIS,
THOUGH, I WILL HAVE. I HOPE YOU WILL SEE THAT
WHAT WE DONE IS NO CRIME, BUT A BRAVE AND
GOOD THING. MISTER BOOTH SAYS THAT MISTER
LINCOLN IS TO BLAME FOR ALL THE MISERY THAT
OUR COUNTRY HAS SUFFERED AND THAT IF HE STAYS
PRESIDENT HE WILL CAUSE EVEN MORE. YOU WILL
LIKELY NEVER SEE ME AGAIN, SO I CAN SAY WHAT I'VE
ALWAYS WANTED TO, THAT I ADMIRE YOU A GREAT
DEAL AND WILL ALWAYS THINK OF YOU FONDLY AND
HOPE THAT NOW AND AGAIN YOU WILL THINK A FEW
KIND THOUGHTS OF ME.

YOURS SINCERELY,

DAVID HEROLD

Miss Fitzpatrick refolds the note and puts it in her reticule. "Please excuse me," she murmurs, and rising, goes downstairs to the main parlor, where she can be alone, for she dislikes public displays of emotion.

"You haven't heard anything from your uncle, I guess?" says Joseph.

Cassandra shakes her head. "I don't expect to, either. If he got away, I don't suppose he'll ever be back."

"What will you do?"

"Miss Fitzpatrick says I can stay with her as long as I like."

"I wish I could offer to let you stay with us, but . . ." Joseph gives a significant glance toward his mother's bedroom. To his surprise, Carolina Ehrlich is standing there in the doorway.

"Joseph tells me," she says, "that you were responsible for saving Mr. Lincoln's life."

Cassandra shrugs. "Not really. I knew it was going to happen, but I didn't know when."

"Nevertheless, you must have a powerful gift."

"That's what my mother always called it. She had it, too."

Carolina comes forward and sits on the sofa next to her son. Joseph notices that she is carrying her reticule by her side, as though—unlikely as it seems—she is planning to go out. "Yes," she says, "I remember my grandmother saying that the Celtic peoples, like the Gypsies, have a long tradition of second sight." She straightens her skirt and clears her throat. "Do you suppose . . . That is, are you still willing to . . . to try to contact my daughter?"

"Of course. Do you have anything that belonged to her?"

Carolina nods, opens the drawstring of her reticule, and takes out Arliss, the stuffed monkey, who was once Margaretta's constant companion and who was rescued by Joseph from the frigid waters of the Delaware River. Clearly embarrassed at having chosen such a childish item, she hands it to Cassandra. "It was her favorite thing," she says apologetically.

"Good," says Cassandra. "Those are best." She clutches the monkey tightly, just the way Margaretta used to do, and closes her eyes. It's fortunate that Cassandra does not mind public displays of emotion as much as Miss Fitzpatrick does, for her face expresses several profound ones in quick succession. It reminds Joseph of the way Margaretta used to shift lightning-quick from one mood to another, sometimes in the middle of a sentence.

"Yes," she says at last, very softly. "I understand." Her eyes open again. Like the eyes of the dying Davy Herold, they seem unable to focus at first on her surroundings. "I got a message," she says. "I think it's from Margaretta."

Carolina raises one hand to her throat in that familiar nervous gesture. "What did she say?"

"I think that she misses you very much, and she knows how much you miss her, but I feel that she would like you to . . . to let her go, to let her move on to . . . whatever is next, and I think . . . I think that she would like you to move on, too."

Joseph had always imagined that Margaretta's stubborn spirit was clinging to them, haunting them. But he realizes now that it was his mother who was the stubborn one, holding on to her memory of Margaretta, seeing her face in the faces of a dozen other girls, refusing to admit that she is gone, refusing to give her up.

For a minute or more, Carolina Ehrlich makes no reply. Her dark face seems to have grown even darker somehow. Joseph is sure that, like the woman who learned that her fiancé was only after her money, his mother is angry with Cassandra for telling her something she didn't wish to hear.

But then she takes a long, wavering breath and says quietly, "Thank you. Would you please tell her for me that I'll try?"

"I don't think I need to. I think she hears you." Cassandra hands the stuffed monkey back to Carolina, who presses it momentarily to her face, in what might be a sort of farewell embrace. Then she holds it out to Cassandra.

"Would you like to keep this? I know you're far too old for it, of course, but I thought . . ."

"Yes," says Cassandra. "I'd like very much to have it."

Miss Fitzpatrick appears at the top of the stairs. "Hello," she says to Carolina. "I don't believe we've met. You must be Joseph's mother."

"Yes."

"I'm Honora Fitzpatrick, Cassandra's tutor." She glances at the earless monkey in Cassandra's hands. "That's interesting," she says, with her trademark touch of sarcasm.

"It belonged to Mrs. Ehrlich's daughter," says Cassandra. "She's given it to me."

"Oh. I don't have to tutor it as well, do I?"

"You can't," says Joseph. "Unless you know sign language."

"As it so happens, I do."

"I might have guessed." Joseph frowns thoughtfully. "You know, I wonder if we could use it in the act. Sign language, I mean, not the monkey."

"You wear a blindfold," Miss Fitzpatrick reminds him. She turns to Carolina Ehrlich. "What do you think of your son's mind-reading abilities?"

"Well . . . to tell you the truth . . ."

"She's never seen us perform," says Joseph.

"Oh, but you must! They're quite amazing, really."

Carolina gives a faint, rare smile. "Well, then, perhaps I shall."

"Are you ready, Cassandra?" asks Miss Fitzpatrick. "We thought that, as we're already out and about, we might as well stop by the ice-cream parlor. Cassandra has become something of an ice-cream fanatic. I don't suppose you'd like to come along?"

Joseph swings his legs gingerly off the sofa. "I think I might manage to walk that far. Mother?"

To his surprise, she gets to her feet and says, a bit dubiously, "Well . . . all right."

Before they've gone three blocks, Carolina Ehrlich has begun to regret her decision. It seems as though the entire population of the city has taken to the streets, enticed by the warm weather and by the festive air that still lingers, more than a week after the war's end.

That's an exaggeration, of course. There are plenty of clerks stuck indoors behind desks and sales counters, and plenty of laborers who can't leave their labors. And then there are all those wounded and dying men who fill the halls of the makeshift hospitals. They won't be strolling through the streets anytime soon.

Perhaps some of them will, eventually. But thousands more, even if they live, will never walk anywhere again, for they have no legs. Some will never again read a book or see a show at the theatre, for they have no eyes. Others will never have a conversation with friends, or eat an ice cream, for they have no mouth.

It would make a pleasant ending to our story, wouldn't it, if Carolina Ehrlich were to suddenly realize how fortunate she is to be able to do all those things? Perhaps she would make up her mind to embrace life, then, to be more outgoing and adventurous. But, for all our tricks and devices, that's one thing we novelists can't do—transform our characters at the drop of a hat. No, Carolina remains just as nervous and withdrawn as ever, just as dismayed by the alarming speed at which the world is moving and changing.

As the four of them turn the corner onto Massachusetts Avenue, a huge horsecar rumbles past them, throwing up dust and making the ground shudder beneath their feet. Though it misses them by a wide margin, the way Carolina Ehrlich reacts, anyone would think it had nearly run her down. She shrinks back against the wall of the building next to her, her heart racing and her hands trembling as she presses a handkerchief to her mouth.

Joseph, who is discussing mesmerism with Miss Fitzpatrick, doesn't notice his mother's distress, but Cassandra does, and she knows exactly what Carolina is feeling—not because she's read the woman's mind but because she so often feels the same way: as though the world is closing in on her, threatening to overwhelm her. Reaching up, she takes hold of Carolina's hand.

This, too, startles Carolina. She hasn't held a child's hand in hers since Margaretta died. Her impulse is to pull away, and she almost does. But to her surprise she finds it somehow comforting, familiar, and she leaves her fingers in the girl's grasp as they continue down the avenue toward the ice-cream parlor, until at last, without her even being quite conscious of it, her hand closes around Cassandra's, as though it's the most natural thing in the world, which it is.

It's time to leave, now. You've learned everything about our characters you need to know; you've seen everything I meant to show you.

And yet you hesitate again, the way you did at the beginning, when I first invited you to come with me—though for a different reason, I imagine. I understand. You've invested a good deal of time and sympathy in these characters. You want to know what will become of them, what lies in store for them.

I wish I could help you. But, as I told you at the outset, when it comes to precognition I'm no use at all. I can't see beyond the boundaries of the story. The best I could manage is an educated guess about what the characters *might* do, based on what they've done so far, and you can make those sorts of guesses yourself.

But I can see that you won't be satisfied until I've given you something more. All right. Just remember, even someone like Cassandra, who has true second sight, can't tell you what *will* happen, only what is likely to happen if things go on as they are.

I suspect that Carolina Ehrlich will never quite manage to let go of Margaretta, but I also suspect that she will grow fond of Cassandra and agree to take her in.

Cassandra, I think, will learn to understand her clairvoyant powers and control them to some extent. Perhaps, in time, she will even come to value them.

I'm confident that Miss Fitzpatrick will find a position at some progressive private school where her inquiring mind and outspoken manner are regarded as an asset, not as a threat, and will teach several generations of fortunate students to think for themselves.

Nicholas and Joseph will undoubtedly tour much of the Re-United States and its territories with their act (though I don't suppose they'll convince Carolina and Cassandra to come along). Perhaps they'll even play the gold-mining camps of the West, as Junius Brutus Booth and his son did. If so, maybe they'll encounter Mrs. McKenna's missing husband, or even Patrick Nolan, who is always seeking an easy way to get rich.

Joseph will take plenty of books with him, of course, for I'm sure he'll continue to be an avid reader—though I would like to think that his tastes will grow more sophisticated and his interests more wide ranging. When he's not on the road, I imagine he will enroll himself at one of the city's academies, where he will expand his intellectual horizons and perhaps discover that he has other talents besides mind reading. After all—to paraphrase Miss Fitzpatrick's motto—you can't be certain what you want to do with your life until you know what all the choices are.

As for Wilkes Booth, I fear that his strand of the story will come to an end very soon, and it will not be a happy one. He did escape from the city, but his leg, which he broke in the leap to the stage, won't let him get far. A large reward has been offered for his capture. But, after turning in such a poor performance in his final role, I doubt that he'll let himself be taken in, to face the jeers of a hostile public.

On the other hand, any or all of those predictions could be wrong. As I pointed out in an earlier chapter, characters in a story, like real people, don't always do what we expect.

Nor does the future always turn out the way we imagine it will. As you have seen, even things that seem inevitable can be changed or prevented, often by people who may appear, at first glance, to be quite ordinary. People like Joseph. People like you.

AFTERWORD

Obviously, novelists have at least one trick that I neglected to tell you about—the ability to change history. You may wonder whether it's fair to play around with the facts that way, to make things turn out differently than they did in real life.

A lot of novelists seem to think so. In fact, there's a special category of fiction called *uchronia,* or alternate history. Alternate history novels ask the question "If some pivotal event in history had taken a slightly different turn, how would it have affected later events?"

Second Sight isn't really alternate history so much as it is *altered* history. And, except for that little matter involving Mr. Lincoln (I won't spell it out, in case you're one of those people who reads the end of the book first), I didn't really change very much. I've tried my best to make the historical background of the story as accurate as possible, down to the dates and times that things actually happened.

The information I've provided about the theatre is true for the most part, too. The mind-reading methods I've described in such detail were actually employed by a number of different illusionists. Nearly all the plays and performers I mention really existed.

In fact, though the Ehrlich family and Patrick Nolan are fictional, the majority of the characters who appear in the book were real historical figures, including Mrs. Surratt and her son, as well as Honora Fitzpatrick, Ward Hill Lamon, Davy Herold, and, of course, John Wilkes Booth. There were several others involved in the assassination plot (which really was, as I've indicated, originally an abduction plot), but I left them out for the sake of simplicity.

Davy Herold met a slightly different fate than the one I assigned him; he was found guilty of treason and hanged, along with most of the other conspirators (and one who may or may not have been a conspirator—Mrs. Surratt). Only John Surratt escaped. Booth managed to elude the authorites for twelve days before he was tracked down and shot.

As for Cassandra Quinn . . . well, there really was a girl of nine or ten who lodged at Mrs. Surratt's boardinghouse, but I could find no reliable information about her aside from her name—Apollonia Dean. Since I had to invent everything else about her, I gave her a new name as well. Isn't it interesting, though, that her real name is derived from Apollo, the Greek god of prophecy?

THE HORSE AND HIS BOY

Mt. Pire

Anvard

narrow gorge

DESER

● Rock

N
W E
S

THE CHRONICLES OF NARNIA

THE LION, THE WITCH AND THE WARDROBE
PRINCE CASPIAN
THE VOYAGE OF THE *Dawn Treader*
THE SILVER CHAIR
THE HORSE AND HIS BOY
(*published by Collins*)

THE MAGICIAN'S NEPHEW
THE LAST BATTLE
(*published by The Bodley Head*)

C. S. LEWIS

The Horse and his Boy

Illustrated by
Pauline Baynes

COLLINS

William Collins Sons & Co Ltd
London · Glasgow · Sydney · Auckland
Toronto · Johannesburg

British Library Cataloguing in Publication Data

Lewis, C.S.
　The horse and his boy.—New ed.
　I. Title　II. Baynes, Pauline
　823'.912[J]　　PZ7
　ISBN 0-00-183182-8
　　First published by Geoffrey Bles 1954
　　　　Second edition 1974
　　　　Third edition 1987
　　Copyright © C.S. Lewis Pte Ltd 1954

Printed and bound in Great Britain
by Robert Hartnoll (1985) Ltd, Bodmin

To David and Douglas Gresham

CONTENTS

HOW SHASTA SET OUT ON HIS TRAVELS

THIS is the story of an adventure that happened in Narnia and Calormen and the lands between, in the Golden Age when Peter was High King in Narnia and his brother and his two sisters were King and Queens under him.

In those days, far south in Calormen on a little creek of the sea, there lived a poor fisherman called Arsheesh, and with him there lived a boy who called him Father. The boy's name was Shasta. On most days Arsheesh went out in his boat to fish in the morning, and in the afternoon he harnessed his donkey to a cart and loaded the cart with fish and went a mile or so southward to the village to sell it. If it had sold well he would come home in a moderately good temper and say nothing to Shasta, but if it had sold badly he would find fault with him and perhaps beat him. There was always something to find fault with for Shasta had plenty of work to do, mending and washing the nets, cooking the supper, and cleaning the cottage in which they both lived.

Shasta was not at all interested in anything that lay south of his home because he had once or twice been to the village with Arsheesh and he knew that there was nothing very interesting there. In the village he only met other men who were just like his father – men with long, dirty robes, and wooden shoes turned up at the toe, and turbans on their heads, and beards, talking to one another very slowly about things that sounded dull. But he was very interested in everything that lay to the North because no one ever went that way and he was never allowed to go there himself. When he was sitting out of doors mending the nets, and all alone, he would often look eagerly to the North. One could see nothing but a grassy slope running up to a level ridge and beyond that the sky with perhaps a few birds in it.

Sometimes if Arsheesh was there Shasta would say, "O my Father, what is there beyond that hill?" And then if the fisherman was in a bad temper he would box Shasta's ears and tell him to attend to his work. Or if he was in a peaceable mood he would say, "O my son, do not allow your mind to be distracted by idle questions. For one of the poets has said, 'Application to business is the root of prosperity, but those who ask questions that do not concern them are steering the ship of folly towards the rock of indigence'."

Shasta thought that beyond the hill there must be some delightful secret which his father wished to hide from him. In reality, however, the fisherman talked like this because he didn't know what lay to the North. Neither did he care. He had a very practical mind.

One day there came from the South a stranger who was unlike any man that Shasta had seen before. He rode upon a strong dappled horse with flowing mane and tail and his stirrups and bridle were inlaid with silver. The spike of a helmet projected from the middle of his silken turban and he wore a shirt of chain mail. By his side hung a curving scimitar, a round shield studded with bosses of brass hung at his back, and his right hand grasped a lance. His face was dark, but this did not surprise Shasta because all the people of Calormen are like that; what did surprise him was the man's beard which was dyed crimson, and curled and gleaming with scented oil. But Arsheesh knew by the gold on the stranger's bare arm that he was a Tarkaan or great lord, and he bowed kneeling before him till his beard touched the earth and made signs to Shasta to kneel also.

The stranger demanded hospitality for the night which of course the fisherman dared not refuse. All the best they had was set before the Tarkaan for supper (and he didn't think much of it) and Shasta, as always happened when the fisherman had company, was given a hunk of bread and turned out of the cottage. On these occasions he usually slept with the donkey in its little thatched stable. But it was much too early to go to sleep yet, and Shasta, who had never learned that it is wrong to listen behind doors, sat down with his ear to a crack in the wooden wall of the cottage to hear what the grown-ups were talking about. And this is what he heard.

"And now, O my host," said the Tarkaan, "I have a mind to buy that boy of yours."

"O my master," replied the fisherman (and Shasta knew by the wheedling tone the greedy look that was probably coming into his face as he said it), "what price could induce your servant, poor though he is, to sell into slavery his only child and his own flesh? Has not one of the poets said, 'Natural affection is stronger than soup and offspring more precious than carbuncles?'"

"It is even so," replied the guest dryly. "But another poet has likewise said, "He who attempts to deceive the judicious is already baring his own back for the scourge." Do not load your aged mouth with falsehoods. This boy is manifestly no son of yours, for your cheek is as dark as mine but the boy is fair and white like the accursed but beautiful barbarians who inhabit the remote North."

"How well it was said," answered the fisherman, "that Swords can be kept off with shields but the Eye of Wisdom pierces through every defence! Know then, O my formidable guest, that because of my extreme poverty I have never married and have no child. But in that same year in which the Tisroc (may he live for ever) began his august and beneficent reign, on a night when the moon was at her full, it pleased the gods to deprive me of my sleep. Therefore I arose from my bed in this hovel and went forth to the beach to refresh myself with looking upon the water and the moon and breathing the cool air. And presently I heard a noise as of oars coming to me across the water and then, as it were, a weak cry. And shortly after, the tide brought to the land a little boat in which there was nothing but a man lean with extreme hunger and thirst who seemed to have died but a few moments before (for he was still warm), and an empty water-skin, and a child, still living. "Doubtless," said I, "these unfortunates have escaped from the wreck of a great ship, but by the admirable designs of the gods, the elder has starved himself to keep the child alive and has perished in sight of land." Accordingly, remembering how the gods never fail to reward those who befriend the destitute, and being moved by compassion (for your servant is a man of tender heart) –"

"Leave out all these idle words in your own praise," interrupted the Tarkaan. "It is enough to know that you took the child – and have had ten times the worth of his daily bread out of him in labour, as anyone can see. And now tell me at once what price you put on him, for I am wearied with your loquacity."

"You yourself have wisely said," answered Arsheesh, "that the boy's labour has been to me of inestimable value. This must be taken into account in fixing the price. For if I sell the boy I must undoubtedly either buy or hire another to do his work."

"I'll give you fifteen crescents for him," said the Tarkaan.

"Fifteen!" cried Arsheesh in a voice that was something between a whine and a scream. "Fifteen! For the prop of my old age and the delight of my eyes! Do not mock my grey beard, Tarkaan though you be. My price is seventy."

At this point Shasta got up and tiptoed away. He had heard all he wanted, for he had often listened when men were bargaining in the village and knew how it was done. He was quite certain that Arsheesh would sell him in the end for something much more than fifteen crescents and much less than seventy, but that he and the Tarkaan would take hours in getting to an agreement.

You must not imagine that Shasta felt at all as you and I would feel if we had just overheard our parents talking about selling us for slaves. For one thing, his life was already little better than slavery; for all he knew, the lordly stranger on the great horse might be kinder to him than Arsheesh. For another, the story about his own discovery in the boat had filled him with excitement and with a sense of relief. He had often been uneasy because, try as he might, he had never been able to love the fisherman, and he knew that a boy ought to love his father. And now, apparently, he was no relation to Arsheesh at all. That took a great weight off his mind. "Why, I might be anyone!" he thought. "I might be the son of a Tarkaan myself – or the son of the Tisroc (may he live for ever) – or of a god!"

He was standing out in the grassy place before the cottage while he thought these things. Twilight was coming on apace and a star or two was already out, but the remains of the sunset could still be seen in the west. Not far away the stranger's horse, loosely tied to an iron ring in the wall of the donkey's stable, was grazing. Shasta strolled over to it and patted its neck. It went on tearing up the grass and took no notice of him.

Then another thought came into Shasta's mind. "I wonder what sort of a man that Tarkaan is," he said out loud. "It would be splendid if he was kind. Some of the slaves in a great lord's house have next to nothing to do. They wear lovely clothes and eat meat every day. Perhaps he'd take me to the wars and I'd save his life in a battle and then he'd set me free and adopt me as his son and give me a palace and a chariot and a suit of armour. But then he might be a horrid cruel man. He might send me to work on the fields in chains. I wish I knew. How can I know? I bet this horse knows, if only he could tell me."

The Horse had lifted its head. Shasta stroked its smooth-as-satin nose and said, "I wish *you* could talk, old fellow."

And then for a second he thought he was dreaming, for quite distinctly, though in a low voice, the Horse said, "But I can."

Shasta stared into its great eyes and his own grew almost as big, with astonishment.

"How ever did *you* learn to talk?" he asked.

"Hush! Not so loud," replied the Horse. "Where I come from, nearly all the animals talk."

"Wherever is that?" asked Shasta.

"Narnia," answered the Horse. "The happy land of Narnia – Narnia of the heathery mountains and the thymy downs, Narnia of the many rivers, the plashing glens, the mossy caverns and the deep forests ringing with the hammers of the Dwarfs. Oh the sweet air of Narnia! An hour's life there is better than a thousand years in Calormen." It ended with a whinny that sounded very like a sigh.

"How did you get here?" said Shasta.

"Kidnapped," said the Horse. "Or stolen, or captured – whichever you like to call it. I was only a foal at the time. My mother warned me not to range the Southern slopes, into Archenland and beyond, but I wouldn't heed her. And by the Lion's Mane I have paid for my folly. All these years I have been a slave to humans, hiding my true nature and pretending to be dumb and witless like *their* horses."

"Why didn't you tell them who you were?"

"Not such a fool, that's why. If they'd once found out I could talk they would have made a show of me at fairs and guarded me more carefully than ever. My last chance of escape would have been gone."

"And why –" began Shasta, but the Horse interrupted him.

"Now look," it said, "we mustn't waste time on idle questions. You want to know about my master the Tarkaan Anradin. Well, he's bad. Not too bad to me, for a war horse costs too much to be treated very badly. But you'd better be lying dead tonight than go to be a human slave in his house tomorrow."

"Then I'd better run away," said Shasta, turning very pale.

"Yes, you had," said the Horse. "But why not run away with me?"

"Are you going to run away too?" said Shasta.

"Yes, if you'll come with me," answered the Horse. "This is the chance for both of us. You see if I run away without a rider, everyone who sees me will say "Stray horse" and be after me as quick as he can. With a rider I've a chance to get through. That's where you can help me. On the other hand, you can't get very far on those two silly legs of yours (what absurd legs humans have!) without being overtaken. But on me you can outdistance any other horse in this country. That's where I can help you. By the way, I suppose you know how to ride?"

"Oh yes, of course," said Shasta. "At least, I've ridden the donkey."

"Ridden the *what*?" retorted the Horse with extreme contempt. (At least, that is what he meant. Actually it came out in a sort of neigh – "Ridden the wha-ha-ha-ha-ha." Talking horses always become more horsy in accent when they are angry.)

"In other words," it continued, "you *can't* ride. That's a drawback. I'll have to teach you as we go along. If you can't ride, can you fall?"

"I suppose anyone can fall," said Shasta.

"I mean can you fall and get up again without crying and mount again and fall again and yet not be afraid of falling?"

"I – I'll try," said Shasta. "Poor little beast," said the Horse in a gentler tone. "I forget you're only a foal. We'll make a fine rider of you in time. And now – we mustn't start until those two in the hut are asleep. Meantime we can make our plans. My Tarkaan is on his way North to the great city, to Tashbaan itself and the court of the Tisroc –"

"I say," put in Shasta in rather a shocked voice, "oughtn't you to say 'May he live for ever'?"

"Why?" asked the Horse. "I'm a free Narnian. And why should I talk slaves' and fools' talk? I don't want him to live for ever, and I know that he's not going to live for ever whether I want him to or not. And I can see you're from the free North too. No more of this Southern jargon between you and me! And now, back to our plans. As I said, my human was on his way North to Tashbaan."

"Does that mean we'd better go to the South?"

"I think not," said the Horse. "You see, he thinks I'm dumb and witless like his other horses. Now if I really were, the moment I got loose I'd go back home to my stable and paddock; back to his palace which is two days' journey South. That's where he'll look for me. He'd never dream of my going on North on my own. And anyway he will probably think that someone in the last village who saw him ride through has followed us to here and stolen me."

"Oh hurrah!" said Shasta. "Then we'll go North. I've been longing to go to the North all my life."

"Of course you have," said the Horse. "That's because of the blood that's in you. I'm sure you're true Northern stock. But not too loud. I should think they'd be asleep soon now."

"I'd better creep back and see," suggested Shasta.

"That's a good idea," said the Horse. "But take care you're not caught."

It was a good deal darker now and very silent except for the sound of the waves on the beach, which Shasta hardly noticed because he had been hearing it day and night as long as he could remember. The cottage, as he approached it, showed no light. When he listened at the front there was no noise. When he went round to the only window, he could hear, after a second or two, the familiar noise of the old fisherman's squeaky snore. It was funny to think that if all went well he would never hear it again. Holding his breath and feeling a little bit sorry, but much less sorry than he was glad, Shasta glided away over the grass and went to the donkey's stable, groped along to a place he knew where the key was hidden, opened the door and found the Horse's saddle and bridle which had been locked up there for the night. He bent forward and kissed the donkey's nose. "I'm sorry we can't take *you*," he said.

"There you are at last," said the Horse when he got back to it. "I was beginning to wonder what had become of you."

"I was getting your things out of the stable," replied Shasta. "And now, can you tell me how to put them on?"

For the next few minutes Shasta was at work, very cautiously to avoid jingling, while the Horse said things like, "Get that girth a bit tighter," or "You'll find a buckle lower down," or "You'll need to shorten those stirrups a good bit." When all was finished it said:

"Now; we've got to have reins for the look of the thing, but you won't be using them. Tie them to the saddle-bow: very slack so that I can do what I like with my head. And, remember – you are not to touch them."

"What are they for, then?" asked Shasta.

"Ordinarily they are for directing me," replied the Horse. "But as I intend to do all the directing on this journey, you'll please keep your hands to yourself. And there's another thing. I'm not going to have you grabbing my mane."

"But I say," pleaded Shasta. "If I'm not to hold on by the reins or by your mane, what *am* I to hold on by?"

"You hold on with your knees," said the Horse. "That's the secret of good riding. Grip my body between your knees as hard as you like; sit straight up, straight as a poker; keep your elbows in. And by the way, what did you do with the spurs?"

"Put them on my heels, of course," said Shasta. "I do know that much."

"Then you can take them off and put them in the saddle-bag. We may be able to sell them when we get to Tashbaan. Ready? And now I think you can get up."

"Ooh! You're a dreadful height," gasped Shasta after his first, and unsuccessful, attempt.

"I'm a horse, that's all," was the reply. "Anyone would think I was a haystack from the way you're trying to climb up me! There, that's better. Now sit *up* and remember what I told you about your knees. Funny to think of me who has led cavalry charges and won races having a potato-sack like you in the saddle! However, off we go." It chuckled, not unkindly.

And it certainly began their night journey with great caution. First of all it went just south of the fisherman's cottage to the little river which there ran into the sea, and took care to leave in the mud some very plain hoof-marks pointing South. But as soon as they were in the middle of the ford it turned upstream and waded till they were about a hundred yards farther inland than the cottage. Then it selected a nice gravelly bit of bank which would take no footprints and came out on the Northern side. Then, still at a walking pace, it went Northward till the cottage, the one tree, the donkey's stable, and the creek – everything, in fact, that Shasta had ever known – had sunk out of sight in the grey summer-night darkness. They had been going up-hill and now were at the top of the ridge – that ridge which had always been the boundary of Shasta's known world. He could not see what was ahead except that it was all open and grassy. It looked endless: wild and lonely and free.

"I say!" observed the Horse. "What a place for a gallop, eh!"

"Oh don't let's," said Shasta. "Not yet. I don't know how to – please, Horse. I don't know your name."

"Breehy-hinny-brinny-hoohy-hah," said the Horse.

"I'll never be able to say that," said Shasta. "Can I call you Bree?"

"Well, if it's the best you can do, I suppose you must," said the Horse. "And what shall I call you?"

"I'm called Shasta."

"H'm," said Bree. "Well, now, there's a name that's *really* hard to pronounce. But now about this gallop. It's a good deal easier than trotting if you only knew, because you don't have to rise and fall. Grip with your knees and keep your eyes straight ahead between my ears. Don't look at the ground. If you think you're going to fall just grip harder and sit up straighter. Ready? Now: for Narnia and the North."

CHAPTER TWO

A WAYSIDE ADVENTURE

It was nearly noon on the following day when Shasta was wakened by something warm and soft moving over his face. He opened his eyes and found himself staring into the long face of a horse; its nose and lips were almost touching his. He remembered the exciting events of the previous night and sat up. But as he did so he groaned.

"Ow, Bree," he gasped. "I'm so sore. All over. I can hardly move."

"Good morning, small one," said Bree. "I was afraid you might feel a bit stiff. It can't be the falls. You didn't have more than a dozen or so, and it was all lovely, soft springy turf that must have been almost a pleasure to fall on. And the only one that might have been nasty was broken by that gorse bush. No: it's the riding itself that comes hard at first. What about breakfast? I've had mine."

"Oh bother breakfast. Bother everything," said Shasta. "I tell you I can't move." But the horse nuzzled at him with its nose and pawed him gently with a hoof till he had to get up. And then he looked about him and saw where they were. Behind them lay a little copse. Before them the turf, dotted with white flowers, sloped down to the brow of a cliff. Far below them, so that the sound of the breaking waves was very faint, lay the sea. Shasta had never seen it from such a height and never seen so much of it before, nor dreamed how many colours it had. On either hand the coast stretched away, headland after headland, and at the points you could see the white foam running up the rocks but making no noise because it was so far off. There were gulls flying overhead and the heat shivered on the ground; it was a blazing day. But what Shasta chiefly noticed was the air. He couldn't think what was missing, until at last he realized that there was no smell of fish in it. For of course, neither in the cottage nor among the nets, had he ever been away from that smell in his life. And this new air was so delicious, and all his old life seemed so far away, that he forgot for a moment about his bruises and his aching muscles and said:

"I say, Bree, didn't you say something about breakfast?"

"Yes, I did," answered Bree. "I think you'll find something in the saddle-bags. They're over there on that tree where you hung them up last night – or early this morning, rather."

They investigated the saddle-bags and the results were cheering – a meat pasty, only slightly stale, a lump of dried figs and another lump of green cheese, a little flask of wine, and some money; about forty crescents in all, which was more than Shasta had ever seen.

While Shasta sat down – painfully and cautiously – with his back against a tree and started on the pasty, Bree had a few more mouthfuls of grass to keep him company.

"Won't it be stealing to use the money?" asked Shasta.

"Oh," said the Horse, looking up with its mouth full of grass, "I never thought of that. A free horse and a talking horse mustn't steal, of course. But I think it's all right. We're prisoners and captives in enemy country. That money is booty, spoil. Besides, how are we to get any food for you without it? I suppose, like all humans, you won't eat natural food like grass and oats."

"I can't."

"Ever tried?"

"Yes, I have. I can't get it down at all. You couldn't either if you were me."

"You're rum little creatures, you humans," remarked Bree.

When Shasta had finished his breakfast (which was by

far the nicest he had ever eaten), Bree said, "I think I'll have a nice roll before we put on that saddle again." And he proceeded to do so. "That's good. That's very good," he said, rubbing his back on the turf and waving all four legs in the air. "You ought to have one too, Shasta," he snorted. "It's most refreshing."

But Shasta burst out laughing and said, "You do look funny when you're on your back!"

"I look nothing of the sort," said Bree. But then suddenly he rolled round on his side, raised his head and looked hard at Shasta, blowing a little.

"Does it really look funny?" he asked in an anxious voice.

"Yes, it does," replied Shasta. "But what does it matter?"

"You don't think, do you," said Bree, "that it might be a thing *talking* horses never do – a silly, clownish trick I've learned from the dumb ones? It would be dreadful to find, when I get back to Narnia, that I've picked up a lot of low, bad habits. What do you think, Shasta? Honestly, now. Don't spare my feelings. Should you think the real, free horses – the talking kind – do roll?"

"How should I know? Anyway I don't think I should bother about it if I were you. We've got to get there first. Do you know the way?"

"I know my way to Tashbaan. After that comes the desert. Oh, we'll manage the desert somehow, never fear. Why, we'll be in sight of the Northern mountains then. Think of it! To Narnia and the North! Nothing will stop us then. But I'd be glad to be past Tashbaan. You and I are safer away from cities."

"Can't we avoid it?"

"Not without going a long way inland, and that would take us into cultivated land and main roads; and I wouldn't know the way. No, we'll just have to creep along the coast. Up here on the downs we'll meet nothing but sheep and rabbits and gulls and a few shepherds. And by the way, what about starting?"

Shasta's legs ached terribly as he saddled Bree and climbed into the saddle, but the Horse was kindly to him and went at a soft pace all afternoon. When evening twilight came they dropped by steep tracks into a valley and found a village. Before they got into it Shasta dismounted and entered it on foot to buy a loaf and some onions and radishes. The Horse trotted round by the fields in the dusk and met Shasta at the far side. This became their regular plan every second night.

These were great days for Shasta, and every day better than the last as his muscles hardened and he fell less often. Even at the end of his training Bree still said he sat like a bag of flour in the saddle. "And even if it was safe, young 'un, I'd be ashamed to be seen with you on the main road." But in spite of his rude words Bree was a patient teacher. No one can teach riding so well as a horse. Shasta learned to trot, to canter, to jump, and to keep his seat even when Bree pulled up suddenly or swung unexpectedly to the left or the right – which, as Bree told him, was a thing you might have to do at any moment in a battle. And then of course Shasta begged to be told of the battles and wars in which Bree had carried the Tarkaan. And Bree would tell of forced marches and the fording of swift rivers, of charges and of fierce fights between cavalry and cavalry when the war horses fought as well as the men, being all fierce stallions, trained to bite and kick, and to rear at the right moment so that the horse's weight as well as the rider's would come down on a enemy's crest in the stroke of sword or battleaxe. But Bree did not want to talk about the wars as often as Shasta wanted to hear about them. "Don't speak of them, youngster," he would say. "They were only the Tisroc's wars and I fought in them as a slave and a dumb beast. Give me the Narnian wars where I shall fight as a free Horse among my own people! Those will be wars worth talking about. Narnia and the North! Bra-ha-ha! Broo hoo!"

Shasta soon learned, when he heard Bree talking like that, to prepare for a gallop.

After they had travelled on for weeks and weeks past more bays and headlands and rivers and villages than Shasta could remember, there came a moonlit night when they started their journey at evening, having slept during the day. They had left the downs behind them and were crossing a wide plain with a forest about half a mile away on their left. The sea, hidden by low sandhills, was about the same distance on their right. They had jogged along for about an hour, sometimes trotting and sometimes walking, when Bree suddenly stopped.

"What's up?" said Shasta.

"S-s-ssh!" said Bree, craning his neck round and twitching his ears. "Did you hear something? Listen."

"It sounds like another horse – between us and the wood," said Shasta after he had listened for about a minute.

"It *is* another horse," said Bree. "And that's what I don't like."

"Isn't it probably just a farmer riding home late?" said Shasta with a yawn.

"Don't tell me!" said Bree. "*That's* not a farmer's riding. Nor a farmer's horse either. Can't you tell by the sound? That's quality, that horse is. And it's being ridden by a real horseman. I tell you what it is, Shasta. There's a Tarkaan under the edge of that wood. Not on his war horse – it's too light for that. On a fine blood mare, I should say."

"Well, it's stopped now, whatever it is," said Shasta.

"You're right," said Bree. "And why should he stop just when we do? Shasta, my boy, I do believe there's someone shadowing us at last."

"What shall we do?" said Shasta in a lower whisper than before. "Do you think he can see us as well as hear us?"

"Not in this light so long as we stay quite still," answered Bree. "But look! There's a cloud coming up. I'll wait till that gets over the moon. Then we'll get off to our right as quietly as we can, down to the shore. We can hide among the sandhills if the worst comes to the worst."

They waited till the cloud covered the moon and then, first at a walking pace and afterwards at a gentle trot, made for the shore.

The cloud was bigger and thicker than it had looked at first and soon the night grew very dark. Just as Shasta was saying to himself, "We must be nearly at those sandhills by now," his heart leaped into his mouth because an appalling noise had suddenly risen up out of the darkness ahead; a long snarling roar, melancholy and utterly savage. Instantly Bree swerved round and began galloping inland again as fast as he could gallop.

"What is it?" gasped Shasta.

"Lions!" said Bree, without checking his pace or turning his head.

After that there was nothing but sheer galloping for some time. At last they splashed across a wide, shallow stream and Bree came to a stop on the far side. Shasta noticed that he was trembling and sweating all over.

"That water may have thrown the brute off our scent," panted Bree when he had partly got his breath again. "We can walk for a bit now."

As they walked Bree said, "Shasta, I'm ashamed of myself. I'm just as frightened as a common, dumb Calormene horse. I am really. I don't feel like a Talking Horse at all. I don't mind swords and lances and arrows but I can't bear – those creatures. I think I'll trot for a bit."

About a minute later, however, he broke into a gallop again, and no wonder. For the roar broke out again, this time on their left from the direction of the forest.

"Two of them," moaned Bree.

When they had galloped for several minutes without any further noise from the lions Shasta said, "I say! That other horse is galloping beside us now. Only a stone's throw away."

"All the b-better," panted Bree. "Tarkaan on it – will have a sword – protect us all."

"But, Bree!" said Shasta. "We might just as well be killed by lions as caught. Or *I* might. They'll hang me for horse-stealing." He was feeling less frightened of lions than Bree because he had never met a lion; Bree had.

Bree only snorted in answer but he did sheer away to his right. Oddly enough the other horse seemed also to be sheering away to the left, so that in a few seconds the space between them had widened a good deal. But as soon as it did so there came two more lions' roars, immediately after one another, one on the right and the other on the left, the horses began drawing nearer together. So, apparently, did the lions. The roaring of the brutes on each side was horribly close and they seemed to be keeping up with the galloping horses quite easily. Then the cloud rolled away. The moonlight, astonishingly bright, showed up everything almost as if it were broad day. The two horses and two riders were galloping neck to neck and knee to knee just as if they were in a race. Indeed Bree said (afterwards) that a finer race had never been seen in Calormen.

Shasta now gave himself up for lost and began to wonder whether lions killed you quickly or played with you as a cat plays with a mouse and how much it would hurt. At the same time (one sometimes does this at the most frightful moments) he noticed everything. He saw that the other rider was a very small, slender person, mail-clad (the moon shone on the mail) and riding magnificently. He had no beard.

Something flat and shining was spread out before them. Before Shasta had time even to guess what it was there was

a great splash and he found his mouth half full of salt water. The shining thing had been a long inlet of the sea. Both horses were swimming and the water was up to Shasta's knees. There was an angry roaring behind them and looking back Shasta saw a great, shaggy, and terrible shape crouched on the water's edge; but only one. "We must have shaken off the other lion," he thought.

The lion apparently did not think its prey worth a wetting; at any rate it made no attempt to take the water in pursuit. The two horses, side by side, were now well out into the middle of the creek and the opposite shore could be clearly seen. The Tarkaan had not yet spoken a word. "But he will," thought Shasta. "As soon as we have landed. What am I to say? I must begin thinking out a story."

Then, suddenly, two voices spoke at his side.

"Oh, I *am* so tired," said the one. "Hold your tongue, Hwin, and don't be a fool," said the other.

"I'm dreaming," thought Shasta. "I could have sworn that other horse spoke."

Soon the horses were no longer swimming but walking and soon with a great sound of water running off their sides and tails and with a great crunching of pebbles under eight hoofs, they came out on the farther beach of the inlet. The Tarkaan, to Shasta's surprise, showed no wish to ask questions. He did not even look at Shasta but seemed anxious to urge his horse straight on. Bree, however, at once shouldered himself in the other horse's way.

"Broo-hoo-hah!" he snorted. "Steady there! I *heard* you, I did. There's no good pretending, Ma'am. *I* heard you. You're a Talking Horse, a Narnian horse just like me."

"What's it got to do with you if she is?" said the strange rider fiercely, laying hand on sword-hilt. But the voice in which the words were spoken had already told Shasta something.

"Why, it's only a girl!" he exclaimed.

"And what business is it of yours if I am *only* a girl?" snapped the stranger. "You're probably only a boy: a rude, common little boy — a slave probably, who's stolen his master's horse."

"That's all *you* know," said Shasta.

"He's not a thief, little Tarkheena," said Bree. "At least, if there's been any stealing, you might just as well say I stole *him*. And as for its not being my business, you wouldn't expect me to pass a lady of my own race in this strange country without speaking to her? It's only natural I should."

"I think it's very natural too," said the mare.

"I wish you'd held your tongue, Hwin," said the girl. "Look at the trouble you've got us into."

"I don't know about trouble," said Shasta. "You can clear off as soon as you like. We shan't keep you."

"No, you shan't," said the girl.

"What quarrelsome creatures these humans are," said Bree to the mare. "They're as bad as mules. Let's try to talk a little sense. I take it, ma'am, your story is the same as mine? Captured in early youth — years of slavery among the Calormenes?"

"Too true, sir," said the mare with a melancholy whinny.

"And now, perhaps — escape?"

"Tell him to mind his own business, Hwin," said the girl.

"No, I won't, Aravis," said the mare putting her ears back. "This is my escape just as much as yours. And I'm sure a noble war-horse like this is not going to betray us. We are trying to escape, to get to Narnia."

"And so, of course, are we," said Bree. "Of course you guessed that at once. A little boy in rags riding (or trying to ride) a war-horse at dead of night couldn't mean anything but an escape of some sort. And, if I may say so, a high-born Tarkheena riding alone at night — dressed up in her brother's armour — and very anxious for everyone to mind their own business and ask her no questions — well, if that's not fishy, call me a cob!"

"All right then," said Aravis. "You've guessed it. Hwin and I are running away. We are trying to get to Narnia. And now, what about it?"

"Why, in that case, what is to prevent us all going together?" said Bree. "I trust, Madam Hwin, you will accept such assistance and protection as I may be able to give you on the journey?"

"Why do you keep talking to my horse instead of to me?" asked the girl.

"Excuse me, Tarkheena," said Bree (with just the slightest backward tilt of his ears), "but that's Calormene talk. We're free Narnians, Hwin and I, and I suppose, if you're running away to Narnia, you want to be one too. In that case Hwin isn't *your* horse any longer. One might just as well say you're *her* human."

The girl opened her mouth to speak and then stopped. Obviously she had not quite seen it in that light before.

"Still," she said after a moment's pause, "I don't know that there's so much point in all going together. Aren't we more likely to be noticed?"

"Less," said Bree; and the mare said, "Oh do let's. I should feel much more comfortable. We're not even certain of the way. I'm sure a great charger like this knows far more than we do."

"Oh come on, Bree," said Shasta, "and let them go their own way. Can't you see they don't want us?"

"We do," said Hwin.

"Look here," said the girl. "I don't mind going with *you*, Mr War-Horse, but what about this boy? How do I know he's not a spy?"

"Why don't you say at once that you think I'm not good enough for you?" said Shasta.

"Be quiet, Shasta," said Bree. "The Tarkheena's question is quite reasonable. I'll vouch for the boy, Tarkheena. He's been true to me and a good friend. And he's certainly either a Narnian or an Archenlander."

"All right, then. Let's go together." But she didn't say anything to Shasta and it was obvious that she wanted Bree, not him.

"Splendid!" said Bree. "And now that we've got the water between us and those dreadful animals, what about you two humans taking off our saddles and our all having a rest and hearing one another's stories."

Both the children unsaddled their horses and the horses had a little grass and Aravis produced rather nice things to eat from her saddle-bag. But Shasta sulked and said No thanks, and that he wasn't hungry. And he tried to put on what he thought very grand and stiff manners, but as a fisherman's hut is not usually a good place for learning grand manners, the result was dreadful. And he half knew that it wasn't a success and then became sulkier and more awkward than ever. Meanwhile the two horses were getting on splendidly. They remembered the very same places in Narnia – "the grasslands up above Beaversdam" and found that they were some sort of second cousins once removed. This made things more and more uncomfortable for the humans until at last Bree said, "And now, Tarkheena, tell us your story. And don't hurry it – I'm feeling comfortable now."

Aravis immediately began, sitting quite still and using a rather different tone and style from her usual one. For in Calormen, story-telling (whether the stories are true or made up) is a thing you're taught, just as English boys and girls are taught essay-writing. The difference is that people want to hear the stories, whereas I never heard of anyone who wanted to read the essays.

CHAPTER THREE

AT THE GATES OF TASHBAAN

"My name," said the girl at once, "is Aravis Tarkheena and I am the only daughter of Kidrash Tarkaan, the son of Rishti Tarkaan, the son of Kidrash Tarkaan, the son of Ilsombreh Tisroc, the son of Ardeeb Tisroc who was descended in a right line from the god Tash. My father is the lord of the province of Calavar and is one who has the right of standing on his feet in his shoes before the face of Tisroc himself (may he live for ever). My mother (on whom be the peace of the gods) is dead and my father has married another wife. One of my brothers has fallen in battle against the rebels in the far west and the other is a child. Now it came to pass that my father's wife, my step-mother, hated me, and the sun appeared dark in her eyes as long as I lived in my father's house. And so she persuaded my father to promise me in marriage to Ahoshta Tarkaan. Now this Ahoshta is of base birth, though in these latter years he has won the favour of the Tisroc (may he live for ever) by flattery and evil counsels, and is now made a Tarkaan and the lord of many cities and is likely to be chosen as the Grand Vizier when the present Grand Vizier dies. Moreover he is at least sixty years old and has a hump on his back and his face resembles that of an ape. Nevertheless my father, because of the wealth and power of this Ahoshta, and being persuaded by his wife, sent messengers offering me in marriage, and the offer was favourably accepted and Ahoshta sent word that he would marry me this very year at the time of high summer.

"When this news was brought to me the sun appeared dark in my eyes and I laid myself on my bed and wept for a day. But on the second day I rose up and washed my face and caused my mare Hwin to be saddled and took with me a sharp dagger which my brother had carried in the western wars and rode out alone. And when my father's house was out of sight and I was come to a green open place in a certain wood where there were no dwellings of men, I dismounted from Hwin my mare and took out the dagger. Then I parted my clothes where I thought the readiest way lay to my heart and I prayed to all the gods that as soon as I was dead I might find myself with my brother. After that I shut my eyes and my teeth and prepared to drive the dagger into my heart. But before I had done so, this mare spoke with the voice of one of the daughters of men and said, "O my mistress, do not by any means destroy yourself, for if you live you may yet have good fortune but all the dead are dead alike."

"I didn't say it half so well as that," muttered the mare.

"Hush, Ma'am, hush," said Bree, who was thoroughly enjoying the story. "She's telling it in the grand Calormene manner and no story-teller in a Tisroc's court could do it better. Pray go on, Tarkheena."

"When I heard the language of men uttered by my mare," continued Aravis, "I said to myself, the fear of death has disordered my reason and subjected me to delusions. And I became full of shame for none of my lineage ought to fear death more than the biting of a gnat. Therefore I addressed myself a second time to the stabbing, but Hwin came near to me and put her head in between me and the dagger and discoursed to me most excellent reasons and rebuked me as a mother rebukes her daughter. And now my wonder was so great that I forgot about killing myself and about Ahoshta and said, 'O my mare, how have you learned to speak like one of the daughters of men?' And Hwin told me what is known to all this company, that in Narnia there are beasts that talk, and how she herself was stolen from thence when she was a little foal. She told me also of the woods and waters of Narnia and the castles and the great ships, till I said, 'In the name of Tash and Azaroth and Zardeenah Lady of the Night, I have a great wish to be in that country of Narnia.' 'O my mistress,' answered the mare, 'if you were in Narnia you would be happy, for in that land no maiden is forced to marry against her will.'

"And when we had talked together for a great time hope returned to me and I rejoiced that I had not killed myself. Moreover it was agreed between Hwin and me that we should steal ourselves away together and we planned it in this fashion. We returned to my father's house and I put on my gayest clothes and sang and danced before my father and pretended to be delighted with the marriage which he had prepared for me. Also I said to him, 'O my father and O the delight of my eyes, give me your licence and permission to go with one of my maidens alone for three days into the woods to do secret sacrifices to Zardeenah, Lady of the Night and of Maidens, as is proper and customary for damsels when they must bid farewell to the service of Zardeenah and prepare themselves for marriage.' And he answered, 'O my daughter and O the delight of my eyes, so shall it be.'

"But when I came out from the presence of my father I went immediately to the oldest of his slaves, his secretary, who had dandled me on his knees when I was a baby and loved me more than the air and the light. And I swore him to be secret and begged him to write a certain letter for me. And he wept and implored me to change my resolution but in the end he said, 'To hear is to obey,' and did all my will. And I sealed the letter and hid it in my bosom."

"But what was in the letter?" asked Shasta.

"Be quiet, youngster," said Bree. "You're spoiling the story. She'll tell us all about the letter in the right place. Go on, Tarkheena."

"Then I called the maid who was to go with me to the woods and perform the rites of Zardeenah and told her to wake me very early in the morning. And I became merry with her and gave her wine to drink; but I had mixed such things in her cup that I knew she must sleep for a night and a day. As soon as the household of my father had committed themselves to sleep I arose and put on an armour of my brother's which I always kept in my chamber in his memory. I put into my girdle all the money I had and certain choice jewels and provided myself also with food, and saddled the mare with my own hands and rode away in the second watch of the night. I directed my course not to the woods where my father supposed that I would go but north and east to Tashbaan.

"Now for three days and more I knew that my father would not seek me, being deceived by the words I had said to him. And on the fourth day we arrived at the city of Azim Balda. Now Azim Balda stands at the meeting of many roads and from it the posts of the Tisroc (may he live for ever) ride on swift horses to every part of the empire: and it is one of the rights and privileges of the greater Tarkaans to send messages by them. I therefore went to the Chief of the Messengers in the House of Imperial Posts in Azim Balda and said, 'O dispatcher of messages, here is a letter from my uncle Ahoshta Tarkaan to Kidrash Tarkaan lord of Calavar. Take now these five crescents and cause it to be sent to him.' And the Chief of the Messengers said, 'To hear is to obey.'

"This letter was feigned to be written by Ahoshta and this was the signification of the writing: 'Ahoshta Tarkaan to Kidrash Tarkaan, salutation and peace. In the name of Tash the irresistible, the inexorable. Be it known to you that as I made my journey towards your house to perform the contract of marriage between me and your daughter Aravis Tarkheena, it pleased fortune and the gods that I fell in with her in the forest when she had ended the rites and sacrifices of Zardeenah according to the custom of maidens. And

when I learned who she was, being delighted with her
beauty and discretion, I became inflamed with love and it
appeared to me that the sun would be dark to me if I did not
marry her at once. Accordingly I prepared the necessary
sacrifices and married your daughter the same hour that I
met her and have returned with her to my own house. And
we both pray and charge you to come hither as speedily as
you may that we may be delighted with your face and
speech; and also that you may bring with you the dowry of
my wife, which, by reason of my great charges and expenses,
I require without delay. And because thou and I are brothers
I assure myself that you will not be angered by the haste of
my marriage which is wholly occasioned by the great love I
bear your daughter. And I commit you to the care of all the
gods.'

"As soon as I had done this I rode on in all haste from
Azim Balda, fearing no pursuit and expecting that my
father, having received such a letter, would send messages to
Ahoshta or go to him himself, and that before the matter
was discovered I should be beyond Tashbaan. And that is

the pith of my story until this very night when I was chased by lions and met you at the swimming of the salt water."

"And what happened to the girl – the one you drugged?" asked Shasta.

"Doubtless she was beaten for sleeping late," said Aravis coolly. "But she was a tool and spy of my stepmother's. I am very glad they should beat her."

"I say, that was hardly fair," said Shasta.

"I did not do any of these things for the sake of pleasing *you*," said Aravis.

"And there's another thing I don't understand about that story," said Shasta. "You're not grown up, I don't believe you're any older than I am. I don't believe you're as old. How could you be getting married at your age?"

Aravis said nothing, but Bree at once said, "Shasta, don't display your ignorance. They're always married at that age in the great Tarkaan families."

Shasta turned very red (though it was hardly light enough for the others to see this) and felt snubbed. Aravis asked Bree for his story. Bree told it, and Shasta thought that he put in a great deal more than he needed about the falls and the bad riding. Bree obviously thought it very funny, but Aravis did not laugh. When Bree had finished they all went to sleep.

Next day all four of them, two horses and two humans, continued their journey together. Shasta thought it had been much pleasanter when he and Bree were on their own. For now it was Bree and Aravis who did nearly all the talking. Bree had lived a long time in Calormen and had always been among Tarkaans and Tarkaans' horses, and so of course he knew a great many of the same people and places that Aravis knew. She would always be saying things like, "But if you were at the fight of Zulindreh you would have seen my cousin Alimash," and Bree would answer, "Oh, yes, Alimash, he was only captain of the ·chariots, you know. I don't quite hold with chariots or the kind of horses who draw chariots. That's not real cavalry. But he is a worthy nobleman. He filled my nosebag with sugar after the taking of Teebeth." Or else Bree would say, "I was down at the lake of Mezreel that summer," and Aravis would say, "Oh, Mezreel! I had a friend there, Lasaraleen Tarkheena. What a delightful place it is. Those gardens, and the Valley of the Thousand Perfumes!" Bree was not in the least trying to leave Shasta out of things, though Shasta sometimes nearly thought he was. People who know a lot of the same things can hardly help talking about them, and if you're there you can hardly help feeling that you're out of it.

Hwin the mare was rather shy before a great war-horse like Bree and said very little. And Aravis never spoke to Shasta at all if she could help it.

Soon, however, they had more important things to think of. They were getting near Tashbaan. There were more, and larger, villages, and more people on the roads. They now did nearly all their travelling by night and hid as best they could during the day. And at every halt they argued and argued about what they were to do when they reached Tashbaan. Everyone had been putting off this difficulty, but now it could be put off no longer. During these discussions Aravis became a little, a very little, less unfriendly to Shasta; one usually gets on better with people when one is making plans than when one is talking about nothing in particular.

Bree said the first thing now to do was to fix a place where they would all promise to meet on the far side of Tashbaan even if, by any ill luck, they got separated in passing the city. He said the best place would be the Tombs of the Ancient Kings on the very edge of the desert. "Things like great stone bee-hives," he said, "you can't possibly miss them. And the best of it is that none of the Calormenes will go near them because they think the place is haunted by ghouls and are afraid of it." Aravis asked if it wasn't really haunted by ghouls. But Bree said he was a free Narnian horse and didn't believe in these Calormene tales. And then Shasta said he wasn't a Calormene either and didn't care a straw about these old stories of ghouls. This wasn't quite true. But it rather impressed Aravis (though at the moment it annoyed her too) and of course she said she didn't mind any number of ghouls either. So it was settled that the Tombs should be their assembly place on the other side of Tashbaan, and everyone felt they were getting on very well till Hwin humbly pointed out that the real problem was not where they should go when they had got through Tashbaan but how they were to get through it.

"We'll settle that tomorrow, Ma'am," said Bree. "Time for a little sleep now."

But it wasn't easy to settle. Aravis's first suggestion was that they should swim across the river below the city during the night and not go into Tashbaan at all. But Bree had two reasons against this. One was that the river-mouth was very wide and it would be far too long a swim for Hwin to do, especially with a rider on her back. (He thought it would be too long for himself too, but he said much less about that). The other was that it would be full of shipping and of course anyone on the deck of a ship who saw two horses swimming past would be almost certain to be inquisitive.

Shasta thought they should go up the river above Tashbaan and cross it where it was narrower. But Bree explained that there were gardens and pleasure houses on both banks of the river for miles and that there would be Tarkaans and Tarkheenas living in them and riding about the roads and having water parties on the river. In fact it would be the most likely place in the world for meeting someone who would recognize Aravis or even himself.

"We'll have to have a disguise," said Shasta.

Hwin said it looked to her as if the safest thing was to go right through the city itself from gate to gate because one was less likely to be noticed in the crowd. But she approved of the idea of disguise as well. She said, "Both the humans will have to dress in rags and look like peasants or slaves. And all Aravis's armour and our saddles and things must be made into bundles and put on our backs, and the children must pretend to drive us and people will think we're only pack-horses."

"My dear Hwin!" said Aravis rather scornfully. "As if anyone could mistake Bree for anything but a war-horse however you disguised him!"

"I should think not, indeed," said Bree, snorting and letting his ears go ever so little back.

"I know it's not a *very* good plan," said Hwin. "But I think it's our only chance. And we haven't been groomed for ages and we're not looking quite ourselves (at least, I'm sure I'm not). I do think if we get well plastered with mud and go along with our heads down as if we're tired and lazy – and don't lift our hooves hardly at all – we might not be noticed. And our tails ought to be cut shorter: not neatly, you know, but all ragged."

"My dear Madam," said Bree. "Have you pictured to yourself how very disagreeable it would be to arrive in Narnia in *that* condition?"

"Well," said Hwin humbly (she was a very sensible mare), "the main thing is to get there."

Though nobody much liked it, it was Hwin's plan which had to be adopted in the end. It was a troublesome one and involved a certain amount of what Shasta called stealing, and Bree called "raiding". One farm lost a few sacks that evening and another lost a coil of rope the next: but some tattered old boy's clothes for Aravis to wear had to be fairly bought and paid for in a village. Shasta returned with them in triumph just as evening was closing in. The others were waiting for him among the trees at the foot of a low range of wooded hills which lay right across their path. Everyone was feeling excited because this was the last hill; when they reached the ridge at the top they would be looking down on Tashbaan. "I do wish we were safely past it," muttered Shasta to Hwin. "Oh I do, I do," said Hwin fervently.

That night they wound their way through the woods up to the ridge by a wood-cutter's track. And when they came out of the woods at the top they could see thousands of lights in the valley down below them. Shasta had had no notion of what a great city would be like and it frightened him. They had their supper and the children got some sleep. But the horses woke them very early in the morning.

The stars were still out and the grass was terribly cold and wet, but daybreak was just beginning, far to their right across the sea. Aravis went a few steps away into the wood and came back looking odd in her new, ragged clothes and carrying her real ones in a bundle. These, and her armour and shield and scimitar and the two saddles and the rest of the horses' fine furnishings were put into the sacks. Bree and Hwin had already got themselves as dirty and bedraggled as they could and it remained to shorten their tails. As the only tool for doing this was Aravis's scimitar, one of the packs had to be undone again in order to get it out. It was a longish job and rather hurt the horses.

"My word!" said Bree, "if I wasn't a Talking Horse what a lovely kick in the face I could give you! I thought you were going to cut it, not pull it out. That's what it feels like."

But in spite of semi-darkness and cold fingers all was done in the end, the big packs bound on the horses, the rope halters (which they were now wearing instead of bridles and reins) in the children's hands, and the journey began.

"Remember," said Bree. "Keep together if we possibly

can. If not, meet at the Tombs of the Ancient Kings, and whoever gets there first must wait for the others."

"And remember," said Shasta. "Don't you two horses forget yourselves and start *talking*, whatever happens."

CHAPTER FOUR

SHASTA FALLS IN WITH THE NARNIANS

AT first Shasta could see nothing in the valley below him but a sea of mist with a few domes and pinnacles rising from it; but as the light increased and the mist cleared away he saw more and more. A broad river divided itself into two streams and on the island between them stood the city of Tashbaan, one of the wonders of the world. Round the very edge of the island, so that the water lapped against the stone, ran high walls strengthened with so many towers that he soon gave up trying to count them. Inside the walls the island rose in a hill and every bit of that hill, up to the Tisroc's palace and the great temple of Tash at the top, was completely covered with buildings – terrace above terrace, street above street, zigzag roads or huge flights of steps bordered with orange trees and lemon trees, roof-gardens, balconies, deep archways, pillared colonnades, spires, battlements, minarets, pinnacles. And when at last the sun rose out of the sea and the great silver-plated dome of the temple flashed back its light, he was almost dazzled.

"Get on, Shasta," Bree kept saying.

The river banks on each side of the valley were such a mass of gardens that they looked at first like forest, until you got closer and saw the white walls of innumerable houses peeping out from beneath the trees. Soon after that, Shasta noticed a delicious smell of flowers and fruit. About fifteen minutes later they were down among them, plodding on a level road with white walls on each side and trees bending over the walls.

"I say," said Shasta in an awed voice. "This is a wonderful place!"

"I daresay," said Bree. "But I wish we were safely through

it and out at the other side. Narnia and the North!"

At that moment a low, throbbing noise began which gradually swelled louder and louder till the whole valley seemed to be swaying with it. It was a musical noise, but so strong and solemn as to be a little frightening.

"That's the horns blowing for the city gates to be open,"

said Bree. "We shall be there in a minute. Now, Aravis, do droop your shoulders a bit and step heavier and try to look less like a princess. Try to imagine you've been kicked and cuffed and called names all your life."

"If it comes to that," said Aravis, "what about you drooping your head a bit more and arching your neck a bit less and trying to look less like a war-horse?"

"Hush," said Bree. "Here we are."

And they were. They had come to the river's edge and the road ahead of them ran along a many-arched bridge. The water danced brightly in the early sunlight; away to their right nearer the river's mouth, they caught a glimpse of ships' masts. Several other travellers were before them on the bridge, mostly peasants driving laden donkeys and mules or carrying baskets on their heads. The children and horses joined the crowd.

"Is anything wrong?" whispered Shasta to Aravis, who had an odd look on her face.

"Oh it's all very well for *you*," whispered Aravis rather savagely. "What would *you* care about Tashbaan? But I ought to be riding in on a litter with soldiers before me and slaves behind, and perhaps going to a feast in the Tisroc's palace (may he live for ever) – not sneaking in like this. It's different for you."

Shasta thought all this very silly.

At the far end of the bridge the walls of the city towered high above them and the brazen gates stood open in the gateway which was really wide but looked narrow because it was so very high. Half a dozen soldiers, leaning on their spears, stood on each side. Aravis couldn't help thinking, "They'd all jump to attention and salute me if they knew whose daughter I am." But the others were only thinking of how they'd get through and hoping the soldiers would not ask any questions. Fortunately they did not. But one of them picked a carrot out of a peasant's basket and threw it at Shasta with a rough laugh, saying:

"Hey! Horse-boy! You'll catch it if your master finds you've been using his saddle-horse for pack work."

This frightened him badly for of course it showed that no one who knew anything about horses would mistake Bree for anything but a charger.

"It's my master's orders, so there!" said Shasta. But it would have been better if he had held his tongue for the soldier gave him a box on the side of his face that nearly knocked him down and said, "Take that, you young filth, to teach you how to talk to freemen." But they all slunk into the city without being stopped. Shasta cried only a very little; he was used to hard knocks.

Inside the gates Tashbaan did not at first seem so splendid as it had looked from a distance. The first street was narrow and there were hardly any windows in the walls on each side. It was much more crowded than Shasta had expected: crowded partly by the peasants (on their way to market) who had come in with them, but also with watersellers, sweetmeat sellers, porters, soldiers, beggars, ragged children, hens, stray dogs, and bare-footed slaves. What you would chiefly have noticed if you had been there was the smells, which came from unwashed people, unwashed dogs, scent, garlic, onions, and the piles of refuse which lay everywhere.

Shasta was pretending to lead but it was really Bree, who knew the way and kept guiding him by little nudges with his nose. They soon turned to the left and began going up a steep hill. It was much fresher and pleasanter, for the road was bordered by trees and there were houses only on the right side; on the other they looked out over the roofs of houses in the lower town and could see some way up the river. Then they went round a hairpin bend to their right and continued rising. They were zigzagging up to the centre of Tashbaan. Soon they came to finer streets. Great statues of the gods and heroes of Calormen – who are mostly impressive rather than agreeable to look at – rose on shining pedestals. Palm trees and pillared arcades cast shadows over the burning pavements. And through the arched gateways of many a palace Shasta caught sight of green branches, cool fountains, and smooth lawns. It must be nice inside, he thought.

At every turn Shasta hoped they were getting out of the crowd, but they never did. This made their progress very slow, and every now and then they had to stop altogether. This usually happened because a loud voice shouted out "Way, way, way, for the Tarkaan", or "for the Tarkheena", or "for the fifteenth Vizier", "or for the Ambassasor", and everyone in the crowd would crush back against the walls;

and above their heads Shasta would sometimes see the great lord or lady for whom all the fuss was being made, lolling upon a litter which four or even six gigantic slaves carried on their bare shoulders. For in Tashbaan there is only one traffic regulation, which is that everyone who is less important has to get out of the way for everyone who is more important; unless you want a cut from a whip or punch from the butt end of a spear.

It was in a splendid street very near the top of the city (the Tisroc's palace was the only thing above it) that the most disastrous of these stoppages occurred.

"Way! Way! Way!" came the voice. "Way for the White Barbarian King, the guest of the Tisroc (may he live for ever)! Way for the Narnian lords."

Shasta tried to get out of the way and to make Bree go back. But no horse, not even a Talking Horse from Narnia, backs easily. And a woman with a very edgy basket in her hands, who was just behind Shasta, pushed the basket hard against his shoulders, and said, "Now then! Who are you shoving!" And then someone else jostled him from the side and in the confusion of the moment he lost hold of Bree. And then the whole crowd behind him became so stiffened and packed tight that he couldn't move at all. So he found himself, unintentionally, in the first row and had a fine sight of the party that was coming down the street.

It was quite unlike any other party they had seen that day. The crier who went before it shouting "Way, way!" was the only Calormene in it. And there was no litter; everyone was on foot. There were about half a dozen men and Shasta had never seen anyone like them before. For one thing, they were all as fair-skinned as himself, and most of them had fair hair. And they were not dressed like men of Calormen. Most of them had legs bare to the knee. Their tunics were of fine, bright, hardy colours – woodland green, or gay yellow, or fresh blue. Instead of turbans they wore steel or silver caps, some of them set with jewels, and one with little wings on each side of it. A few were bare-headed. The swords at their sides were long and straight, not curved like Calormene scimitars. And instead of being grave and mysterious like most Calormenes, they walked with a swing and let their arms and shoulders go free, and chatted and laughed. One was whistling. You could see that they were ready to be friends with anyone who was friendly and didn't give a fig for anyone who wasn't. Shasta thought he had never seen anything so lovely in his life.

But there was not time to enjoy it for at once a really dreadful thing happened. The leader of the fair-headed men suddenly pointed at Shasta, cried out, "There he is! There's our runaway!" and seized him by the shoulder. Next moment he gave Shasta a smack – not a cruel one to make you cry but a sharp one to let you know you are in disgrace – and added, shaking:

"Shame on you, my lord! Fie for shame! Queen Susan's eyes are red with weeping because of you. What! Truant for a whole night! Where have you been?"

Shasta would have darted under Bree's body and tried to make himself scarce in the crowd if he had had the least chance; but the fair-haired men were all round him by now and he was held firm.

Of course his first impulse was to say that he was only poor Arsheesh the fisherman's son and that the foreign lord must have mistaken him for someone else. But then, the very last thing he wanted to do in that crowded place was to start explaining who he was and what he was doing. If he started on that, he would soon be asked where he had got his horse from, and who Aravis was – and then, goodbye to any chance of getting through Tashbaan. His next impulse was to look at Bree for help. But Bree had no intention of letting all the crowd know that he could talk, and stood looking just as stupid as a horse can. As for Aravis, Shasta did not even dare to look at her for fear of drawing attention. And there was no time to think, for the leader of the Narnians said at once:

"Take one of his little lordship's hands, Peridan, of your courtesy, and I'll take the other. And now, on. Our royal sister's mind will be greatly eased when she sees our young scapegrace safe in our lodging."

And so, before they were half-way through Tashbaan, all their plans were ruined, and without even a chance to say good-bye to the others Shasta found himself being marched off among strangers and quite unable to guess what might be going to happen next. The Narnian King – for Shasta began to see by the way the rest spoke to him that he must be a king – kept on asking him questions; where he had been, how he had got out, what he had done with his clothes, and didn't he know that he had been very naughty. Only the king called it "naught" instead of naughty.

And Shasta said nothing in answer, because he couldn't think of anything to say that would not be dangerous.

"What! All mum?" asked the king. "I must plainly tell you, prince, that this hangdog silence becomes one of your blood even less than the scape itself. To run away might pass for a boy's frolic with some spirit in it. But the king's son of Archenland should avouch his deed; not hang his head like a Calormene slave."

This was very unpleasant, for Shasta felt all the time that this young king was the very nicest kind of grown-up and would have liked to make a good impression on him.

The strangers led him – held tightly by both hands – along a narrow street and down a flight of shallow stairs and then up another to a wide doorway in a white wall with two tall, dark cypress trees, one on each side of it. Once through the arch, Shasta found himself in a courtyard which was also a garden. A marble basin of clear water in the centre was kept continually rippling by the fountain that fell into it. Orange trees grew round it out of smooth grass, and the four white walls which surrounded the lawn were covered with climbing roses. The noise and dust and crowding of the streets seemed suddenly far away. He was led rapidly across the garden and then into a dark doorway. The crier remained outside. After that they took him along a corridor, where the stone floor felt beautifully cool to his hot feet, and up some stairs. A moment later he found himself blinking in the light of a big, airy room with wide open windows, all looking North so that no sun came in. There was a carpet on the floor more wonderfully coloured than anything he had ever seen and his feet sank down into it as if he were treading in thick moss. All round the walls there were low sofas with rich cushions on them, and the room seemed to be full of people; very queer people some of them, thought Shasta. But he had no time to think of that before the most beautiful lady he had ever seen rose from her place and threw her arms round him and kissed him, saying:

"Oh Corin, Corin, how could you? And thou and I such close friends ever since thy mother died. And what should I have said to thy royal father if I came home without thee? Would have been a cause almost of war between Archenland and Narnia which are friends time out of mind. It was naught, playmate, very naught of thee to use us so."

"Apparently," thought Shasta to himself, "I'm being mistaken for a prince of Archenland, wherever that is. And these must be the Narnians. I wonder where the real Corin is?" But these thoughts did not help him say anything out loud.

"Where hast been, Corin?" said the lady, her hands still on Shasta's shoulders.

"I – I don't know," stammered Shasta.

"There it is, Susan," said the King. "I could get no tale out of him, true or false."

"Your Majesties! Queen Susan! King Edmund!" said a voice: and when Shasta turned to look at the speaker he nearly jumped out of his skin with surprise. For this was one of these queer people whom he had noticed out of the corner of his eye when he first came into the room. He was about the same height as Shasta himself. From the waist upwards he was like a man, but his legs were hairy like a goat's, and shaped like a goat's and he had goat's hooves and a tail. His skin was rather red and he had curly hair and a short pointed beard and two little horns. He was in fact a Faun, which is a creature Shasta had never seen a picture of or even heard of. And if you've read a book called *The Lion, the Witch and the Wardrobe* you may like to know that this was the very same Faun, Tumnus by name, whom Queen Susan's sister Lucy had met on the very first day when she found her way into Narnia. But he was a good deal older now for by this time Peter and Susan and Edmund and Lucy had been Kings and Queens of Narnia for several years.

"Your Majesties," he was saying, "His little Highness has had a touch of the sun. Look at him! He is dazed. He does not know where he is."

Then of course everyone stopped scolding Shasta and asking him questions and he was made much of and laid on a sofa and cushions were put under his head and he was given iced sherbet in a golden cup to drink and told to keep very quiet.

Nothing like this had ever happened to Shasta in his life before. He had never even imagined lying on anything so comfortable as that sofa or drinking anything so delicious as that sherbet. He was still wondering what had happened to the others and how on earth he was going to escape and meet them at the Tombs, and what would happen when the real Corin turned up again. But none of these worries seemed so pressing now that he was comfortable. And perhaps, later on, there would be nice things to eat!

Meanwhile the people in that cool airy room were very interesting. Besides the Faun there were two Dwarfs (a kind of creature he had never seen before) and a very large Raven.

The rest were all humans; grown-ups, but young, and all of them, both men and women, had nicer faces and voices than most Calormenes. And soon Shasta found himself taking an interest in the conversation. "Now, Madam," the King was saying to Queen Susan (the lady who had kissed Shasta). "What think you? We have been in this city fully three weeks. Have you yet settled in your mind whether you will marry this dark-faced lover of yours, this Prince Rabadash, or no?"

The lady shook her head. "No, brother," she said, "not for all the jewels in Tashbaan." ("Hullo!" thought Shasta. "Although they're king and queen, they're brother and sister, not married to one another.")

"Truly, sister," said the King, "I should have loved you the less if you had taken him. And I tell you that at the first coming of the Tisroc's ambassadors into Narnia to treat of this marriage, and later when the Prince was our guest at Cair Paravel, it was a wonder to me that ever you could find it in your heart to show him so much favour."

"That was my folly, Edmund," said Queen Susan, "of which I cry you mercy. Yet when he was with us in Narnia, truly this Prince bore himself in another fashion than he does now in Tashbaan. For I take you all to witness what marvellous feats he did in that great tournament and hastilude which our brother the High King made for him, and how meekly and courteously he consorted with us the space of seven days. But here, in his own city, he has shown another face."

"Ah!" croaked the Raven. "It is an old saying: see the bear in his own den before you judge of his conditions."

"That's very true, Sallowpad," said one of the Dwarfs. "And another is, Come, live with me and you'll know me."

"Yes," said the King. "We have now seen him for what he is: that is, a most proud, bloody, luxurious, cruel, and self-pleasing tryant."

"Then in the name of Aslan," said Susan, "let us leave Tashbaan this very day."

"There's the rub, sister," said Edmund. "For now I must open to you all that has been growing in my mind these last two days and more. Peridan, of your courtesy look to the door and see that there is no spy upon us. All well? So. For now we must be secret."

Everyone had begun to look very serious. Queen Susan jumped up and ran to her brother. "Oh, Edmund," she cried. "What is it? There is something dreadful in your face."

CHAPTER FIVE

PRINCE CORIN

"My dear sister and very good Lady," said King Edmund, "you must now show your courage. For I tell you plainly we are in no small danger."

"What is it, Edmund?" asked the Queen.

"It is this," said Edmund. "I do not think we shall find it easy to leave Tashbaan. While the Prince had hope that you would take him, we were honoured guests. But by the Lion's Mane, I think that as soon as he has your flat denial we shall be no better than prisoners."

One of the Dwarfs gave a low whistle.

"I warned your Majesties, I warned you," said Sallowpad the Raven. "Easily in but not easily out, as the lobster said in the lobster pot!"

"I have been with the Prince this morning," continued Edmund. "He is little used (more's the pity) to having his will crossed. And he is very chafed at your long delays and doubtful answers. This morning he pressed very hard to know your mind. I put it aside – meaning at the same time to diminish his hopes – with some light common jests about women's fancies, and hinted that his suit was likely to be cold. He grew angry and dangerous. There was a sort of threatening, though still veiled under a show of courtesy, in every word he spoke."

"Yes," said Tumnus. "And when I supped with the Grand Vizier last night, it was the same. He asked me how I like Tashbaan. And I (for I could not tell him I hated every stone of it and I would not lie) told him that now, when high summer was coming on, my heart turned to the cool woods and dewy slopes of Narnia. He gave a smile that meant no good and said, 'There is nothing to hinder you from dancing there again, little goatfoot; *always provided you leave us in exchange a bride for our prince.'*"

"Do you mean he would make me his wife by force?" exclaimed Susan.

"That's my fear, Susan," said Edmund. "Wife: or slave which is worse."

"But how can he? Does the Tisroc think our brother the High King would suffer such an outrage?"

"Sire," said Peridan to the King. "They would not be so mad. Do they think there are no swords and spears in Narnia?"

"Alas," said Edmund. "My guess is that the Tisroc has very small fear of Narnia. We are a little land. And little lands on the borders of a great empire were always hateful to the lords of the great empire. He longs to blot them out, gobble them up. When first he suffered the Prince to come to Cair Paravel as your lover, sister, it may be that he was only seeking an occasion against us. Most likely he hopes to make one mouthful of Narnia and Archenland both."

"Let him try," said the second Dwarf. "At sea we are as big as he is. And if he assaults us by land, he has the desert to cross."

"True, friend," said Edmund. "But is the desert a sure defence? What does Sallowpad say?"

"I knew that desert well," said the Raven. "For I have flown above it far and wide in my younger days," (you may be sure that Shasta pricked up his ears at this point). "And this is certain; that if the Tisroc goes by the great oasis he can never lead a great army across it into Archenland. For though they could reach the oasis by the end of their first day's march, yet the springs there would be too little for the thirst of all those soldiers and their beasts. But there is another way."

Shasta listened more attentively still.

"He that would find that way," said the Raven, "must start from the Tombs of the Ancient Kings and ride northwest so that the double peak of Mount Pire is always straight ahead of him. And so, in a day's riding or a little more, he shall come to the head of a stony valley, which is so narrow that a man might be within a furlong of it a thousand times and never know that it was there. And looking down this valley he will see neither grass nor water nor anything else good. But if he rides on down it he will come to a river and can ride by the water all the way into Archenland."

"And do the Calormenes know of this Western way?" asked the Queen.

"Friends, friends," said Edmund, "what is the use of all this discourse? We are not asking whether Narnia or Calormen would win if war arose between them. We are asking how to save the honour of the Queen and our own lives out of this devilish city. For though my brother, Peter the High King, defeated the Tisroc a dozen times over, yet long before that day our throats would be cut and the Queen's grace would be the wife, or more likely, the slave, of this prince."

"We have our weapons, King," said the first Dwarf. "And this is a reasonably defensible house."

"As to that," said the King, "I do not doubt that every one of us would sell our lives dearly in the gate and they would not come at the Queen but over our dead bodies. Yet we should be merely rats fighting in a trap when all's said."

"Very true," croaked the Raven. "These last stands in a house make good stories, but nothing ever came of them. After their first few repulses the enemy always set the house on fire."

"I am the cause of all this," said Susan, bursting into tears. "Oh, if only I had never left Cair Paravel. Our last happy day was before those ambassadors came from Calormen. The Moles were planting an orchard for us . . . oh . . . oh."

And she buried her face in her hands and sobbed.

"Courage, Su, courage," said Edmund. "Remember – but what is the matter with *you*, Master Tumnus?" For the Faun was holding both his horns with his hands as if he were trying to keep his head on by them and writhing to and fro as if he had a pain in his inside.

"Don't speak to me, don't speak to me," said Tumnus. "I'm thinking. I'm thinking so that I can hardly breathe. Wait, wait, do wait."

There was a moment's puzzled silence and then the Faun looked up, drew a long breath, mopped its forehead and said:

"The only difficulty is how to get down to our ship – with some stores, too – without being seen and stopped."

"Yes," said a Dwarf dryly. "Just as the beggar's only difficulty about riding is that he has no horse."

"Wait, wait," said Mr Tumnus impatiently. "All we need is some pretext for going down to our ship today and taking stuff on board."

"Yes," said King Edmund doubtfully.

"Well, then," said the Faun, "how would it be if your majesties bade the Prince to a great banquet to be held on board our own galleon, the *Spendour Hyaline*, tomorrow night? And let the message be worded as graciously as the Queen can contrive without pledging her honour: so as to give the Prince a hope that she is weakening."

"This is very good counsel, Sire," croaked the Raven.

"And then," continued Tumnus excitedly, "everyone will expect us to be going down to the ship all day, making preparations for our guests. And let some of us go to the bazaars and spend every minim we have at the fruiterers and the sweetmeat sellers and the wine merchants, just as we would if we were really giving a feast. And let us order magicians and jugglers and dancing girls and flute players, all to be on board tomorrow night."

"I see, I see," said King Edmund, rubbing his hands.

"And then," said Tumnus, "we'll all be on board tonight. And as soon as it is quite dark –"

"Up sails and out oars –!" said the King.

"And so to sea," cried Tumnus, leaping up and beginning to dance.

"And our nose Northward," said the first Dwarf.

"Running for home! Hurrah for Narnia and the North!" said the other.

"And the Prince waking next morning and finding his birds flown!" said Peridan, clapping his hands.

"Oh Master Tumnus, dear Master Tumnus," said the Queen, catching his hands and swinging with him as he danced. "You have saved us all."

"The Prince will chase us," said another lord, whose name Shasta had not heard.

"That's the least of my fears," said Edmund. "I have seen all the shipping in the river and there's no tall ship of war nor swift galley there. I wish he may chase us! For the *Splendour Hyaline* could sink anything he has to send after her – if we were overtaken at all."

"Sire," said the Raven. "You shall hear no better plot than the Faun's though we sat in council for seven days. And now, as we birds say, nests before eggs. Which is as much as to say, let us all take our food and then at once be about our business."

Everyone arose at this and the doors were opened and the lords and the creatures stood aside for the King and Queen to go out first. Shasta wondered what he ought to do, but Mr Tumnus said, "Lie there, your Highness, and I will bring you up a little feast to yourself in a few moments. There is no need for you to move until we are all ready to embark."

Shasta laid his head down again on the pillows and soon he was alone in the room.

"This is perfectly dreadful," thought Shasta. It never came into his head to tell these Narnians the whole truth and ask for their help. Having been brought up by a hard, close-fisted man like Arsheesh, he had a fixed habit of never telling

grown-ups anything if he could help it: he thought they would always spoil or stop whatever you were trying to do. And he thought that even if the Narnian King might be friendly to the two horses, because they were Talking Beasts of Narnia, he would hate Aravis, because she was a Calormene, and either sell her for a slave or send her back to her father. As for himself, "I simply daren't tell them I'm not Prince Corin *now*," thought Shasta. "I've heard all their plans. If they knew I wasn't one of themselves, they'd never let me out of this house alive. They'd be afraid I'd betray them to the Tisroc. They'd kill me. And if the real Corin turns up, it'll all come out, and they *will*!" He had, you see, no idea of how noble and free-born people behave.

"What am I to do? What am I to do?" he kept saying to

himself. "What – hullo, here comes that goaty little creature again."

The Faun trotted in, half dancing, with a tray in its hands which was nearly as large as itself. This he set on an inlaid table beside Shasta's sofa, and sat down himself on the carpeted floor with his goaty legs crossed.

"Now, princeling," he said. "Make a good dinner. It will be your last meal in Tashbaan."

It was a fine meal after the Calormene fashion. I don't know whether you would have liked it or not, but Shasta did. There were lobsters, and salad, and snipe stuffed with almonds and truffles, and a complicated dish made of chicken-livers and rice and raisins and nuts, and there were cool melons and gooseberry fools and mulberry fools, and every kind of nice thing that can be made with ice. There was also a little flagon of the sort of wine that is called "white" though it is really yellow.

While Shasta was eating, the good little Faun, who thought he was still dazed with sunstroke, kept talking to him about the fine times he would have when they all got home; about his good old father King Lune of Archenland and the little castle where he lived on the southern slopes of the pass. "And don't forget," said Mr Tumnus, "that you are promised your first suit of armour and your first war horse on your next birthday. And then your Highness will begin to learn how to tilt and joust. And in a few years, if all goes well, King Peter has promised your royal father that he himself will make you Knight at Cair Paravel. And in the meantime there will be plenty of comings and goings between Narnia and Archenland across the neck of the mountains. And of course you remember you have promised to come for a whole week to stay with me for the Summer Festival, and there'll be bonfires and all-night dances of Fauns and Dryads in the heart of the woods and, who knows? – we might see Aslan himself!"

When the meal was over the Faun told Shasta to stay quietly where he was. "And it wouldn't do you any harm to have a little sleep," he added. "I'll call you in plenty of time to get on board. And then, Home. Narnia and the North!"

Shasta had so enjoyed his dinner and all the things Tumnus had been telling him that when he was left alone his thoughts took a different turn. He only hoped now that the real Prince Corin would not turn up until it was too late and that he would be taken away to Narnia by ship. I am afraid he did not think at all of what might happen to the real Corin when he was left behind in Tashbaan. He was a little worried about Aravis and Bree waiting for him at the Tombs. But then he said to himself, "Well, how can I help it?" and, "Anyway, that Aravis thinks she's too good to go about with me, so she can jolly well go alone," and at the same time he couldn't help feeling that it would be much nicer going to Narnia by sea than toiling across the desert.

When he had thought all this he did what I expect you would have done if you had been up very early and had a long walk and a great deal of excitement and then a very good meal, and were lying on a sofa in a cool room with no noise in it except when a bee came buzzing in through the wide open windows. He fell asleep.

What woke him was a loud crash. He jumped up off the

sofa, staring. He saw at once from the mere look of the room – the lights and shadows all looked different – that he must have slept for several hours. He saw also what had made the crash: a costly porcelain vase which had been standing on the window-sill lay on the floor broken into about thirty pieces. But he hardly noticed all these things. What he did

notice was two hands gripping the window-sill from outside. They gripped harder and harder (getting white at the knuckles) and then up came a head and a pair of shoulders. A moment later there was a boy of Shasta's own age sitting astride the sill with one leg hanging down inside the room.

Shasta had never seen his own face in a looking-glass. Even if he had, he might not have realized that the other boy was (at ordinary times) almost exactly like himself. At the moment this boy was not particularly like anyone for he had the finest black eye you ever saw, and a tooth missing, and his clothes (which must have been splendid ones when he put them on) were torn and dirty, and there was both blood and mud on his face.

"Who are you?" said the boy in a whisper.

"Are you Prince Corin?" said Shasta.

"Yes, of course," said the other. "But who are you?"

"I'm nobody, nobody in particular, I mean," said Shasta. "King Edmund caught me in the street and mistook me for you. I suppose we must look like one another. Can I get out the way you've got in?"

"Yes, if you're any good at climbing," said Corin. "But why are you in such a hurry? I say: we ought to be able to get some fun out of this being mistaken for one another."

"No, no," said Shasta. "We must change places at once. It'll be simply frightful if Mr Tumnus comes back and finds us both here. I've had to pretend to be you. And you're starting tonight – secretly. And where were you all this time?"

"A boy in the street made a beastly joke about Queen Susan," said Prince Corin, "so I knocked him down. He ran howling into a house and his big brother came out. So I knocked the big brother down. Then they all followed me until we ran into three old men with spears who are called the Watch. So I fought the Watch and they knocked me down. It was getting dark by now. Then the Watch took me along to lock me up somewhere. So I asked them if they'd like a stoup of wine and they said they didn't mind if they did. Then I took them to a wine shop and got them some and they all sat down and drank till they feel asleep. I thought it was time for me to be off so I came out quietly and then I found the first boy – the one who had started all the trouble – still hanging about. So I knocked him down again. After that I climbed up a pipe on to the roof of a house and lay quiet till it began to get light this morning. Ever since that I've been finding my way back. I say, is there anything to drink?"

"No, I drank it," said Shasta. "And now, show me how

you got in. There's not a minute to lose. You'd better lie down on the sofa and pretend – but I forgot. It'll be no good with all those bruises and black eye. You'll just have to tell them the truth, once I'm safely away."

"What else did you think I'd be telling them?" asked the Prince with a rather angry look. "And who are *you*?"

"There's no time," said Shasta in a frantic whisper. "I'm a Narnian, I believe; something Northern anyway. But I've been brought up all my life in Calormen. And I'm escaping: across the desert; with a talking Horse called Bree. And now, quick! How do I get away?"

"Look," said Corin. "Drop from this window on to the roof of the verandah. But you must do it lightly, on your toes, or someone will hear you. Then along to your left and you can get up to the top of that wall if you're any good at all as a climber. Then along the wall to the corner. Drop onto the rubbish heap you will find outside, and there you are."

"Thanks," said Shasta, who was already sitting on the sill. The two boys were looking into each other's faces and suddenly found that they were friends.

"Good-bye," said Corin. "And *good* luck. I do hope you get safe away."

"Good-bye," said Shasta. "I say, you have been having some adventures."

"Nothing to yours," said the Prince. "Now drop; lightly – I say," he added as Shasta dropped. "I hope we meet in Archenland. Go to my father King Lune and tell him you're a friend of mine. Look out! I hear someone coming."

CHAPTER SIX

SHASTA AMONG THE TOMBS

SHASTA ran lightly along the roof on tiptoes. It felt hot to his bare feet. He was only a few seconds scrambling up the wall at the far end and when he got to the corner he found himself looking down into a narrow, smelly street, and there was a rubbish heap against the outside of the wall just as Corin had told him. Before jumping down he took a rapid glance round him to get his bearings. Apparently he had now come over the crown of the island-hill on which Tashbaan is built. Everything sloped away before him, flat roofs below flat roofs, down to the towers and battlements of the city's Northern wall. Beyond that was the river and beyond the river a short slope covered with gardens. But beyond that again there was something he had never seen the like of – a great yellowish-grey thing, flat as a calm sea, and stretching for miles. On the far side of it were huge blue things, lumpy but with jagged edges, and some of them with white tops. "The desert! the mountains!" thought Shasta.

He jumped down on to the rubbish and began trotting along downhill as fast as he could in the narrow lane, which soon brought him into a wider street where there were more people. No one bothered to look at a little ragged boy running along on bare feet. Still, he was anxious and uneasy till he turned a corner and there saw the city gate in front of him. Here he was pressed and jostled a bit, for a good many other people were also going out; and on the bridge beyond the gate the crowd became quite a slow procession, more like a queue than a crowd. Out there, with clear running water on each side, it was deliciously fresh after the smell and heat and noise of Tashbaan.

When once Shasta had reached the far end of the bridge he

found the crowd melting away; everyone seemed to be going either to the left or right along the river bank. He went straight ahead up a road that did not appear to be much used, between gardens. In a few paces he was alone, and a few more brought him to the top of the slope. There he stood and stared. It was like coming to the end of the world for all the grass stopped quite suddenly a few feet before him and the sand began: endless level sand like on a sea shore but a bit rougher because it was never wet. The mountains, which now looked further off than before, loomed ahead. Greatly to his relief he saw, about five minutes' walk away on his left, what must certainly be the Tombs, just as Bree had described them; great masses of mouldering stone shaped like gigantic bee-hives, but a little narrower. They looked very black and grim, for the sun was now setting right behind them.

He turned his face West and trotted towards the Tombs. He could not help looking out very hard for any sign of his friends, though the setting sun shone in his face so that he could see hardly anything. "And anyway," he thought, "of course they'll be round on the far side of the farthest Tomb, not this side where anyone might see them from the city."

There were about twelve Tombs, each with a low arched doorway that opened into absolute blackness. They were dotted about in no kind of order, so that it took a long time, going round this one and going round that one, before you could be sure that you had looked round every side of every tomb. This was what Shasta had to do. There was nobody there.

It was very quiet here out on the edge of the desert; and now the sun had really set.

Suddenly from somewhere behind him there came a terrible sound. Shasta's heart gave a great jump and he had to bite his tongue to keep himself from screaming. Next

moment he realized what it was: the horns of Tashbaan
blowing for the closing of the gates. "Don't be a silly little
coward," said Shasta to himself. "Why, it's only the same
noise you heard this morning." But there is a great difference between a noise heard letting you in with your friends
in the morning, and a noise heard alone at nightfall, shutting

you out. And now that the gates were shut he knew there
was no chance of the others joining him that evening.
"Either they're shut up in Tashbaan for the night," thought
Shasta, "or else they've gone on without me. It's just the sort
of thing that Aravis would do. But Bree wouldn't. Oh, he
wouldn't. – now, would he?"

In this idea about Aravis Shasta was once more quite
wrong. She was proud and could be hard enough but she
was as true as steel and would never have deserted a companion, whether she liked him or not.

Now that Shasta knew he would have to spend the night
alone (it was getting darker every minute) he began to like
the look of the place less and less. There was something very

uncomfortable about those great, silent shapes of stone. He had been trying his hardest for a long time not to think of ghouls: but he couldn't keep it up any longer.

"Ow! Ow! Help!" he shouted suddenly, for at that very moment he felt something touch his leg. I don't think anyone can be blamed for shouting if something comes up from behind and touches him; not in such a place and at such a time, when he is frightened already. Shasta at any rate was too frightened to run. Anything would be better than being chased round and round the burial places of the Ancient Kings with something he dared not look at behind him. Instead, he did what was really the most sensible thing he could do. He looked round; and his heart almost burst with relief. What had touched him was only a cat.

The light was too bad now for Shasta to see much of the cat except that it was big and very solemn. It looked as if it might have lived for long, long years among the Tombs, alone. Its eyes made you think it knew secrets it would not tell.

"Puss, puss," said Shasta. "I suppose you're not a *talking* cat."

The cat stared at him harder than ever. Then it started walking away, and of course Shasta followed it. It led him right through the tombs and out on the desert side of them. There it sat down bolt upright with its tail curled round its feet and its face set towards the desert and towards Narnia and the North, as still as if it were watching for some enemy. Shasta lay down beside it with his back against the cat and his face towards the Tombs, because if one is nervous there's nothing like having your face towards the danger and having something warm and solid at your back. The sand wouldn't have seemed very comfortable to you, but Shasta had been sleeping on the ground for weeks and hardly noticed it. Very soon he fell asleep, though even in his dreams he went on wondering what had happened to Bree and Aravis and Hwin.

He was wakened suddenly by a noise he had never heard before. "Perhaps it was only a nightmare," said Shasta to himself. At the same moment he noticed that the cat had gone from his back, and he wished it hadn't. But he lay quite still without even opening his eyes because he felt sure he would be more frightened if he sat up and looked round at the Tombs and the loneliness: just as you or I might lie still with the clothes over our heads. But then the noise came again – a harsh, piercing cry from behind him out of the desert. Then of course he had to open his eyes and sit up.

The moon was shining brightly. The Tombs – far bigger and nearer than he had thought they would be – looked grey in the moonlight. In fact, they looked horribly like huge people, draped in grey robes that covered their heads and faces. They were not at all nice things to have near you when spending a night alone in a strange place. But the noise had come from the opposite side, from the desert. Shasta had to turn his back on the Tombs (he didn't like that much) and stare out across the level sand. The wild cry rang out again.

"I hope it's not more lions," thought Shasta. It was in fact not very like the lion's roars he had heard on the night when they met Hwin and Aravis, and was really the cry of a jackal. But of course Shasta did not know this. Even if he had known, he would not have wanted very much to meet a jackal.

The cries rang out again and again. "There's more than one of them, whatever they are," thought Shasta. "And they're coming nearer."

I suppose that if he had been an entirely sensible boy he would have gone back through the Tombs nearer to the river where there were houses, and wild beasts would be less likely to come. But then there were (or he thought there were) the ghouls. To go back through the Tombs would mean going past those dark openings in the Tombs; and what might come out of them? It may have been silly, but Shasta felt he would rather risk the wild beasts. Then, as the cries came nearer and nearer, he began to change his mind.

He was just going to run for it when suddenly, between him and the desert, a huge animal bounded into view. As the moon was behind it, it looked quite black, and Shasta did not know what it was, except that it had a very big, shaggy head and went on four legs. It did not seem to have noticed Shasta, for it suddenly stopped, turned its head towards the desert and let out a roar which re-echoed through the Tombs and seemed to shake the sand under Shasta's feet. The cries of the other creatures suddenly stoppd and he thought he could hear feet scampering away. Then the great beast turned to examine Shasta.

"It's a lion, I know it's a lion," thought Shasta. "I'm done. I wonder will it hurt much. I wish it was over. I wonder does anything happen to people after they're dead. O-o-oh! Here it comes!" And he shut his eyes and his teeth tight.

But instead of teeth and claws he only felt something warm lying down at his feet. And when he opened his eyes he said, "Why, it's not nearly as big as I thought! It's only half the size. No, it isn't even quarter the size. I do declare it's only the cat!! I must have dreamed all that about its being as big as a horse."

And whether he really had been dreaming or not, what was now lying at his feet, and staring him out of countenance with its big, green, unwinking eyes, was the cat; though certainly one of the largest cats he had ever seen.

"Oh, Puss," gasped Shasta. "I *am* so glad to see you again. I've been having such horrible dreams." And he at once lay down again, back to back with the cat as they had been at the beginning of the night. The warmth from it spread all over him.

"I'll never do anything nasty to a cat again as long as I live," said Shasta, half to the cat and half to himself. "I did once, you know. I threw stones at a half-starved mangy old stray. Hey! Stop that." For the cat had turned round and given him a scratch. "None of that," said Shasta. "It isn't as if you could understand what I'm saying." Then he dozed off.

Next morning when he woke, the cat was gone, the sun was already up, and the sand hot. Shasta, very thirsty, sat up and rubbed his eyes. The desert was blindingly white and, though there was a murmur of noises from the city behind him, where he sat everything was perfectly still. When he looked a little left and west, so that the sun was not in his eyes, he could see the mountains on the far side of the desert, so sharp and clear that they looked only a stone's throw away. He particularly noticed one blue height that divided into two peaks at the top and decided that it must be Mount Pire. "That's our direction, judging by what the Raven said," he thought, "so I'll just make sure of it, so as not to waste any time when the others turn up." So he made a good, deep straight furrow with his foot pointing exactly to Mount Pire.

The next job, clearly, was to get something to eat and drink. Shasta trotted back through the Tombs – they looked quite ordinary now and he wondered how he could ever have been afraid of them – and down into the cultivated land by the river's side. There were a few people about but not very many, for the city gates had been open several hours and the early morning crowds had already gone in. So he had no diffculty in doing a little "raiding" (as Bree called it). It involved a climb over a garden wall and the results were three oranges, a melon, a fig or two, and a pomegranate. After that, he went down to the river bank, but not too near the bridge, and had a drink. The water was so nice that he took off his hot, dirty clothes and had a dip; for of course Shasta, having lived on the shore all his life, had learned to swim almost as soon as he had learned to walk. When he came out he lay on the grass looking across the water at Tashbaan – all the splendour and strength and glory of it. But that made him remember the dangers of it too. He suddenly realized that the others might have reached the Tombs while he was bathing ("and gone on without me, as likely as not"), so he dressed in a fright and tore back at such a speed that he was all hot and thirsty when he arrived and so the good of his bathe was gone.

Like most days when you are alone and waiting for something this day seemed about a hundred hours long. He had plenty to think of, of course, but sitting alone, just thinking, is pretty slow. He thought a good deal about the Narnians and especially about Corin. He wondered what had happened when they discovered that the boy who had been lying on the sofa and hearing all their secret plans wasn't really Corin at all. It was very unpleasant to think of all those nice people imagining him a traitor.

But as the sun slowly, slowly climbed up to the top of the sky and then slowly, slowly began going downwards to the West, and no one came and nothing at all happened, he began to get more and more anxious. And of course he now realized that when they arranged to wait for one another at the Tombs no one had said anything about How Long. He couldn't wait here for the rest of his life! And soon it would be dark again, and he would have another night just like last night. A dozen different plans went through his head, all wretched ones, and at last he fixed on the worst plan of all. He decided to wait till it was dark and then go back to the river and steal as many melons as he could carry and set out for Mount Pire alone, trusting for his direction to the line he had drawn that morning in the sand. It was a crazy idea and if he had read as many books as you have about journeys over deserts he would never have dreamed of it. But Shasta had read no books at all.

Before the sun set something did happen. Shasta was sitting in the shadow of one of the Tombs when he looked up and saw two horses coming towards him. Then his heart gave a great leap, for he recognized them as Bree and Hwin. But the next moment his heart went down into his toes again. There was no sign of Aravis. The Horses were being led by a strange man, an armed man pretty handsomely dressed like an upper slave in a great family. Bree and Hwin were no longer got up like pack-horses, but saddled and bridled. And what could it all mean? "It's a trap," thought Shasta. "Somebody has caught Aravis and perhaps they've tortured her and she's given the whole thing away. They want me to jump out and run up and speak to Bree and then I'll be caught too! And yet if I don't, I may be losing my only chance to meet the others. Oh I do wish I knew what had happened." And he skulked behind the Tomb, looking out every few minutes, and wondering which was the least dangerous thing to do.

CHAPTER SEVEN

ARAVIS IN TASHBAAN

WHAT had really happened was this. When Aravis saw
Shasta hurried away by the Narnians and found herself
alone with two horses who (very wisely) wouldn't say a
word, she never lost her head even for a moment. She grabbed Bree's halter and stood still, holding both the horses;
and though her heart was beating as hard as a hammer, she
did nothing to show it. As soon as the Narnian lords had
passed she tried to move on again. But before she could take
a step, another crier ("Bother all these people" thought
Aravis) was heard shouting out, "Way, way, way! Way for
the Tarkheena Lasaraleen!" and immediately, following the
crier, came four armed slaves and then four bearers carrying
a litter which was all a-flutter with silken curtains and all
a-jingle with silver bells and which scented the whole street
with perfumes and flowers. After the litter, female slaves in
beautiful clothes, and then a few grooms, runners, pages,
and the like. And now Aravis made her first mistake.

She knew Lasaraleen quite well – almost as if they had
been at school together – because they had often stayed in
the same houses and been to the same parties. And Aravis
couldn't help looking up to see what Lasaraleen looked like
now that she was married and a very great person indeed.

It was fatal. The eyes of the two girls met. And
immediately Lasaraleen sat up in the litter and burst out at
the top of her voice.

"Aravis! What on earth are you doing here? Your father –"

There was not a moment to lose. Without a second's delay
Aravis let go the Horses, caught the edge of the litter, swung
herself up beside Lasaraleen and whispered furiously in her
ear.

"Shut up! Do you hear! Shut up. You must hide me. Tell your people —"

"But darling —" began Lasaraleen in the same loud voice. (She didn't in the least mind making people stare; in fact she rather liked it.)

"Do what I tell you or I'll never speak to you again," hissed Aravis. "Please, please be quick, Las. It's frightfully important. Tell your people to bring those two horses along. Pull all the curtains of the litter and get away somewhere where I can't be found. And do *hurry*."

"All right, darling," said Lasaraleen in her lazy voice. "Here. Two of you take the Tarkheena's horses." (This was to the slaves.) "And now home. I say, darling, do you think we really want the curtains drawn on a day like this? I mean to say—"

But Aravis had already drawn the curtains, enclosing Lasaraleen and herself in a rich and scented, but rather stuffy, kind of tent.

"I mustn't be seen," she said. "My father doesn't know I'm here. I'm running away."

"My dear, how perfectly thrilling," said Lasaraleen. "I'm dying to hear all about it. Darling, you're sitting on my dress. Do you mind? That's better. It is a new one. Do you like it? I got it at—"

"Oh, Las, do be serious," said Aravis. "Where is my father?"

"Didn't you know?" said Lasaraleen. "He's here, of course. He came to town yesterday and is asking about you everywhere. And to think of you and me being here together and his not knowing anything about it! It's the funniest thing I ever heard." And she went off into giggles. She always had been a terrible giggler, as Aravis now remembered.

"It isn't funny at all," she said. "It's dreadfully serious. Where can you hide me?"

"No difficulty at all, my dear girl," said Lasaraleen. "I'll take you home. My husband's away and no one will see you. Phew! It's not much fun with the curtains drawn. I want to see people. There's no point in having a new dress on if one's to go about shut up like this."

"I hope no one heard you when you shouted out to me like that," said Aravis.

"No, no, of course, darling," said Lasaraleen absentmindedly. "But you haven't even told me yet what you think of the dress."

"Another thing," said Aravis. "You must tell your people

to treat those two horses very respectfully. That's part of the secret. They're really Talking Horses from Narnia."

"Fancy!" said Lasaraleen. "How exciting! And oh, darling, have you seen the barbarian queen from Narnia? She's staying in Tashbaan at present. They say Prince Rabadash is madly in love with her. There have been the most wonderful parties and hunts and things all this last fortnight. I can't see that she's so very pretty myself. But some of the Narnian *men* are lovely. I was taken out on a river party the day before yesterday, and I was wearing my –"

"How shall we prevent your people telling everyone that you've got a visitor – dressed like a beggar's brat – in your house? It might so easily get round to my father."

"Now don't keep on fussing, there's a dear," said Lasaraleen. "We'll get you some proper clothes in a moment. And here we are!"

The bearers had stopped and the litter was being lowered. When the curtains had been drawn Aravis found that she was in a courtyard-garden very like the one that Shasta had been taken into a few minutes earlier in another part of the city. Lasaraleen would have gone indoors at once but Aravis reminded her in a frantic whisper to say something to the slaves about not telling anyone of their mistress's strange visitor.

"Sorry, darling, it had gone right out of my head," said Lasareleen. "Here. All of you. And you, doorkeeper. No one is to be let out of the house today. And anyone I catch talking about this young lady will be first beaten to death and then burned alive and after that be kept on bread and water for six weeks. There."

Although Lasaraleen had said she was dying to hear Aravis's story, she showed no sign of really wanting to hear it at all. She was, in fact, much better at talking than at listening. She insisted on Aravis having a long and luxurious bath (Calormene baths are famous) and then dressing her up in the finest clothes before she would let her explain anything. The fuss she made about choosing the dresses nearly drove Aravis mad. She remembered now that Lasaraleen had always been like that, interested in clothes and parties

and gossip. Aravis had always been more interested in bows and arrows and horses and dogs and swimming. You will guess that each thought the other silly. But when at last they were both seated after a meal (it was chiefly of the whipped cream and jelly and fruit and ice sort) in a beautiful pillared room (which Aravis would have liked better if Lasaraleen's spoiled pet monkey hadn't been climbing about it all the time) Lasaraleen at last asked her why she was running away from home.

When Aravis had finished telling her story, Lasaraleen said, "But, darling, why *don't* you marry Ahoshta Tarkaan? Everyone's crazy about him. My husband says he is beginning to be one of the greatest men in Calormen. He has just been made Grand Vizier now old Axartha has died. Didn't you know?"

"I don't care. I can't stand the sight of him," said Aravis.

"But, darling, only think! Three palaces, and one of them that beautiful one down on the lake at Ilkeen. Positively ropes of pearls, I'm told. Baths of asses' milk. And you'd see such a lot of *me*."

"He can keep his pearls and palaces as far as I'm concerned," said Aravis.

"You always *were* a queer girl, Aravis," said Lasaraleen. "What more *do* you want?"

In the end, however, Aravis managed to make her friend believe that she was in earnest and even to discuss plans. There would be no difficulty now about getting the two horses out of the North gate and then on to the Tombs. No one would stop or question a groom in fine clothes leading a war horse and a lady's saddle horse down to the river, and Lasaraleen had plenty of grooms to send. It wasn't so easy to decide what to do about Aravis herself. She suggested that she could be carried out in the litter with the curtains drawn. But Lasaraleen told her that litters were only used in the city and the sight of one going out through the gate would be certain to lead to questions.

When they had talked for a long time – and it was all the longer because Aravis found it hard to keep her friend to the point – at last Lasaraleen clapped her hands and said, "Oh, I have an idea. There is *one* way of getting out of the city without using the gates. The Tisroc's garden (may he live for ever!) runs right down to the water and there is a little water-door. Only for the palace people of course – but then you know, dear (here she tittered a little) we almost *are* palace people. I say, it is lucky for you that you came to *me*. The dear Tisroc (may he live for ever!) is *so* kind. We're asked to the palace almost every day and it is like a second home. I love all the dear princes and princesses and I positively *adore* Prince Rabadash. I might run in and see any of the palace ladies at any hour of the day or night. Why shouldn't I slip in with you, after dark, and let you out by the water-door? There are always a few punts and things tied up outside it. And even if we were caught –"

"All would be lost," said Aravis.

"Oh darling, don't get so excited," said Lasaraleen. "I was going to say, even if we were caught everyone would only say it was one of my mad jokes. I'm getting quite well known for them. Only the other day – do listen, dear, this is frightfully funny –"

"I meant, all would be lost *for me*," said Aravis a little sharply.

"Oh – ah – yes – I *do* see what you mean, darling. Well, can you think of any better plan?"

Aravis couldn't, and answered, "No. We'll have to risk it. When can we start?"

"Oh, not tonight," said Lasaraleen. "Of course not tonight. There's a great feast on tonight (I must start getting my hair done for it in a few minutes) and the whole place will be a blaze of lights. And such a crowd too! It would have to be tomorrow night."

This was bad news for Aravis, but she had to make the best of it. The afternoon passed very slowly and it was a relief when Lasaraleen went out to the banquet, for Aravis was very tired of her giggling and her talk about dresses and parties, weddings and engagements and scandals. She went to bed early and that part she did enjoy: it was so nice to have pillows and sheets again.

But the next day passed very slowly. Lasaraleen wanted to go back on the whole arrangement and kept on telling Aravis that Narnia was a country of perpetual snow and ice

inhabited by demons and sorcerers, and she was mad to
think of going there. "And with a peasant boy, too!" said
Lasaraleen. "Darling, think of it! It's not Nice." Aravis had
thought of it a good deal, but she was so tired of
Lasaraleen's silliness by now that, for the first time, she
began to think that travelling with Shasta was really rather
more fun than fashionable life in Tashbaan. So she only
replied, "You forget that I'll be nobody, just like him, when
we get to Narnia. And anyway, I promised."

"And to think," said Lasaraleen, almost crying, "that if
only you had sense you could be the wife of a Grand Vizier!"
Aravis went away to have a private word with the horses.

"You must go with a groom a little before sunset down to
the Tombs," she said. "No more of those packs. You'll be
saddled and bridled again. But there'll have to be food in
Hwin's saddle-bags and a full water-skin behind yours,
Bree. The man has orders to let you both have a good long
drink at the far side of the bridge."

"And then, Narnia and the North!" whispered Bree. "But
what if Shasta is not at the Tombs."

"Wait for him of course," said Aravis. "I hope you've
been quite comfortable."

"Never better stabled in my life," said Bree. "But if the
husband of that tittering Tarkheena friend of yours is paying his head groom to get the best oats, then I think the head
groom is cheating him."

Aravis and Lasaraleen had supper in the pillared room.

About two hours later they were ready to start. Aravis
was dressed to look like a superior slave-girl in a great house
and wore a veil over her face. They had agreed that if any
questions were asked Lasaraleen would pretend that Aravis
was a slave she was taking as a present to one of the
princesses.

The two girls went out on foot. A very few minutes

brought them to the palace gates. Here there were of course soldiers on guard but the officer knew Lasaraleen quite well and called his men to attention and saluted. They passed at once into the Hall of Black Marble. A fair number of courtiers, slaves and others were still moving about here but this only made the two girls less conspicuous. They passed on into the Hall of Pillars and then into the Hall of Statues and down the colonnade, passing the great beaten-copper doors of the throne room. It was all magnificent beyond description; what they could see of it in the dim light of the lamps.

Presently they came out into the garden-court which sloped downhill in a number of terraces. On the far side of that they came to the Old Palace. It had already grown almost quite dark and they now found themselves in a maze of corridors lit only by occasional torches fixed in brackets to the walls. Lasaraleen halted at a place where you had to go either left or right.

"Go on, do go on," whispered Aravis, whose heart was beating terribly and who still felt that her father might run into them at any corner.

"I'm just wondering . . ." said Lasaraleen. "I'm not absolutely sure which way we go from here. I *think* it's the left. Yes, I'm almost sure it's the left. What fun this is!"

They took the left hand way and found themselves in a passage that was hardly lighted at all and which soon began going down steps.

"It's all right," said Lasaraleen. "I'm sure we're right now. I remember these steps." But at that moment a moving light appeared ahead. A second later there appeared from round a distant corner, the dark shapes of two men walking backwards and carrying tall candles. And of course it is only before royalties that people walk backwards. Aravis felt Lasaraleen grip her arm – that sort of sudden grip which is almost a pinch and which means that the person who is gripping you is very frightened indeed. Aravis thought it odd that Lasaraleen should be so afraid of the Tisroc if he were really such a friend of hers, but there was no time to go on thinking. Lasaraleen was hurrying her back to the top of the steps, on tiptoes, and groping wildly along the wall.

"Here's a door," she whispered. "Quick."

They went in, drew the door very softly behind them, and found themselves in pitch darkness. Aravis could hear by Lasaraleen's breathing that she was terrified.

"Tash preserve us!" whispered Lasaraleen. "What *shall* we do if he comes in here. Can we hide?"

There was a soft carpet under their feet. They groped forward into the room and blundered on to a sofa.

"Let's lie down behind it," whimpered Lasaraleen. "Oh, I *do* wish we hadn't come."

There was just room between the sofa and the curtained wall and the two girls got down. Lasaraleen managed to get the better position and was completely covered. The upper part of Aravis's face stuck out beyond the sofa, so that if anyone came into that room with a light and happened to look in exactly the right place they would see her. But of course, because she was wearing a veil, what they saw would not at once look like a forehead and a pair of eyes. Aravis shoved desperately to try to make Lasaraleen give her a little more room. But Lasaraleen, now quite selfish in her panic, fought back and pinched her feet. They gave it up and lay still, panting a little. Their own breath semed dreadfully noisy, but there was no other noise.

"Is it safe?" said Aravis at last in the tiniest possible whisper.

"I – I – *think* so," began Lasaraleen. "But my poor nerves –" and then came the most terrible noise they could have heard at that moment: the noise of the door opening. And then came light. And because Aravis couldn't get her head any further in behind the sofa, she saw everything.

First came the two slaves (deaf and dumb, as Aravis rightly guessed, and therefore used at the most secret councils) walking backwards and carrying the candles. They took up their stand one at each end of the sofa. This was a good thing, for of course it was now harder for anyone to see Aravis once a slave was in front of her and she was looking between his heels. Then came an old man, very fat, wearing a curious pointed cap by which she immediately knew that he was the Tisroc. The least of the jewels with which he was covered was worth more than all the clothes and weapons of the Narnian lords put together: but he was so fat and such a mass of frills and pleats and bobbles and buttons and tassels and talismans that Aravis couldn't help thinking the Narnian fashions (at any rate for men) looked nicer. After him came a tall young man with a feathered and jewelled turban on his head and an ivory-sheathed scimitar at his side. He seemed very excited and his eyes and teeth flashed fiercely in the candlelight. Last of all came a little hump-backed, wizened old man in whom she recognized with a shudder the new Grand Vizier and her own betrothed husband, Ahoshta Tarkaan himself.

As soon as all three had entered the room and the door was shut, the Tisroc seated himself on the divan with a sigh of contentment, the young man took his place, standing before him, and the Grand Vizier got down on his knees and elbows and laid his face flat on the carpet.

CHAPTER EIGHT

IN THE HOUSE OF THE TISROC

"Oh-my-father-and-oh-the-delight-of-my-eyes," began the young man, muttering the words very quickly and sulkily and not at all as if the Tisroc *were* the delight of his eyes. "May you live for ever, but you have utterly destroyed me. If you had given me the swiftest of the galleys at sunrise when I first saw that the ship of the accursed barbarians was gone from her place I would perhaps have overtaken them. But you persuaded me to send first and see if they had not merely moved round the point into better anchorage. And now the whole day has been wasted. And they are gone – gone – out of my reach! The false jade, the –" and here he added a great many descriptions of Queen Susan which would not look at all nice in print. For of course this young man was Prince Rabadash and of course the false jade was Susan of Narnia.

"Compose yourself, O my son," said the Tisroc. "For the departure of guests makes a wound that is easily healed in the heart of a judicious host."

"But I *want* her," cried the Prince. "I must have her. I shall die if I do not get her – false, proud, black-hearted daughter of a dog that she is! I cannot sleep and my food has no savour and my eyes are darkened because of her beauty. I must have the barbarian queen."

"How well it was said by a gifted poet," observed the Vizier, raising his face (in a somewhat dusty condition) from the carpet, "that deep draughts from the fountain of reason are desirable in order to extinguish the fire of youthful love."

This seemed to exasperate the Prince. "Dog," he shouted, directing a series of well-aimed kicks at the hindquarters of the Vizier, "do not dare to quote the poets to me. I have had maxims and verses flung at me all day and I can endure them no more." I am afraid Aravis did not feel at all sorry for the Vizier.

The Tisroc was apparently sunk in thought, but when, after a long pause, he noticed what was happening, he said tranquilly:

"My son, by all means desist from kicking the venerable and enlightened Vizier: for as a costly jewel retains its value even if hidden in a dung-hill, so old age and discretion are to be respected even in the vile persons of our subjects. Desist therefore, and tell us what you desire and propose."

"I desire and propose, O my father," said Rabadash, "that you immediately call out your invincible armies and invade the thrice-accursed land of Narnia and waste it with fire and sword and add it to your illimitable empire, killing their High King and all of his blood except the queen Susan. For I must have her as my wife, though she shall learn a sharp lesson first."

"Understand, O my son," said the Tisroc, "that no words you can speak will move me to open war against Narnia."

"If you were not my father, O ever-living Tisroc," said the Prince, grinding his teeth, "I should say that was the word of a coward."

"And if you were not my son, O most inflammable Rabadash," replied his father, "your life would be short and your death slow when you had said it." (The cool, placid voice in which he spoke these words made Aravis's blood run cold.)

"But why, O my father," said the Prince – this time in a much more respectful voice, "why should we think twice about punishing Narnia any more than about hanging an idle slave or sending a worn-out horse to be made into dog's-meat? It is not the fourth size of one of your least provinces. A thousand spears could conquer it in five weeks. It is an unseemly blot on the skirts of your empire."

"Most undoubtedly," said the Tisroc. "These little barbarian countries that call themselves *free* (which is as much as to say, idle, disordered, and unprofitable) are hateful to the gods and to all persons of discernment."

"Then why have we suffered such a land as Narnia to remain thus long unsubdued?"

"Know, O enlightened Prince," said the Grand Vizier, "that until the year in which your exalted father began his salutary and unending reign, the land of Narnia was covered with ice and snow and was moreover ruled by a most powerful enchantress."

"This I know very well, O loquacious Vizier," answered the Prince. "But I know also that the enchantress is dead. And the ice and snow have vanished, so that Narnia is now wholesome, fruitful, and delicious."

"And this change, O most learned Prince, has doubtless been brought to pass by the powerful incantations of those wicked persons who now call themselves kings and queens of Narnia."

"I am rather of the opinion," said Rabadash, "that it has

come about by the alteration of the stars and the operation of natural causes."

"All this," said the Tisroc, "is a question for the disputations of learned men. I will never believe that so great an alteration, and the killing of the old enchantress, were effected without the aid of strong magic. And such things are to be expected in that land, which is chiefly inhabited by demons in the shape of beasts that talk like men, and monsters that are half man and half beast. It is commonly reported that the High King of Narnia (whom may the gods utterly reject) is supported by a demon of hideous aspect and irresistible maleficence who appears in the shape of a Lion. Therefore the attacking of Narnia is a dark and doubtful enterprise, and I am determined not to put my hand out farther than I can draw it back."

"How blessed is Calormen," said the Vizier, popping up his face again, "on whose ruler the gods have been pleased to bestow prudence and circumspection! Yet as the irrefutable and sapient Tisroc has said it is very grievous to be constrained to keep our hands off such a dainty dish as Narnia. Gifted was that poet who said —" but at this point Ahoshta noticed an impatient movement of the Prince's toe and became suddenly silent.

"It is very grievous," said the Tisroc in his deep, quiet voice. "Every morning the sun is darkened in my eyes, and every night my sleep is the less refreshing, because I remember that Narnia is still free."

"O my father," said Rabadash. "How if I show you a way by which you can stretch out your arm to take Narnia and yet draw it back unharmed if the attempt prove unfortunate?"

"If you can show me that, O Rabadash," said the Tisroc, "you will be the best of sons."

"Hear then, O father. This very night and in this hour I

will take but two hundred horse and ride across the desert. And it shall seem to all men that you know nothing of my going. On the second morning I shall be at the gates of King Lune's castle of Anvard in Archenland. They are at peace with us and unprepared and I shall take Anvard before they have bestirred themselves. Then I will ride through the pass above Anvard and down through Narnia to Cair Paravel. The High King will not be there; when I left them he was already preparing a raid against the giants on his northern border. I shall find Cair Paravel, most likely with open gates, and ride in. I shall exercise prudence and courtesy and spill as little Narnian blood as I can. And what then remains but to sit there till the *Splendour Hyaline* puts in, with Queen Susan on board, catch my strayed bird as she sets foot ashore, swing her into the saddle, and then, ride, ride, ride back to Anvard?"

"But is it not probable, O my son," said the Tisroc, "that at the taking of the woman either King Edmund or you will lose his life?"

"They will be a small company," said Rabadash, "and I will order ten of my men to disarm and bind him: restraining my vehement desire for his blood so that there shall be no deadly cause of war between you and the High King."

"And how if the *Splendour Hyaline* is at Cair Paravel before you?"

"I do not look for that with these winds, O my father."

"And lastly, O my resourceful son," said the Tisroc, "you have made clear how all this might give you the barbarian woman, but not how it helps me to the over-throwing of Narnia."

"O my father, can it have escaped you that though I and my horsemen will come and go through Narnia like an arrow from a bow, yet we shall have Anvard for ever? And when you hold Anvard you sit in the very gate of Narnia, and your garrison in Anvard can be increased by little and little till it is a great host."

"It is spoken with understanding and foresight. But how do I draw back my arm if all this miscarries?"

"You shall say that I did it without your knowledge and against your will, and without your blessing, being constrained by the violence of my love and the impetuosity of youth."

"And how if the High King then demands that we send back the barbarian woman, his sister?"

"O my father, be assured that he will not. For though the fancy of a woman has rejected this marriage, the High King Peter is a man of prudence and understanding who will in no way wish to lose the high honour and advantage of being allied to our House and seeing his nephew and grand nephew on the throne of Calormen."

"He will not see that if I live for ever as is no doubt your wish," said the Tisroc in an even drier voice than usual.

"And also, O my father and O the delight of my eyes," said the Prince, after a moment of awkward silence, "we shall write letters as if from the Queen to say that she loves me and has no desire to return to Narnia. For it is well known that women are as changeable as weathercocks. And even if they do not wholly believe the letters, they will not dare to come to Tashbaan in arms to fetch her."

"O enlightened Vizier," said the Tisroc, "bestow your wisdom upon us concerning this strange proposal."

"O eternal Tisroc," answered Ahosta, "the strength of paternal affection is not unknown to me and I have often heard that sons are in the eyes of their fathers more precious than carbuncles. How then shall I dare freely to unfold to you my mind in a matter which may imperil the life of this exalted Prince?"

"Undoubtedly you will dare," replied the Tisroc.

"Because you will find that the dangers of not doing so are at least equally great."

"To hear is to obey," moaned the wretched man. "Know then, O most reasonable Tisroc, in the first place, that the danger of the Prince is not altogether so great as might appear. For the gods have withheld from the barbarians the light of discretion, as that their poetry is not, like ours, full of choice apophthegms and useful maxims, but is all of love and war. Therefore nothing will appear to them more noble and admirable than such a mad enterprise as this of – ow!" For the Prince, at the word "mad", had kicked him again.

"Desist, O my son," said the Tisroc. "And you, estimable Vizier, whether he desists or not, by no means allow the flow of your eloquence to be interrupted. For nothing is more suitable to persons of gravity and decorum than to endure minor inconveniences with constancy."

"To hear is to obey," said the Vizier, wriggling himself round a little so as to get his hinder parts further away from Rabadash's toe. "Nothing, I say, will seem as pardonable, if not estimable, in their eyes as this – er – hazardous attempt, especially because it is undertaken for the love of a woman. Therefore, if the Prince by misfortune fell into their hands, they would assuredly not kill him. Nay, it may even be, that though he failed to carry off the queen, yet the sight of his great valour and of the extremity of his passion might incline her heart to him."

"That is a good point, old babbler," said Rabadash. "Very good, however it came into your ugly head."

"The praise of my masters is the light of my eyes," said Ahoshta. "And secondly, O Tisroc, whose reign must and shall be interminable, I think that with the aid of the gods it is very likely that Anvard will fall into the Prince's hands. And if so, we have Narnia by the throat."

There was a long pause and the room became so silent

that the two girls hardly dared to breathe. At last the Tisroc spoke.

"Go, my son," he said. "And do as you have said. But expect no help nor countenance from me. I will not avenge you if you are killed and I will not deliver you if the barbarians cast you into prison. And if, either in success or failure, you shed a drop more than you need of Narnian noble blood and open war arises from it, my favour shall never fall upon you again and your next brother shall have

your place in Calormen. Now go. Be swift, secret, and fortunate. May the strength of Tash the inexorable, the irresistible be in your sword and lance."

"To hear is to obey," cried Rabadash, and after kneeling for a moment to kiss his father's hands he rushed from the room. Greatly to the disappointment of Aravis, who was now horribly cramped, the Tisroc and Vizier remained.

"O Vizier," said the Tisroc, "is it certain that no living soul knows of this council we three have held here tonight?"

"O my master," said Ahoshta, "it is not possible that any

should know. For that very reason I proposed, and you in your wisdom agreed, that we should meet here in the Old Palace where no council is ever held and none of the household has any occasion to come."

"It is well," said the Tisroc. "If any man knew, I would see to it that he died before an hour had passed. And do you also, O prudent Vizier, forget it. I sponge away from my own heart and from yours all knowledge of the Prince's plans. He is gone without my knowledge or my consent, I know not whither, because of his violence and the rash and disobedient disposition of youth. No man will be more

astonished than you and I to hear that Anvard is in his hands."

"To hear is to obey," said Ahoshta.

"That is why you will never think even in your secret heart that I am the hardest hearted of fathers who thus send my first-born son on an errand so likely to be his death; pleasing as it must be to you who do not love the Prince. For I see into the bottom of your mind."

"O impeccable Tisroc," said the Vizier. "In comparison with you I love neither the Prince nor my own life nor bread nor water nor the light of the sun."

"Your sentiments," said the Tisroc, "are elevated and correct. I also love none of these things in comparison with the glory and strength of my throne. If the Prince succeeds, we have Archenland, and perhaps hereafter Narnia. If he fails – I have eighteen other sons and Rabadash, after the manner of the eldest sons of kings, was beginning to be dangerous. More than five Tisrocs in Tashbaan have died before their time because their eldest sons, enlightened princes, grew tired of waiting for their throne. He had better cool his blood abroad than boil it in inaction here. And now, O excellent Vizier, the excess of my paternal anxiety inclines me to sleep. Command the musicians to my chamber. But before you lie down, call back the pardon we wrote for the third cook. I feel within me the manifest prognostics of indigestion."

"To hear is to obey," said the Grand Vizier. He crawled backwards on all fours to the door, rose, bowed, and went out. Even then the Tisroc remained seated in silence on the divan till Aravis almost began to be afraid that he had dropped asleep. But at last with a great creaking and sighing he heaved up his enormous body, signed to the slaves to precede him with the lights, and went out. The door closed behind him, the room was once more totally dark, and the two girls could breathe freely again.

CHAPTER NINE

ACROSS THE DESERT

"How dreadful! How perfectly dreadful!" whimpered Lasaraleen. "Oh darling, I *am* so frightened. I'm shaking all over. Feel me."

"Come on," said Aravis, who was trembling herself. "They've gone back to the new palace. Once we're out of this room we're safe enough. But it's wasted a terrible time. Get me down to that water-gate as quick as you can."

"Darling, how *can* you?" squeaked Lasaraleen. "I can't do anything – not now. My poor nerves! No: we must just lie still a bit and then go back."

"Why back?" asked Aravis.

"Oh, you don't understand. You're so unsympathetic," said Lasaraleen, beginning to cry. Aravis decided it was no occasion for mercy.

"Look here!" she said, catching Lasaraleen and giving her a good shake. "If you say another word about going back, and if you don't start taking me to that water-gate at once – do you know what I'll do? I'll rush out into that passage and scream. Then we'll both be caught."

"But we shall both be k-k-killed!" said Lasaraleen. "Didn't you hear what the Tisroc (may he live for ever) said?"

"Yes, and I'd sooner be killed than married to Ahosht. So come *on*."

"Oh you *are* unkind," said Lasaraleen. "And I in such a state!"

But in the end she had to give in to Aravis. She led the way down the steps they had already descended, and along another corridor and so finally out into the open air. They were now in the palace garden which sloped down in terraces to the city wall. The moon shone brightly. One of the drawbacks about adventures is that when you come to the most beautiful places you are often too anxious and hurried to appreciate them; so that Aravis (though she remembered them years later) had only a vague impression of grey lawns, quietly bubbling fountains, and the long black shadows of cypress trees.

When they reached the very bottom and the wall rose frowning above them, Lasaraleen was shaking so that she could not unbolt the gate. Aravis did it. There, at last, was the river, full of reflected moonlight, and a little landing stage and a few pleasure boats.

"Good-bye," said Aravis, "and thank you. I'm sorry if I've been a pig. But think what I'm flying from!"

"Oh Aravis darling," said Lasaraleen. "Won't you change your mind? Now that you've seen what a very great man Ahoshta is!"

"Great man!" said Aravis. "A hideous grovelling slave who flatters when he's kicked but treasures it all up and hopes to get his own back by egging on that horrible Tisroc to plot his son's death. Faugh! I'd sooner marry my father's scullion than a creature like that."

"Oh Aravis, Aravis! How can you say such dreadful things; and about the Tisroc (may he live for ever) too. It must be right if *he's* going to do it!"

"Good-bye," said Aravis, "and I thought your dresses lovely. And I think your house is lovely too. I'm sure you'll have a lovely life – though it wouldn't suit me. Close the door softly behind me."

She tore herself away from her friend's affectionate embraces, stepped into a punt, cast off, and a moment later was out in midstream with a huge real moon overhead and a huge reflected moon down, deep down, in the river. The air was fresh and cool and as she drew near the farther bank she heard the hooting of an owl. "Ah! That's better!" thought Aravis. She had always lived in the country and had hated every minute of her time in Tashbaan.

When she stepped ashore she found herself in darkness for the rise of the ground, and the trees, cut off the moonlight. But she managed to find the same road that Shasta had found, and came just as he had done to the end of the grass and the beginning of the sand, and looked (like him) to her left and saw the big, black Tombs. And now at last, brave girl though she was, her heart quailed. Supposing the others weren't there! Supposing the ghouls were! But she stuck out her chin (and a little bit of her tongue too) and went straight towards them.

But before she had reached them she saw Bree and Hwin and the groom.

"You can go back to your mistress now," said Aravis (quite forgetting that he couldn't, until the city gates opened next morning). "Here is money for your pains."

"To hear is to obey," said the groom, and at once set off at a remarkable speed in the direction of the city. There was no need to tell him to make haste: he also had been thinking a good deal about ghouls.

For the next few seconds Aravis was busy kissing the noses and patting the necks of Hwin and Bree just as if they were quite ordinary horses.

"And here comes Shasta! Thanks be to the Lion!" said Bree.

Aravis looked round, and there, right enough, was Shasta who had come out of hiding the moment he saw the groom going away.

"And now," said Aravis. "There's not a moment to lose." And in hasty words she told them about Rabadash's expedition.

"Treacherous hounds!" said Bree, shaking his mane and

stamping with his hoof. "An attack in time of peace, without defiance sent! But we'll grease his oats for him. We'll be there before he is."

"Can we?" said Aravis, swinging herself into Hwin's saddle. Shasta wished he could mount like that.

"Brooh-hoo!" snorted Bree. "Up you get, Shasta. Can we! And with a good start too!"

"He said he was going to start at once," said Aravis.

"That's how humans talk," said Bree. "But you don't get a company of two hundred horse and horsemen watered and victualled and armed and saddled and started all in a minute. Now: what's our direction? Due North?"

"No," said Shasta. "I know about that. I've drawn a line. I'll explain later. Bear a bit to our left, both you horses. Ah – here it is!"

"Now," said Bree. "All that about galloping for a day and a night, like in stories, can't really be done. It must be walk and trot: but brisk trots and short walks. And whenever we walk you two humans can slip off and walk too. Now. Are you ready, Hwin? Off we go. Narnia and the North!"

At first it was delightful. The night had now been going on for so many hours that the sand had almost finished giving back all the sun-heat it had received during the day, and the air was cool, fresh, and clear. Under the moonlight the sand, in every direction and as far as they could see, gleamed as if it were smooth water or a great silver tray. Except for the noise of Bree's and Hwin's hoofs there was not a sound to be heard. Shasta would nearly have fallen asleep if he had not had to dismount and walk every now and then.

This seemed to last for hours. Then there came a time when there was no longer any moon. They seemed to ride in the dead darkness for hours and hours. And after that there came a moment when Shasta noticed that he could see Bree's neck and head in front of him a little more clearly than before; and slowly, very slowly, he began to notice the vast grey flatness on every side. It looked absolutely dead, like something in a dead world; and Shasta felt quite terribly tired and noticed that he was getting cold and that his lips were dry. And all the time the squeak of the leather, the jingle of the bits, and the noise of the hoofs – not *Propputty-propputty* as it would be on a hard road, but *Thubbudy-thubbudy* on the dry sand.

At last, after hours of riding, far away on his right there came a single long streak of paler grey, low down on the horizon. Then a streak of red. It was the morning at last, but without a single bird to sing about it. He was glad of the walking bits now, for he was colder than ever.

Then suddenly the sun rose and everything changed in a moment. The grey sand turned yellow and twinkled as if it was strewn with diamonds. On their left the shadows of Shasta and Hwin and Bree and Aravis, enormously long, raced beside them. The double peak of Mount Pire, far ahead, flashed in the sunlight and Shasta saw they were a little out of the course. "A bit left, a bit left," he sang out. Best of all, when you looked back, Tashbaan was already small and remote. The Tombs were quite invisible: swallowed up in that single, jagged-edged hump which was the city of the Tisroc. Everyone felt better.

But not for long. Though Tashbaan looked very far away when they first saw it, it refused to look any further away as they went on. Shasta gave up looking back at it, for it only gave him the feeling that they were not moving at all. Then the light became a nuisance. The glare of the sand made his eyes ache: but he knew he mustn't shut them. He must screw them up and keep on looking ahead at Mount Pire and shouting out directions. Then came the heat. He noticed it for the first time when he had to dismount and walk: as he slipped down to the sand the heat from it struck up into his face as if from the opening of an oven door. Next time it was worse. But the third time, as his bare feet touched the sand he screamed with pain and got one foot back in the stirrup and the other half over Bree's back before you could have said knife.

"Sorry, Bree," he gasped. "I can't walk. It burns my feet."
"Of course!" panted Bree. "Should have thought of that myself. Stay on. Can't be helped."

"It's all right for *you*," said Shasta to Aravis who was walking beside Hwin. "You've got shoes on."

Aravis said nothing and looked prim. Let's hope she didn't mean to, but she did.

On again, trot and walk and trot, jingle-jingle-jingle, squeak-squeak-squeak, smell of hot horse, smell of hot self, blinding glare, headache. And nothing at all different for mile after mile. Tashbaan would never look any further away. The mountains would never look any nearer. You felt this had been going on for always –. jingle-jingle-jingle, squeak-squeak-squeak, smell of hot horse, smell of hot self.

Of course one tried all sorts of games with oneself to try to make the time pass: and of course they were all no good. And one tried very hard not to think of drinks – iced sherbet in a palace in Tashbaan, clear spring water tinkling with a dark earthy sound, cold, smooth milk just creamy enough and not too creamy – and the harder you tried not to think, the more you thought.

At last there was something different – a mass of rock sticking up out of the sand about fifty yards long and thirty feet high. It did not cast much shadow, for the sun was now very high, but it cast a little. Into that shade they crowded. There they ate some food and drank a little water. It is not easy giving a horse a drink out of a skin bottle, but Bree and Hwin were clever with their lips. No one had anything like enough. No one spoke. The Horses were flecked with foam and their breathing was noisy. The children were pale.

After a very short rest they went on again. Same noises, same smells, same glare, till at last their shadows began to fall on their right, and then got longer and longer till they seemed to stretch out to the Eastern end of the world. Very slowly the sun drew nearer to the Western horizon. And now at last he was down and, thank goodness, the merciless glare was gone, though the heat coming up from the sand was still as bad as ever. Four pairs of eyes were looking out eagerly for any sign of the valley that Sallowpad the Raven had spoken about. But, mile after mile, there was nothing but level sand. And now the day was quite definitely done, and most of the stars were out, and still the Horses thundered on and the children rose and sank in their saddles, miserable with thirst and weariness. Not till the moon had risen did Shasta – in the strange, barking voice of someone whose mouth is perfectly dry – shout out:

"There it is!"

There was no mistaking it now. Ahead, and a little to their right, there was at last a slope: a slope downward and hummocks of rock on each side. The Horses were far too tired to speak but they swung round towards it and in a minute or

two they were entering the gully. At first it was worse in there than it had been out in the open desert, for there was a breathless stuffiness between the rocky walls and less moonlight. The slope continued steeply downwards and the rocks on either hand rose to the height of cliffs. Then they began to meet vegetation – prickly cactus-like plants and coarse grass of the kind that would prick your fingers. Soon the horse-hoofs were falling on pebbles and stones instead of sand. Round every bend of the valley – and it had many bends – they looked eagerly for water. The Horses were nearly at the end of their strength now, and Hwin, stumbling and panting, was lagging behind Bree. They were almost in despair before at last they came to a little muddiness and a tiny trickle of water through softer and better grass. And the trickle became a brook, and the brook became a stream with bushes on each side, and the stream became a river and there came (after more disappointments than I could possibly describe) a moment when Shasta, who had been in a kind of doze, suddenly realized that Bree had stopped and found himself slipping off. Before them a little cataract of water poured into a broad pool: and both the Horses were already in the pool with their heads down, drinking, drinking, drinking. "O-o-oh," said Shasta and plunged in – it was about up to his knees – and stooped his head right into the cataract. It was perhaps the loveliest moment in his life.

It was about ten minutes later when all four of them (the two children wet nearly all over) came out and began to notice their surroundings. The moon was now high enough to peep down into the valley. There was soft grass on both sides of the river, and beyond the grass, trees and bushes sloped up to the bases of the cliffs. There must have been some wonderful flowering shrubs hidden in that shadowy undergrowth for the whole glade was full of the coolest and most delicious smells. And out of the darkest recess among the trees there came a sound Shasta had never heard before – a nightingale.

Everyone was much too tired to speak or to eat. The Horses, without waiting to be unsaddled, lay down at once. So did Aravis and Shasta.

About ten minutes later the careful Hwin said, "But we mustn't go to sleep. We've got to keep ahead of that Rabadash."

"No," said Bree very slowly. "Mustn't go sleep. Just a little rest."

Shasta knew (for a moment) that they would all go to sleep if he didn't get up and do something about it, and felt that he ought to. In fact he decided that he would get up and persuade them to go on. But presently; not yet: not just yet . . .

Very soon the moon shone and the nightingale sang over two horses and two human children, all fast asleep.

It was Aravis who awoke first. The sun was already high in the heavens and the cool morning hours were already wasted. "It's my fault," she said to herself furiously as she jumped up and began rousing the others. "One wouldn't expect Horses to keep awake after a day's work like that, even if they *can* talk. And of course that Boy wouldn't; he's had no decent training. But *I* ought to have known better."

The others were dazed and stupid with the heaviness of their sleep.

"Heigh-ho – broo-hoo," said Bree. "Been sleeping in my saddle, eh? I'll never do that again. Most uncomfortable –"

"Oh come on, come on," said Aravis. "We've lost half the morning already. There isn't a moment to spare."

"A fellow's got to have a mouthful of grass," said Bree.

I'm afraid we can't wait," said Aravis.

"What's the terrible hurry?" said Bree. "We've crossed the desert, haven't we?"

"But we're not in Archenland yet," said Aravis. "And we've got to get there before Rabadash."

"Oh, we must be miles ahead of him," said Bree. "Haven't we been coming a shorter way? Didn't that Raven friend of yours say this was a short cut, Shasta?"

"He didn't say anything about *shorter*," answered Shasta. "He only said *better*, because you got to a river this way. If the oasis is due North of Tashbaan, then I'm afraid this may be longer."

"Well I can't go on without a snack," said Bree. "Take my bridle off, Shasta."

"P-please," said Hwin, very shyly, "I feel just like Bree that I *can't* go on. But when Horses have humans (with spurs and things) on their backs, aren't they often made to go on when they're feeling like this? and then they find they can. I m-mean – oughtn't we to be able to do even more, now that we're free. It's all for Narnia."

"I think, Ma'am," said Bree very crushingly, "that I know a little more about campaigns and forced marches and what a horse can stand than you do."

To this Hwin made no answer, being, like most highly bred mares, a very nervous and gentle person who was easily put down. In reality she was quite right, and if Bree had had a Tarkaan on his back at that moment to make him go on, he would have found that he was good for several hours' hard going. But one of the worst results of being a slave and being forced to do things is that when there is no one to force you any more you find you have almost lost the power of forcing yourself.

So they had to wait while Bree had a snack and a drink, and of course Hwin and the children had a snack and a drink too. It must have been nearly eleven o'clock in the morning before they finally got going again. And even then Bree took things much more gently than yesterday. It was really Hwin, though she was the weaker and more tired of the two, who set the pace.

The valley itself, with its brown, cool river, and grass and moss and wild flowers and rhododendrons, was such a pleasant place that it made you want to ride slowly.

CHAPTER TEN

THE HERMIT OF THE
SOUTHERN MARCH

AFTER they had ridden for several hours down the valley, it widened out and they could see what was ahead of them. The river which they had been following here joined a broader river, wide and turbulent, which flowed from their left to their right, towards the east. Beyond this new river a delightful country rose gently in low hills, ridge beyond ridge, to the Northern Mountains themselves. To the right there were rocky pinnacles, one or two of them with snow clinging to the ledges. To the left, pine-clad slopes, frowning cliffs, narrow gorges, and blue peaks stretched away as far as the eye could reach. He could no longer make out Mount Pire. Straight ahead the mountain range sank to a wooded saddle which of course must be the pass from Archenland into Narnia.

"Broo-hoo-hoo, the North, the green North!" neighed Bree: and certainly the lower hills looked greener and fresher than anything that Aravis and Shasta, with their southern-bred eyes, had ever imagined. Spirits rose as they clattered down to the water's-meet of the two rivers.

The eastern-flowing river, which was pouring from the higher mountains at the western end of the range, was far too swift and too broken with rapids for them to think of swimming it; but after some casting about, up and down the bank, they found a place shallow enough to wade. The roar and clatter of water, the great swirl against the horses' fetlocks, the cool, stirring air and the darting dragon-flies, filled Shasta with a strange excitement.

"Friends, we are in Archenland!" said Bree proudly as he splashed and churned his way out on the Northern bank.

"I think that river we've just crossed is called the Winding Arrow."

"I hope we're in time," murmured Hwin.

Then they began going up, slowly and zigzagging a good deal, for the hills were steep. It was all open park-like country with no roads or houses in sight. Scattered trees, never thick enough to be a forest, were everywhere. Shasta, who had lived all his life in an almost tree-less grassland, had never seen so many or so many kinds. If you had been there you would probably have known (he didn't) that he was seeing oaks, beeches, silver birches, rowans, and sweet chestnuts. Rabbits scurried away in every direction as they advanced, and presently they saw a whole herd of fallow deer making off among the trees.

"Isn't it simply glorious!" said Aravis.

At the first ridge Shasta turned in the saddle and looked back. There was no sign of Tashbaan; the desert, unbroken except by the narrow green crack which they had travelled down, spread to the horizon.

"Hullo!" he said suddenly. "What's that!"

"What's what?" said Bree, turning round. Hwin and Aravis did the same.

"That," said Shasta, pointing. "It looks like smoke. Is it a fire?"

"Sand-storm, I should say," said Bree.

"Not much wind to raise it," said Aravis.

"Oh!" exclaimed Hwin. "Look! There are things flashing in it. Look! They're helmets – and armour. And it's moving: moving this way."

"By Tash!" said Aravis. "It's the army. It's Rabadash."

"Oh course it is," said Hwin. "Just what I was afraid of. Quick! We must get to Anvard before it." And without another word she whisked round and began galloping

North. Bree tossed his head and did the same.

"Come *on*, Bree, come on," yelled Aravis over her shoulder.

The race was very gruelling for the Horses. As they topped each ridge they found another valley and another ridge beyond it; and though they knew they were going in more or less the right direction, no one knew how far it was to Anvard. From the top of the second ridge Shasta looked back again. Instead of a dust-cloud well out in the desert he now saw a black, moving mass, rather like ants, on the far bank of the Winding Arrow. They were doubtless looking for a ford.

"They're on the river!" he yelled wildly.

"Quick! Quick!" shouted Aravis. "We might as well not have come at all if we don't reach Anvard in time. Gallop, Bree, gallop. Remember you're a war-horse."

It was all Shasta could do to prevent himself from shouting out similar instructions; but he thought, "The poor chap's doing all he can already," and held his tongue. And certainly both Horses were doing, if not all they could, all they thought they could; which is not quite the same thing. Bree had caught up with Hwin and they thundered side by

side over the turf. It didn't look as if Hwin could possibly keep it up much longer.

At that moment everyone's feelings were completely altered by a sound from behind. It was not the sound they had been expecting to hear – the noise of hoofs and jingling armour, mixed, perhaps, with Calormene battle-cries. Yet Shasta knew it at once. It was the same snarling roar he had heard that moonlit night when they first met Aravis and Hwin. Bree knew it too. His eyes gleamed red and his ears lay flat back on his skull. And Bree now discovered that he had not really been going as fast – not quite as fast – as he could. Shasta felt the change at once. Now they were really going all out. In a few seconds they were well ahead of Hwin.

"It's not fair," thought Shasta. "I *did* think we'd be safe from lions here!"

He looked over his shoulder. Everything was only too clear. A huge tawny creature, its body low to the ground, like a cat streaking across the lawn to a tree when a strange dog has got into the garden, was behind them. And it was nearer every second and half second.

He looked forward again and saw something which he

did not take in, or even think about. Their way was barred by a smooth green wall about ten feet high. In the middle of that wall there was a gate, open. In the middle of the gateway stood a tall man dressed, down to his bare feet, in a robe coloured like autumn leaves, leaning on a straight staff. His beard fell almost to his knees.

Shasta saw all this in a glance and looked back again. The lion had almost got Hwin now. It was making snaps at her hind legs, and there was no hope now in her foam-flecked, wide-eyed face.

"Stop," bellowed Shasta in Bree's ear. "Must go back. Must help!"

Bree always said afterwards that he never heard, or never understood this; and as he was in general a very truthful horse we must accept his word.

Shasta slipped his feet out of the stirrups, slid both his legs over the left side, hesitated for one hideous hundredth of a second, and jumped. It hurt horribly and nearly winded him; but before he knew how it hurt him he was staggering back to help Aravis. He had never done any-thing like this in his life before and hardly knew why he was doing it now.

One of the most terrible noises in the world, a horse's scream, broke from Hwin's lips. Aravis was stooping low over Hwin's neck and seemed to be trying to draw her sword. And now all three – Aravis, Hwin, and the lion – were almost on top of Shasta. Before they reached him the lion rose on its hind legs, larger than you would have believed a lion could be, and jabbed at Aravis with its right paw. Shasta could see all the terrible claws extended. Aravis screamed and reeled in the saddle. The lion was tearing her shoulders. Shasta, half mad with horror, man-aged to lurch towards the brute. He had no weapon, not even a stick or a stone. He shouted out, idiotically, at the lion as one would at a dog. "Go home! Go home!" For a fraction of a second he was staring right into its wide-opened, raging mouth. Then, to his utter astonishment, the lion, still on its hind legs, checked itself suddenly, turned head over heels, picked itself up, and rushed away.

Shasta did not for a moment suppose it had gone for good. He turned and raced for the gate in the green wall which, now for the first time, he remembered seeing. Hwin, stumbling and nearly fainting, was just entering the gate: Aravis still kept her seat but her back was covered with blood.

"Come in, my daughter, come in," the robed and bearded man was saying, and then "Come in, my son" as Shasta panted up to him. He heard the gate closed behind him; and the bearded stranger was already helping Aravis off her horse.

They were in a wide and perfectly circular enclosure, protected by a high wall of green turf. A pool of perfectly still water, so full that the water was almost exactly level with the ground, lay before him. At one end of the pool, completely overshadowing it with its branches, there grew the hugest and most beautiful tree that Shasta had ever seen. Beyond the pool was a little low house of stone roofed with deep and ancient thatch. There was a sound of bleating and over at the far side of the enclosure there were some goats. The level ground was completely covered with the finest grass.

"Are – are – are you," panted Shasta. "Are you King Lune of Archenland?"

The old man shook his head. "No," he replied in a quiet voice, "I am the Hermit of the Southern March. And now, my son, waste no time on questions, but obey. This damsel is wounded. Your horses are spent. Rabadash is at this moment finding a ford over the Winding Arrow. If you run now, without a moment's rest, you will still be in time to warn King Lune."

Shasta's heart fainted at these words for he felt he had no strength left. And he writhed inside at what seemed the cruelty and unfairness of the demand. He had not yet learned that if you do one good deed your reward usually is to be set to do another and harder and better one. But all he said out loud was:

"Where is the King?"

The Hermit turned and pointed with his staff. "Look," he said. "There is another gate, right opposite to the one you entered by. Open it and go straight ahead: always straight ahead, over level or steep, over smooth or rough, over dry or wet. I know by my art that you will find King Lune straight ahead. But run, run: always run."

Shasta nodded his head, ran to the northern gate and disappeared beyond it. Then the Hermit took Aravis, whom he had all this time been supporting with his left arm, and half led, half carried her into the house. After a long time he came out again.

"Now, cousins," he said to the Horses. "It is your turn."

Without waiting for an answer – and indeed they were too exhausted to speak – he took the bridles and saddles off both of them. Then he rubbed them both down, so well that a groom in a King's stable could not have done it better.

"There, cousins," he said, "dismiss it all from your minds and be comforted. Here is water and there is grass. You shall have a hot mash when I have milked my other cousins, the goats."

"Sir," said Hwin, finding her voice at last, "will the Tarkheena live? Has the lion killed her?"

"I who know many present things by my art," replied the Hermit with a smile, "have yet little knowledge of things future. Therefore I do not know whether any man or woman or beast in the whole world will be alive when the sun sets tonight. But be of good hope. The damsel is likely to live as long as any of her age."

When Aravis came to herself she found that she was lying on her face on a low bed of extraordinary softness in a cool, bare room with walls of undressed stone. She couldn't understand why she had been laid on her face; but when she tried to turn and felt the hot, burning pains all over her back, she remembered, and realized why. She couldn't understand what delightfully springy stuff the bed was made of, because it was made of heather (which is the best bedding) and heather was a thing she had never seen or heard of.

The door opened and the Hermit entered, carrying a large wooden bowl in his hand. After carefully setting this down, he came to the bedside, and asked:

"How do you find yourself, my daughter?"

"My back is very sore, father," said Aravis, "but there is nothing else wrong with me."

He knelt beside her, laid his hand on her forehead, and felt her pulse.

"There is no fever," he said. "You will do well. Indeed there is no reason why you should not get up tomorrow. But now, drink this."

He fetched the wooden bowl and held it to her lips. Aravis couldn't help making a face when she tasted it, for goats' milk is rather a shock when you are not used to it. But she was very thirsty and managed to drink it all and felt better when she had finished.

"Now, my daughter, you may sleep when you wish," said the Hermit. "For your wounds are washed and dressed and though they smart they are no more serious than if they had been the cuts of a whip. It must have been a very strange lion; for instead of catching you out of the saddle and getting his teeth into you, he has only drawn his claws across your back. Ten scratches: sore, but not deep or dangerous."

"I say!" said Aravis. "I *have* had luck."

"Daughter," said the Hermit, "I have now lived a hundred and nine winters in this world and have never yet met any such thing as Luck. There is something about all this that I do not understand: but if ever we need to know it, you may be sure that we shall."

"And what about Rabadash and his two hundred horse?" asked Aravis.

"They will not pass this way, I think," said the Hermit. "They must have found a ford by now well to the east of us. From there they will try to ride straight to Anvard."

"Poor Shasta!" said Aravis. "Has he far to go? Will he get there first?"

"There is good hope of it," said the old man.

Aravis lay down again (on her side this time) and said, "Have I been asleep for a long time? It seems to be getting dark."

The Hermit was looking out of the only window, which faced north. "This is not the darkness of night," he said presently. "The clouds are falling down from Stormness Head. Our foul weather always comes from there in these parts. There will be thick fog tonight."

Next day, except for her sore back, Aravis felt so well that after breakfast (which was porridge and cream) the Hermit said she could get up. And of course she at once went out to speak to the Horses. The weather had changed and the whole of that green enclosure was filled, like a great green cup, with sunlight. It was a very peaceful place, lonely and quiet.

Hwin at once trotted across to Aravis and gave her a horse-kiss.

"But where's Bree?" said Aravis when each had asked after the other's health and sleep.

"Over there," said Hwin, pointing with her nose to the far side of the circle. "And I wish you'd come and talk to him. There's something wrong, I can't get a word out of him."

They strolled across and found Bree lying with his face towards the wall, and though he must have heard them coming, he never turned his head or spoke a word.

"Good morning, Bree," said Aravis. "How are you this morning?"

Bree muttered something that no one could hear.

"The Hermit says that Shasta probably got to King Lune in time," continued Aravis, "so it looks as if all our troubles are over. Narnia, at last, Bree!"

"I shall never see Narnia," said Bree in a low voice.

"Aren't you well, Bree dear?" said Aravis.

Bree turned round at last, his face mournful as only a horse's can be.

"I shall go back to Calormen," he said.

"What?" said Aravis. "Back to slavery!"

"Yes," said Bree. "Slavery is all I'm fit for. How can I ever show my face among the free Horses of Narnia? — I who left a mare and a girl and a boy to be eaten by lions while I galloped all I could to save my own wretched skin!"

"We all ran as hard as we could," said Hwin.

"Shasta didn't!" snorted Bree. "At least he ran in the right direction: ran *back*. And that is what shames me most of all. I, who called myself a war-horse and boasted of a hundred fights, to be beaten by a little human boy — a child, a mere foal, who had never held a sword nor had any good nurture or example in his life!"

"I know," said Aravis. "I felt just the same. Shasta was marvellous. I'm just as bad as you, Bree. I've been snubbing him and looking down on him ever since you met us and now he turns out to be the best of us all. But I think it would be better to stay and say we're sorry than to go back to Calormen."

"It's all very well for you," said Bree. "You haven't disgraced yourself. But I've lost everything."

"My good Horse," said the Hermit, who had approached them unnoticed because his bare feet made so little noise on that sweet, dewy grass. "My good Horse, you've lost nothing but your self-conceit. No, no, cousin. Don't put back your ears and shake your mane at me. If you are really so humbled as you sounded a minute ago, you must learn to listen to sense. You're not quite the great Horse you had come to think, from living among poor dumb horses. Of course you were braver and cleverer than *them*. You could hardly help being that. It doesn't follow that you'll be anyone very special in Narnia. But as long as you know you're nobody special, you'll be a very decent sort of Horse, on the whole, and taking one thing with another. And now, if you and my other four-footed cousin will come round to the kitchen door we'll see about the other half of that mash."

CHAPTER ELEVEN

THE UNWELCOME
FELLOW TRAVELLER

WHEN Shasta went through the gate he found a slope of grass and a little heather running up before him to some trees. He had nothing to think about now and no plans to make: he had only to run, and that was quite enough. His limbs were shaking, a terrible stitch was beginning in his side, and the sweat that kept dropping into his eyes blinded them and made them smart. He was unsteady on his feet too, and more than once he nearly turned his ankle on a loose stone.

The trees were thicker now than they had yet been and in the more open spaces there was bracken. The sun had gone in without making it any cooler. It had become one of those hot, grey days when there seem to be twice as many flies as usual. Shasta's face was covered with them; he

didn't even try to shake them off – he had too much else to do.

Suddenly he heard a horn – not a great throbbing horn like the horns of Tashbaan but a merry call, Ti-ro-to-to-ho! Next moment he came out into a wide glade and found himself in a crowd of people.

At least, it looked a crowd to him. In reality there were about fifteen or twenty of them, all gentlemen in green hunting-dress, with their horses; some in the saddle and some standing by their horses' heads. In the centre someone was holding the stirrup for a man to mount. And the man he was holding it for was the jolliest, fat, apple-cheeked, twinkling-eyed King you could imagine.

As soon as Shasta came in sight this King forgot all about mounting his horse. He spread out his arms to Shasta, his face lit up, and he cried out in a great, deep voice that seemed to come from the bottom of his chest:

"Corin! My son! And on foot, and in rags! What –"

"No," panted Shasta, shaking his head. "Not Prince Corin. I – I – know I'm like him . . . saw his Highness in Tashbaan . . . sent his greetings."

The King was staring at Shasta with an extraordinary expression on his face.

"Are you K-King Lune?" gasped Shasta. And then, without waiting for an answer, "Lord King – fly – Anvard – shut the gates – enemies upon you – Rabadash and two hundred horse."

"Have you assurance of this, boy?" asked one of the other gentlemen.

"My own eyes," said Shasta. "I've seen them. Raced them all the way from Tashbaan."

"On foot?" said the gentleman, raising his eyebrows a little.

"Horses – with the Hermit," said Shasta.

"Question him no more, Darrin," said King Lune. "I see truth in his face. We must ride for it, gentlemen. A spare horse there, for the boy. You can ride fast, friend?"

For answer Shasta put his foot in the stirrup of the horse which had been led towards him and a moment later he was in the saddle. He had done it a hundred times with

Bree in the last few weeks, and his mounting was very different now from what it had been on that first night when Bree had said that he climbed up a horse as if he were climbing a haystack.

He was pleased to hear the Lord Darrin say to the King, "The boy has a true horseman's seat, Sire. I'll warrant there's noble blood in him."

"His blood, aye, there's the point," said the King. And he stared hard at Shasta again with that curious expression, almost a hungry expression, in his steady, grey eyes.

But by now the whole party was moving off at a brisk canter. Shasta's seat was excellent but he was sadly puzzled what to do with his reins, for he had never touched the reins while he was on Bree's back. But he looked very carefully out of the corners of his eyes to see what the others were doing (as some of us have done at parties when we weren't quite sure which knife or fork we were meant to use) and tried to get his fingers right. But he didn't dare to try really directing the horse; he trusted it would follow the rest. The horse was of course an ordinary horse, not a Talking Horse; but it had quite wits enough to realize that the strange boy on its back had no whip and no spurs and was not really master of the situation. That was why Shasta soon found himself at the tail end of the procession.

Even so, he was going pretty fast. There were no flies now and the air in his face was delicious. He had got his breath back too. And his errand had succeeded. For the first time since the arrival at Tashbaan (how long ago it seemed!) he was beginning to enjoy himself.

He looked up to see how much nearer the mountain tops had come. To his disappointment he could not see them at all: only a vague greyness, rolling down towards them. He had never been in mountain country before and was surprised. "It's a cloud," he said to himself, "a cloud coming down. I see. Up here in the hills one is really in the sky. I shall see what the inside of a cloud is like. What fun! I've often wondered." Far away on his left and a little behind him, the sun was getting ready to set.

They had come to a rough kind of road by now and were making very good speed. But Shasta's horse was still the last of the lot. Once or twice when the road made a bend (there was now continuous forest on each side of it) he lost sight of the others for a second or two.

Then they plunged into the fog, or else the fog rolled

over them. The world became grey. Shasta had not realized
how cold and wet the inside of a cloud would be; nor how
dark. The grey turned to black with alarming speed.

Someone at the head of the column winded the horn
every now and then, and each time the sound came from a
little farther off. He couldn't see any of the others now, but
of course he'd be able to as soon as he got round the next
bend. But when he rounded it he still couldn't see them. In
fact he could see nothing at all. His horse was walking
now. "Get on, Horse, get on," said Shasta. Then came the
horn, very faint. Bree had always told him that he must
keep his heels well turned out, and Shasta had got the idea
that something very terrible would happen if he dug his
heels into a horse's sides. This seemed to him an occasion
for trying it. "Look here, Horse," he said, "if you don't
buck up, do you know what I'll do? I'll dig my heels into
you. I really will." The horse, however, took no notice of
this threat. So Shasta settled himself firmly in the saddle,
gripped with his knees, clenched his teeth, and punched
both the horse's sides with his heels as hard as he could.

The only result was that the horse broke into a kind of
pretence of a trot for five or six paces and then subsided
into a walk again. And now it was quite dark and they
seemed to have given up blowing that horn. The only
sound was a steady drip-drip from the branches of the
trees.

"Well, I suppose even a walk will get us somewhere
sometime," said Shasta to himself. "I only hope I shan't
run into Rabadash and his people."

He went on for what seemed a long time, always at a
walking pace. He began to hate that horse, and he was also
beginning to feel very hungry.

Presently he came to a place where the road divided into
two. He was just wondering which led to Anvard when he

was startled by a noise from behind him. It was the noise of trotting horses. "Rabadash!" thought Shasta. He had no way of guessing which road Rabadash would take. "But if I take one," said Shasta to himself, "he *may* take the other: and if I stay at the cross-roads I'm *sure* to be caught." He dismounted and led his horse as quickly as he could along the right-hand road.

The sound of the cavalry grew rapidly nearer and in a minute or two Shasta realized that they were at the cross-roads. He held his breath, waiting to see which way they would take.

There came a low word of command "Halt!" then a moment of horsey noises – nostrils blowing, hoofs pawing, bits being champed, necks being patted. Then a voice spoke.

"Attend, all of you," it said. "We are now within a furlong of the castle. Remember your orders. Once we are in Narnia, as we should be by sunrise, you are to kill as little as possible. On this venture you are to regard every drop of Narnian blood as more precious than a gallon of your own. On *this* venture, I say. The gods will send us a happier hour and then you must leave nothing alive between Cair Paravel and the Western Waste. But we are not yet in Narnia. Here in Archenland it is another thing. In the assault on this castle of King Lune's, nothing matters but speed. Show your mettle. It must be mine within an hour. And if it is, I give it all to you. I reserve no booty for myself. Kill me every barbarian male within its walls, down to the child that was born yesterday, and everything else is yours to divide as you please – the women, the gold, the jewels, the weapons, and the wine. The man that I see hanging back when we come to the gates shall be burned alive. In the name of Tash the irresistible, the inexorable – forward!"

With a great cloppitty-clop the column began to move, and Shasta breathed again. They had taken the other road.

Shasta thought they took a long time going past, for though he had been talking and thinking about "two hundred horse" all day, he had not realized how many they really were. But at last the sound died away and once more he was alone amid the drip-drip from the trees.

He now knew the way to Anvard but of course he could not now go there: that would only mean running into the arms of Rabadash's troopers. "What on earth am I to do?" said Shasta to himself. But he remounted his horse and continued along the road he had chosen, in the faint hope of finding some cottage where he might ask for shelter and a meal. He had thought, of course, of going back to Aravis and Bree and Hwin at the hermitage, but he couldn't because by now he had not the least idea of the direction.

"After all," said Shasta, "this road is bound to get to somewhere."

But that all depends on what you mean by somewhere. The road kept on getting to somewhere in the sense that it got to more and more trees, all dark and dripping, and to colder and colder air. And strange, icy winds kept blowing the mist past him though they never blew it away. If he had been used to mountain country he would have realized that this meant he was now very high up – perhaps right at the top of the pass. But Shasta knew nothing about mountains.

"I *do* think," said Shasta, "that I must be the most un-fortunate boy that ever lived in the whole world. Every-thing goes right for everyone except me. Those Narnian lords and ladies got safe away from Tashbaan; I was left behind. Aravis and Bree and Hwin are all as snug as any-thing with that old Hermit: of course I was the one who was sent on. King Lune and his people must have got safely into the castle and shut the gates long before Rabadash arrived, but I get left out."

And being very tired and having nothing inside him, he felt so sorry for himself that the tears rolled down his cheeks.

What put a stop to all this was a sudden fright. Shasta discovered that someone or somebody was walking beside him. It was pitch dark and he could see nothing. And the Thing (or Person) was going so quietly that he could hardly hear any footfalls. What he could hear was breathing. His invisible companion seemed to breathe on a very large scale, and Shasta got the impression that it was a very large creature. And he had come to notice this breathing so gradually that he had really no idea how long it had been there. It was a horrible shock.

It darted into his mind that he had heard long ago that there were giants in these Northern countries. He bit his lip in terror. But now that he really had something to cry about, he stopped crying.

The Thing (unless it was a Person) went on beside him so very quietly that Shasta began to hope he had only imagined it. But just as he was becoming quite sure of it, there suddenly came a deep, rich sigh out of the darkness beside him. That couldn't be imagination! Anyway, he had felt the hot breath of that sigh on his chilly left hand.

If the horse had been any good – or if he had known how to get any good out of the horse – he would have risked everything on a breakaway and a wild gallop. But he knew he couldn't make that horse gallop. So he went on at a walking pace and the unseen companion walked and breathed beside him. At last he could bear it no longer.

"Who are you?" he said, scarcely above a whisper.

"One who has waited long for you to speak," said the Thing. Its voice was not loud, but very large and deep.

"Are you – are you a giant?" asked Shasta.

"You might call me a giant," said the Large Voice. "But I am not like the creatures you call giants."

"I can't see you at all," said Shasta, after staring very hard. Then (for an even more terrible idea had come into his head) he said, almost in a scream, "You're not – not something *dead*, are you? Oh please – please do go away. What harm have I ever done you? Oh, I am the unluckiest person in the whole world!"

Once more he felt the warm breath of the Thing on his hand and face. "There," it said, "that is not the breath of a ghost. Tell me your sorrows."

Shasta was a little reassured by the breath: so he told how he had never known his real father or mother and had been brought up sternly by the fisherman. And then he told the story of his escape and how they were chased by lions and forced to swim for their lives; and of all their dangers in Tashbaan and about his night among the tombs and how the beasts howled at him out of the desert. And he told about the heat and thirst of their desert journey and how they were almost at their goal when another lion chased them and wounded Aravis. And also, how very long it was since he had had anything to eat.

"I do not call you unfortunate," said the Large Voice.

"Don't you think it was bad luck to meet so many lions?" said Shasta.

"There was only one lion," said the Voice.

"What on earth do you mean? I've just told you there were at least two the first night, and –"

"There was only one: but he was swift of foot."

"How do you know?"

"I was the lion." And as Shasta gaped with open mouth and said nothing, the Voice continued. "I was the lion who forced you to join with Aravis. I was the cat who comforted you among the houses of the dead. I was the lion who drove the jackals from you while you slept. I was the lion who gave the Horses the new strength of fear for the last mile so that you should reach King Lune in time. And I was the lion you do not remember who pushed the boat in which you lay, a child near death, so that it came to shore where a man sat, wakeful at midnight, to receive you."

"Then it was you who wounded Aravis?"

"It was I."

"But what for?"

"Child," said the Voice, "I am telling you your story, not hers. I tell no one any story but his own."

"Who *are* you?" asked Shasta.

"Myself," said the Voice, very deep and low so that the earth shook: and again "Myself", loud and clear and gay: and then the third time "Myself", whispered so softly you could hardly hear it, and yet it seemed to come from all round you as if the leaves rustled with it.

Shasta was no longer afraid that the Voice belonged to something that would eat him, nor that it was the voice of a ghost. But a new and different sort of trembling came over him. Yet he felt glad too.

The mist was turning from black to grey and from grey to white. This must have begun to happen some time ago, but while he had been talking to the Thing he had not been noticing anything else. Now, the whiteness around him became a shining whiteness; his eyes began to blink. Somewhere ahead he could hear birds singing. He knew the night was over at last. He could see the mane and ears and head of his horse quite easily now. A golden light fell on them from the left. He thought it was the sun.

He turned and saw, pacing beside him, taller than the horse, a Lion. The horse did not seem to be afraid of it or else could not see it. It was from the Lion that the light came. No one ever saw anything more terrible or beautiful.

Luckily Shasta had lived all his life too far south in Calormen to have heard the tales that were whispered in Tashbaan about a dreadful Narnian demon that appeared in the form of a lion. And of course he knew none of the true stories about Aslan, the great Lion, the son of the Emperor-over-the-sea, the King above all High Kings in Narnia. But after one glance at the Lion's face he slipped out of the saddle and fell at its feet. He couldn't say anything but then he didn't want to say anything, and he knew he needn't say anything.

The High King above all kings stooped towards him. Its mane, and some strange and solemn perfume that hung about the mane, was all round him. It touched his forehead with its tongue. He lifted his face and their eyes met. Then instantly the pale brightness of the mist and the fiery brightness of the Lion rolled themselves together into a swirling glory and gathered themselves up and disappeared. He was alone with the horse on a grassy hillside under a blue sky. And there were birds singing.

CHAPTER TWELVE

SHASTA IN NARNIA

"Was it all a dream?" wondered Shasta. But it couldn't have been a dream for there in the grass before him he saw the deep, large print of the Lion's front right paw. It took one's breath away to think of the weight that could make a footprint like that. But there was something more remarkable than the size about it. As he looked at it, water had already filled the bottom of it. Soon it was full to the brim, and then overflowing, and a little stream was running downhill, past him, over the grass.

Shasta stooped and drank – a very long drink – and then dipped his face in and splashed his head. It was extremely cold, and clear as glass, and refreshed him very much. After that he stood up, shaking the water out of his ears and flinging the wet hair back from his forehead, and began to take stock of his surroundings.

Apparently it was still very early morning. The sun had only just risen, and it had risen out of the forests which he saw low down and far away on his right. The country which he was looking at was absolutely new to him. It was a green valley-land dotted with trees through which he caught the gleam of a river that wound away roughly to the North-West. On the far side of the valley there were high and even rocky hills, but they were lower than the mountains he had seen yesterday. Then he began to guess where he was. He turned and looked behind him and saw that the slope on which he was standing belonged to a range of far higher mountains.

"I see," said Shasta to himself. "Those are the big mountains between Archenland and Narnia. I was on the other side of them yesterday. I must have come through the pass in the night. What luck that I hit it! – at least it wasn't luck at all really, it was *Him*. And now I'm in Narnia."

He turned and unsaddled his horse and took off its bridle – "Though you *are* a perfectly horrid horse," he said. It took no notice of this remark and immediately began eating grass. That horse had a very low opinion of Shasta.

"I wish I could eat grass!" thought Shasta. "It's no good going back to Anvard, it'll all be besieged. I'd better get lower down into the valley and see if I can get anything to eat."

So he went on downhill (the thick dew was cruelly cold to his bare feet) till he came into a wood. There was a kind of track running through it and he had not followed this for many minutes when he heard a thick and rather wheezy voice saying to him.

"Good morning, neighbour."

Shasta looked round eagerly to find the speaker and presently saw a small, prickly person with a dark face who had just come out from among the trees. At least, it was small for a person but very big indeed for a hedgehog, which was what it was.

"Good morning," said Shasta. "But I'm not a neighbour. In fact I'm a stranger in these parts."

"Ah?" said the Hedgehog inquiringly.

"I've come over the mountains – from Archenland, you know."

"Ah, Archenland," said the Hedgehog. "That's a terrible long way. Never been there myself."

"And I think, perhaps," said Shasta, "someone ought to be told that there's an army of savage Calormenes attacking Anvard at this very moment."

"You don't say so!" answered the Hedgehog. "Well, think of that. And they do say that Calormen is hundreds and thousands of miles away, right at the world's end, across a great sea of sand."

"It's not nearly as far as you think," said Shasta. "And oughtn't something to be done about this attack on Anvard? Oughtn't your High King to be told?"

"Certain sure, something ought to be done about it," said the Hedgehog. "But you see I'm just on my way to bed for a good day's sleep. Hullo, neighbour!"

The last words were addressed to an immense biscuit-coloured rabbit whose head had just popped up from somewhere beside the path. The Hedgehog immediately told the Rabbit what it had just learned from Shasta. The Rabbit agreed that this was very remarkable news and that somebody ought to tell someone about it with a view to doing something.

And so it went on. Every few minutes they were joined by other creatures, some from the branches overhead and some from little underground houses at their feet, till the party consisted of five rabbits, a squirrel, two magpies, a goat-foot faun, and a mouse, who all talked at the same time and all agreed with the Hedgehog. For the truth was that in that golden age when the Witch and the Winter had gone and Peter the High King ruled at Cair Paravel, the smaller woodland people of Narnia were so safe and happy that they were getting a little careless.

Presently, however, two more practical people arrived in the little wood. One was a Red Dwarf whose name appeared to be Duffle. The other was a stag, a beautiful lordly creature with wide liquid eyes, dappled flanks and legs so thin and graceful that they looked as if you could break them with two fingers.

"Lion alive!" roared the Dwarf as soon as he had heard the news. "And if that's so, why are we all standing still, chattering? Enemies at Anvard! News must be sent to Cair Paravel at once. The army must be called out. Narnia must go to the aid of King Lune."

"Ah!" said the Hedgehog. "But you won't find the High King at the Cair. He's away to the North trouncing those giants. And talking of giants, neightbours, that puts me in mind –"

"Who'll take our message?" interrupted the Dwarf. "Anyone here got more speed than me?"

"I've got speed," said the Stag. "What's my message? How many Calormenes?"

"Two hundred: under Prince Rabadash. And –" But the Stag was already away – all four legs off the ground at once, and in a moment its white stern had disappeared among the remoter trees.

"Wonder where he's going," said a Rabbit. "He won't find the High King at Cair Paravel, you know."

"He'll find Queen Lucy," said Duffle. "And then – hullo! What's wrong with the Human? It looks pretty green. Why, I do believe it's quite faint. Perhaps it's mortal hungry. When did you last have a meal, youngster?"

"Yesterday morning," said Shasta weakly.

"Come on, then, come on," said the Dwarf, at once throwing his thick little arms round Shasta's waist to support him. "Why, neighbours, we ought all to be ashamed of ourselves! You come with me, lad. Breakfast! Better than talking."

With a great deal of bustle, muttering reproaches to itself, the Dwarf half led and half supported Shasta at a great speed further into the wood and a little downhill. It was a longer walk than Shasta wanted at that moment and his legs had begun to feel very shaky before they came out from the trees on to bare hillside. There they found a little house with a smoking chimney and an open door, and as they came to the doorway Duffle called out,

"Hey, brothers! A visitor for breakfast."

And immediately, mixed with a sizzling sound, there came to Shasta a simply delightful smell. It was one he had never smelled in his life before, but I hope you have. It was, in fact, the smell of bacon and eggs and mushrooms all frying in a pan.

"Mind your head, lad," said Duffle a moment too late, for Shasta had already bashed his forehead against the low lintel of the door. "Now," continued the Dwarf, "sit you down. The table's a bit low for you, but then the stool's low too. That's right. And here's porridge – and here's a jug of cream – and here's a spoon."

By the time Shasta had finished his porridge, the Dwarf's two brothers (whose names were Rogin and Bricklethumb) were putting the dish of bacon and eggs and mushrooms, and the coffee pot and the hot milk, and the toast, on the table.

It was all new and wonderful to Shasta for Calormene

food is quite different. He didn't even know what the slices of brown stuff were, for he had never seen toast before. He didn't know what the yellow soft thing they smeared on the toast was, because in Calormen you nearly always get oil instead of butter. And the house itself was quite different from the dark, frowsty, fish-smelling hut of Arsheesh and from the pillared and carpeted halls in the palaces of Tashbaan. The roof was very low, and everything was made of wood, and there was a cuckoo-clock and a red-and-white checked table-cloth and a bowl of wild flowers and little curtains on the thick-paned windows. It was also rather troublesome having to use dwarf cups and plates and knives and forks. This meant that helpings were very small, but then there were a great many helpings, so that Shasta's plate or cup was being filled every moment, and every moment the Dwarfs themselves were saying, "Butter please", or "Another cup of coffee," or "I'd like a few more mushrooms," or "What about frying another egg or so?" And when at last they had all eaten as much as they possibly could the three Dwarfs drew lots for who would do the washing-up, and Rogin was the unlucky one. Then Duffle and Bricklethumb took Shasta outside to a bench which ran against the cottage wall, and they all stretched out their legs and gave a great sigh of contentment and the two Dwarfs lit their pipes. The dew was off the grass now and the sun was warm; indeed, if there hadn't been a light breeze, it would have been too hot.

"Now, Stranger," said Duffle, "I'll show you the lie of the land. You can see nearly all South Narnia from here, and we're rather proud of the view. Right away on your left, beyond those near hills, you can just see the Western Mountains. And that round hill away on your right is called the Hill of the Stone Table. Just beyond —"

But at that moment he was interrupted by a snore from Shasta who, what with his night's journey and his excellent breakfast, had gone fast asleep. The kindly Dwarfs, as soon as they noticed this, began making signs to each other not to wake him, and indeed did so much whispering and nodding and getting up and tiptoeing away that they certainly would have waked him if he had been less tired.

He slept pretty well nearly all day but woke up in time for supper. The beds in that house were all too small for him but they made him a fine bed of heather on the floor, and he never stirred nor dreamed all night. Next morning they had just finished breakfast when they heard a shrill, exciting sound from outside.

"Trumpets!" said all the Dwarfs, as they and Shasta all came running out.

The trumpets sounded again: a new noise to Shasta, not huge and solemn like the horns of Tashbaan nor gay and merry like King Lune's hunting horn, but clear and sharp and valiant. The noise was coming from the woods to the East, and soon there was a noise of horse-hoofs mixed with it. A moment later the head of the column came into sight.

First came the Lord Peridan on a bay horse carrying the great banner of Narnia – a red lion on a green ground. Shasta knew him at once. Then came three people riding abreast, two on great chargers and one on a pony. The two on the chargers were King Edmund and a fair-haired lady with a very merry face who wore a helmet and a mail shirt and carried a bow across her shoulder and a quiver full of arrows at her side. ("The Queen Lucy," whispered Duffle.) But the one on the pony was Corin. After that came the main body of the army: men on ordinary horses, men on Talking Horses (who didn't mind being ridden on proper occasions, as when Narnia went to war), centaurs, stern, hard-bitten bears, great Talking Dogs, and last of all six giants. For there are good giants in Narnia. But though he knew they were on the right side Shasta at first could hardly bear to look at them; there are some things that take a lot of getting used to.

Just as the King and Queen reached the cottage and the Dwarfs began making low bows to them, King Edmund called out,

"Now, friends! Time for a halt and a morsel!" and at once there was a great bustle of people dismounting and haversacks being opened and conversation beginning when Corin came running up to Shasta and seized both his hands and cried,

"What! *You* here! So you got through all right? I *am* glad. Now we shall have some sport. And isn't it luck! We only got into harbour at Cair Paravel yesterday morning and the very first person who met us was Chervy the Stag with all this news of an attack on Anvard. Don't you think –"

"Who is your Highness's friend?" said King Edmund who had just got off his horse.

"Don't you see, Sire?" said Corin. "It's my double: the boy you mistook me for at Tashbaan."

"Why, so he is your double," exclaimed Queen Lucy. "As like as two twins. This is a marvellous thing."

"Please, your Majesty," said Shasta to King Edmund, "I was no traitor, really I wasn't. And I couldn't help hearing your plans. But I'd never have dreamed of telling them to your enemies."

"I know now that you were no traitor, boy," said King Edmund, laying his hand on Shasta's head. "But if you would not be taken for one, another time try not to hear what's meant for other ears. But all's well."

After that there was so much bustle and talk and coming and going that Shasta for a few minutes lost sight of Corin

and Edmund and Lucy. But Corin was the sort of boy whom one is sure to hear of pretty soon and it wasn't very long before Shasta heard King Edmund saying in a loud voice:

"By the Lion's Mane, prince, this is too much! Will your Highness never be better? You are more of a heart's-scald than our whole army together! I'd as lief have a regiment of hornets in my command as you."

Shasta wormed his way through the crowd and there saw Edmund, looking very angry indeed, Corin looking a little ashamed of himself, and a strange Dwarf sitting on the ground making faces. A couple of fauns had apparently just been helping it out of its armour.

"If I had but my cordial with me," Queen Lucy was saying, "I could soon mend this. But the High King has so strictly charged me not to carry it commonly to the wars and to keep it only for great extremities!"

What had happened was this. As soon as Corin had

spoken to Shasta, Corin's elbow had been plucked by a Dwarf in the army called Thornbut.

"What is it, Thornbut?" Corin had said.

"Your Royal Highness," said Thornbut, drawing him aside, "our march today will bring us through the pass and right to your royal father's castle. We may be in battle before night."

"I know," said Corin. "Isn't it splendid!"

"Splendid or not," said Thornbut, "I have the strictest orders from King Edmund to see to it that your Highness is not in the fight. You will be allowed to see it, and that's treat enough for your Highness's little years."

"Oh what nonsense!" Corin burst out. "Of course I'm going to fight. Why, the Queen Lucy's going to be with the archers."

"The Queen's grace will do as she pleases," said Thornbut. "But you are in my charge. Either I must have your solemn and princely word that you'll keep your pony beside mine – not half a neck ahead – till I give your

Highness leave to depart: or else – it is his Majesty's word – we must go with our wrists tied together like two prisoners."

"I'll knock you down if you try to bind me," said Corin.

"I'd like to see your Highness do it," said the Dwarf.

That was quite enough for a boy like Corin and in a second he and the Dwarf were at it hammer and tongs. It would have been an even match for, though Corin had longer arms and more height, the Dwarf was older and tougher. But it was never fought out (that's the worst of fights on a rough hillside) for by very bad luck Thornbut trod on a loose stone, came flat down on his nose, and found when he tried to get up that he had sprained his ankle: a real excruciating sprain which would keep him from walking or riding for at least a fortnight.

"See what your Highness has done," said King Edmund. "Deprived us of a proved warrior on the very edge of battle."

"I'll take his place, Sire," said Corin.

"Pshaw," said Edmund. "No one doubts your courage. But a boy in battle is a danger only to his own side."

At that moment the King was called away to attend to something else, and Corin, after apologizing handsomely to the Dwarf, rushed up to Shasta and whispered,

"Quick. There's a spare pony now, and the Dwarf's armour. Put it on before anyone notices."

"What for?" said Shasta.

"Why, so that you and I can fight in the battle of course! Don't you want to?"

"Oh – ah, yes, of course," said Shasta. But he hadn't been thinking of doing so at all, and began to get a most uncomfortable prickly feeling in his spine.

"That's right," said Corin. "Over your head. Now the sword-belt. But we must ride near the tail of the column and keep as quiet as mice. Once the battle begins everyone will be far too busy to notice us."

CHAPTER THIRTEEN

THE FIGHT AT ANVARD

BY about eleven o'clock the whole company was once more on the march, riding westward with the mountains on their left. Corin and Shasta rode right at the rear with the Giants immediately in front of them. Lucy and Edmund and Peridan were busy with their plans for the battle and though Lucy once said, "But where is his goosecap Highness?" Edmund only replied, "Not in the front, and that's good news enough. Leave well alone."

Shasta told Corin most of his adventures and explained that he had learned all his riding from a horse and didn't really know how to use the reins. Corin instructed him in this, besides telling him all about their secret sailing from Tashbaan.

"And where is the Queen Susan?"

"At Cair Paravel," said Corin. "She's not like Lucy, you know, who's as good as a man, or at any rate as good as a boy. Queen Susan is more like an ordinary grown-up lady. She doesn't ride to the wars, though she is an excellent archer."

The hillside path which they were following became narrower all the time and the drop on their right hand became steeper. At last they were going in single file along the edge of a precipice and Shasta shuddered to think that he had done the same last night without knowing it. "But of course," he thought, "I was quite safe. That is why the Lion kept on my left. He was between me and the edge all the time."

Then the path went left and south away from the cliff and there were thick woods on both sides of it and they went steeply up and up into the pass. There would have been a splendid view from the top if it were open ground but among all those trees you could see nothing – only, every now and then, some huge pinnacle of rock above the tree-tops, and an eagle or two wheeling high up in the blue air.

"They smell battle," said Corin, pointing at the birds. "They know we're preparing a feed for them."

Shasta didn't like this at all.

When they had crossed the neck of the pass and come a good deal lower they reached more open ground and from here Shasta could see all Archenland, blue and hazy, spread out below him and even (he thought) a hint of the desert beyond it. But the sun, which had perhaps two hours or so to go before it set, was in his eyes and he couldn't make things out distinctly.

Here the army halted and spread out in a line, and there was a great deal of rearranging. A whole detachment of very dangerous-looking Talking Beasts whom Shasta had not noticed before and who were mostly of the cat kind (leopards, panthers, and the like) went padding and growling to take up their positions on the left. The giants were ordered to the right, and before going there they all took off something they had been carrying on their backs and sat down for a moment. Then Shasta saw that what they had been carrying and were now putting on were pairs of boots: horrid, heavy, spiked boots which came up to their knees. Then they sloped their huge clubs over their shoulders and marched to their battle position. The archers, with Queen Lucy, fell to the rear and you could first see them bending their bows and then hear the twang-twang as they tested the strings. And wherever you looked you could see people tightening girths, putting on helmets, drawing swords, and throwing cloaks to the ground. There was hardly any talking now. It was very solemn and very dreadful. "I'm in for it now – I really am in for it now," thought Shasta. Then there came noises far ahead: the sound of many men shouting and a steady thud-thud-thud.

"Battering ram," whispered Corin. "They're battering the gate."

Even Corin looked quite serious now.

"Why doesn't King Edmund get *on*?" he said. "I can't stand this waiting about. Chilly too."

Shasta nodded: hoping he didn't look as frightened as he felt.

The trumpet at last! On the move now – now trotting – the banner streaming out in the wind. They had topped a low ridge now, and below them the whole scene suddenly opened out; a little, many-towered castle with its gate towards them. No moat, unfortunately, but of course the gate shut and the portcullis down. On the walls they could see, like little white dots, the faces of the defenders. Down below, about fifty of the Calormenes, dismounted, were steadily swinging a great tree trunk against the gate. But at once the scene changed. The main bulk of Rabadash's men had been on foot ready to assault the gate. But now he had seen the Narnians sweeping down from the ridge. There is no doubt those Calormenes are wonderfully trained. It seemed to Shasta only a second before a whole line of the enemy were on hoseback again, wheeling round to meet them, swinging towards them.

And now a gallop. The ground between the two armies grew less every moment. Faster, faster. All swords out now, all shields up to the nose, all prayers said, all teeth clenched. Shasta was dreadfully frightened. But it suddenly came into his head, "If you funk this, you'll funk every battle all your life. Now or never."

But when at last the two lines met he had really very little idea of what happened. There was a frightful confusion and an appalling noise. His sword was knocked clean out of his hand pretty soon. And he'd got the reins tangled somehow. Then he found himself slipping. Then a spear came straight at him and as he ducked to avoid it he rolled right off his horse, bashed his left knuckles terribly against someone else's armour, and then –

But it is no use trying to describe the battle from Shasta's point of view; he understood too little of the fight in general and even of his own part in it. The best way I can tell you what really happened is to take you some miles away to where the Hermit of the Southern March sat gazing into the smooth pool beneath the spreading tree, with Bree and Hwin and Aravis beside him.

For it was in this pool that the Hermit looked when he wanted to know what was going on in the world outside the green walls of his hermitage. There, as in a mirror, he could see, at certain times, what was going on in the streets of cities far farther south than Tashbaan, or what ships were putting into Redhaven in the remote Seven Isles, or what robbers or wild beasts stirred in the great Western forests between Lantern Waste and Telmar. And all this day he had hardly left his pool, even to eat or drink, for he knew that great events were on foot in Archenland. Aravis and the Horses gazed into it too. They could see it was a magic pool: instead of reflecting the tree and the sky it revealed cloudy and coloured shapes moving, always moving, in its depths. But they could see nothing clearly. The Hermit could and from time to time he told them what he saw. A little while before Shasta rode into his first battle, the Hermit had begun speaking like this:

"I see one – two – three eagles wheeling in the gap by Stormness Head. One is the oldest of all the eagles. He would not be out unless battle was at hand. I see him wheel to and fro, peering down sometimes at Anvard and some- times to the east, behind Stormness. Ah – I see now what Rabadash and his men have been so busy at all day. They have felled and lopped a great tree and they are now com- ing out of the woods carrying it as a ram. They have learned something from the failure of last night's assult. He would have been wiser if he had set his men to making ladders: but it takes too long and he is impatient. Fool that he is! He ought to have ridden back to Tashbaan as soon as the first attack failed, for his whole plan depended on speed and surprise. Now they are bringing their ram into position. King Lune's men are shooting hard from the walls. Five Calormenes have fallen: but not many will. They have their shields above their heads. Rabadash is giving his orders now. With him are his most trusted lords, fierce Tarkaans from the eastern provinces. I can see their faces. There is Corradin of Castle Tormunt, and Azrooh, and Chlamash, and Ilgamuth of the twisted lip, and a tall Tarkaan with a crimson beard –"

"By the Mane, my old master Anradin!" said Bree.

"S-s-sh," said Aravis.

"Now the ram has started. If I could hear as well as see, what a noise that would make! Stroke after stroke: and no gate can stand it for ever. But wait! Something up by

Stormness has scared the birds. They're coming out in masses. And wait again . . . I can't see yet . . . ah! Now I can. The whole ridge, up on the east, is black with horsemen. If only the wind would catch that standard and spread it out. They're over the ridge now, whoever they are. Aha! I've seen the banner now. Narnia, Narnia! It's the red lion. They're in full career down the hill now. I can see King Edmund. There's a woman behind among the archers. Oh! –"

"What is it?" asked Hwin breathlessly.

"All his Cats are dashing out from the left of the line."

"Cats?" said Aravis.

"Great cats, leopards and such," said the Hermit impatiently. "I see, I see. The Cats are coming round in a circle to get at the horses of the dismounted men. A good stroke. The Calormene horses are mad with terror already. Now the Cats are in among them. But Rabadash has reformed his line and has a hundred men in the saddle. They're riding to meet the Narnians. There's only a hundred yards between the two lines now. Only fifty. I can see King Edmund, I can see the Lord Peridan. There are two mere children in the Narnian line. What can the King be about to let them into battle? Only ten yards – the lines have met. The Giants on the Narnian right are doing wonders . . . but one's down . . . shot through the eye, I suppose. The centre's all in a muddle. I can see more on the left. There are the two boys again. Lion alive! one is Prince Corin. The other, like him as two peas. It's your little Shasta. Corin is fighting like a man. He's killed a Calormene. I can see a bit of the centre now. Rabadash and Edmund almost met then, but the press has separated them –"

"What about Shasta?" said Aravis.

"Oh the fool!" groaned the Hermit. "Poor, brave little

fool. He knows nothing about this work. He's making no use at all of his shield. His whole side's exposed. He hasn't the faintest idea what to do with his sword. Oh, he's remembered it now. He's waving it wildly about . . . nearly cut his own pony's head off, and he will in a moment if he's not careful. It's been knocked out of his hand now. It's mere murder sending a child into the battle; he can't live five minutes. Duck, you fool – oh, he's down."

"Killed?" asked three voices breathlessly.

"How can I tell?" said the Hermit. "The Cats have done their work. All the riderless horses are dead or escaped now: no retreat for the Calormenes on *them*. Now the Cats are turning back into the main battle. They're leaping on the rams-men. The ram is down. Oh, good! good! The gates are opening from the inside: there's going to be a sortie. The first three are out. It's King Lune in the middle: the brothers Dar and Darrin on each side of him. Behind them are Tran and Shar and Cole with his brother Colin. There are ten – twenty – nearly thirty of them out by now. The Calormen line is being forced back upon them. King Edmund is dealing marvellous strokes. He's just slashed Corradin's head off. Lots of Calormenes have thrown down their arms and are running for the woods. Those that remain are hard pressed. The Giants are closing in on the right – Cats on the left – King Lune from their rear. The Calormenes are a little knot now, fighting back to back. Your Tarkaan's down, Bree. Lune and Azrooh are fighting hand to hand; the King looks like winning – the King is keeping it up well – the King has won. Azrooh's down. King Edmund's down – no, he's up again: he's at it with Rabadash. They're fighting in the very gate of the castle. Several Calormenes have surrendered. Darrin has killed Ilgamuth. I can't see what's happened to Rabadash. I think he's dead, leaning against the castle wall, but I don't know.

Chlamash and King Edmund are still fighting but the battle is over everywhere else. Chlamash has surrendered. The battle *is* over. The Calormenes are utterly defeated."

When Shasta fell off his horse he gave himself up for lost. But horses, even in battle, tread on human beings very much less than you would suppose. After a very horrible ten minutes or so Shasta realized suddenly that there were no longer any horses stamping about in the immediate

neighbourhood and that the noise (for there were still a good many noises going on) was no longer that of a battle. He sat up and stared about him. Even he, little as he knew of battles, could soon see that the Archenlanders and Narnians had won. The only living Calormenes he could see were prisoners, the castle gates were wide open, and King Lune and King Edmund were shaking hands across the battering ram. From the circle of lords and warriors around them there arose a sound of breathless and excited, but obviously cheerful conversation. And then, suddenly, it all united and swelled into a great roar of laughter.

Shasta picked himself up, feeling uncommonly stiff, and ran towards the sound to see what the joke was. A very curious sight met his eyes. The unfortunate Rabadash appeared to be suspended from the castle walls. His feet, which were about two feet from the ground, were kicking wildly. His chain-shirt was somehow hitched up so that it was horribly tight under the arms and came half way over his face. In fact he looked just as a man looks if you catch him in the very act of getting into a stiff shirt that is a little too small for him. As far as could be made out afterwards (and you may be sure the story was well talked over for many a day) what happened was something like this. Early in the battle one of the Giants had made an unsuccessful stamp at Rabadash with his spiked boot: unsuccessful because it didn't crush Rabadash, which was what the Giant had intended, but not quite useless because one of the spikes tore the chain mail, just as you or I might tear an ordinary shirt. So Rabadash, by the time he encountered Edmund at the gate, had a hole in the back of his hauberk. And when Edmund pressed him back nearer and nearer to the wall, he jumped up on a mounting block and stood there raining down blows on Edmund from above. But then, finding that this position, by raising him above the heads of everyone else, made him a mark for every arrow from the Narnian bows, he decided to jump down again. And he meant to look and sound – no doubt for a moment he *did* look and sound – very grand and very dreadful as he jumped, crying, "The bolt of Tash falls from above." But he had to jump sideways because the crowd in front of him left him no landing place in that direction. And then, in the neatest way you could wish, the tear in the back of his hauberk caught on a hook in the wall. (Ages ago this hook had had a ring in it for tying horses to.) And there he found himself, like a piece of washing hung up to dry, with everyone laughing at him.

"Let me down, Edmund," howled Rabadash. "Let me down and fight me like a king and a man; or if you are too great a coward to do that, kill me at once."

"Certainly," began King Edmund, but King Lune interrupted.

"By your Majesty's good leave," said King Lune to Edmund. "Not so." Then turning to Rabadash he said, "Your royal Highness, if you had given that challenge a week ago, I'll answer for it there was no one in King Edmund's dominion, from the High King down to the smallest Talking Mouse, who would have refused it. But by attacking our castle of Anvard in time of peace without defiance sent, you have proved yourself no knight, but a traitor, and one rather to be whipped by the hangman than to be suffered to cross swords with any person of honour. Take him down, bind him, and carry him within till our pleasure is further known."

Strong hands wrenched Rabadash's sword from him and he was carried away into the castle, shouting, threatening, cursing, and even crying. For though he could have faced torture he couldn't bear being made ridiculous. In Tashbaan everyone had always taken him seriously.

At that momemt Corin ran up to Shasta, seized his hand and started dragging him towards King Lune. "Here he is, Father, here he is," cried Corin.

"Aye, and here *thou* art, at last," said the King in a very gruff voice. "And hast been in the battle, clean contrary to your obedience. A boy to break a father's heart! At your age a rod to your breech were fitter than a sword in your fist, ha!" But everyone, including Corin, could see that the King was very proud of him.

"Chide him no more, Sire, if it please you," said Lord

Darrin. "His Highness would not be your son if he did not inherit your conditions. It would grieve your Majesty more if he had to be reproved for the opposite fault."

"Well, well," grumbled the King. "We'll pass it over for this time. And now –"

What came next surprised Shasta as much as anything that had ever happened to him in his life. He found himself suddenly embraced in a bear-like hug by King Lune and kissed on both cheeks. Then the King set him down again and said, "Stand here together, boys, and let all the court see you. Hold up your heads. Now, gentlemen, look on them both. Has any man any doubts?"

And still Shasta could not understand why everyone stared at him and at Corin nor what all the cheering was about.

CHAPTER FOURTEEN

HOW BREE BECAME A WISER HORSE

WE must now return to Aravis and the Horses. The Hermit, watching his pool, was able to tell them that Shasta was not killed or even seriously wounded, for he saw him get up and saw how affectionately he was greeted by King Lune. But as he could only see, not hear, he did not know what anyone was saying and, once the fighting had stopped and the talking had begun, it was not worth while looking in the pool any longer.

Next morning, while the Hermit was indoors, the three of them discussed what they should do next.

"I've had enough of this," said Hwin. "The Hermit has been very good to us and I'm very much obliged to him I'm sure. But I'm getting as fat as a pet pony, eating all day and getting no exercise. Let's go on to Narnia."

"Oh not today, Ma'am," said Bree. "I wouldn't hurry things. Some other day, don't you think?"

"We must see Shasta first and say good-bye to him – and – and apologize," said Aravis.

"Exactly!" said Bree with great enthusiasm. "Just what I was going to say."

"Oh, of course," said Hwin. "I expect he is in Anvard. Naturally we'd look in on him and say good-bye. But that's on our way. And why shouldn't we start at once? After all, I thought it was Narnia we all wanted to get to?"

"I suppose so," said Aravis. She was beginning to wonder what exactly she would do when she got there and was feeling a little lonely.

"Of course, of course," said Bree hastily. "But there's no need to rush things, if you know what I mean."

"No, I don't know what you mean," said Hwin. "Why don't you want to go?"

"M-m-m, broo-hoo," muttered Bree. "Well, don't you see, Ma'am – it's an important occasion – returning to one's country – entering society – the best society – it is so essential to make a good impression – not perhaps looking quite ourselves, yet, eh?"

Hwin broke out into a horse-laugh. "It's your tail, Bree! I see it all now. You want to wait till your tail's grown again! And we don't even know if tails are worn long in Narnia. Really, Bree, you're as vain as that Tarkheena in Tashbaan!"

"You *are* silly, Bree," said Aravis.

"By the Lion's Mane, Tarkheena, I'm nothing of the sort," said Bree indignantly. "I have a proper respect for myself and for my fellow horses, that's all."

"Bree," said Aravis, who was not very interested in the cut of his tail, "I've been wanting to ask you something for a long time. Why do you keep on swearing By the Lion and By the Lion's Mane? I thought you hated lions."

"So I do," answered Bree. "But when I speak of *the* Lion of course I mean Aslan, the great deliverer of Narnia who drove away the Witch and the Winter. All Narnians swear by *him*."

"But is he a lion?"

"No, no, of course not," said Bree in a rather shocked voice.

"All the stories about him in Tashbaan say he is," replied Aravis. "And if he isn't a lion why do you call him a lion?"

"Well, you'd hardly understand that at your age," said Bree. "And I was only a little foal when I left so I don't quite fully understand it myself."

(Bree was standing with his back to the green wall while

he said this, and the other two were facing him. He was talking in rather a superior tone with his eyes half shut; that was why he didn't see the changed expression in the faces of Hwin and Aravis. They had good reason to have open mouths and staring eyes; because while Bree spoke they saw an enormous lion leap up from outside and balance itself on the top of the green wall; only it was a brighter yellow and it was bigger and more beautiful and more alarming than any lion they had ever seen. And at once it jumped down inside the wall and began approaching Bree from behind. It made no noise at all. And Hwin and Aravis couldn't make any noise themselves, no more than if they were frozen.)

"No doubt," continued Bree, "when they speak of him as a Lion they only mean he's as strong as a lion or (to our enemies, of course) as fierce as a lion. Or something of that kind. Even a little girl like you, Aravis, must see that it would be quite absurd to suppose he is a *real* lion. Indeed it would be disrespectful. If he was a lion he'd have to be a Beast just like the rest of us. Why!" (and here Bree began to laugh) "If he was a lion he'd have four paws, and a tail, and *Whiskers*! . . . Aie, ooh, hoo-hoo! Help!"

For just as he said the word *Whiskers* one of Aslan's had actually tickled his ear. Bree shot away like an arrow to the other side of the enclosure and there turned; the wall was too high for him to jump and he could fly no farther. Aravis and Hwin both started back. There was about a second of intense silence.

Then Hwin, though shaking all over, gave a strange little neigh, and trotted across to the Lion.

"Please," she said, "you're so beautiful. You may eat me if you like. I'd sooner be eaten by you than fed by anyone else."

"Dearest daughter," said Aslan, planting a lion's kiss on

her twitching, velvet nose, "I knew you would not be long in coming to me. Joy shall be yours."

Then he lifted his head and spoke in a louder voice.

"Now, Bree," he said, "you poor, proud frightened Horse, draw near. Nearer still, my son. Do not dare not to dare. Touch me. Smell me. Here are my paws, here is my tail, these are my whiskers. I am a true Beast."

"Aslan," said Bree in a shaken voice, "I'm afraid I must be rather a fool."

"Happy the Horse who knows that while he is still young. Or the Human either. Draw near, Aravis my daughter. See! My paws are velveted. You will not be torn this time."

"This time, sir?" said Aravis.

"It was I who wounded you," said Aslan. "I am the only lion you met in all your journeyings. Do you know why I tore you?"

"No, sir."

"The scratches on your back, tear for tear, throb for throb, blood for blood, were equal to the stripes laid on the back of your stepmother's slave because of the drugged sleep you cast upon her. You needed to know what it felt like."

"Yes, sir. Please —"

"Ask on, my dear," said Aslan.

"Will any more harm come to her by what I did?"

"Child," said the Lion, "I am telling you your story, not hers. No one is told any story but their own." Then he shook his head and spoke in a lighter voice.

"Be merry, little ones," he said. "We shall meet soon again. But before that you will have another visitor." Then in one bound he reached the top of the wall and vanished from their sight.

Strange to say, they felt no inclination to talk to one

another about him after he had gone. They all moved slowly away to different parts of the quiet grass and there paced to and fro, each alone, thinking.

About half an hour later the two Horses were summoned to the back of the house to eat something nice that the Hermit had got ready for them and Aravis, still walking and thinking, was startled by the harsh sound of a trumpet outside the gate.

"Who is there?" asked Aravis.

"His Royal Highness Prince Cor of Archenland," said a voice from outside.

Aravis undid the door and opened it, drawing back a little way to let the strangers in.

Two soldiers with halberds came first and took their stand at each side of the entry. Then followed a herald, and the trumpeter.

"His Royal Highness Prince Cor of Archenland desires an audience of the Lady Aravis," said the Herald. Then he and the trumpeter drew aside and bowed and the soldiers saluted and the Prince himself came in. All his attendants withdrew and closed the gate behind them.

The Prince bowed, and a very clumsy bow for a Prince it was. Aravis curtsied in the Calormene style (which is not at all like ours) and did it very well because, of course, she had been taught how. Then she looked up and saw what sort of person this Prince was.

She saw a mere boy. He was bare-headed and his fair hair was encircled with a very thin band of gold, hardly thicker than a wire. His upper tunic was of white cambric, as fine as a handkerchief, so that the bright red tunic beneath it showed through. His left hand, which rested on his enamelled sword hilt, was bandaged.

Aravis looked twice at his face before she gasped and said, "Why! It's Shasta!"

Shasta all at once turned very red and began speaking very quickly. "Look here, Aravis," he said, "I do hope you won't think I'm got up like this (and the trumpeter and all) to try to impress you or make out that I'm different or any rot of that sort. Because I'd far rather have come in my old clothes, but they're burnt now, and my father said –"

"Your father?" said Aravis.

"Apparently King Lune is my father," said Shasta. "I might really have guessed it. Corin being so like me. We were twins, you see. Oh, and my name isn't Shasta, it's Cor."

"Cor is a nicer name than Shasta," said Aravis.

"Brothers' names run like that in Archenland," said Shasta (or Prince Cor as we must now call him). "Like Dar and Darrin, Cole and Colin and so on."

"Shasta – I mean Cor," said Aravis. "No, shut up. There's something I've got to say at once. I'm sorry I've been such a pig. But I did change before I knew you were a Prince, honestly I did: when you went back, and faced the Lion."

"It wasn't really going to kill you at all, that Lion," said Cor.

"I know," said Aravis, nodding. Both were still and solemn for a moment as each saw that the other knew about Aslan.

Suddenly Aravis remembered Cor's bandaged hand. "I say!" she cried, "I forgot! You've been in a battle. Is that a wound?"

"A mere scratch," said Cor, using for the first time a rather lordly tone. But a moment later he burst out laughing and said, "If you want to know the truth, it isn't a proper wound at all. I only took the skin off my knuckles just as any clumsy fool might do without going near a battle."

"Still you were in the battle," said Aravis. "It must have been wonderful."

"It wasn't at all like what I thought," said Cor.

"But Sha – Cor, I mean – you haven't told me anything yet about King Lune and how he found out who you were."

"Well, let's sit down," said Cor. "For it's rather a long story. And by the way, Father's an absolute brick. I'd be just as pleased – or very nearly – at finding he's my father even if he wasn't a king. Even though Education and all sorts of horrible things are going to happen to me. But you want the story. Well, Corin and I were twins. And about a week after we were both born, apparently, they took us to a wise old Centaur in Narnia to be blessed or something. Now this Centaur was a prophet as a good many Centaurs are. Perhaps you haven't seen any Centaurs yet? There were some in the battle yesterday. Most remarkable people, but I can't say I feel quite at home with them yet. I

say, Aravis, there are going to be a lot of things to get used to in these Northern countries."

"Yes, there are," said Aravis. "But get on with the story."

"Well, as soon as he saw Corin and me, it seems this Centaur looked at me and said, A day will come when that boy will save Archenland from the deadliest danger in which ever she lay. So of course my Father and Mother were very pleased. But there was someone present who wasn't. This was a chap called the Lord Bar who had been Father's Lord Chancellor. And apparently he'd done something wrong – *bezzling* or some word like that – I didn't understand that part very well – and Father had had to dismiss him. But nothing else was done to him and he was allowed to go on living in Archenland. But he must have been as bad as he could be, for it came out afterwards he had been in the pay of the Tisroc and had sent a lot of secret information to Tashbaan. So as soon as he heard I was going to save Archenland from a great danger he decided I must be put out of the way. Well, he succeeded in kidnapping me (I don't exactly know how) and rode away down the Winding Arrow to the coast. He'd had everything prepared and there was a ship manned with his own followers lying ready for him and he put out to sea with me on board. But Father got wind of it, though not quite in time, and was after him as quickly as he could. The Lord

Bar was already at sea when Father reached the coast, but not out of sight. And Father was embarked in one of his own warships within twenty minutes.

"It must have been a wonderful chase. They were six days following Bar's galleon and brought her to battle on the seventh. It was a great sea-fight (I heard a lot about it yesterday evening) from ten o'clock in the morning till sunset. Our people took the ship in the end. But I wasn't there. The Lord Bar himself had been killed in the battle. But one of his men said that, early that morning, as soon as he saw he was certain to be overhauled, Bar had given me to one of his knights and sent us both away in the ship's boat. And that boat was never seen again. But of course that was the same boat that Aslan (he seems to be at the back of all the stories) pushed ashore at the right place for Arsheesh to pick me up. I wish I knew that knight's name, for he must have kept me alive and starved himself to do it."

"I suppose Aslan would say that was part of someone else's story," said Aravis.

"I was forgetting that," said Cor.

"And I wonder how the prophecy will work out," said Aravis, "and what the great danger is that you're to save Archenland from."

"Well," said Cor rather awkwardly, "they seem to think I've done it already."

Aravis clapped her hands. "Why, of course!" she said. "How stupid I am. And how wonderful! Archenland can never be in much greater danger than it was when Rabadash had crossed the Arrow with his two hundred horse and you hadn't yet got through with your message. Don't you feel proud?"

"I think I feel a bit scared," said Cor.

"And you'll be living at Anvard now," said Aravis rather wistfully.

"Oh!" said Cor, "I'd nearly forgotten what I came about. Father wants you to come and live with us. He says there's been no lady in the court (they call it the court, I don't know why) since Mother died. Do, Aravis. You'll like Father – and Corin. They're not like me; they've been properly brought up. You needn't be afraid that –"

"Oh stop it," said Aravis, "or we'll have a real fight. Of course I'll come."

"Now let's go and see the Horses," said Cor.

There was a great and joyous meeting between Bree and Cor, and Bree, who was still in a rather subdued frame of mind, agreed to set out for Anvard at once: he and Hwin would cross into Narnia on the following day. All four bade an affectionate farewell to the Hermit and promised that they would soon visit him again. By about the middle of the morning they were on their way. The Horses had expected that Aravis and Cor would ride, but Cor explained that except in war, where everyone must do what he can do best, no one in Narnia or Archenland ever dreamed of mounting a Talking Horse.

This reminded poor Bree again of how little he knew about Narnian customs and what dreadful mistakes he

might make. So while Hwin strolled along in a happy dream, Bree got more nervous and more self-conscious with every step he took.

"Buck up, Bree," said Cor. "It's far worse for me than for you. You aren't going to be *educated*. I shall be learning reading and writing and heraldry and dancing and history and music while you'll be galloping and rolling on the hills of Narnia to your heart's content."

"But that's just the point," groaned Bree. "*Do* Talking Horses roll? Supposing they don't? I can't bear to give it up. What do you think, Hwin?"

"I'm going to roll anyway," said Hwin. "I don't suppose any of them will care two lumps of sugar whether you roll or not."

"Are we near that castle?" said Bree to Cor.

"Round the next bend," said the Prince.

"Well," said Bree, "I'm going to have a good one now: it may be the last. Wait for me a minute."

It was five minutes before he rose again, blowing hard and covered with bits of bracken.

"Now I'm ready," he said in a voice of profound gloom. "Lead on, Prince Cor, Narnia and the North."

But he looked more like a horse going to a funeral than a long-lost captive returning to home and freedom.

CHAPTER FIFTEEN

RABADASH THE RIDICULOUS

THE next turn of the road brought them out from among
the trees and there, across green lawns, sheltered from the
north wind by the high wooded ridge at its back, they saw
the castle of Anvard. It was very old and built of a warm,
reddish-brown stone.

Before they had reached the gate King Lune came out to
meet them, not looking at all like Aravis's idea of a king
and wearing the oldest of old clothes; for he had just come
from making a round of the kennels with his Huntsman
and had only stopped for a moment to wash his doggy
hands. But the bow with which he greeted Aravis as he
took her hand would have been stately enough for an
Emperor.

"Little lady," he said, "we bid you very heartily welcome. If my dear wife were still alive we could make you
better cheer but could not do it with a better will. And I am
sorry that you have had misfortunes and been driven from
your father's house, which cannot but be a grief to you. My
son Cor has told me about your adventures together and
all your valour."

"It was he who did all that, Sir," said Aravis. "Why, he
rushed at a lion to save me."

"Eh, what's that?" said King Lune, his face brightening.
"I haven't heard that part of the story."

Then Aravis told it. And Cor, who had very much
wanted the story to be known, though he felt he couldn't
tell it himself, didn't enjoy it so much as he had expected,
and indeed felt rather foolish. But his father enjoyed it very
much indeed and in the course of the next few weeks told it
to so many people that Cor wished it had never happened.

Then the King turned to Hwin and Bree and was just as polite to them as to Aravis, and asked them a lot of questions about their families and where they had lived in Narnia before they had been captured. The Horses were rather tongue-tied for they weren't yet used to being talked to as equals by Humans – grown-up Humans, that is. They didn't mind Aravis and Cor.

Presently Queen Lucy came out from the castle and joined them and King Lune said to Aravis, "My dear, here is a loving friend of our house, and she has been seeing that your apartments are put to rights for you better than I could have done it."

"You'd like to come and see them, wouldn't you?" said Lucy, kissing Aravis. They liked each other at once and soon went away together to talk about Aravis's bedroom and Aravis's boudoir and about getting clothes for her, and all the sort of things girls do talk about on such an occasion.

After lunch, which they had on the terrace (it was cold birds and cold game pie and wine and bread and cheese), King Lune ruffled up his brow and heaved a sigh and said, "Heigh-ho! We have still that sorry creature Rabadash on our hands, my friends, and must needs resolve what to do with him."

Lucy was sitting on the King's right and Aravis on his left. King Edmund sat at one end of the table and the Lord Darrin faced him at the other. Dar and Peridan and Cor and Corin were on the same side as the King.

"Your Majesty would have a perfect right to strike off his head," said Peridan. "Such an assault as he made puts him on a level with assassins."

"It is very true," said Edmund. "But even a traitor may mend. I have known one that did." And he looked very thoughtful.

"To kill this Rabadash would go near to raising war with the Tisroc," said Darrin.

"A fig for the Tisroc," said King Lune. "His strength is in numbers and numbers will never cross the desert. But I have no stomach for killing men (even traitors) in cold blood. To have cut his throat in the battle would have eased my heart mightily: but this is a different thing."

"By my counsel," said Lucy, "your Majesty shall give him another trial. Let him go free on strait promise of fair dealing in the future. It may be that he will keep his word."

"Maybe Apes will grow honest, Sister," said Edmund. "But, by the Lion, if he breaks it again, may it be in such time and place that any of us could swap off his head in clean battle."

"It shall be tried," said the King: and then to one of the attendants, "Send for the prisoner, friend."

Rabadash was brought before them in chains. To look at him anyone would have supposed that he had passed the night in a noisome dungeon without food or water; but in reality he had been shut up in quite a comfortable room and provided with an excellent supper. But as he was sulking far too furiously to touch the supper and had spent the whole night stamping and roaring and cursing, he naturally did not now look his best.

"Your royal Highness needs not to be told," said King Lune, "that by the law of nations as well as by all reasons of prudent policy, we have as good right to your head as ever one mortal man had against another. Nevertheless, in consideration of your youth and the ill nurture, devoid of all gentilesse and courtesy, which you have doubtless had in the land of slaves and tyrants, we are disposed to set you free, unharmed, on these conditions: first, that —"

"Curse you for a barbarian dog!" spluttered Rabadash. "Do you think I will even hear your conditions? Faugh!

You talk very largely of nurture and I know not what. It's easy, to a man in chains, ha! Take off these vile bonds, give me a sword, and let any of you who dares then debate with me."

Nearly all the lords sprang to their feet, and Corin shouted:

"Father! Can I *box* him? Please."

"Peace! Your Majesties! My Lords!" said King Lune. "Have we no more gravity among us than to be so chafed by the taunt of a pajock? Sit down, Corin, or shalt leave the table. I ask your Highness again, to hear our conditions."

"I hear no conditions from barbarians and sorcerers," said Rabadash. "Not one of you dare touch a hair of my head. Every insult you have heaped on me shall be paid with oceans of Narnian and Archenlandish blood. Terrible shall the vengeance of the Tisroc be: even now. But kill me, and the burnings and torturings in these northern lands shall become a tale to frighten the world a thousand years hence. Beware! Beware! Beware! The bolt of Tash falls from above!"

"Does it ever get caught on a hook half-way?" asked Corin.

"Shame, Corin," said the King. "Never taunt a man save when he is stronger than you: then, as you please."

"Oh you foolish Rabadash," sighed Lucy.

Next moment Cor wondered why everyone at the table had risen and was standing perfectly still. Of course he did the same himself. And then he saw the reason. Aslan was among them though no one had seen him coming. Rabadash started as the immense shape of the Lion paced softly in between him and his accusers.

"Rabadash," said Aslan. "Take heed. Your doom is very near, but you may still avoid it. Forget your pride (what have you to be proud of?) and your anger (who has done you wrong?) and accept the mercy of these good kings."

Then Rabadash rolled his eyes and spread out his mouth into a horrible, long mirthless grin like a shark, and wagged his ears up and down (anyone can learn how to do this if they take the trouble). He had always found this very effective in Calormen. The bravest had trembled when he made these faces, and ordinary people had fallen to the floor, and sensitive people had often fainted. But what Rabadash hadn't realized is that it is very easy to frighten people who know you can have them boiled alive the moment you give the word. The grimaces didn't look at all alarming in Archenland; indeed Lucy only thought Rabadash was going to be sick.

"Demon! Demon! Demon!" shrieked the Prince. "I know you. You are the foul fiend of Narnia. You are the enemy of the gods. Learn who *I* am, horrible phantasm. I am descended from Tash, the inexorable, the irresistible. the curse of Tash is upon you. Lightning in the shape of scorpions shall be rained on you. The mountains of Narnia shall be ground into dust. The –"

"Have a care, Rabadash," said Aslan quietly. "The doom is nearer now: it is at the door: it has lifted the latch."

"Let the skies fall," shrieked Rabadash. "Let the earth gape! Let blood and fire obliterate the world! But be sure I will never desist till I have dragged to my palace by her hair the barbarian queen, the daughter of dogs, the –"

"The hour has struck," said Aslan: and Rabadash saw, to his supreme horror, that everyone had begun to laugh.

They couldn't help it. Rabadash had been wagging his ears all the time and as soon as Aslan said, "The hour has struck!" the ears began to change. They grew longer and more pointed and soon were covered with grey hair. And

while everyone was wondering where they had seen ears
like that before, Rabadash's face began to change too. It
grew longer, and thicker at the top and larger eyed, and the
nose sank back into the face (or else the face swelled out
and became all nose) and there was hair all over it. And his
arms grew longer and came down in front of him till his
hands were resting on the ground: only they weren't hands,
now, they were hoofs. And he was standing on all fours,
and his clothes disappeared, and everyone laughed louder
and louder (because they couldn't help it) for now what
had been Rabadash was, simply and unmistakably, a
donkey. The terrible thing was that his human speech
lasted just a moment longer than his human shape, so that
when he realized the change that was coming over him, he
screamed out:

"Oh, not a Donkey! Mercy! If it were even a horse – e'en
– a hor – eeh – auh, eeh-auh." And so the words died away
into a donkey's bray.

"Now hear me, Rabadash," said Aslan. "Justice shall be
mixed with mercy. You shall not always be an Ass."

At this of course the Donkey twitched its ears forward –
and that also was so funny that
everybody laughed all the more. They
tried not to, but they tried in vain.

"You have appealed to Tash," said
Aslan. "And in the temple of Tash you
shall be healed. You must stand before
the altar of Tash in Tashbaan at the great
Autumn Feast this year and there, in the
sight of all Tashbaan, your ass's shape
will fall from you and all men will know
you for Prince Rabadash. But as long as
you live, if ever you go more than ten
miles away from the great temple in

Tashbaan you shall instantly become again as you now are. And from that second change there will be no return."

There was a short silence and then they all stirred and looked at one another as if they were waking from sleep. Aslan was gone. But there was a brightness in the air and on the grass, and a joy in their hearts, which assured them that he had been no dream: and anyway, there was the donkey in front of them.

King Lune was the kindest-hearted of men and on seeing his enemy in this regrettable condition he forgot all his anger.

"Your royal Highness," he said. "I am most truly sorry that things have come to this extremity. Your Highness will bear witness that it was none of our doing. And of course we shall be delighted to provide your Highness with shipping back to Tashbaan for the – er – treatment which Aslan has prescribed. You shall have every comfort which your Highness's situation allows: the best of the cattle-boats – the freshest carrots and thistles –"

But a deafening bray from the Donkey and a well-aimed kick at one of the guards made it clear that these kindly offers were ungratefully received.

And here, to get him out of the way, I'd better finish off the story of Rabadash. He (or it) was duly sent back by boat to Tashbaan and brought into the temple of Tash at the great Autumn Festival, and then he became a man again. But of course four or five thousand people had seen the transformation and the affair could not possibly be hushed up. And after the old Tisroc's death when Rabadash became Tisroc in his place he turned out the most peaceable Tisroc Calormen had ever known. This was because, not daring to go more than ten miles from Tashbaan, he could never go on a war himself: and he didn't want his Tarkaans to win fame in the wars at his expense, for that is the way Tisrocs get overthrown. But though his reasons were selfish, it made things much more comfortable for all the smaller countries round Calormen. His own peole never forgot that he had been a donkey. During his reign, and to his face, he was called Rabadash the Peacemaker, but after his death and behind his back he was called Rabadash the Ridiculous, and if you look him up in a good History of Calormen (try the local library) you will find him under that name. And to this day in Calormene schools, if you do anything unusually stupid, you are very likely to be called "a second Rabadash".

Meanwhile at Anvard everyone was very glad that he had been disposed of before the real fun began, which was a grand feast held that evening on the lawn before the castle, with dozens of lanterns to help the moonlight. And the wine flowed and tales were told and jokes were cracked, and then silence was made and the King's poet with two fiddlers stepped out into the middle of the circle. Aravis and Cor prepared themselves to be bored, for the only poetry they knew was the Calormene kind, and you know now what that was like. But at the very first scrape of the fiddles a rocket seemed to go up inside their heads, and the poet sang the great old lay of Fair Olvin and how he fought the Giant Pire and turned him into stone (and that is the origin of Mount Pire – it was a two-headed Giant) and won the Lady Liln for his bride; and when it was over they wished it was going to begin again. And though Bree couldn't sing he told the story of the fight at Zalindreh. And Lucy told again (they had all, except Aravis and Cor, heard it many times but they all wanted it again) the tale of the Wardrobe and how she and King Edmund and Queen Susan and Peter the High King had first come into Narnia.

And presently, as was certain to happen sooner or later,

King Lune said it was time for young people to be in bed. "And tomorrow, Cor," he added, "shalt come over all the castle with me and see the estres and mark all its strength and weakness: for it will be thine to guard when I'm gone."

"But Corin will be the King then, Father," said Cor.

"Nay, lad," said King Lune, "thou art my heir. The crown comes to thee."

"But I don't want it," said Cor. "I'd far rather –"

"'Tis no question what thou wantest, Cor, nor I either. 'Tis in the course of law."

"But if we're twins we must be the same age."

"Nay," said the King with a laugh. "One must come first. Art Corin's elder by full twenty minutes. And his better too, let's hope, though that's no great mastery." And he looked at Corin with a twinkle in his eyes.

"But, Father, couldn't you make whichever you like to be the next King?"

"No. The king's under the law, for it's the law makes him a king. Hast no more power to start away from thy crown than any sentry from his post."

"Oh dear," said Cor. "I don't want to at all. And Corin – I am most dreadfully sorry. I never dreamed my turning up was going to chisel you out of your kingdom."

"Hurrah! Hurrah!" said Corin. "I shan't have to be King. I shan't have to be King. I'll always be a prince. It's princes have all the fun."

"And that's truer than thy brother knows, Cor," said King Lune. "For this is what it means to be a king: to be first in every desperate attack and last in every desperate retreat, and when there's hunger in the land (as must be now and then in bad years) to wear finer clothes and laugh louder over a scantier meal than any man in your land."

When the two boys were going upstairs to bed Cor again

asked Corin if nothing could be done about it. And Corin said:

"If you say another word about it, I'll – I'll knock you down."

It would be nice to end the story by saying that after that the two brothers never disagreed about anything again, but I am afraid it would not be true. In reality they quarrelled and fought just about as often as any other two boys would, and all their fights ended (if they didn't begin) with Cor getting knocked down. For though, when they had both grown up and become swordsmen, Cor was the more dangerous man in battle, neither he nor anyone else in the North Countries could ever equal Corin as a boxer. That was how he got his name of Corin Thunder-Fist; and how he performed his great exploit against the Lapsed Bear of Stormness, which was really a Talking Bear but had gone back to Wild Bear habits. Corin climbed up to its lair on the Narnian side of Stormness one winter day when the snow was on the hills and boxed it without a time-keeper for thirty-three rounds. And at the end it couldn't see out of its eyes and became a reformed character.

Aravis also had many quarrels (and, I'm afraid, even fights) with Cor, but they always made it up again: so that years later, when they were grown up, they were so used to quarrelling and making it up again that they got married so as to go on doing it more conveniently. And after King Lune's death they made a good King and Queen of Archenland and Ram the Great, the most famous of all the kings of Archenland, was their son. Bree and Hwin lived happily to a great age in Narnia and both got married but not to one another. And there weren't many months in which one or both of them didn't come trotting over the pass to visit their friends at Anvard.